TAG

Simon Royle

Also by Simon Royle

Bangkok Burn
Bangkok Wet

About the author

Simon Royle was born in Manchester, England in 1963. He has been variously a yachtsman, advertising executive, and a senior management executive in software companies. He lives in Bangkok, with his wife and two children.

TAG

Simon Royle

PRESS

First published in Thailand by I & I Press 2010

This I&I Press trade paperback edition 2010

Copyright © 2010 Simon Royle
Afterword copyright © 2010 Simon Royle
Cover copyright © 2010 Simon Royle

This is a work of fiction. Any similarities to people or
places, living or dead, is purely coincidental.

ISBN 978 616 90769 0 2

A CIP catalogue record for this title is available from the
National Library of Thailand.

Typeset in Adobe Garamond Pro and BankGothic for Chapter Headings.

The moral right of the author has been asserted.

I&I Press
249/17 Lat Phrao 122,
Lat Phrao Road,
Wang Thonglang,
Bangkok 10310

WWW.SIMON-ROYLE.COM

For Pim

The luckiest day when I met you,
Hurtling through the Stars,
Not revolving around the sun, I am,
Dawn, dusk, and night, your Moon.
My Earth is you.

An UNPOL Case File

Date: Monday, December 2, 2109
Case #: JM-Bgk-2109
Location: UNPOL Section Office, Pratunam, Bangkok
Log Time: 3:30pm
Subject: Jibril Muraz Personal Unique Identifier (PUI): 230963UK
Containment Officer/s: Somchai Pisanulock; Jirasak Pancharoen
Charge/s: Illegal Wiretapping, Identity Fraud, Counterfeiting.
Statement:

Acting on information from a confidential informant, we entered an unlicensed gambling den. Upon entering the premises, we found that an illegal migration operation was in place and immediately enacted a containment order on all individuals and equipment. Further investigation of the equipment led us to believe that Jibril Muraz was, in fact, assisting criminals listed on UNPOL's Most Wanted to evade detection using counterfeit PUIs. Subject did not resist containment and did not offer a statement.

Date: Tuesday, December 3, 2109
Case #: JM-Bgk-2109
Location: Pratunam, Bangkok
Log Time: 4:30pm
Subject: Jibril Muraz Personal Unique Identifier (PUI): 230963UK
Charge/s: Illegal Wiretapping, Identity Fraud, Counterfeiting.
Transfer Order:

By request of Serious Crimes Unit, UNPOL HQ, New Singapore. Please arrange immediate transfer of subject to New Singapore UNPOL HQ. Containment Unit prepared to receive at Changi Levport.

Date: Wednesday, December 4, 2109
Case #: JM-Bgk-2109
Request: Truth Treatment.
Location: Level 10, UNPOL

Log Time: 12:30am
Subject: Jibril Muraz
Request Filed by: Agent Sharon Cochran
Requested Authorized for Submission: Director of UNPOL: Thomas Bartholomew Oliver
Request Authorized: Judge Miriam Wu
Truth Treatment Transcript:

Cochran: I'd like to start by asking a couple of basic questions that you should have no trouble answering. Is that okay? A yes or no answer is sufficient.

Muraz: Yes.

Cochran: Your name is Jibril Muraz? And your PUI is 230963UK?

Muraz: No.

Cochran: Your identification and PUI were gathered from your Dev at the time of your containment in Bangkok; are you saying that this is not your true identity?

Muraz: Yes.

Cochran: Could you tell us your real identity?

Muraz: Yes.

Cochran: Good, excellent. We do appreciate your cooperation. Now perhaps you could give us more information about who you are beyond a simple yes or no answer. What is your real identity?

Muraz: My real identity is Unknown.

Cochran: Um, yes, I see. All right, let's move on. We can come back to the issue of your identity later. Your fixed abode is listed as 61 Sholle Street, Paddington, London; however, we have checked that address, and it doesn't exist. Can you tell us where you normally live?

Muraz: Yes.

Cochran: And where is that, then?

Muraz: I live in another dimension. It is alien to you.

Cochran: I see. Perhaps you could tell me more about this dimension. Where is it?

Muraz: I can't explain it to you. You do not have the mental capacity or knowledge to understand any answer I could give you about that dimension.

Cochran: Well, why don't we try at least, could you tell me more about this dimension?

Muraz: No.

End of Truth Treatment Transcript

Subject refused to answer the last question, and biometrics for the subject indicated that he fell asleep after saying "no".

Truth Treatment concluded. The effectiveness of the truth treatment is in doubt in this case. The results are inconclusive and provide no further information for trace unit, other than what is already known.

Date: Wednesday, December 4, 2109
Location: Level 10, UNPOL
Log Time: 11:30pm
Subject requested to produce an oral statement for the court.
Transcript of Statement: Jibril Muraz 230963UK
Attending Officer: Agent Sharon Cochran
Statement follows:

I was working as an illegal runner in a small shop in Bangkok. Life was simple. Eat, sleep, work. The rate was good, too good. We were running illegals, mostly out of the China Geographic but some from other Geographics too. If you could come up with the 50k cred for the counterfeit Personal Unique Identifiers we spent our days scripting, then you were eligible. We'd been at it for six weeks operating in shifts, two shifts, twelve to a shift, each of us running between three and eight illegals. At 50k per illegal, good rates were being made by us all: 50% in cred cards, paid then and there, each time we got someone through the security zones to their agreed destination.

The guy running the shop was a bastard, a real mean, sadistic son of a bitch. He kept the temperature down, said it kept us awake. The shop was cold; I had to keep blowing into my hands just to keep my fingers from freezing. The booths had no heating. It was just horrible, but warmth, comfort, ethics, morals, rights and wrongs, well, it was easy to forget all that with the amount of cred we were making.

I've been a 'gun for hire' since I was fourteen, and here we are twenty years down that track. You want to know what happened and why. I can tell you the what. The why I'm still working out.

[At this point, the subject Jibril Muraz requested, under article 3 of the United Nation Containment Code, that he be allowed to meet with arbitrator Jonah James Oliver. Request was formally denied on grounds of level 1 security threat.]
Statement continued:

3

The light show didn't work. The drugs haven't worked, and in another half an hour, everything you know about me will disappear from your systems and you will not know who or what I am. Better get me what I want or you'll come out of this with nothing you want or need.

[At this point subject appeared to adopt a meditation position and began to meditate.]

THE REQUEST

"At which point, all trace of Mr Jibril Muraz disappeared from our systems, and he hasn't said a word after that." The woman who had just presented raised her eyebrows as if to invite a question from me. We were sitting in a small conference room on the new Biosense office seats that procurement had seen fit to torture us with.

"And he was drugged?" Well, it might be stating the obvious, but she was clearly expecting me to say something, and I still had last night's leaving party for Milo banging around in my head. The last thing I needed was a runner.

She looked at me like I was some kind of novice. "Yes, of course he was drugged. Under the circumstances, this was natural, and after clearing his medical, we proceeded with the Truth Treatment."

"I see, and how did he respond to that treatment?"

At this, Agent Sharon Cochran looked just a little perturbed, and a slight edge of doubt crept into her voice. "He, um, appeared to resist the Truth Treatment, although that is hard to prove."

I sensed she was dodging around something here that she didn't want to talk about.

"Well, in what way was it hard to prove that he was resisting?"

She looked me in the eye. "Under the Truth Treatment he stated that he was an alien being from another dimension."

I spat my Starbucks latte over the table in front of me. "He what?" I couldn't help it, and Sharon raised an eyebrow.

"He claimed he was an alien being. Look, this case is a problem. We're under intense time pressure to get it cracked, and all we have is a runner who claims he's from another planet or dimension or whatever. I don't have time to debate the how and the why. We need answers, and we need them quick. Can you talk to him or should I call someone else?" With this last thrust of her best executive power-presenting performance, she looked at her watch and then frowned at my latte splattered all over the table.

5

"Why me? I'm an arbitrator. Why don't you take this up with the prosecutors' staff?" I rose from the Biosense chair and dabbed at the spilt latte with my handkerchief. I really didn't need this right now. I had a huge caseload already, and this pro bono work for UNPOL was just something I did to appease my uncle.

"He doesn't want to talk to any arbitrator. He wants to talk to you." She smiled as she saw the frown on my face and again looked me right in the eyes. "He asked for you by name."

I sat back down.

"Okay, Sharon, maybe you'd better start at the beginning because a sec ago you said you'd be happy to call someone else, and now you're saying he knows me and wants only to talk to me!"

"First of all, I didn't say I'd be happy to call someone else. I said I would if you wouldn't take the job," she said, leaning over the table so her face was only cents away from mine. "And secondly, this guy was running sixteen illegals at the same time, all of them grade one, which is something we have never heard of, never mind seen, and we only discovered him by complete accident. At this exact moment in time, we have sixteen of the most wanted people in the universe running around, and we haven't got a clue where they are. We need him to talk and fast. Can you help?"

I really wanted to have Sharon right there and then on the table, having been thoroughly dominated and turned on by her power shakedown. I resorted to the male primeval of telling her this with my eyes. There were only two problems with that: one, she was happily married, and two, she was a lesbian and one hundred percent committed to her partner, both of which were facts she communicated right back with her eyes, basically telling me to fuck off and hell would freeze over before I got within touching distance of her body.

"Okay, I'll talk to him."

"Thank you. The complete file is in there. Don't worry, it's a standalone, and this room is silent," she said, indicating the Dev with a wave of her hand and smiling, almost in pity I thought, as she left the room. The door clicked shut.

"Shit," I spat out, my lips compressed tightly in annoyance. I should have turned it down flat. It had trouble written all over it, and my stupid fantasies about Cochran had led me into a place I really didn't need to be. I blew out my cheeks and let out a long sigh. This had been a dumb move, but then Milo's party was partly to blame – I'd drunk too many alkys for my own good. I stood and ran my hand through my hair, doing a quick inventory of what I'd said and thought while with Cochran. "Shit, shit, shit," I said and was hitting the table with my fist when out of the corner of my eye I saw the door open, and Sharon pop her head back in. I froze and shifted to try and make it look as if I always sat like this.

Sharon frowned and said, "Oh, and Jonah, the director would like to see you before you talk to the runner." With a last quick flash of that feline smile and a quirky raise of the eyebrows, she was gone, closing the door behind her.

The director of UNPOL is Sir Thomas Bartholomew Oliver, my uncle. He'd never asked to see me about any official matter in all my time in New Singapore. UNPOL really did have a problem if he was getting involved at this level. If he was involved, then it was very serious, and the runner had asked for me by name. I had to see why my name was in there.

I turned to the Dev on the table in front of me and said, "This is Arbitrator Jonah James Oliver, sign on." The device snapped on with the Center's Portal set as the landing page. I saw that the detached icon was displayed, so the Dev was disconnected from the network, and my credentials and icon came up in the bottom corner. "Provide me with the case file on Jibril Muraz."

The screen filled with the data stream dating back from today with referenced digital information on Jibril Muraz. There wasn't much, but what there was, I couldn't believe. This guy had been running sixteen of the most wanted criminals on earth. Then, when they were interrogating him, all reference data to his PUI had disappeared, along with all the reference data related to the criminals he was running. He was forty-six years old and registered to a non-existent address at Sholle Street, Paddington, London. Scanning his transcript, I saw that he claimed to have been doing this since he was fourteen. How many other illegals had he placed in society? He was being kept in Level Ten, 'The Deep', as they called it here at UNPOL.

I said, "Show me references to Oliver."

The Devscreen resized around the scant information and zoomed to the end of the transcript just before he had sat down and meditated. The transcript didn't give me his exact words, which I would have liked to have seen, just that he requested to see me.

This was a big case. It was interesting too. Most of the pro bono work I did for UNPOL was incredibly routine and dull, albeit occasionally gratifying in helping someone out of a mess, but this case was going to be big news. My mind suddenly conjured up an image of the cases I had stacked up at my regular contribution. Although the case was interesting, I should pass. Let someone else have the limelight on this one. I was just too busy.

I popped my Devstick into the Dev and, taking a copy of the data, logged the copy.

"This is UN Operative Jonah James Oliver, sign off." I got up from the table and steeled myself for the coming encounter. Time to see the director.

The Director

"Jonah, come in. Take a seat. How are you, my boy?" Sir Thomas said with a smile and a jab of his hand indicating the chairs in front of his desk.

"I am well, Uncle, thank you," I said and walked across the room to Sir Thomas's desk and sat down on one of the two straight-backed wooden chairs facing him, and waited for him to speak. He looked at me, his eyes large in the rimless glasses. An affectation, technology rendering the glasses unnecessary, but Sir Thomas refused the surgery and preferred the round, rimless glasses. He fiddled with a trackball on his desk and then looked directly at me again.

"Jonah, I have to ask you this, as a matter of protocol, and whatever the answer, I need the absolute truth from you. This man who's requested to meet with you: do you know him?" Sir Thomas held my eyes with a solemn expression. I had a flashback to a moment when a vase had been broken in his study and he'd asked me then for the absolute truth. The answer that time had been yes I had broken it and hidden the evidence. This time I was sure I was innocent. Somehow even at thirty-four years of age, my uncle could make me feel like a little boy again.

"No, sir, I'd never met or heard of him before this morning's events."

Sir Thomas stared at me hard, looking deep into my eyes with his enlarged pupils, and the corners of his mouth twitched upwards.

"Good. I believe you. Any idea why he is requesting to see you?"

"No, sir, I have given it some thought, and I checked back cases for any references to his name, but I haven't come up with anything."

"No, neither have we. So it seems we need you to talk to him. Are you comfortable with that?"

"Honestly? No. My caseload is fairly heavy right now, and I really don't have the time. However, judging from the evidence and the seriousness of the alleged offenses, it would seem that we don't have any choice."

"Quite so, quite so," Sir Thomas said, nodding his nearly bald head up and down. I thought it was remarkable how little we actually resembled each other

9

given that I was his brother's son. I broke my thoughts to focus: Sir Thomas was speaking again.

"Yes, I read of your recent victory in the Schilling vs. Bauer case. Excellent work, that. You saved them 130 million cred. I was – am – very proud of you."

"Thank you, sir." I wasn't surprised that he'd heard of the case; it had been dragging on for four years by the time it reached me at Coughington and Scuttle.

Sir Thomas sat forward in his Siteazy and, clasping his hands together, rested them on his dark wooden desk. "Yes, well, I have taken the liberty of asking the Board of Governors to send a note to Bill Scuttle requesting an immediate leave of absence for you in connection with your pro bono contribution here at UNPOL. We haven't given them any details of your role here other than to say it is of vital importance to the Nation. Something that won't do your Contributory Record any harm either. Now take a look at the wall screen," he said, indicating the wall behind me.

I stood up and turned the straight-backed wooden chair to an angle that would allow me to talk to Sir Thomas and have an easy view of the screen. I sat back down and folded my hands into my lap.

An image appeared of a man sitting naked on a Biosense chair in white space. Jibril Muraz. He sat in the lotus position, his eyes closed. He seemed perfectly still, and were it not for his bio data indicating his vital signs streaming across the bottom of the screen in a constant flow, like a stock ticker, you might have thought him dead.

Sir Thomas cleared his throat and said, "This is how he has been since he requested to see you. He's in the White Room in the Deep. The White Room is a new development here, and we only use it in extreme cases. This one qualifies. Basically you feel as if you're in a cloud, with no sense of depth or orientation. You wake up sitting on that chair without a floor beneath your feet. It's experimental, but so far we've had good results. So far, that is, until Mr Jibril Muraz. He's resisted Truth Treatment, which is highly unusual with all that rubbish about being an alien, and he has obviously penetrated our information systems because of the data loss. So irrespective of the sixteen criminals who are now scattered around the universe – and we haven't a clue who or where they are – the fact that this Jibril Muraz is in our systems is enough cause for huge concern. We need you to bring all your skills to bear as a negotiator and draw him out, get him to speak."

I waited for Sir Thomas to continue, and when he didn't, I asked, "Do I have to conduct the interview in the White Room?" There it was, my final acceptance that I had to take this role, but then I'd really accepted the instant I heard he'd asked for me. My mind flashed a quick image of Cochran, and I pushed it away. Focus.

"No, but we would prefer it if you did."

I took out my Devstick and, looking at the case file information, said, "According to this, the timing between his request for a meeting with me and the sudden disappearance of all of his related data was almost instantaneous. That couldn't have been a planned coincidence – wouldn't that indicate that he has an accomplice?"

"Yes, that's possible and our current most likely scenario. That or he planted a data time bomb and counted, which we haven't ruled out. Either way, the implications are extremely serious."

"Yes, I understand. Is it possible that his accomplice is still in the system and watching us?"

"Yes, it is possible, and there is a risk."

I turned to face Sir Thomas, and he studied me with his serious look and said, "If his accomplice is in the systems, he may be able to manipulate the building's various alarms and defenses. We have our best digital trace and infrastructure people on this, but they still haven't been able to detect the source of the deleted data, so …"

Just leaving that 'so' dangling like that didn't give me much comfort at this sudden turn of events. The day was not improving.

"What defenses and alarms are we talking about?"

"Well, in a worst-case scenario, paralyzing sound will be released, nerve gas will flood the room, and the partition between you and the prisoner will rise while the door to the room will stay locked."

"I see."

"I want you to take a stun device with you as protection. Both of you would most probably be unconscious the sec anything happened, but just in case, as a purely precautionary measure, I'd feel more comfortable if you took the stun gun."

He pulled open a drawer in his very traditional battleship of a desk, took out a black, squat-looking device, and laid it on the dark green blotter in front of him. It seemed out of place in this antique throwback of an office. Even his title was antique, one of the last Knighthoods given for services to the Realm before that Realm was merged with all others after the Last Great War of 2056. He was just twenty-one years old when knighted by the King of England.

I had never had to take a weapon to a meeting before. It was a strange feeling, a feeling I didn't enjoy. Like most humans, I despised violence in any form and, apart from the very occasional hormone-inspired scuffles of my youth, had never experienced it in its physical form.

"I'd rather not. I want to go in naked, as he is. Either that, or clothe him before our interview," I said and swiveled in the chair to face Sir Thomas directly.

Sir Thomas sat back in his Siteazy and frowned, lifting a hand to stroke his slightly dimpled, fleshy chin.

I mentally assembled my arguments to convince him that what I was proposing made sense, but he interrupted my thoughts by saying, "All right. No stun gun and you go in naked."

"Thank you, sir," I said, nodding to him in acknowledgement of his acquiescence.

"Not at all, Jonah – thank you. We'll be monitoring everything that goes on, and at the first sign of any trouble, we'll get you out. I've put a Special Ops team on standby, and they'll be outside the door to the room." Sir Thomas stood up and held out his hand, smiling. Most of us don't shake hands anymore: we've borrowed the practice of 'wai' from the Thai and Indian cultures, but everything about Sir Thomas is antique, including his handshake. I took his hand, shaking firmly. His palm felt sweaty in my grip, and I resisted the urge to wipe my palm on my trouser leg.

Leaving Sir Thomas's office, the path under my feet lit the way to the nearest Lev ports. I followed the directional arrows, their subtle light blinking direction in time with my steps.

The Lev politely enquired, "Where do you wish to go, Arbitrator Oliver?"

"Er, yes, take me to Jibril Muraz. And I want to travel off-line, please."

"Certainly, Arbitrator Oliver, eight minutes to destination," the Lev said as the Lev capsule started to move.

I sat down. You couldn't really feel it moving, but the portal on the Devscreen next to the Lev door changed from the spinning UN icon to show how the capsule was moving through the complex. Only newer buildings have Levs; the older buildings still have the Lev's forefather, the elevator. A touch of the keypad or voice instruction could display your position relative to the universe if you really wanted to know that or simply your exact location on Earth. It could also display others traveling around you. Useful when you're lonely and looking for company, but right now I wanted to travel incognito, as far as I could be incognito when all those I reported to, and a fair few I didn't, could track my tag in a milsec if they wanted to. The portal showed I was about five hundred meters from the surface and tracking deeper, as well as in an easterly direction from my uncle's office.

"Destination is now estimated to be reached in approximately six minutes, Arbitrator Oliver."

Six minutes. My thoughts were still flashing across the inside of my forehead. I could feel them. My temples started to throb. Six minutes and I'm there. It wasn't much time, and usually I'd prepare for days, even months before a meeting, but there was no time. I took out my Devstick and reviewed the data that I had copied earlier. There wasn't much, but what there was, I read three times. The Lev spoke again.

"Arrived at destination, Arbitrator Oliver. Have a good day."

I rose from the Biosense chair in the Lev capsule a calm man. I felt like I could use a really strong alky, but I was calm.

THE RUNNER

Stepping out of the Lev that had brought me from Sir Thomas's office on the 244th floor of UNPOL headquarters just below Topside, I was now at the lowest level in New Singapore – Level Ten. The Deep. Apart from the lack of sky ports, the corridor looked almost like the one I had just left, except this one had no carpet. But then it wasn't an executive floor. I smoothed the suit I was wearing. Finest Italian wool, if a bit rumpled, as it was the same one I'd attended Milo's leaving party in. I straightened my back and traced the directional lighting with a firm step leading me towards the prisoner Jibril Muraz.

The Special Ops team, wearing full body armor, gas masks and black ear protectors, were standing in a group, all eight of them. The directional lights stopped about a meter in front of where the group was standing. I stopped in front of them and took off my upper outer, laying it on the floor. Then the upper inner and I was bare-chested. I could just see through the masks that three of the team were female. I stripped the rest of my clothes off and stood naked in front of them. One of the females deliberately tilted her face mask down to look at my crotch and then, looking up at me, smiled and gave me a thumbs-up. She made me feel better, and I grinned in spite of the situation. The group leader also gave me a thumbs up, and I realized that it meant I was good to go.

I turned to face a door. You could only tell it was a door because of its slightly different shade of color from the rest of the elongated tube I'd been walking in. I stepped up to the eye-level Dev and said, "Arbitrator Jonah James Oliver." Forcing myself not to pay attention to that quiver in my voice, I stood straighter and held my eyes open as the scan was done. The door swished open.

I took a step forward and found myself in white space. The room was entirely white, a matt white. I couldn't tell where floor, walls or ceilings began or ended – it was like being in a cloud. I turned to my left and saw at the opposite end of the room, seemingly floating in space, a man sitting on a Biosense chair, much like the ones in the conference room, although this one was in the room's same uniform matt white and almost invisible.

14

Jibril was still sitting in the lotus position. I took a tentative step forward and then another. My feet made no sound on the floor. I took another step and then another, and then I sensed something and put out my hand. Nothing. Another step with my hand held out in front of me, and then my hand touched something solid. Despite my foreknowledge of the partition, I still felt a quick surge of relief flow through me at the physical touch of this transparent wall between us. I looked down and around and saw a Biosense come out of the floor just behind me. I sat down. The Biosense felt cool on my buttocks. I wondered how many people were watching this.

"I'm Jonah James Oliver, arbitrator, but my friends call me JJ. You asked to see me." From what I could tell, Jibril was tall, brown hair, greying at the temples, with a pale, almost translucent complexion. His eyes blinked open.

"I know," he said and smiled. It was the first genuine smile of warmth that I had received all day or, for that matter, a very long time. The more I looked at the smile, the more I felt its warmth, and the more I wanted to smile back. I didn't, but I wanted to.

"Do you know what the name Jonah means?" he asked. His voice was very soft but firm and clear. There was a pure quality to it, each word enunciated perfectly.

"It means bad luck," I said.

"That's but one interpretation of the meaning and a rather literal one at that. According to the Ancient texts, Jonah was a Messenger of God. Do you believe in God, Jonah?" His eyebrows raised slightly as he waited for my answer.

I was thinking that this conversation was not going as planned, but then who was I kidding? What plan? The only plan that I was following was the 'fly by the seat of your pants' plan, so I decided to go along for the flight.

"Well, yes and no."

"Ah, Jonah," he said, with what I could have sworn was a twinkle in his eye, "belief in God is not a yes and no issue. You either do or you do not. The word belief is the crucial one there. It does not allow for fence-sitting or quibbling. So do you?"

"Maybe."

"Perhaps I shouldn't be asking such personal questions so early in our relationship, but then I feel as if I have known you for so many years." He shifted his position and, with both hands resting on his knees, looked comfortable despite the fact that he was naked. Yes, he was tall, judging by the height of his torso, at least one hundred and ninety cents, perhaps taller.

"Jonah was a prophet for all religions, the Son of Truth, a dove. He appears in the Old and New Testaments, the Koran, and the Jewish bible, not to mention the Bahai faith. In each he is seen as a Messenger of God, and a fairly strict one at that. Are you strict, Jonah? Will you request God to strike me down for my sins, or having sought repentance of Him, shall I be saved as you were vomited from the great fish's mouth onto the shores of Nineveh?"

I was thinking that this runner had quaffed a spike too many in his running days, but held the thoughts and didn't speak them out.

"You're probably thinking that I am totally crazy." He chuckled, a hand coming up to cover his mouth as if to hide his mirth at my totally readable expression.

"No, no, not at all. I just haven't heard that story of my name before. It's very interesting."

Again I lapsed into silence. I hadn't a clue what to say, and in those circumstances, it's usually better to keep your mouth shut and let everyone think that you may be a fool rather than opening it and removing all doubt.

"I don't think you're a fool, Jonah. Yes, Jonah, that is right."

Wait. I heard that, but his lips didn't move. He didn't say anything, but I heard him say that I was right – right about thinking he might be a telepath. This guy was freaking me out. Was I that readable? He continued to smile with a warmth that enveloped me, and I felt embraced by it, even in my shock. Nothing in my training came close to enabling me to deal with this situation. As arbitrators, our thoughts are our refuge, and if mine were on open display with him, then I had nothing left.

"Yes, Jonah, I am in your mind, but perhaps all of us are in each other's minds. However, that philo discussion will have to wait for another day, for we do not have much time. Jonah, we will have two conversations. One will be for the people monitoring our meeting, and the other will be for you and me. Of course, you are free to divulge to your superiors both of our conversations, but I ask that you hold off until we have finished. Now what we need to do here is very complex and usually takes months of training to get right. Obviously we don't have that much time. So this is how you do it. I have every faith in you, Jonah. I know you can do this.

"You will ask me a question using your voice. When you have finished, I will tell you something using my mind. As I am replying to your question using my voice, you will reply to my question using your mind, and so we will continue. Are you ready, Jonah?"

I thought, "Yes," and said, "You know my name and, indeed, seem remarkably well acquainted with it, so how should I address you?"

Just before I finished saying this, my mind was assaulted in a way that I can only describe as what I imagine insanity to be. His words, transmitted to my mind, overrode what I was saying, and it was a struggle to not repeat what he was saying in my mind, but I succeeded, just barely managing to strangle out the last spoken phrase.

In my mind he said, "I came here to enlist your help on urgent matters of global importance; there is a conspiracy that, if successful, will send this planet, and the colonies on the Moon and Mars, back into the Dark Ages."

I raised my eyebrows as if waiting for a response to my question, but it was more a reaction to the assault on my mind.

His voice said, "Names and PUIs aren't that relevant to me as a runner, Jonah. Look at you. You have carried your name for all your life without understanding its true meaning. However, for the purposes of ease of conversation, you may call me Jibril."

The smile had gone from his face to be replaced by a slight frown. I wondered if this was as a result of his having to concentrate on what I was thinking while he was talking.

I thought, "Why me?"

And said, "So, Jibril, you have admitted that you are a runner and have agreed to produce a statement of your activities for purpose of judgment under Article 2 of United Nation Containment Code, but you stopped the process and insisted on seeing me. How is it that you know of me?"

While saying this, again my mind was overlaid with his thoughts. Somehow I managed to get the words out, but now my temples were throbbing in pain at the effort of conducting these two conversations.

His thought said, "Jonah, your name is not Jonah, your uncle is not your uncle, and you are not you, as you know you. My real name is Gabriel – Jibril is Arabic for Gabriel. You must trust me, Jonah, it is vital for the future of this planet that you do."

I heard his voice say, "You represented an illegal that I once ran. He said you were kind and fair to him, which was good enough for me, and so I asked for you." I saw a bead of sweat roll from his temple down his jaw line and fall onto his chest.

I thought, "How can I trust you when I don't know who you are or where you come from?"

I said, "Do you perhaps remember which illegal this was? I mean the one who said that I treated him fairly?" My voice was strained; I hoped those monitoring this didn't notice.

"Your voice sounds natural enough, Jonah, and we're nearly finished. Proof of what I say and my trust in you is that in less than eight hours I will be gone from this room."

This thought overrode everything I was thinking, and then his voice said, "Who the illegal was is of no importance. The important thing is that I know the whereabouts of sixteen of the most wanted people in the universe, and your superiors want that information. To get it, they're going to have to give me what I want."

While he said this, I thought, "How does your disappearance provide me with the proof that I can trust you or that anything you have claimed is real?"

And I said, "Well, Jibril, perhaps if you tell me what it is that you want, I would be happy to relay that to the appropriate people."

I felt a trickle of sweat run from my armpit down my ribs. This wasn't easy, this dual conversation stuff. His thoughts again crowded in, swamping my thoughts of sweat, piercing into my head.

"Jonah, the proof is that I came here to meet with you to give you this message. When I leave, you will realize that the only reason I allowed myself to be caught was because this was the only way that I could reach you without causing suspicion to fall upon you."

"Ten million units, a full pardon and a drop off in the outlands of the region of South America," he said and smiled, sitting even further back in his chair. "Then with the aid of a Dev, I will track all sixteen of the illegals who were dropped when I was so rudely interrupted in my work."

I couldn't think of anything. I froze. My mind was a shattered nothing. I just looked blankly at him.

"That's enough for now, Jonah, I can feel you're at the breaking point. When the time comes, you will know what to do, and you will do the right thing. Don't trust Agent Cochran: she's a telepath as you are, so be very careful when you are in the same room with her to think of anything but this conversation or else you will find yourself here in the Deep, or worse."

Somehow my mind cleared enough for me to say, "Do you have anything else to add to that or is that the sum of your requests?"

Immediately after I'd spoken, I thought, "All right. I will wait eight hours, and if you're gone, then what do I wait for? And did you say I was a telepath?"

"No, I don't want anything else. That is all I require," he said and closed his eyes.

I stood up and turned around. As the door behind me opened, a final thought entered my head.

"You were born a telepath like your father, the man your so-called uncle captured, tortured, and then killed, but you are untrained, so unless you must use it to save your life, then do not. When the time comes, we will send you a sign, and you will do the right thing. Goodbye, my brother, for that is who you are. I await the day with eagerness when we will meet again."

I was dripping with sweat, sopping wet, and I felt wrung out mentally and physically. It was all I could do to walk through the door and retrace the steps to the Lev port. One of the Special Ops team handed me my clothes and wanted to take me by the elbow, but I shrugged him off and followed the lights. My brain was frozen, and I couldn't muster a single thought to my command. My exhaustion dominated all else. I entered the Lev port and sat down.

The Lev said, "I am instructed that your next destination is the director's office, Arbitrator Oliver. You will arrive there in approximately eight minutes."

The door slid shut silently, and eight minutes was the time I had to recover from what I had been told by Gabriel. My head was still a mess, and I could hardly recall our spoken conversation but our unspoken conversation was as clear as if it had been printed on the inside of my forehead. I could see every word and feel the emotion behind them. I sat back in the Biosense and shut my eyes.

"Off-line travel, please, Lev." I started putting my clothes on again.

Suddenly life had changed. That single thought dominated. I opened my eyes and, taking my Devstick out, looked at the time. In less than twenty-four minutes, the time it had taken since I had left the Lev to the time that I was sitting here right now, my entire life had changed.

When I was twenty-six, I had driven a car – it was a bright red Tesla Mach 4 with a beautiful raked back windscreen – into the back of another car. The anti-collision had failed, and I went through the windshield at about eighty kilos an hour. Two days and a hundred and twenty staples later, I was sitting outside in the hospital's garden under a huge banyan tree, feeling like the happiest guy on earth. Everything petty had just washed off me like mud off a sluice. I had felt so light that I thought I might float right up into the arms of the tree. Well, okay, the painkillers they'd given me probably accounted for some of my happiness, but the point is, I was having such a moment again. Only this time I didn't feel happy, I felt scared. But I wasn't crying over spilt latte either. I became focused upon my own survival.

"Destination is estimated to be reached in approximately six minutes, Arbitrator Oliver."

I realized, as if awakening to a whole new dimension of life, that suddenly circumstances had created a situation in which I might be a central figure to a plot of global significance. More indeed than simply significant, the future of the universe as we know it perhaps depended on my successful actions, whatever they turned out to be.

Don't panic. Focus. Right, okay. Me, save the planet. Right, no problem. I let out a long breath, emptying my lungs of every milcube of oxygen, until my diaphragm was pressed against my spine, and I held that moment. Then with a slight gasp, I drew in a breath as long as its exhaling partner. The only immediate solution, being the rational arbitrator that I was trained to be, was to re-evaluate the evidence surrounding this circumstance in another eight hours.

Gabriel had said that proof of his message would be in his disappearance, and that would happen within eight hours. Therefore I had everything to gain and nothing to lose by being the old me for another eight hours. I would banish, no, wipe out, all thoughts of my little mental chat with Gabriel and simply wait.

I mean the whole thing could be a set-up. This could all be part of some elaborate training exercise designed to test me under adverse circumstances.

What if they've got an internal and external transcript of the discussion? Do they have that kind of technology? I mean, I know they can read heart rate, blood pressure and temperature, that kind of stuff. Can they record your mind while you're having a chat? I don't know. Then don't worry about it. If they do, you're finished, but if Gabriel's telling the truth and you do walk into Uncle's office and spew out everything you two talked about, then you're headed for brain wipe or worse.

"Destination is estimated to be reached in approximately four minutes, Arbitrator Oliver."

THE DIRECTOR'S REVIEW

Sir Thomas paused the image of Jonah as he was just leaving the White Room after his discussion with the prisoner Jibril Muraz.

He turned sideways in his Siteazy and leaned towards Agent Cochran. "So, what do you think?" he asked, without any expression on his face.

Agent Cochran rose from the chair in front of Sir Thomas's desk and walked over to the wall screen. The image cut off as her body intercepted the light from the Dev, and turning to face the director, she said, "I don't like it, but I don't know what I don't like. If all the runner wanted was a free ticket to the wilds and a bunch of cred, why didn't he come out with that at the beginning and save himself from the Truth Treatment? That doesn't make sense."

"Perhaps he felt that he needed someone who he knew he could trust to deliver the right message on his behalf. Have you checked the list of illegals that my nephew has so kindly and fairly represented in his time as arbitrator?"

"Yes, Sir Thomas, I have. We're looking at fourteen individuals over the past eighteen months as our initial scan. In total, though, your nephew has dispensed his kindness with over eighty-five illegals cases, so we plan to run through and interview the last eighteen months first, and if we get nothing solid there, we'll track back further. All of the digital information on record has, of course, already been analyzed, but no hits there."

Sir Thomas tapped the Dev console set into the arm of the Siteazy, and the screen flashed on again – the sudden light a reminder to Agent Cochran that she was talking to the director. She quickly sat down, straight-backed, on the wooden chair and awaited Sir Thomas's pleasure.

He leaned towards her and in a conspirative tone said, "And what did you think of Jonah's reaction to the question 'You probably think I'm totally crazy?' Didn't anything odd strike you about that? Hmm?" Sir Thomas then said, "Dev, take the scene back to where Muraz talks about being crazy, please."

The image on the screen changed into a close-up shot of Jibril's face. His pulse, body temperature, heartbeat, and heat signature were all displayed at the bottom of the image. They were all within normal parameters, except the pulse rate which seemed a tad below normal.

As Jonah said on screen, 'No, no, not at all, I just haven't heard that story of my name before. It's very interesting', Sir Thomas leant over to Agent Cochran and again almost whispering said, "There, start watching there, and tell me what you see," jabbing with his forefinger at the wall screen and fixing her with a look that would make ice cubes if he cared to put it to that use.

Agent Cochran studied the images again, from Jonah to the runner. And as the runner said, 'You represented an illegal that I once ran. He said you were kind and fair to him, which was good enough for me, and so I asked for you,' she said, "Please stop the image there and focus on Muraz. There, yes, advance one, another. There, do you see that, Sir Thomas? The bead of sweat running down his temple. All his readings are normal, room temp was set at optimal for the core body heat of the two people in the room, so why the bead of sweat?"

The director smiled at her. She felt like it was a threat and smiled as non-threateningly as possible back. Sir Thomas lifted his eyes towards the door of his office and nodded to her. She turned to face in that direction as the director looked at his watch and said, "Now, you have two minutes before my nephew walks through that door, so get yourself ready."

She quickly ran through a list of the routines she could choose. Her mind games. She wanted to wait, let him settle down before she probed. Get right at what he was thinking while he was answering a question, so he'd be as naked in his mind as he was in the White Room. An image of Jonah naked flashed in her mind. And then an image of Jibril. She squirmed on the straight-backed wooden seat.

She slowed her breathing and let the present thoughts fall away. Focusing on breathing through her nose, feeling the passage of its life-sustaining force pass under the tip of her nose, she kept her eyes wide open and saw everything but nothing as she cleared her mind for the task ahead. Focused, she heard Sir Thomas speak.

"Dev, please open the door for my nephew," and Cochran prepared to cast her mind into Jonah's.

***

Sir Thomas and Agent Cochran were sitting down, both looking at the space where the door was when I walked in. Their attention turned to me.

I had chaired and participated in many debriefings after interview sessions.

The monitor was almost always immediately played to key sponsors as soon as the interview had finished, which might have just been possible since I'd had to relieve my bladder after leaving the Lev.

"Jonah, please take a seat." Sir Thomas waved his hand at the chair to Cochran's right.

I advanced across the Kurdish carpet and noticed that the weave changed colors as I walked over it. I sat down.

"Agent Cochran and I have been reviewing the monitor of your interview with the runner. It all seems to have gone remarkably well, wouldn't you say?" Sir Thomas said this with a slight smile on his face that made me very nervous. I could feel my heart racing.

"Well, yes, sir, it seems relatively straightforward," I replied, thinking, "I wish I could be like my uncle – he is so together."

"Right," Sir Thomas said, holding his smile in place. "Any other impressions of the runner, this Jibril, as he calls himself?"

"Um, well, I did think it strange that he wanted to see me in the first place. As Agent Cochran said in our earlier meeting, he's been through Truth Treatment, so I wonder why he didn't simply state these terms earlier. Frankly, I haven't been able to discern why he chose to wait to speak to me before asking for what he wants, and there was one other thing that I thought a little odd, but can likewise find no reason for."

"Well, spit it out, Jonah. What is this other thing you thought was odd?" Sir Thomas had changed his smile, and now regarded me with pursed lips and a slight frown.

"Well, at one point I noticed that a single bead of sweat rolled off him and fell on his stomach. Room temp was optimal for us so it wasn't heat. Therefore, it must have been stress. However, what he was talking about at that time wasn't particularly stressful, and so I cannot really figure out why he was sweating."

"Do you see me, Jonah?"

The words pierced into my mind from nowhere. I quickly thought, "I really want to be like my uncle. I hope that I can win his respect through this case. I must bring this case to a successful conclusion."

My uncle smiled and said, "Yes, well, Jonah, you've done well. I think you should take the rest of the day off, but remain ready to come back in if we need you."

"Thank you, sir." Rising, I smiled at Agent Cochran, who smiled back. I kept thinking, "It's great that my uncle thinks I handled that well," and held that thought until I was out of my uncle's office, once again following the lights' direction back to the Lev port.

***

As soon as the door slid shut behind Jonah, Sir Thomas said, "Well?"

"He was thinking about how much he admires you and wants to be like you."

"Did he realize that you were in his mind?"

"No. He had no idea. I only did a brief probe, but it turned up nothing. He simply admires you and hopes that this case will lead you to respect him more."

Sir Thomas nodded and, leaning back in the Siteazy, said, "And what do we make of our runner, then? Give him what he wants and hope that he plays ball, or put him through treatment again?"

"I think we should wait, Sir Thomas. Let him sweat for a while. It is highly unlikely that anyone else could have picked up where he left the illegals, so only he knows where they all are. With no one to run them if they move without him, they'll be picked up, which might give us a little more leverage than we have now." Agent Cochran was still straight-backed as could be and on delivering this last opinion seemed, if it could be possible, to straighten out even more.

Ambitious and talented, thought Sir Thomas. Very ambitious and certainly ruthless – she wants my job or more. Well, I'm not quite ready to move on yet, and she's not quite ready to take over. But in time, really, there is no one else – although hinting that Jonah may be my top choice for my replacement may cast an interesting element into the mix.

As Sir Thomas pondered succession, and her ambition, Agent Cochran sat perfectly still. She could, if required, remain absolutely still for over thirty-six hours.

Sir Thomas made a steeple of his hands and, bringing them to his lips, said, "Right, we've had him in containment for 56 hours and 34 minutes, so let's keep him where he is, no food, no water and no access to waste facilities. It's 1:38 now, let him stew in his own excrement for another 15 hours, and we'll interview again at 3am-ish, by which time he may be more amenable to seeing things our way."

TOPSIDE

I headed straight towards the Lev port nearest the director's office for the third time in one day and in my life to date. Right now I wanted as much distance as I could get between me and Cochran and my uncle. I was scared and glad to be out of there.

The Lev politely enquired, "Where do you wish to go, Arbitrator Oliver?"

"Take me Topside, nearest Lev port, please." I didn't bother sitting down; we were only a level below Topside.

"Certainly, Arbitrator Oliver. Half a minute to destination."

I kept a straight face, but it was very hard. I felt like smiling. I felt like smiling a huge smile, a gigantic smile, but I didn't. Instead, I let that smile grow inside me, spreading its warmth through to every pore, and I now wanted sun and sky. I had to control my breathing, and my heart felt as if it were trying to break out of my chest, but I had to control it. How much do they monitor, and were they monitoring me right now in this executive Lev? I didn't know, but it occurred to me that if I was going to survive this, then I had better find out and fast. This is how a criminal must think. I'm thinking like a criminal. It was a shocking thought, but it was true.

"Lev, what's the weather like outside?"

"Temperature is twenty-three degrees cel with scattered nimbus clouds, and a forty-five percent chance of rain. Wind is out of the southeast and at eight to twelve kilos: a light breeze."

"Travel off-line, please."

Score one for Gabriel, I thought. The bitch from hell did try to get in my mind while I was in there, but my plan seemed to have worked. At least I am free. When I came out of the Lev before going to the director's office, I remembered Gabriel's warning about Agent Cochran with a vengeance. It scared me enough that the urge to relieve myself was desperate. I headed for the nearest outlet to have a think, and I came up with the idea that I would simply report exactly what had happened in the room and the rest of the time all I would think about was what a great guy the director was and how much I would like to be like him.

It is impossible to think of two things at the same time; we're not dimensional enough to do that. It should be possible for our brains to do parallel processing, but we're just not there yet. So if anyone did attempt to read what was in my mind, then all they would get was that I really admired the director.

And I assume it had worked. The debrief had gone perfectly from my point of view, and I could now just wait until eight hours passed or something happened that meant I had to go back. Either way, the fact that Agent Cochran did read my mind meant that Gabriel had told the truth about at least one thing, and on that score, he was doing better than anyone else so far today.

"Arrived at destination, Arbitrator Oliver. Have a good day."

The Lev door opened, and I stepped out into a covered area. In front of me was the entrance to the UNPOL Executive Club, to my left the railed walkway that ran around Topside. I took out my Devstick and said, "Give me a map of the Topside area nearest to me." The map came up; I thumbed down to zoom in and said, "Find me nearest relax lounge outside of one kilom from where I am." A kilom ought to be enough distance between me and UNPOL staffers.

It was a bit early to have an alky and, strictly speaking, was against the rules because although I had the day off, I was on standby and therefore supposed to remain clean. But somehow, under the circumstances, I reckoned I'd be forgiven this small indulgence and headed for a Sky Level relax lounge. A name came up attached to a lounge icon on the map. Polar Nights. I thumbed 'Go To' and the shortest route was indicated with a thin red line. The directional arrow on my map pointed left, so I obeyed and started walking.

The Topside area on Jurong Island is mostly new, except over near the wharves on the side closest to the mainland of New Singapore. There it narrows to a one hundred and eighty meter wide stretch that arches over the water between the mainland and the island of Jurong. The idea of a Topside had been voted in by New Singapore residents in 2085 – they were one of the early adopters although now most of the major cities have a Topside. By connecting all the high-rise buildings with a structure that could accommodate the weight of full landscaping and maximum two-storey buildings, a new landscape was created on top of the city.

Topside is mostly for relaxation and greenery, providing green open spaces for people who would otherwise be surrounded by metal, plastic and other manmade materials all of their lives. There aren't any electric or other vehicles on Topside, except walkers and bicycles. I had taken the easterly route that would lead me in a half circle around the UNPOL golf course to the wharf area. Of course, the wharves themselves are fifteen hundred meters below Topside, but it was still called the wharf area.

The rubberized walkway was mostly deserted as I walked along. A jogger in UNPOL tracksuit outers jogged past me and gave me a smile. I controlled my paranoia and smiled back. Discreet directional arrows set into the walkway beat a time with the directional arrow in the map on my Devstick and led me around a par three.

I heard a golfer exclaim, "Shit," as his ball hit the water in the pond between him and the green. His companions laughed. A mother pushing her child along in a stroller also smiled at me, and I felt the paranoia increase. This is ridiculous, Jonah, I thought. Calm down. I decided to change the route I was on and turned left onto a path running between the golf course and a park. For a sec or two my Devstick squawked at me as the directional arrow on it blinked red. I ignored it and kept walking.

I couldn't smile just in case I'd been tagged and they were tracking my every image whether digital or physical. I just had to act normally. That way no one would suspect anything. Breaking with routine should be okay, but I had to do something natural. Having a strong alky and needing somewhere to reflect is natural behavior after what I had been through, and then I'd head straight back to my Envplex where I would simply wait. I took another look at my Devstick. It had responded to my change in course and provided a new route based upon my current direction. I took another turn, right this time, and checked the Devstick again. About another fifteen hundred meters to go.

The sun and breeze on my face felt great, and in the time it took me to reach Polar Nights, I had come to the conclusion that everything Gabriel had said was true. The entrance to Polar Nights at my back, I took in the view from Sky Level over to the mainland, resting my arms on the safety rail that ran along the edge of the walkway. Fifteen hundred meters below me, the surface looked green and tranquil, the Travways cleverly hidden from the view from above by the designers of New Singapore.

I thought about Gabriel's claim that what I did would have significance for the future of the planet and help prevent a conspiracy that could send us back to the Dark Ages. The Charter came to mind. The revised Charter of the United Nation, wherein individual nations were all consolidated, first published in 2063, seven years after the last Great War. The preamble says:

to save succeeding generations from the scourge of war, which is potentially catastrophic and devastating to mankind, and

to reaffirm faith in fundamental human rights, in the dignity and worth of the human person, in the equal rights of all humans, and

to establish conditions under which justice and respect for the obligations arising from treaties and other sources of Global Law can be maintained, and

to promote social progress and better standards of life in larger freedom, and

to promote the spread of humankind through the universe.

I had learnt this preamble as a student, as we all do, and then again with all the treaties, laws, and codicils therein when I had decided on being an arbitrator as an element of my purpose. And now, according to Gabriel, this preamble, this premise that every human capable of reasoned thought takes for granted, was in my hands.

Gabriel's conversation in my mind was clear now, but like a memory from a dream, I could also recall our words spoken for the benefit of those monitoring our interview. I had no doubt that, by this time, those images and sounds as well as all the other data attached to that interview would have been dissected and analyzed thousands of times over by many pairs of eyes, but it seemed as if we had pulled off our private chat without any suspicion falling on us.

In less than eight hours, Gabriel would disappear from the interview room. I had no idea what he meant by disappear. Escape or vaporize, I simply could not imagine how one could do either. The Deep was approximately two thousand meters down from the surface and no one had ever escaped. Gabriel's level one status meant he was under constant monitoring. Even if his Tag had disappeared off the Grid, his physical presence was under containment. Somehow I had no doubt that what Gabriel had said he would do would happen.

I noticed that a rather wet-looking cloud was about to envelop the walkway I was on and headed into the Polar Nights, which the Dev by the door advertised as a little piece of heaven designed primarily for hetros but welcome to all, and ambled my way over to the 'Males' entrance. A young couple came out of the Unisex entrance and kissed as I walked through into the dimly lit interior. As advertised, the emphasis was on hetro, and a young woman wearing a beautiful smile and not much else came up to me.

"Hi, welcome to Polar Nights. Are you meeting anyone in particular, or can

I just help you find a seat?"

"Uhm … I'd like to have a seat and just relax by myself for a while, thanks," I said and smiled back at her.

"Sure, please come this way, we've just upgraded our Siteazys, and the Aurora section of the lounge is empty right now. How does that sound?" she asked as she led me through the dark lounge to a huge Siteazy with a Dev beside it. I looked at the Aurora Borealis massively cast on the floor-to-ceiling Devscreen. Perfect, I thought, and sat down in the Siteazy.

The first woman left, and a second arrived. "Hi, my name's Sahara." She flashed me another beautiful smile. She was about the same height as me, about one hundred and eighty-six cent, with the blondest hair I had ever seen. "Can I get you any refreshment, and would you like a leg massage while relaxing?"

"Yes to the refreshment, and no to the massage, thanks, Sahara. I'd like a very strong alky, but not paralytic if you know what I mean."

"Sure. We have a cocktail called the Endorpho 80, which is really great. It'll put your mind into a semi-meditative state within thirty secs and complete muscle relaxation within forty-five," she rattled this off and finished with another of those brilliant smiles, and I just nodded, lying back in the Siteazy. I thought the day had definitely taken a turn for the better.

The alky arrived borne by the radiant and young Sahara who left me with a charming, "If you need absolutely anything, I am here to serve you," and swished away with an alluring little sway of her buttocks. I smiled to myself and took a long draught of this Endorpho. It had a slight minty flavor but wasn't too sweet and slipped down nicely.

I felt the drink hit, as promised. I'd forgotten to ask how long I would stay in this most pleasantly aware but relaxed state, but with these kind of loaded alkys, the hit usually lasted at least an hour, so I just laid back and enjoyed it. Before I relaxed too completely, I punched out a quick command on my Devstick to send me fresh clothes, both inners and outers, from my Envplex to the Polar Nights and told the Dev at the side of Siteazy to have Sahara deliver these once the effects of the Endorpho 80 wore off. With a slight chuckle to myself, I wondered if they had an Endorpho 100 and decided not to go there. I would need my wits about me for whatever was to come.

The tension in my body flowed out as the drink hit my nervous system, and my thoughts turned once again to Gabriel and his final words.

Gabriel was my brother, and my uncle was not my uncle, but he was the man who had killed my father. Not only killed, but tortured as well. My uncle, if this was true, was the personification of what our Charter purported to protect us from.

Despite the Endorpho, I tensed, a quiet rage surfacing, but with purpose I pushed that rage aside and turned my thoughts to planning my action ahead. We cannot know the future, but we can plan based upon likely scenarios, and it was these scenarios that I started running through my head like a data stream on free flow.

A Boring Machine

Gabriel sat in exactly the same position as when Jonah had left the interview room over seven hours and thirty-four minutes ago. The fact that Gabriel knew to the second when Jonah had left the room was a testament to his mental strength and his prowess in matters of mind control. Gabriel had been counting since his capture in Bangkok, which had happened two hundred and twenty-eight thousand, eight hundred and forty seconds ago. Or to be less precise, sixty-three and a half hours ago.

Some time in the next twenty-five minutes or so, he would be rescued. That is what they had calculated when profiling the capture and containment. That they had been correct up to this point was due to their research into the methods of UNPOL.

Gabriel stopped counting now that the time was so close and instead prepared his breathing for what was coming. Once the room was breached, it and the attached corridor tube would be flooded with paralyzing nerve gas and paralyzing sound. Anyone taking but a single breath or exposing their eardrums to the sound would be instantly immobilized.

Suddenly in the stillness of the room he felt a slight tremor under his bare feet, and it grew rapidly until the Biosense chair, which he quickly rose from, was visibly shaking. Standing upright, Gabriel took a deep breath and held it. Placing his hands over his ears, he looked straight ahead to where he felt the direction of the shaking was coming from. A faint noise began to accompany the shaking and increased rapidly until it was a roar, and the room partition shattered with the movement into an opaque-glazed mess. A large black circle appeared in the wall in front of him, cut by the teeth of a revolving blade. Twenty panels opened in the lower part of white wall, and nozzles spraying a mustard-colored gas poked out as a bone-wrenching cacophony of sound assaulted Gabriel's eardrums through his hands.

The circular piece of wall crashed forward into the room, revealing a large machine. In the middle of the hub that held the cutting blade, a small door opened, and two figures wearing bright red ear protectors and body armor stepped quickly out of the door and rushed over to Gabriel. In the face mask he made out Maloo's flat nose wrinkled with his laughter as, grasping Gabriel's arm, they moved quickly to the door of the giant boring machine, the 'Mole'. Maloo pushed Gabriel through first into the tiny airlock and then climbed in after with the other member of the extraction team. The door's bolts slid home with a pneumatic swoosh, and the air in the airlock was filtered with the giant extractor, pulling the tight bodysuits in its direction with its force.

The 'clean air' light went on, and Maloo leaned over Gabriel and hit the button to open the door to the main capsule. The Mole disengaged from the White Room with a jolt and began its journey back up the tunnel it had created getting there.

***

Cochran and her partner, Sunita Shido, had just finished their appetizers when Cochran's Devstick screen flashed red. She picked it up and held it to her ear, glancing around at the other people seated near her in La Maison.

Her mouth open, she gasped and exclaimed, "What!" Cochran's eyes flitted around at the people near her again to see if they had noticed. No one had heard her except Sunita, who laid her knife and fork down on her plate and placed her hands on the table beside it. Sunita swallowed the oyster that was on her tongue and reached for her glass of red wine.

"When did this happen?" she heard Cochran rasp in a harsh whisper into her Devstick. "Ten minutes! Why have you taken this long to notify me? Never mind, there is no excuse. All right, lock down the area and no news of his escape is to be broadcast, not until I'm there, do you understand?"

She put the Devstick back on the table in front of her and, picking up her wine glass, swallowed its contents. Sunita said, "Trouble at UNPOL?"

"The runner I was telling you about just escaped. I've got to go," Cochran said and stood, picking up her Chanel purse. "Don't wait for me – this could take some time."

Sunita nodded and took another sip of wine. "Go, Sharon, go, stay safe," and tilting her head towards the French doors behind Cochran, she smiled.

Cochran gave her a small tight smile back and, with a slight shrug of her shoulders, turned on her heel, head down, and strode out of the restaurant, leaving through the sliding glass French doors, her Devstick to her mouth as she walked. They had chosen La Maison, the intimate Topside French restaurant of the Hyatt Hotel. Just off to the right of the restaurant was its tropical Balinese garden with a large area of green lawn stepped at different levels framed by shallow swimming lanes. As she walked over the patio, a Heliocopter glided down, its electrically driven propellers turning silently in the dark cool of the evening. It was twenty-one degrees cel, a cool night for New Singapore.

The reflection of the flashing blue light slowly shrank in size on the green lawn as the Heliocopter came in to land. The door slid open to receive Cochran as, Devstick still held to her mouth, she gave instructions, speaking urgently. "Place immediate satimage coverage of Jurong. If we don't get him within the next five minutes, expand that coverage to New Singapore and the equivalent ocean area. I assume that you have locked down all transit points. Please confirm."

She climbed into the Heliocopter, and the door clunked shut. Already in the air, the craft dipped its nose slightly and headed for Jurong Island eight kiloms to the southwest. The craft quickly picked up height and speed, and soon the chopwhir of the propellers was audible in the cabin. Cochran sat listening to and watching the different voice and image channels coming in over her Devstick, her thumb frantically scrolling the images.

She flicked from the image of the Lev and airship ports of Changi. He wouldn't be crazy enough to try to get through there, she thought. He's got to be somewhere close, and he'll try to get out by sea. That's what I would do. Again she held the Devstick to her mouth. "Make sure all ocean and port areas are covered. Get all UNPOL marine vessels on high alert. Anything that has moved from port to ocean in the last five minutes, board and search. Use UNPOL Blue Notice as required, upon my authority."

She listened and watched as the activity driven by her commands picked up pace. He couldn't have gone far. She checked the time on the Devstick: 8:45pm. She realized she was seriously panicked. How could this have happened on her watch?

Sitting on the hard metal seats that ran along the cabin, she didn't bother with the safety webbing, couldn't waste the time to put it on as she was focused on the action on the screen of the Devstick. The Heliocopter came in fast, landing with a thump, a bounce and slight grind of a skid on the roof of the UNPOL Executive Club. She disembarked, one hand heaving her out of the cabin, and ran in a crouch towards the stairs leading to the Lev port that would take her down to the command center. She had to catch him: this couldn't happen, not on her watch.

***

The Mole shot out of the hole it had first made six days ago in the floor of the warehouse in Jurong Port, and skidded to a stop just before hitting the wall. Gabriel glanced at the time on the Devscreen hanging from the ceiling of the Mole, 8:40pm, and hit the open door release. The door hissed open and swung free. He jumped up from his crouched position and, one hand on the circular titanium frame of the door, jumped to the floor of the warehouse. Maloo and Isaac quickly followed, and the three of them walked over to a large plastic sheet laid on the floor of the warehouse. No one spoke. They knew what they had to do, and they had already agreed on the best way to do it. Maloo and Isaac stripped off everything they were wearing, dropping it to the plastic sheet. Gabriel, already naked, walked over to a shelf with three deep-sided trays stacked one on top of the other. He picked the stack up and walked back to Maloo and Isaac, who had finished stripping and were folding the plastic sheet into a small block.

Gabriel laid out the three trays side by side with a meter in between, and the three men each sat in front of a tray. Inside was the identity, the person they would become to enable their escape. Running. An identity designed to be anonymous, to fit in with the masses, to not be an anomaly, and therefore to pass under the radar to the other side. In the single nation an individual can travel anywhere provided he acknowledges the right of the nation to know who he is and what he is doing at any time.

As individuals travel through security zones, PUIs, or Tags as they are called, are activated and visually compared to known statistics and images. Everywhere on the Earth, the Moon and Mars, the three 'worlds' human beings occupy, this invasion of privacy is accepted for the right to travel anywhere freely. Every day in New Singapore, half a million people travel through the city and its surrounding area. To run, you need an identity that will appear in its movements and digital actions not to be suspicious, but to be normal. And they each had a tray of normality.

Gabriel, on the far right of the others, glanced to his left. Maloo was struggling into the brown boots he'd selected. With a final tug, he laid back his elbows on the cement floor and said, "Well, brother, do we look like Haulers?"

"You'll do," Gabriel said and walked over to the wall of the warehouse. A section of the wall stood detached, leaving a space that was just big enough for them to squeeze through. Gabriel went first, and the others followed, each turning sideways through the narrow gap. Once on the other side, Gabriel and Maloo pulled the piece of the wall into place, and Isaac picked up a tube of instant cement. As soon as the wall fit, he pulled the trigger, and the cement gun spurted a thin tube of expanding cement from its nozzle. Gabriel and Maloo quickly walked across the floor of the warehouse and went through the next space.

Two warehouses over from the one the Mole had made its exit in, a seventy-five meter articulated chrome-plated long-hauler stood waiting with all systems running. With the last wall space closed and cemented, the three men headed for the entrance to the long hauler. The door was open, and Gabriel made his way up the winding staircase until he reached the bridge. He sat down in the primary driver's seat and pulled the View Devscreen closer to his eye position. Maloo climbed into the seat next to him, and Isaac disappeared down the companionway stairs.

"Activate mapped course to Jakarta, full autopilot on," Gabriel said into the mic that distended from the edge of the Devscreens. It looked like a fly hovering just a cent from his mouth. Telemetric data from the vehicle flooded the Devscreen with numbers scrolling in a constant flow across images which showed the warehouse from the front, rear, side and top of the vehicle.

Gabriel looked out of the front windshield of the bridge, over the sloped chromed snub-nose of the long-hauler, at the cement floor twenty meters below him. The roof of the warehouse was just high enough, with only ten cents clearance between the top of the long-hauler and the ceiling. The doors to the warehouse slowly slid open, and the long-hauler pulled out onto Wharf One of Old Jurong Port. Gabriel glanced at the time set into the sweeping console of the bridge in front of him. 8:49pm – slightly ahead of schedule.

On Her Watch

The Active Trace Command Center (ATCC) at UNPOL Headquarters is the largest single user of Devscreen displays in the world. It is designed to provide a global, real-time surveillance and interdiction capability to UNPOL to safeguard the citizens of the world. Capable of reading a watch face, cameras circling the planet capture movement and display that movement on the Devscreens. Actions are compared against an optional set of parameters for a given area. Parameters might include humans, vehicles, walking, running or driving, and when any of these are triggered, the camera can zoom down to a minute detail, Tag the movement and bring up any associated information attached to it. Or, in the case of a human being tagged, its Personal Unique Identifier (PUI).

There are approximately six point three million people living and moving around in New Singapore at any one time. Tracking this amount of movement by human eyeballs is possible but requires too many people. ATCC instead relies on its computational ability to solve this problem. Everything from washing machines and mobile phones to electric automobiles has computational ability. This computational ability is called a Dev. ATTC's Devs are huge, occupying four floors in the massive complex and drawing seven percent of the total power output of New Singapore.

Cochran entered the command center at a fast walk and immediately headed to the primary Devcockpit console set high and at the rear of the room. Picking up the helmet that lay on the console, she put it on, adjusting the mic to the right angle for her mouth. The room was buzzing with activity. She thumbed a switch on the console, and the room's buzz was replaced with the sound of two UNPOL officers questioning a suspect. The image on her Dev had a blue frame to show it was the active screen that she was listening to.

She said, "Change," and the image and sound switched to another suspect being questioned, this time aboard a ship on the ocean just off UNPOL Headquarters. From the Devcockpit she had a view of all the Devscreens in the room.

36

She immediately issued an UNPOL Blue Notice requesting assistance in arrest and containment or any information related to the whereabouts of Jibril Muraz. The Blue Notice also contained the line 'suspect is believed to be armed and dangerous' and was flashed to UNPOL offices globally. Scanning the Devscreens arrayed in front of her, she looked up, hands on her hips, and surveyed the rest of the room. It was busy and had been since Muraz had escaped. UNPOL was on high alert, and all shifts had been called in.

The Devs do their work in spotting suspicious movement or actions, and then human eyeballs take over to provide analysis and interpretation. Everyone's Devstick carries their PUI, and the log of that PUI can be pulled up for inspection. Everything we've achieved and everything we do digitally is attached to our log and transparent to UNPOL. This is their right, just as we have the right to investigate UNPOL and seek access to all files or information that is on record, unless blocked by court order for reasons of National Security or the safety of others.

Cochran surveyed the list of tagged PUIs and noted their position on the overlay map of New Singapore. The number was around one hundred suspicious acts in progress, but this number rose and fell according to tags being cleared off and new tags being added. The Geographic area of New Singapore had a total of thirty-two thousand, three hundred and thirty-five crimes committed so far this year, an average of eighty-eight point five eight crimes per day. Today, that average was up over ten percent, but Cochran didn't care about the other ninety-seven point eight seven. The whole department was focused on a single crime; one that was unique in the history of UNPOL, that of Jibril Muraz escaping the Deep.

Most of New Singapore was within ten minutes' reach. As UNPOL units contacted each suspect and cleared them off the list, the number of suspicious tags started dropping. Within five minutes, this had fallen to an average of ten suspicious acts going on at any one time. The Devscreen showed the images of the suspects being halted and questioned, but none of the images showed what she wanted. She glanced at the time again: 8:53pm. She felt the panic rise in a surge and squashed it down, focusing on the Devscreens in front of her.

A Devscreen to her far left told of events in the tunnel made by the Mole. Mines had been left and the bomb disposal unit was still trying to figure out how to defuse them. Still no progress.

"Send in a remote control unit to sweep. We might lose a couple, but it will be faster than this," Cochran said into the microphone. The UNPOL BDU officer in the tunnel nodded his head. She changed the active Devscreen again. Still nothing. Where, where, where? Where is he? He must have gone out to sea, but everything there had checked out as normal.

A chrome-plated long-hauler pulling out of Old Jurong Port driving along Wharf One caught her eye. She made it the active screen. Three male occupants. She ordered a check of the vehicle. A closed-circuit camera at the exit of Wharf One gave her a close-up image of the two men sitting high up on the long-hauler's bridge. One was black and had the features of an aborigine from Australia, hair in dreadlocks. The other was white, bearded, with dark hair over his shoulders and wearing a blue NY Yankees baseball cap. The PUIs checked out – they were regular drivers and their PUI images matched their image on the closed-circuit cameras. She flipped the active Devscreen, her fingers drumming a steady beat on the console.

***

In the bridge of the long-hauler, Gabriel had his Devstick folded out on his lap, fingers and voice giving commands. On his Devscreen he had images of all the closed-circuit cameras and satimages that were focused on his route. The satimages he didn't worry about, as they could only see the top of the long-hauler, and this was a regularly scheduled trip. The closed-circuit cameras were another matter, and those required the intervention of his actions. He had made his early living being a runner; it was his craft, and he was one of the best. Each time they approached a camera, his intervention through his Devstick caused the digital signals to be changed – substituting the correct PUIs and the images from footage that they had captured from the same cameras that were now trying to track them. Normality is the hardest thing to detect, and everything about their profile was normal.

He checked the time: 8:55pm. In another five minutes, they'd clear New Singapore and be on the Australasia Travway. Once there, the long-hauler would increase speed to six hundred kilos an hour. They'd be rolling through Jakarta by 10:30pm. At the Australasia long-hauler park, just outside of Jakarta, they'd swap with the real drivers in the food court. He smiled and thought, three very wealthy drivers, and focused his attention on the upcoming main security zone for the on-ramp to the Australasia Travway – the huge eight lanes either way transport route running from Auckland to Osaka.

They reached the on-ramp, and the long-hauler slowed in the queue of traffic waiting, attached now to the mag lev tracks set into the surface of the Travway. The traffic around them was mostly long-haulers with a few EVs, electric vehicles, in the far right lane. They were on the far left lane. The security zone had sixteen cameras. Gabriel had all the cameras up on his Dev. As each scanned the bridge of the vehicle, he altered the signal in the camera, sending the images he had on his dev of the real drivers. They moved up in the queue, and a light on the Dev console of the long-hauler flashed green as their speed picked up, and they went up the ramp. As they crested, Gabriel looked at the speed indicator on the Devscreen set into the console of the bridge, two hundred and fifty kilos and climbing. Home free.

***

Cochran checked, for the hundredth time. The time was 10:35pm. He'd escaped. She knew it in the marrow of her tired, defeated bones, and it cut like a hot knife in her gut. She showed no emotion and kept issuing commands, even though she knew it was futile. Rage and despair warred for dominance in her. Rage won. She wasn't going to just capture this Jibril, she was going to kill him, but only after she'd made him suffer. She was as sure of that as she was that he had escaped. On her watch! The only ever escape from the Deep. The hot knife twisted. She sucked in, evil thoughts of revenge racing in her mind.

A Normal Life

Jonah's Env, Unit A, 20th floor, Woodlands
Envplex, Woodlands, New Singapore.
Thursday, 12 December 2109, 5:15am +8 UTC

As I woke up, I realized that what had been nagging at the edges of my brain had worked itself out. I knew why I trusted Gabriel, or Jibril in Arabic. It was his eyes: they were like mine.

The escape of Jibril Muraz was reported on newsfeeds globally, and an UNPOL Blue Notice, Contain on Site, was issued. All the major newsfeeds carried it, and his image, this time clothed, was broadcast continuously with appeals for further information. The manner of his escape, however, was a closely guarded secret and known only to those who had to know in order to do their work.

I learned of it in my briefing with the director, the evening of Gabriel's escape. My part in the matter of Gabriel had not been released to the feeds. Whereas the bitch from hell, Agent Cochran, had her image repeatedly broadcast and was reported as saying that Muraz would soon be contained and, "No further comment for the moment, thank you."

I tried to keep busy, but it was impossible to think of anything else except what I had been told in that exhausting mind conversation. I had a brief chat with Bill Scuttle, the senior partner in the firm, and cleared with him that I was going to take a few days self-time and that I'd be back to contribute by Monday. I confirmed with UNPOL that there were no pressing pro bono duties, and I stayed in my Envplex waiting for the sign.

I thought about the sign all the time, worried about missing it. I also thought about my uncle, my so-called uncle. He had murdered my father and was in a conspiracy to send the planet back into the Dark Ages. It sounded crazy, but I believed it. The fact that I believed it made me think I might be going crazy, but I believed it to my core.

I looked at the Devscreen next to the sleeper. 5:15am. I folded my arms behind my head on the pillow and stared at the ceiling. Usually I am good at waiting. I can be very patient – it's part of being an arbitrator. But this wasn't some spat between two corporate enterprises, Ents, raging at each other over infringed copyrights. This was my life. I had so many questions that I couldn't ask. Who am I? Who is Sir Thomas? Why did he kill my father? What is the conspiracy? Was I under suspicion? Was I being more closely watched? Is my Env bugged? This last thought caused a quick surge of adrenalin, and I sat up and looked around my Env. I let out a long slow breath. If it was bugged and I suddenly started looking for them, it would be suspicious. If they were there, the only thing I could do was act normally. As long as they can't tell what I'm thinking, they can't know what I know.

Lying there, I tried to recall my first known memory. I was surprised that the earliest really solid memory was of when I was ten years old. On my tenth birthday I had boarded a flight. It was a holiday, and I was flying to a summer camp in Italy from London. As I was an unaccompanied child, an Alitalia air staffer was assigned to get me on the airship. When she saw from my PUI on my Devstick that it was my birthday, she gave me a big smile and, putting her face close to mine with that big smile on it, proceeded to tug my right ear lobe ten times. It hurt. And I wished she would stop. That is my first real memory.

I can remember things from when I was five years old, but not clearly. They're impressionist memories. But from ten years old, I can remember things quite clearly. People, events, the schools, knowledge learned, decisions made, these memories are more solid. My uncle had told me that my parents died just after I was born, and this is an impressionist memory. A sad little boy standing in front of his uncle, being told why his parents did not visit him like the other children's parents. I feel and remember the sadness but the exact time, place and circumstances have faded.

Another reason I believed Gabriel is that Sir Thomas and I look nothing alike. And from what I had seen from the very scant images of my parents, I didn't look much like my supposed father, Sir Thomas's brother. If what Gabriel had said was true, and I chose to believe it was, then everything that had been told to me about the origins of my existence was a lie.

I have the images of their funeral service, but apart from that, only two other images of my parents exist. I am in none of them. I had always thought that strange. Don't mothers always hold their babies and have an image taken? As a boy, it was hard to build fantasies around such flimsy evidence of existence, but still I tried. I can remember that. Lying in my sleeper in the dormitory at night, imagining that in the morning my parents would be there to take me home. I tried to remember what I dreamed about, after I turned ten, but drew a blank.

I tried to remember what I dreamed about last week. I don't dream, I realized. I have no dreams.

It was hard to frame Sir Thomas in my mind as an evil person. My inheritance from my parents, under Sir Thomas's management until I turned eighteen, had grown substantially, and I didn't need to contribute to earn cred. Sir Thomas had also seen to my education and placed me in different schools throughout my youth. He said in speeches that my circumstances were what led him to form the Oliver Foundation, a globally recognized scholarship program for orphaned children.

We had neither lived, nor traveled together. We would meet usually in a meeting room set aside for the purpose at the school or academy I was attending. In one sense I grew up surrounded by people, in another I grew up totally alone. It struck me how little I actually knew about my uncle, and I realized that this was not a good thing. I had to know more.

Why did you murder my father? Just to think of that spun the thoughts in my head into a whirlwind. As a society we abhor violence in any form, mental or physical. We are taught from a young age that it is the basest of behaviors, that murder is the most heinous of all violence. The finality of it extinguishes all hope and leaves nothing but negative energy. That my uncle could be capable of such a thing shocked me to my core. Somewhere out there was a man who had answers for me, my brother, he had said, and I believed that too.

Perhaps it was this unsubstantiated, born in the gut sureness that had thrown my thoughts into such confusion. I couldn't work it out. Usually I am a skeptical person. Not negative. I'm optimistic, but I'm also pragmatic, and therefore skeptical. It wasn't usual for me to believe in something without having solid evidence to justify that belief. Here I had no such evidence, only an event foretold coming to pass. But there was something else that made me believe Gabriel and it had nothing to do with evidence. It was his eyes.

As much as I wanted to just lie in the sleeper, the lack of a sign gnawed at my conscience. He had told me that he needed my help on a matter of 'global importance'. It was difficult to sleep with those words constantly in my brain, and I felt guilty just lying there. I should be doing something, but what? Wait for the sign. I tried to think what he would have wanted me to do, and the only thing I could come up with was to make myself available for discreet contact.

A part of me, a really significant part of me, was afraid of my uncle. To my knowledge, I had never met a murderer and just to know that about someone was terrifying. I pushed that thought away with the less sure one that Sir Thomas didn't know that I knew what he was. The trifling comfort it provided allowed me to sketch out a plan of action. Act normal, but try to find out more about Sir Thomas. If Gabriel was smart enough to figure out how to get into and out of the Deep just to meet me, then for sure he was smart enough to send me the sign irrespective of what I was doing. I climbed out of my sleeper and walked naked over to the Clearfilm desk in front of the window that looked out over the causeway to Johor.

I was about to turn on the Dev on the desk, but my hand stopped before it touched the small red button that would bring it alive. What was I going to do on the Dev? Was anyone watching? Would not using the Dev create suspicion? I had to keep up appearances. I had to make it look as if everything was exactly the same in my life. The Dev suddenly became a threat in my mind. We called it Dev, short for Device, the ubiquitous apparatus that provided us with the means of communication. In the twentieth century when personal computers were first invented, they were indeed personal, but by the end of that century most of them were connected to the Internet. The Internet and another invention, the mobile phone, caused the convergence, Dev, that made terms like phone, computer and camera almost obsolete.

I had always thought of the various Devs that I have owned as 'friends'. Not in the sense that I want to take them out for dinner, although I have done that often, but rather that whenever I have been alone, I have always had the Dev to keep me company. Music, flicks, even characters that had conversations with me, some of which I created, the Dev was always there to fill that gap. With my newly acquired habit of thinking like a criminal … no that isn't right, not a criminal, a spy, yes, that is how I have to think, as a spy would think … Devs had become dangerous.

I pressed the red button, and the Devscreen instantly came alive. The time in the bottom right corner read 5:30am. The usual time I woke up.

I said, "Global newsfeeds, main living space screen." The floor-to-ceiling screen, which ran along half the wall occupied by my double sleeper and the relax space with its long sofa and two Siteazys, displayed the global newsfeeds. I had the large center image set on Bloomberg-Reuters, a financial news channel. Around this large square, twenty other news channels displayed. I could change channel by voice command or Devstick, which was tuned to function as a remote control for the main Dev in my Env.

"This is Kathy Peterson reporting for Bloomberg-Reuters, back to you, Jeff." Commodity prices ran along the bottom of the screen: gold was down, titanium up. I switched channels to legal news. The screen showed an earnest-looking, blonde-haired lady, perhaps in her sixties. Although age is hard to tell, she looked like she could be someone's grandmother. She was listening to a question from an interviewer who was off-image.

"… and then what are the implications for privacy? The government knows where you are at all times …"

I turned the volume up a little and walked over to the food prep area just off the relax space. I was lucky to find this Env. It was large, big enough for a family of seven, and I had taken it on a long lease with the condition of significant remodeling. I had retained one of the rooms for guests. It had never been used. The rest of the walls in the Env had been knocked down to leave one large space. In that, I had created four distinct sections: the food prep area, the relax area, and the sleeping and working areas. The open space of the Env was about three hundred square meters, large by anyone's standards, but I had taken the lease at the time when the economy was in a down cycle.

The interviewer was still speaking. "You're online, literally on display to the globe, so what does this mean for our privacy? We're already open at all times to government inspection. Doesn't this mean that anyone anywhere can tune in to where we are and track us? Isn't that an enormous security concern?"

I opened up my fridge and pulled out a carton of orange juice. The freshness indicator on the box showed green, so I poured myself a glass and, taking it with me, walked over to the relax area and sat in the Siteazy in front of the screen. I took a sip of the orange juice.

The blonde woman nodded her head. "Barry, before I answer your question, I'd like to get this into perspective because there's a few assumptions in your question that are simply incorrect. Firstly, the new Personal Unique Identification Law, or to call it by its commonly known name, the 'Tag Law', does not mean that anyone can suddenly zoom in on an image of you. Far from it. The same processes and protection we have as individuals today will still be in place. No one is advocating removing those. Through your own personalized profile page you will be able to set up more privacy conditions than what we have now. The only difference between this law and the last is that having an embedded PUI is a lot more convenient than having to carry around a Devstick. This law is about more privacy, not less. Bo Vinh's words on this are appropriate, and I quote …"

"We'll have to hold it there, June, while we take a quick suggestion break. Don't change feed – we'll be right back with June Masters and the rest of our panel to talk about the 'Tag Law' and what it means for you."

The feed switched into a suggestion for the new Mercedes-Benz electric vehicle. The EV looked sporty enough, but I wasn't tempted. Living in New Singapore and spending most of my time in the city, I had little need for an EV. I changed channels. It occurred to me that I was probably behind in voting and changed to the UN Vote channel. The popular vote, 'Popvote', was Bo Vinh's idea, and he used it to great effect in ridding the world of the nation states. He set up the first online voting site where, through authentication of your identity, you could vote on any issue happening in the world of politics. Pulling people of all nations to the site with his commentary, he used it as a platform to demonstrate to nation leaders how far off the mark they were with some of their policies. And in many cases, how far they had drifted from the wishes of the people that had voted for them.

I was behind in voting. It is compulsory to vote, and if you don't, your vote is counted as undecided, and depending on the ranked importance of the vote, you can be fined. It isn't a large fine and can be paid in either contributing time to a listed cause or in cred. I scanned through the list of votes, scrolling down from the most current through to the last vote I'd made. The list was mostly City council votes for New Singapore, as a resident there I had to vote on those, and there was only one global vote that I had missed. That had been to develop a new City in the ocean off the Maldives. I would have voted yes but was too late. I credded the fine and changed the channel back to the panel discussion. A suggestion for a new slimming regen unit was just finishing, yours for five thousand nine hundred and ninety-nine cred, and then a tanned and serious-looking Barry came back.

"Thanks for staying with us. We're talking about the new 'Tag Law', set for global Popvote Saturday 15 March 2110. Joining me on the panel are June Masters, president of the Goldman School for Public Policy; Andy Haas, former head justice of the Permanent Court of Arbitration and currently advisor to the New Aspiration Party responsible for proposing the 'Tag Law'; Dan Quigley, of the Conservative Christian Party who support the Law; and last but certainly not least, Annika Bardsdale of the Social Responsibility Party, who are opposed to the new Law. June, if I can start with you. Just before we went to the break, you were talking about the difference between the existing law and the new law."

"Yes, Barry, thank you. As I was saying, the new 'Tag Law' provides more privacy. In the words of Bo Vinh: 'Having nothing to hide from each other is the first step to having nothing to fear from each other,' and that is what this Law is all about. No more carrying around a Devstick to prove our identity – it becomes a part of us. What could be more human?"

"That's a dangerous thought, June, using technology to define what is human. Suppose the Tagged identities are hacked? What then? Your entire life is on display to someone?"

"Annika, our entire lives are on display right now. If a hacker wants to get into us and they're skilled enough, they can steal your identity right now – it happens all the time. With the Tag, that will become much harder because you are the device. The Tag embedded in your arm is protection against identity theft because any action that doesn't match your current location will immediately be seen for what it is. You have to go beyond emotion here and understand the logic."

I took another sip of my orange juice. I can't say I liked the idea of having anything inserted into my body, but the idea of the Tag appealed to me on a number of levels. Firstly, it would cut down crime, which has been rising steadily. Secondly, there really was no difference between an embedded Tag and a PUI on a Devstick. Well, the only difference is that your hands are free – but I guess you could say your hands are free if your Devstick is in a pocket or clipped to a belt. Even so, a one mil tag embedded in your upper arm is still more convenient to carry around.

I thought it would make shopping easier. Just step up to any Dev in any shop space and speak or key in your password. No more waving your Devstick at the shop Dev. If I understood it correctly – and privacy is not my area of expertise under the law – but location and other personal data belong to you. Ents have to delete any data that is yours within one month of acquiring it, unless you give them permission not to. In which case, they can hold your data but not resell it to any other party without your express permission. You have access to any data the government holds about you, except where such access is deemed to be a threat to the Nation, and then you require a court order.

The security around personal data is massive, but then again, I'd also just seen what Gabriel could do to those systems and that worried me about the Tag. What if someone could hack the data? What could they do? Well, nothing more than what they can do now, and that was why I though the Tag Law would be passed. March 15 – I had to remember to vote. I picked up my Devstick and marked it in my calendar. The time on the Devstick showed it was nearly 5:45am. I got up and swallowed the rest of the orange juice, taking the empty glass back to the food prep area. After putting the glass into the sanitizer, I headed for the shower.

I think up some of my best ideas while showering, but not this time, and I got it over with as quickly as possible. "Fast dry," I said, and a blast of warm air hit me from above, driving the wet from my body with its force. No sign yet, a ton of questions and I have to maintain a normal life. That summed it up, but it didn't help. Frustrated with it all, I looked at myself in the mirror. Who are you?

Standing there, examining my reflection, I realized something else, something I recognized but wasn't familiar with – fear. I was scared. I ran my hands through my hair and down my jaw line, feeling the stubble that had grown there. I had to get a grip: these thoughts were leading me nowhere, and being scared, while a natural response, was counterproductive. I had to do something, but what? And that's when it hit me. Take a vac. Get away from all of this. If Gabriel needed to find me, he could, I was sure of that, and suddenly the idea of taking a vac grew. Would it look suspicious? No, not if I told Sir Thomas in advance and made it seem like I was rewarding myself with a hard-earned spell of relaxation.

Feeling a surge of energy, I went back out to the living area and said to the Dev, "Find me a list of VacEnvs within one hour's travel time from here. Search criteria: clean white sand beach, stand-alone bedroom or cabin, occupancy less than twenty percent, with sailing craft for rent within one kilom of VacEnv." A list of VacEnvs came up. It wasn't a long list as December is always high season in Southeast Asia, which is where the map and list had focused, given my criteria. While looking down the list, I thought about what I would write to Sir Thomas. It would be better to send him an email, as I didn't trust myself not to show emotion if I was looking at him. I'd just write something short but ask if he had any further leads on the runner – that way it would look as if I knew nothing. I called up my comms program on the Dev and, selecting Sir Thomas from my list of contacts, dictated.

Dear Sir Thomas,

Hope you are well. I am planning on taking a vac. I just wanted to check with you that I personally am in no danger from the runner that escaped? I was thinking about going to a beach in the Southern Thailand Geographic. In your opinion, is it safe for me to do so? I should be gone for three or four days – I'll bring you back some of that whisky you like.

With warm regards,

Your nephew,

Jonah.

Jonah James Oliver

Arbitrator at Law

Coughington and Scuttle

My signature appended itself to the message automatically. The 'Chatnip' app gave me a list of my 'ums' and 'ahs' to delete, which I did. I thought it looked a bit too formal, but then, I always attach my signature to my emails. Just stay normal, keep everything as normal as possible, I thought, and said, "Send."

I turned my attention back to the list of VacEnvs, and one looked particularly interesting. A tiny VacEenv in a small village called Tha Sala, about fifteen kiloms north from Nakorn Si Thammarat further up along the coast. Using the Changi Lev port, I could reach Phuket within ten mins and then catch an airship transport across to Nakorn Si Thammarat. I could be on the beach in Tha Sala within an hour of leaving New Singapore. The Lev between New Singapore had only finished construction last year. The final section of tube was put in place in November, ready for pumping out the air. The resulting vacuum allows us to travel at eight thousand kilos per hour, with high-speed mag-lev, in the little sixteen-seat pods that we call Levs. The idea was adopted for building elevators and many buildings now have the Lev tubes coiled up like a giant spring either inside or outside of the structures to which they provide transport. They were first called Vactrains, but when the pods came along and they were put in buildings, trains just didn't fit anymore. The Transatlantic Lev can take you from London to New York in less than an hour.

The Geographic of Thailand had standardized on Southeast Asia Time (SEAT) back in 2020, as had Indonesia, so I hit the comms button next to their name. The hands of a little clock started spinning where my finger had touched the screen. The hands spun some more, and then I realized I was still naked. I quickly turned off the cam on my Dev and went to voice-only mode on my side. The clock hands disappeared, and a man, standing on a beach, his back to the ocean, appeared on my Devscreen. He looked Thai, was wearing a sarong, and had a large fish dangling from a meaty fist.

"Sawasdee Khrap, good morning, Mr Oliver, my name is Bank. Please excuse the fish – I was just on my way to the kitchen when I heard your call. How can I be of service, sir?"

"Good morning, Khun Bank. I'm thinking of staying at your VacEnv for a few days. Do you still have beach-front cottages available?"

"Yes, we do, Mr Oliver. We've just opened and are still in soft launch, so we're not doing any marketing right now. In fact, we only have two other guests staying here tonight. When were you planning on arriving, sir?"

"I was thinking about coming over there before lunch. Could you arrange a car for me? I'll call you when I'm boarding the airship."

"Certainly, Mr Oliver. And I take it you would like one of our beach cottages, is that right, sir?"

"Yes, that's right. As near to the sea as possible, okay?"

"Yes, Mr Oliver, thank you. So we'll look forward to seeing you around lunchtime, then."

"Yes, thanks, and save me some of that fish for later," I said.

His face broke into a grin, and he gave me a thumbs-up as I cut the call. I felt better. At least I was doing something, moving. It had to be an improvement on sitting around brooding over the circumstances I found myself in. I looked across the room at the clothes racks by the sleeper and frowned. I didn't have any clothes that were suitable for the beach. Everything I had was either formal or smart-casual. Do clothes define a person? Probably not, but they do tell you a lot about someone's lifestyle, and mine spoke volumes. The last time that I had taken any time off, 'self-time', was when I had just arrived in New Singapore from the Scotland Geographic. All I ever do is contribute and sleep a dreamless sleep.

THE GANG OF FOUR

Martine Shorne was the eldest in the team– 'The Gang of Four' as they were unofficially known: Marty, as she was usually called, plus Dom, Fatima, and Stanislav, the boy from the Urals Geographic. Together they traced the untraceable. They got the cases that others found impossible, and Case #JM-2109 was somewhere out there beyond impossible. But there was always something.

They had been given the case at 4:45pm yesterday, six days after his escape. They'd heard about the escape along with the rest of the planet's population by mid-noon on the Friday when it had been released to the newsfeeds globally. The news quickly became the most commented upon topic online and off.

Marty had gone over the entire timeline and absorbed all the data. It amounted to nothing. By the second degree of separation, everything disappeared. The lead from the tip-off that led to the raid, the capture, transportation to New Singapore, the footage of the interviews, containment, and finally the clouded-out, gas-filled image of the black hole in the wall of the White Room and the blunt cylindrical rear end of the Mole.

The Devcockpit they'd recovered gave them nothing; neither did the Mole, found six kiloms away in a warehouse in Old Jurong Port and completely destroyed with a magnesium bomb. She smiled: she had to admire the planning and execution. Altogether it was a work of art. From the fake mines in the tunnel, the collapsed roof of the tunnel three-quarters of the way down, to the electromagnetic pulse mines that had destroyed the remote control bomb disposal units, it was all beautifully planned and flawlessly executed.

The sixteen grade-one illegals had also disappeared, their PUIs a complete falsification. She knew they were dealing with someone brilliant, but then the 'Gang of Four' were pretty stellar too, and now it was their turn to play. Trace Operations had its hereditary roots in the profiling of serial murderers by the Federal Bureau of Investigation (FBI) in the twentieth century; their primary role being to predict where the accused was and what they were likely to do next.

They played 'what if' all day and often all night long until they had worked out what was the most plausible course of action for any given individual, group or event. In a sense, they made predictions. In another, they were fortunetellers, but a far more sophisticated truth is that everything they did was based on intuition, insight, experience and derived from fact. They also loved a challenge.

They had half a floor of the northern tower of the UNPOL Complex to themselves. Two thousand square meters of cool rubberized black floor space. The walls were Devscreens, and the ceiling appeared to be whatever they wanted it to be, on any given day. It was a huge Devscreen separated from the floor by a height of fifteen meters. Today, as per usual, it was black to match the floor. Despite the size of the room, there was no echo, and their name for it was the Cave.

No one entered their space without asking first. It was an unwritten rule, but one enforced by the threat of what might happen to one's digital history if unheeded. There was a rumor, carefully cultivated, that a senior level UNPOL officer had barged into their space without invitation. That night he had gone to dinner and found that he no longer existed as a person. His PUI had been wiped along with his ability to cred the dinner. He'd been contained and a full investigation into his past had begun before his PUI had reappeared. No one could tell how it had disappeared, or how it had come back, and although everyone suspected the 'Gang of Four', no one could prove it, and therefore no one dared say anything.

Marty looked at the image of the naked man sitting on the Biosense, his feet not touching the ground in the White Room. Jibril Muraz, a name from the Lebanese culture, Jibril meaning Gabriel in Arabic. The man didn't look as if he was of Arabic background, and his DNA didn't match that of the common Lebanese ancestry streams. He could have chosen a common Caucasian origin name, but he didn't. That was an interesting question. Given that everything this man had done was carefully planned, she had to assume that the choice of name was deliberate.

If he chose an Arabic name, then is there a relationship to that Geographic? Or is the fact that he is a Caucasian more relevant and the name is meant to be translated? If the first name means something, then so does the surname, Muraz. There isn't a straightforward translation into English for Muraz, unlike with Gabriel. Therefore if it isn't straightforward, perhaps it is an anagram.

She stood and stretched. Her one hundred and seventy-eight cents frame twisted to the right and left to work out the knots in her spine which sounded with satisfying pops as she wrenched it sideways again. She straightened and walked across the black floor barefoot until she reached Dom sitting in the northeastern corner of the room. Dominique, 'just call me Dom', Signora was an anthropologist with triple degrees in social, biological and cultural anthropology, and he loved jazz.

She said, "Have you got anything on his DNA?"

Dom swiveled in his Siteazy to face her, his hands on his thighs. "No matches. Nothing. Of course, this guy's too good. But his DNA is fascinating."

"Why?" she asked and sat cross-legged on the floor beside him. He turned the Siteazy back to the Dev in front of him and tapped a key on the console.

"Look at this," he said, pointing to the DNA chart. He had constructed a most likely origin from the DNA – matching it with other known DNA and bringing it down back through time to its various sources. "This is some mix. French, Polynesian, English, and Greek. How's that for a combo? These are the most obvious strands. Do you know how many matches we have on record?"

"No, not off the top my head," said Marty with an innocent smile.

"Sorry, of course you don't. Well, the answer is none, and the probability of that …"

"Yes. Off the scale. That I do know."

Dom stretched out his legs in front of him and folded his hands behind his head. He said, "I'm thinking about his whole meditation thing as well. He had to learn that somewhere, and certainly his demeanor is really more Asian than anything else. Well, the point is, when you throw that into the DNA mix the whole picture becomes even more confusing because now it adds Asian culture into that mix."

"What about the linguistics of the statement?"

"Ah, the linguini," Dom said and smiled at his own joke, his eyes darting to Marty to see if she smiled too. "I was hoping you'd ask me that because it rounds out my current theory nicely. The answer is the linguistics are almost deliberately American in Geographic origin. Which supports my theory that this Jibril comes from everywhere." At this, Dom let out a burst of laughter, and Marty had to smile.

"All right. Go down the strands again, and see if you find any close matches," she said, rising in a fluid motion, not using her hands to push herself off the floor. She turned and walked southwest to the opposite corner of the room.

Entering the University of Dubai at fourteen, and before she had finished her first year in behavioral sciences there, Fatima Farzi had written a book on behavior that became the course book for the first year students the following year. By her second year, she had passed the level of knowledge acquisition required to become a doctor and asked her professors what she was going to study in her third year. Typically, a Masters in behavioral sciences was a four-year course. Her professors, with nothing left to give, asked her to keep writing. She had just turned seventeen when she produced the new course material for the whole four years. Working on it full-time, she finished it within six months. She was now nineteen, a virgin, extremely shy, and perhaps the most brilliant member of the team.

Marty laid a hand on the teenager's shoulder and leant forward to see what she was working on. Fatima jumped slightly and turned to Marty. On seeing it was her, she relaxed and smiled. She loved Marty like a big sister, and Marty felt the same way about Fatima, protecting her from the masses of UNPOL.

"Anything?" she asked and nodded at the image of Jibril, or Gabriel, on the screen.

"Yes, the absence of behavior is a behavior in and of itself, and that is all I've got. Sorry."

"That's okay, it's not your fault. I've got nothing either, just ideas and they keep changing. But what do you mean, the absence of behavior?"

Fatima smiled her shy smile, which Marty knew meant that she was about to hear something very clever and unique.

"I cataloged his behaviors from the moment of containment to his escape. He gives away nothing. There is no behavior. He doesn't get angry, sad, happy, confused or mad. The whole time, he maintains a singular behavior. And that is his behavior. He is totally under control at all times. His behavior is no behavior. Which means his behavior is control."

"Okay," Marty said, "and where does that leave us? What else?"

Fatima chewed her bottom lip as if debating whether or not to share with Marty what she knew. Marty waited patiently, softly smiling an encouraging smile. Fatima blurted out, "I think he's really handsome," and blushed bright red, her eyes flashing and looking around the room to see if Dom or Stanislav had heard.

"So do I," Marty said and squeezed Fatima's shoulder lightly. "Very handsome. But how about his behavior? Is there anything else you sense?"

Fatima had been feeling guilty, but on seeing Marty's smile and hearing her confirmation, felt better about what she had really been thinking about Jibril. She said, "If he is controlling his behaviors to the extent that he can hide all of them from our observation, then the conclusion we can draw is that he is operating on at least two levels. One level is his public persona, and the other is his real persona. The important thing here is that we believe his public persona is his real persona when, in fact, it is a fabrication. This means that he is capable of controlling not just his behavior but the behavior of others so they perceive him incorrectly. He exploits the concept of 'at face value' and projects that face value convincingly through his passivity. Getting people to perceive something when you're doing nothing is quite a skill."

"Yes. That's good thinking, Fatima. Excellent. How about why? Why is he doing this? You've given me what he's doing, and I agree with you, but why is he doing it?"

"Don't know."

"Can you think about that for us?"

Fatima smiled. "That's what I've been doing. I'll think some more, though. Are you hungry yet?"

"Not yet. Why don't you wait. I should be ready in another hour, and then we can eat together, okay?"

Fatima rolled her eyes at Marty's look and stance. Fatima loved to eat, and her body reflected that. At ninety kilogs in weight and only one hundred and fifty cents tall, Fatima was a plump girl with the most beautiful eyes that Marty had ever seen. "Okay, Marty, another hour."

Marty smiled at her and straightened up. With a pat on Fatima's shoulder, she walked across the room to Stanislav. Stanislav sat in between and equidistant from Dom and Fatima, in the southeast section of the circular room. Marty had chosen the northwest area in honor of one her favorite flicks, and she and Dom guarded the door that entered from the northernmost point of the room. They each had a quarter circle of Devscreen that could be divided up or made single at a touch on the trackballs in their Devcockpit consoles.

Stanislav entered the 'School of Hard Knocks' the day he was born, traveling the hardest road of them all to the 188th floor of UNPOL Headquarters Deep Trace Operations Unit. An orphan raised by the City of Tyumen, Stanislav was brilliant at mathematics. The Tyumen Technopark had been his gateway to being recognized, as his skill in cryptography and eavesdropping was first exploited by the Russian mafia. Upon leaving the squat cement block of a school where his brilliance at mathematics was ignored by his teachers, he was recruited by the Russkaya Mafiya and placed in Tyumen Technopark to steal secrets.

He was seventeen when he was arrested for supplying confidential information gleaned from the airwaves of the Corps and Ents operating in Tyumen. Ordered to contribute a year of his time to working with UNPOL, cracking criminal gangs operating in the Urals, he was so successful that within four months he was transferred to UNPOL Headquarters and given the opportunity to work with them on a permanent basis. As thin as Fatima was fat, Stanislav was one hundred and eighty cents tall and weighed fifty-five kilogs. He was also an albino.

Stanislav was hopelessly in love with Fatima, but never dared to say it. He didn't have to because Fatima knew it, but she was hopelessly in love with Dom, who also knew it, but he was hopelessly in love with Marty and hoped she didn't know it. Marty loved them all, but she had already given her heart to another, and all that was left was for her to guide them and love them with what was left over. Misfits all, including Dom, who was so handsome, and so perfect, and so chronically insecure. The Cave was their sanctuary, and Marty, through being 'normal', was their leader and representative. The thought made her smile. She was the biggest misfit of them all.

Martine Shorne, Marty, Queen of the Dev. She understood more about the labyrinths of the digital landscape than anyone she knew. Most people have blood running through their veins, but she had Dev code running through hers. Somehow, and she didn't know how, it had just always been there. She saw the essence of data and was able to perceive its origin and meaning.

Stanislav was laid out on his sleeper, a Dev helmet over his head, the mirrored visor reflecting the black of the ceiling.

She left him alone and walked back to her Devcockpit.

A Change of Plan

Picking up my Devstick, I smiled thinking of the trip ahead. I couldn't remember feeling this excited about anything in a long time. My smile faded as I remembered Gabriel's thoughts again inside my head, 'You are not Jonah', and I remembered that the only thing of me that I really knew for sure was mine was my thoughts. The door to the Env swished open, and I headed out.

I got on my Devstick and called up a map of walkys around the Envplex my Env was in, and planned a trip on the walkys that would take me around the edge of New Singapore to the main Lev ports that allow travel to Phuket. Taking a vac was unusual behavior for me, but I believed that my message to Sir Thomas and the little shopping excursion I was planning would allay suspicions. I rode the Lev down to the surface and walked over to the nearest walky that took me to the main southeast walky from my Complex in Woodlands down to Tampines and Changi – the main Lev concourse and airship port. It was a sunny day but humid. Soon my cotton outer was soaking up the sweat tracking off me in little streams, but it felt good to be out and about as I traveled the walky with my hand on the rail as advised by the safety warnings.

At Tampines there was an old open-air market where all kinds of things were sold and purchased. It was here that I planned to use my cred to buy some beach clothes. The morning's late starters had all but gone by the time I entered Tampines. I got off the PSE1 walky and headed over to the Lev that would take me to Sun Plaza Park. It was just after ten, and if I could get the shopping done quickly, I could still make it to Tha Sala before lunch.

The Sun Plaza open-air market was a mass of white sails and brightly colored banners, each proclaiming the wares of the stalls under the sails. I entered into a narrow aisle between the stalls and asked my Devstick to give me a layout of the market. The map came up, and the clothes stalls were two rows over from where I was. I cut through the aisles selling fashionable teenage outers and footwear. A pair of white cloth shoes caught my eye, hanging from the sail of one of the stalls.

A fat Chinese woman, sat on a blue plastic stool which was placed on a

56

low wooden table, looked down at me from within the stall. I reached up and touched the shoes with my hand and said, "Do you have these in a size 10?" She nodded and using a long plastic pole with a hook on it, extracted another pair and dipped the pole. They slid down to my hand.

"How much?"

"Twenty cred."

I nodded. I could have bargained, but that wasn't why I was here. In my pro bono work with UNPOL, the one thing I see time and again is how criminals are caught because someone else is caught. Your name comes up because you bought something or called the person who has been contained and as such you get tagged for surveillance. I assumed that since I was the last person to talk with Jibril, that no matter how innocent I may appear, I would be tagged. With my call to the VacEnv, my message to Sir Thomas and buying beach clothes on cred in Tampines market, I hoped to show whoever might be watching me that I was going to the beach.

I called up my cred and held up my Devstick, the fat woman held up hers, and I checked to see that only twenty cred had been deducted from mine. "Thanks," I said and got a smile in return as I walked on.

Two rows over, all of the stores were selling clothing, inners and outers of all descriptions. About twenty meters down the lane, between the stalls, I spotted what I was looking for – the stall I had seen when I had been here before. I headed towards a sign saying 'Life's a Beach', which had a smiling droopy mustached guy standing on a beach, wearing nothing but a sombrero, next to the name written in red on a white background.

The guy behind the stall was about one hundred and fifty cents tall and couldn't have been older than nineteen, with a beard that refused to be and a mustache equally struggling to define itself. He looked up at me and, with a smile, said, "Hi, man, you need some threads for the beach?"

He had a very high-toned squeaky voice, and stifling a laugh, I said, "Yeah."

"Awesome," he replied, smiling even more broadly. He had braces on his teeth. "So where you headed to, dude?"

I returned his smile and said, "I'm heading up the coast to the Thai Geographic for a few days."

"Cool."

I spotted a pair of black knee-length swimming shorts and asked, "How much?"

"Oh, those, they're great, man, super-fast dry and the color never fades. Only fifteen cred and I'll throw in a 'Life's a Beach' T-shirt."

"I tell you what, I'll give you thirty creds for the shorts and that white cotton – that is cotton, right? – shirt hanging there, and that bag," I said, pointing first at the shirt hanging on the wall of the stall behind him and then a 'Life's a Beach' white cloth bag on the side of the stall.

His eyes suddenly got older and wiser, and dropping the beach bum slang, he said, "I'll tell you what, forty creds and it's a deal."

I looked at him, smiled, and said, "Deal."

He climbed up on a stool to get the shirt and, grabbing the shorts and my free T-shirt, stuffed them into the cloth bag and handed them to me with another smile. I held up my Devstick and swiped the transaction.

"Stay loose, dude," he said, dropping back into his beach character now the deal was done.

I retraced my steps out of the market and back to the Lev that had brought me here. Twenty minutes after I'd left the PSE1 walky, I was back on it. Mission done, my thoughts turned to the travel that was ahead of me and especially the fact that within a couple of hours at most I'd be by the sea on a white, sandy beach.

Reaching Changi ten minutes later, I headed for the Lev port that would take me to Phuket. The massive domed concourse of the Changi Lev and airship port was as busy as any place that operates on a continuous time cycle with zero downtime. In the cool muted echoes of the concourse, I checked the times for the Levs to Phuket and saw that I had at least twenty minutes to spare before a Lev with an empty seat was available.

I was hungry. I hadn't had anything to eat that day, and I'd been awake for over four hours. I headed down a short walky to the lower level of the concourse, where travelers of all Geographics were taking a time out. Just off the walky there was a small café set by a fountain with a violinist entertaining the people while they ate.

I took a table near the fountain and studied the Devscreen set into its surface, selecting a croque monsieur and a latte as I confirmed the deduction from my cred. Three servbots were serving food and taking orders, their squat white bodies shining and bearing the blue Panasonic logo. One of them dispatched itself from the serving hub and propelled itself towards me around the edge of all the tables. With a polite 'thank you for your custom', it deposited the toasted sandwich and latte carefully on my table and left. The violinist was playing a jaunty tune with her eyes shut, and swaying to the music. She looked young and was probably a student picking up extra cred doing a double.

I had left the Dev on, and the screen was scrolling through suggestions. This perfume, that timepiece, toys for kids … Suddenly my eye caught a suggestion that sent a thrill through me. I hit pause on the Devscreen, and the feed stopped scrolling. The suggestion was for travel to the Moon, but what had caught my eye was the particular resort which was being suggested. 'Buy two, get three free nights at the Nineveh Hot Springs Resort.' The word 'Nineveh' seemed to get larger and more focused the more I looked at it. I quickly glanced around me, but no one was paying any attention. Gabriel had said that Jonah was vomited out onto the shores of Nineveh.

Was this it? Was this the sign? Gabriel had said that a sign would come and when I saw it I would know it and do the right thing. A quick-find on the Devscreen mapped out the route to the Moon travel port which was situated at the right of the Changi concourse. Did he mean literally do the right thing, meaning go to the right?

I was in a dilemma. I'd spent all morning thinking about being normal, and now I was confronted with doing something very abnormal. I had never been to the Moon. Never even thought about going to the Moon. Not only that, but my actions in the morning would look doubly suspicious. Shit! Okay, think. I checked the Dev again for the departure times for the Moon. My message inbox light was flashing red on my Devstick. I had ten mins before the next flight took off for the Moon and after that an hour's wait. I opened my inbox and saw that there was a reply from Sir Thomas. I opened it.

Dear Jonah,
Have a good trip. I like that Mekong whiskey, a bottle of that would be wonderful, thank you.
TBO

I hit reply, my mind made up.

Dear Sir Thomas,
Change of plans. I've decided to travel to the Moon. Never been in space. Want to see what it's like. I'll bring you back some moonshine instead of the Mekhong.
Best wishes,
Your nephew,

Jonah.
Jonah James Oliver
Arbitrator at Law
Coughington and Scuttle

I was decided. If they were watching me, then they'd stop me at the security zone, but I wasn't hiding anything, I'd already told the director of UNPOL where I was headed. There was just enough time to catch a ship to the Orbiter, travel to the Moon and be back again before my self-time was up on Thursday. After a quick gulp of my latte, I rose and, with croque monsieur and 'Life's a Beach' bag in hand, hurried my way over to the Lev.

Exiting the Lev corridor, I walked into the Moon travel port and found myself a seat. Other Moon travelers were sitting around, reading, talking, and in some cases standing, waiting patiently for the Lev that would take us to the ship. I had been just in time, as the door opened, and we all filed in an orderly manner into the Lev.

"Four and a half minutes to Virgin Galactic Moon Port," the Lev said once we were all seated.

I looked at my Devstick. No urgent messages, no recalls, and I hadn't been stopped as I'd passed through the security zone. I had never been in space before, and I was excited. Most of my fellow travelers looked as if they contributed to Ents or Corps and my outers marked me as a tourist.

The Lev docked with the ship, and I followed my arrows to my designated seat on the right side of the ship just aft of the wings. I sat down, and a screen set in the headrest of the seat in front of me took me through the safety procedures. I glanced over to my left and watched what the guy in the seat next to me was doing. He looked like he'd done this before, and he was wearing coveralls with the Broken Hills Mining Ents logo over the breast pocket. Removing all detachable objects on my person and changing my footwear for the pair in the locker by my feet was about all there was. The door closed, and we taxied out. I could see over our wing to the cockpit of the mother ship. A warning sign in the headrest screen told me to sit back and have my arms at my side as the seat restraint emerged from the modified Siteazy I was in. The inflatable cushion pressured me lightly into my seat.

With a powerful thrust, we were quickly using up the spaceport runway at Changi, and then we were airborne, banking left over the open sea. The autopilot kicked in the thrusters, and we hurtled through the sky at just over mach one.

As we reached the apogee of flight for the mother ship, there was a loud clunk, which made me start and then smile sheepishly to myself. The last crash of a space ship had been more than twenty years ago. Space travel was statistically far safer than cars. With the release, I watched as our capsule dropped and the mother ship peeled away heading back to Changi, and then I was punched back in my seat as we went from mach one to mach three. Mach three is not a pleasant experience, but it was over within ninety secs. I felt the inflatable cushion release me, and then my body floated to the confines of the seat restraint. I was in space.

A Trip to the Moon

You have never seen a night sky until you have been to space. I was awed and thrilled. I had looked at the stars through some very powerful lenses and as images on a Devscreen, but nothing compares to being in space. The travelers around me relaxed, and reaching into the hole set into the locker by my Siteazy, I pulled out my Devstick. While looking through the port, I brought the Devstick up to my lips and said, "Find route from here to Moon spaceport to Nineveh Hot Springs Resort." My Devstick started the timer countdown for my estimated time of arrival at the resort.

We were coming up to the second phase of the journey where we would dock with the orbital spaceport and then transfer to the actual Moon landing craft for the trip and descent to the Moon. Compared to the aerodynamic beauty of the craft we were in, the image of the Moon landing craft on my Devstick looked more like a shipping container with portholes set into its side. It had a blunt black nose and a massive propulsion unit in the rear end. Well, as long as it's quick and safe, I thought, and put my Devstick back into the locker.

As we powered into the Orbiter's arrivals bay and docked on, the screen in the headrest warned me to turn on my gravity boots. A smiling Virgin Galactic staffer demonstrated how to turn on the gravity field by pressing on a button set into the top of the boot. As I copied his actions, I felt my feet attach themselves firmly to the floor beneath them. I had wondered about that and smiled to myself as I imagined us all suddenly floating about the cabin.

The traveler in the seat next to me asked, "First time in space?"

"Yes, it is," I replied with a smile. "Is it that obvious?"

"Frankly, yes," and giving me a wai and a smile, the traveler said, "My name's David – my friends call me Dave."

In the wake of the massive flu epidemics that swept the world in the twenties, the wai had become the standard form of greeting. The only person I knew who still shook hands was Sir Thomas. An image of his sweaty hand grasping mine came to mind. I waied him back and smiled as our fingertips missed each other's.

This weightlessness would take a little bit of getting used to, I thought.

"You've been here often, Dave?"

"I live here. I've just been visiting relatives on Earth, but my purpose is here. I contribute to the mining Ent at Broken Hills. If you're interested, I have some self-time left over, and I'd be delighted to show you around. I'm without a sexual partner at the moment, and I find you very attractive. I've got a three-hundred-square-metre cozy on Polar Edge."

"Actually, Dave, I was looking to get some serious self-time in. But thanks for the offer."

"Well," he smiled and, lifting his Devstick, offered a transfer from his Devstick to mine, "if you change your mind, here are my contact details."

I pressed accept and smiled back.

"Are you, by any chance, homo?" he asked, which strictly speaking was on the outer edges of socially acceptable public communication, but I put that down to him being in the colonies where social comms are a bit more unusual and sometimes much more direct than those of Earth's.

"No, up to now I've only explored hetro," I said, still smiling. "But thanks for the contact, and if I find myself at a loose end, I'll get in touch." The screen told me that I should use the carry on provided in my locker to pack my personal belongings in and to make sure that I sealed it properly, which would be indicated by a flashing green light on the lock.

The door of our craft opened, and with my personal belongings recaptured in the carry on with a huge Virgin Galactic logo emblazoned across it, I walked out of the craft and through a corridor into the Orbiter.

As we entered the spaceport, some of the travelers reached down and switched off the gravity in their boots and pushed off. I didn't feel comfortable enough to do that yet and instead walked following the lights called up by my Devstick to the nearest port, where a ship would take me to the Moon. Another glance at my Devstick told me I had a fifty-minute wait before I could pick up a connecting flight. Because I was grounded by the artificial gravity of the boots, I wasn't disoriented – something that the Dev in the headrest had warned me about. In fact, I was hungry and headed over to a food stand.

Near the food dispenser was a measuring stand where, for a cred, you could see how much taller you were in space. A couple of kids with gravity boots on were laughing and having their image taken. I consulted my Devstick again and checked my data stream. Still nothing. I might be extremely lucky and no one in the UNPOL unit charged with tracking down Gabriel would pick up on the Nineveh reference, but somehow I doubted it. It was too unusual and when taken with my decision to travel to the Moon would definitely cause a flag. I reasoned that when interviewed I would simply say that the idea struck me to go to the Moon and on a whim I went. Without any other evidence, they would have to believe me. That is, if they restricted themselves to a simple debrief. If I was subjected to Truth Treatment, then the discussion with Gabriel that had taken place in our minds would be revealed.

The man who was tethered to the food dispenser just above me let out a loud fart. Another of the effects of weightlessness was gas in the body tends to go out through the bottom rather than the top half of our bodies. He smiled apologetically at me, and I just waved a hand about to indicate it was normal. I credded a few units and bought a ProCarboVite bar that promised to give me all the protein, carbohydrates and vitamins my eighty kilog body mass would need for the next twenty-four hours, and also a space sickness pill as I had felt a slight headache and nasal stuffiness come over me. This was normal, according to the FAQ in my Devstick, and the Aspamo pill from Pfizer that I had just taken would provide 'Instant, long-lasting relief from headache and nasal congestion caused by space sickness'.

A bunch of little kids were floating around in something called the 'Ball Cage'. Filled with hundreds of hand-sized foam balls of all different colors, a huge net enclosed the kids, with their parents tethered to railings around the exterior of the net. Their shrieks and laughter echoed in the huge cylindrical port and somehow lent an air of a family outing to the moment. About three hundred meters away, off to my left and up from where I was tethered, I saw the entrance to a relax lounge. Its large circular structure was painted a dark grey and padded as was the rest of the interior of the port. Well, I thought, if I am to look like I'm trying out space travel, then it would be very natural for me to have a go at flying.

There's a kid in all of us, and I'm no exception. In fact, there are those who say I still have way too much kid in me and not enough adult. I strapped my carry on to my outers and, clicking off the button on my grav boots, pushed off from the food stall, just missing the legs of the guy who had just again farted. Flying unaided by anything other than the propulsion of your push off is awesome. I loved it and flipped a somersault as I approached the entrance. Unfortunately my somersault led to me getting totally lost, and I struggled to get some sense of where I was. A tether from a fixed newsfeed screen was just within reach. I grabbed it, stopping my tumble. It took a moment, but I reoriented myself with the relax lounge and pushed off again, this time restricting my enthusiasm to stretching out my arms and pretending I was a plane. As I neared the entrance, a tether was floated out to me by the woman on the door, and I grabbed it.

"Hi," she said with a big smile. "I thought you were going to fly right past us there for a minute. Welcome to Orbital Dreams, sir." Pulling the tether in, she reached down and turned my grav boots back on. When I was firmly anchored to the floor outside the entrance, she asked me, "How are you looking to relax today, sir?"

"I've been travelling since this morning – I wouldn't mind a shower if you have one," I replied, giving her my best smile.

"We do have shower cubes; however, can I recommend the assisted sponge bath and happy ending," she said and continued in the same singsong twangy voice that marked her as having come from the Geographic of the west coast of America. "Showers are a bit amazing in space, and if you haven't had one before, you tend to choke on the water. And ejaculations in space are just fabulous," she gushed, with an attempt at a coy smile and a flutter of her eyelashes.

I hadn't been with a woman sexually since the night of Milo's leaving party, and the thought of this beauty or someone like her giving me a sponge bath was very appealing, but a quick glance at my Devstick told me I only had thirty-five minutes to my flight.

"Um, actually, I think I'll skip the shower and just have an alky, okay?"

"Sure," she said and led me into the interior. She handed me a tether and reached down to turn off my grav boots. "The tether will take you to the lounge, and my colleague will take care of you there." With that, the tether started reeling me towards another circular structure seemingly suspended from what passed for a ceiling – or was it a floor – by a single thick band of polymer tubing. Reaching the entrance, I was pulled inside, and another woman clicked on the button on my grav boots again. I was beginning to see how all this moving around in space was done.

Leading me down a corridor, the woman held my arm in a light grip, and by the end of the corridor, I was walking as normally as I would be on Earth. I took a seat around a plush circular table. In the middle of the table was a woman with a small globe of the Earth floating from a chain attached to her belly button.

"My name's Christine; what can I do you for?" she said, and leaning forward, her rather saggy breasts floated unevenly at eye level. She was quite a bit older than the beauty at the door and space wasn't being kind to her wrinkles. I felt glad that I hadn't gone for the sponge bath.

"Have you got an Endorpho 80?" I asked.

"Sorry, we don't have that, but we do have a Marsmellow. It's a mild psychoactive that lets you view the world through a rose-tinted hue that lasts for about an hour and a half." She had really long nipples, and they were pointing in opposite directions.

"Hmm, I'm not really looking for something hallucinogenic – space is trippy enough. How about something that just takes the edge off but leaves me in full cognitive control?" I said with a smile at her, regretting my unkind thought about her wrinkly body. That we are all beautiful, and each of us is a unique miracle, is something that every morals class teaches from when we are the age of three. But somehow physical attraction is still a main qualifier when it comes to sexual partners.

"How about the Valkyrie?" she said. The smile in her eyes told me she'd picked up on my glance at her elongated tits waving around in front of her. "It'll give you a real lift, and if you're on a long haul, you'll have a great sleep after an hour of great flying." Her lips stretched into a warm smile, and returning it, I gave her a nod and leaned back in the Siteazy.

I took out my Devstick and glanced at my data stream. Nothing had changed. There was the usual chatter from my contribution, spam, and weather updates for New Singapore and surrounding cities. My current location was shown, but because I had my profile on silent self-time, all my contacts knew that I might be receiving but I wouldn't be updating.

Christine handed me the alky and went back to the poker game she was playing on the Dev beside her. The alky tasted sweet, too much so for my taste, but I was thirsty so I took a long drink of it. Only twenty minutes to go and I still had to navigate myself down to the Moon port for the six-hour journey to the Moon. The timer on my Devstick calculated my time to the port and told me I could relax for another five minutes and then I should go. I flashed my cred over the Dev in the arm of the Siteazy and paid for the alky.

The alky hit. I swallowed the rest of it, which tasted like crap but felt great, and stood up. I braced myself and, looking down, checked that I had grav turned on. I was flying already, and I wanted my feet firmly on the ground. My Devstick picked out the directional lights for me to follow, and with a light stride, I made my way back out to the main concourse of the Orbiter.

My seat was on an O'RionSpace craft which, at a bargain price of one thousand and one hundred cred, had offered me a full-body-length Siteazy and gravity simulation suit sleeper for the six-hour travel time to the Moon. On leaving the lounge, I grabbed a tether leading to the nearest gravwalk and left my boots turned on. The Valkyrie had a bit more kick to it than I had thought it would. This was going to be fun.

THE MAN IN THE MOON

I woke up with a headache and a runny nose. The rapidly deploying seat restraint had woken me. Looking out of the porthole, I could see the battered surface of the Moon writ large as we were coming in to land at the Moon Base on Peary Crater.

We were about one thousand meters off the surface of the Moon and descending at a fast glide. The lights of the runway track were bright in the shadow of the southern end of the crater where my Devstick had told me I'd be landing. The seat restraint settled firmly over my shoulders, and after a distinct braking motion as we powered down, we hit the runway with a jolt, followed by the rapid deceleration as we rolled down towards the arrivals bay. The sun was glinting off the solar panels bathed in eternal light on the far ridge of the crater over seventy kiloms away. I could see them clearly, but then they were massive energy farms providing virtually all of the electricity for the Lunar Colony.

As I left the compartment, the craft staffer offered me a smile and a cheery request to fly with O'RionSpace again soon. I smiled in return and, feeling healthy and strong, checked my Devstick as I entered Peary Moon Base. I passed through the security zone, waving my Devstick over the scanner. No alarms went off, nor did any gas nozzles appear in the walls of the corridor. I guess my luck was holding, as it had been just under eight hours since I'd left my Cozy that morning.

Exiting from the Moon port, I came into a large open area with a see-through ceiling – the night sky and earth shining brightly in blue-green. Consulting my Devstick for directions, I set off a new stream of color in the lights inlaid into the walkway. I turned on my grav boots and headed for the Lev port that would take me to Shackleton Moonbase on the Far Side of the Moon. There, buried fifty meters below ground and with access to the surface of the Moon, was the Nineveh Hot Springs Resort.

Taking a seat in the Lev, I relaxed as I called up the map on my Devstick. It showed the little Lev oval tracking its way through a maze of tubes within the Moon's core. The route to Shackleton Moonbase took us to within twenty kiloms of the Moon's molten core and was the fastest route available at a total distance of about three thousand five hundred kiloms. Traveling at just over one thousand three hundred and fifty kilos per hour, I would arrive at Shackleton in another two hours and forty minutes or so.

I watched the new global events datafeed in the Lev for a while but kept the volume off. I was bone tired. I felt a little surge of guilt and excitement as UNPOL reported that they still hadn't caught Jibril and again warned the public that he was dangerous. Then the whole screen turned bright yellow, and white letters on a black strip scrolled across the screen: Breaking News. An earnest woman with a bad haircut stood outside the remains of what looked like it had been a café. Bright aluminum chairs and glass were scattered amid pools of blood, mingled in with the food that people had been eating. The text running along the bottom told of a bomb being set off in Paris in the Geographic of France – fifteen dead and forty-five wounded. No one had claimed responsibility, but coming so soon after the UNPOL report, it was obvious they were tying the bomb to Jibril. Possible reasons given for the blast were religious extremism, political or business motives and terror tactics. No evidence was given as to who was supposed to be terrified and why. Right after this, the mayor of Paris came on, and subtitles told me that this act of terror on innocent Christmas shoppers had to be punished – and that if the Tag Law had been implemented, this wouldn't have happened. I thought that was a giant and mistaken leap in logic, but nevertheless, I could feel his anguish as his hand waved wildly in the direction of the destruction behind him. The next image was that of Sir Thomas, as director of UNPOL. I turned the sound up.

"… The perpetrators of this crime against humanity shall be hunted down like the beasts they are and caged as such. We have not seen this kind of action in European cities for many years, and unfortunately, it shows that we have become complacent in our security. There are those in society who would seek to impose their will or their doctrine on free-thinking citizens, and it is our sworn duty to defend against that imposition. Our condolences and thoughts are with the families and friends of the deceased, and we wish the wounded a speedy and whole recovery in regen. However, our grief will not dissuade nor delay us in our task of hunting down these violent, base criminals. Thank you, that is all I have to say. I have work to do."

The woman with the bad hairdo came back on, standing in the Paris street outside the bombed café. "That was Sir Thomas Oliver, director of UNPOL, telling us that they are working on this case, and that their thoughts …"

I turned down the volume, shocked by what I had read and heard. A bomb. I looked around the Lev, its normal interior suddenly threatening, and turned off the feed. I felt strangely proud of Sir Thomas and what he'd said. Not just that, but the way he had handled himself and how sincere he looked. Was Gabriel certain that this earnest, sincere man who I called uncle had killed my father? Trying to reconcile these thoughts within myself was too much for my brain in this tired state.

It was 9:05pm New Singapore time when I emerged from the Lev port at Shackleton Moonbase. Consulting the Devstick ,I pulled up the map that would route me through to the Nineveh. It was now fifteen hours since I'd woken up, and I needed to have a clean and get some sleep. Checking my image on the Devstick brought up red eyes with bags underneath them, tussled, sleep-mashed light brown hair and a slight but discernible stubble across my chin and jaw. A shower or, better still, an assisted sponge bath with or without a happy ending, beckoned.

The Shack, as it is called Far Side, is the least populated of the Moon's six bases, and there were only a few other people in the tube that I was walking down. A small entranceway, cut into the side of the tube with a white trellis set into it, was where the lights indicated I should go next. I walked into the entrance and took a look at my Devstick to confirm the route. I had looked at this route a hundred times in the last few hours, but still it had not etched itself firmly enough in my memory for me to trust the recall. The datafeed from Earth showed that service was temporarily unavailable now that I had left the craft and was actually on the surface of the Moon. Of course, the network of satellites usually kept us online, even on the Far Side of the Moon not visible to Earth, where radio waves are blocked by the Moon itself. Must be a sun flare, I thought, and checked the local map. My Devstick had defaulted to the Shack's environment, providing me with the map I was following and local news. There wasn't much of it.

Suddenly the map on my Devstick disappeared. I said, "Find Nineveh Hot Springs Resort," but a glance confirmed that there were no hits for my current location. The tube was quite dark, and a door opening about ten meters away cast a yellow glow through to where I was standing. A man came out and stood in the doorway. I looked at him, and taking a step towards him so that I could ask where the Nineveh was, I stopped.

"Hello, Jonah," Gabriel said and, holding his arms wide, walked towards me haloed by a golden light. He reached me and smiled into my eyes, wrapping his arms around me in a tight hug that nearly squeezed the air out of me. Putting his arm around my shoulder and pulling me towards the open door, he said, "We have much to talk about, brother, but first, you must eat and rest."

At first glance, the room inside the doorway was a storage unit for tube cleaners, and with a grin at the puzzled expression on my face, Gabriel walked to the far end of the small room and pulled a shelving rack out to reveal another smaller door set into the wall. We went through the door, and inside was a hole in the floor about two meters in diameter with a spiral staircase going down. Gabriel led the way as we wound our way down the stairs.

"This was one of the early titanium mines," he said over his shoulder, "but was abandoned, and we took it over." About five minutes later, we reached the bottom and emerged into a larger chamber about fifty meters in diameter, lit by a single string of lights suspended from its ceiling and disappearing around what seemed like a downward curve. In the middle of the chamber was a golf cart. It looked incongruous in the setting, but Gabriel climbed into the driver's seat and I into the passenger seat. With a flip of the red switch between us, he pressed his foot on the accelerator, and away we went down the tube.

We could talk forever, talking on the Moon

"Jonah, Jonah, wake up." I felt a hand lightly shaking and squeezing my shoulder. Turning my head away from the wall, I saw Gabriel sitting on the edge of the sleeper I was in. I pushed myself up and lay back, resting my weight on my elbows.

"What time is it?"

"It's 1:45am New Singapore time. You've slept for four hours. Here take this, it'll get you back on your feet." He handed me a cup, warm on the outside. "We have until 6am. Then we have to get you visible again. Comms are down across the sector, but we can only hold that for another four hours, and then we have to put you in a hot tub in the Nineveh." With this last softly spoken comment, Gabriel smiled and patted me on my knee. He crossed the room to a small table in its center.

I looked around the concrete-walled room. It was Spartan: two sleepers lengthwise against each wall, polymer storage racks, black rubberized flooring, and next to the small table in the center of the room was a mobile Devcockpit. There must have been at least fifty Devscreens arrayed in a semicircle in front of a Siteazy. It was the largest I had ever seen. In contrast to the setting it was in, it looked singularly out of place. Like a shiny high-cred luxury unpacked from a drab package.

Gabriel turned to me and, indicating the Siteazy next to the Devcockpit, said, "Come over here and take a seat. I've calculated that it would take me eighteen days and about forty-six minutes to tell you of all that has happened in the time that we have been separated from each other. Unfortunately, we don't have that kind of time on our hands, so I'm going to have to stick to the problem we have and how we think you can resolve it."

"Eighteen days," I asked. "Has that much happened since last week?"

Gabriel smiled, his hand resting on the headrest of the Siteazy, but he looked sad to me. "No, I meant since we were parted thirty-four years, fifty-three days, and three hours ago. You were twenty-eight days old, and I was twelve. I'll tell you what I can in any time we have left over, if we can come up with a solution to our problem."

I got out of the sleeper and went and sat in the Siteazy. Gabriel sat on the Biosense in the middle of the Devcockpit but, turning to the opening of the cockpit, put his feet up on the Dev's manual entry panel, his hands folded into his lap.

I said, "Just do me a favor, okay?"

"Name it."

"Just speak to me with your voice, okay? No getting into my mind stuff."

Gabriel laughed loudly and slapped his hand on his thigh.

"Okay, we won't do that." His face turning serious, he looked me in the eye and said, "But I will have to give you some mental training on how to survive the Truth Treatment and avoid scrutiny from Cochran."

"Good," I said and smiled at him. "Now can you please tell me about this conspiracy, and how I am supposed to save the universe?"

Gabriel grinned a little sheepishly. "Well, I might have been just a bit overdramatic with that one, but then again, it depends how you look at it, and from where I'm sitting, it's not far from the truth."

The screen of the Dev was split into a multitude of past and present images, text and sounds, arranged in a two hundred and seventy degree arc extending upwards at about a forty-five degree angle. I couldn't see the side nearest me, but on the wall behind Gabriel I could see images of UNPOL units on the Moon.

"We're safe," Gabriel said, noticing my look and glancing at the screen. "We could stay here for another decade, and they wouldn't find us, but we have to get you back and in position if we're going to stop the carnage that Sir Thomas is planning. That is, if you will help? I don't think I've ever formally asked. I apologize, of course, but I just assumed."

"I'm glad you assumed – please don't apologize. You were right to. Go ahead, and tell me what he's planning."

"Sit back, relax, and put those on," Gabriel said, nodding at a set of earphones on the arm of my Siteazy and reaching for his own on the panel next to his feet. I laid back in the chair, put the earphones on, and a screen appeared over my waist, while the sound of Gabriel talking filled my ears.

"Sir Thomas is part of a select group of individuals who regard themselves as the elite of the universe. This is, in fact, true if you accept the concept of elitism. By definition, entry criteria for this group defines it as elite: you must be of the highest Intelligence Score – over one hundred and forty-five – and have the most accumulated wealth and position of influence to gain entry. You also need to be totally ruthless, coldly logical, and entirely selfish. We call them the Hawks, they call us Doves.

"The term 'WarHawk' was first used in 1812 to describe a group of congressman in the twelth Congress of the United States who advocated war against the empire of Great Britain in 1812. It wasn't until the early 1900s, however, that the current confederation of Hawks was born, in a small farmhouse in Brittany, France. The ten men and two women who attended that meeting came together as a consequence of the first peace conference held during the previous year and the resulting Hague Convention.

"Another factor was the perception that peace would inevitably increase the influence of the common man. Sweeping Europe, and already established to some extent in France and the United States, the common man was a growing influence like never before in history. To the men and women in the meeting, these were problems that had to be dealt with. A simple but very effective plan, with two principle criteria as its objectives, was developed over the course of the next three days. The first was to maintain control of the common man, and the second was to keep his numbers down to manageable levels. The meeting concluded with the name 'Hawks' being adopted, as the discussions had led them to an inescapable truth. War would achieve both of the objectives that they set for themselves. This was a time-proven historical fact.

"What we are dealing with today are the children of those twelve. If you regard them as the trunk of a tree, then today we are dealing with the leaves, and the leaves are thick enough that you cannot see the branches. We know that there is an induction ceremony and that it involves vigorous questioning, sometimes to the extent of torture and many times involving truth drugs or Truth Treatments, as UNPOL like to call them. Once past that questioning, the induction ceremony is not elaborate, but each Hawk is given a dagger, usually by an elder member of their family.

"Hawks operate within their own sphere of influence. There is no secret handshake, hidden tattoo or code words. You either know someone is definitely a Hawk or you do not treat them as one. This makes them extremely difficult to penetrate. They meet, but not often, and word is discreetly passed along the original branches and out to the new branches. Representatives are sent to meet and talk. And what has been decided upon is then passed along to the leaves.

"It was the Hawks who drove us to the last three so-called Great Wars – WWI in 1914, WWII in 1939, and WWIII in 2056 – and why they label wars 'great' is a mystery to me. However, that aside, it was the Hawks who presented a plan that unleashed the endgame potential of global nuclear conflict. It was them who said, 'Fire first, otherwise they will. Fire first, and we will win'. It was them who caused the massive loss of life. They have been quiet, but not silent, for a long time since then. You might say investing their time in the current plan."

I turned my attention away from the Devscreen in front of me and looked at Gabriel. He was watching me, and he paused, his eyebrows raised slightly in question. In my mind I could see the small group of twelve, and I knew he was telling the truth. I nodded at him to continue.

Gabriel's soft voice continued clearly. "Sir Thomas was initiated into the Hawks on his sixteenth birthday in 2051. As the son of a Hawk, and of course satisfying at least some of the criteria, he is a very smart and very dangerous opponent, with an IS of 153. At the time of the Great War, Sir Thomas was a mere youth of twenty-one, but he had already risen to a superior position in NATO forces. There is lots of trace for more than rumor that Sir Thomas had a significant hand in initiating a nuclear attack on the Geographic of Romania. By dissolving the political base for war in the dissolution of individual countries, but maintaining them as Geographic regions for the people who remained in those spaces, the global elite that remained after the Great War came to the conclusion that it was in everyone's interest to disarm.

"The problem for the Hawks is that without conflict and with all humans being treated as equal, their share, their quota, is shrinking. The fundamental premise of the Hawks is that Earth has limited resources and those resources should be used by those who are most capable of fully realizing the potential of those resources. Embracing Darwin's concepts of evolution, they seek on a periodic basis to reduce the strain on the Earth's resources and improve the gene pool that survives. Who really dies in wars, disease, starvation and natural disasters? Sure, maybe some percentage of the elite do, but even the estimated ten percent of one percent is still a very small number compared to ten percent of fifty percent. But generally, the vast proportion of the population can smell a rotten meal when they're being fed it, and since the Global Popvote of 2066, global disarmament and consolidation of the nation states into the United Nation of Earth, the ability for the Hawks to create catastrophic devastation resulting in large loss of human life has greatly diminished.

"A cornered beast is a dangerous one, Jonah. Given the compulsion of Hawks to control a disproportionate share of the world's wealth and power, Sir Thomas has come up with a way to get rid of about sixty-five percent of the global population, without spreading a virus, or bombs. Worse, he's come up with a way whereby sixty-five percent will volunteer for their own deaths."

I was stunned and raised my hand for him to pause.

"Sir Thomas has figured out a way to persuade sixty-five percent of the planet's population to volunteer to kill themselves?"

"You've seen the suggestions for the Tag Law on the newsfeeds. Did you see the news on the Paris bombing yesterday?" Gabriel asked, pausing to take a sip of what looked like water in a clear bottle.

"Yes, I have."

I turned my thoughts to the Tag suggestions I'd seen and the safer life they portrayed for everyone. It was a huge issue. One of privacy, but then, how much privacy do we really have now? I had seen the comms and tracking unit's main console back in UNPOL's complex in New Singapore. Devs the size of long-haulers and screens that could relay thousands of life-size images laid over a grid of where the circumstances were happening.

We may not have Tags embedded in our arms yet, but for the amount of privacy we have now through the PUIs on our Devsticks, we may as well. The pros of the suggestions focused on the benefits of the uplink and downlink to the Tag. The ability to read an internal biocheck and have it tracked in real time. A monitor for those in the care of children: never would youngsters be rushed late to healthcare again, nor would they be mislaid thanks to the map overlay updated constantly on your Devstick.

Gabriel put the bottle down and continued, "Well, that was the Hawks, and it is the start of the endgame in Sir Thomas and the other Hawks' plan to make sure that every new special Tag contains a toxic wafer. On a command relayed through the downlink to the Tag, the wafer will melt, releasing the toxin into all tagged humans with an Intelligence Score of less than a hundred. Within a week of the command, the first victims will start to die. Before the end of the second week, we estimate that about six point three billion people will be dead."

Again, I had to pause to let the scale of what Gabriel had said sink in before signaling him to go on.

"At this point, the Hawks will move globally to declare a national disaster and proclaim that the deaths are probably an attack from an alien power that we have been unable to detect. Despite there being no evidence to support this theory, the Military Security Council will then issue a global state of emergency and, acting on behalf of the United Nation of Earth Security Council, declare martial law. Under martial law, many of our basic freedoms will be suspended."

The enormity of this struck me full on. My body reacted. I vomited. A hot flash had spiked through my guts as the realization of the importance of where I was hit me. It was simply too much because in my gut, my 'gut feel', I knew that everything Gabriel had told me and shown me was the truth.

Luckily there was a recycler next to the Dev, and after I had vented my stomach of the ProCarboVite bar in it, I spat and looked up at Gabriel, wiping my mouth with the sleeve of my outers. He looked back. There was no expression on his face, it was just him. It said there is no artifice here, no hidden agenda. This is real.

Seeing the panic in my face, Gabriel said, "It's okay, Jonah. We can stop it – you and I and our friends – we can. This thing cannot happen, but we know when they want it to happen. We know which Ents are building the wafers, which scientists perfected the formula for the toxin, and whether they were murdered after completing their work. And we know that the Intelligence Score limit has been set to one hundred. But what we don't know is which people are connected with the planned moves directly after the extermination. If we can find out who those people are, then when we blow the whistle we have a chance to block them. But if we blow the whistle now, they'll either fade away to fight another day, or move to implement immediately and through perhaps messier means.

"The Tag Law is due to be put up for global Popvote on 15 March 2110. We probably have a week after that, maybe two, in which the Tags will be distributed. We understand that the tag can be self-administered and has a fool-proof delivery mechanism. So they'll probably be delivered to each person's home. If you haven't injected it, you'll be noticed by your absence online and requested to report to a nearby hospital to have it administered to you. That's what we know about the delivery.

"Shortly after it is confirmed to have been delivered to all households and individuals, the implementation suggestions will start. Globally the deadline to inject the Tag will be two weeks so that by 1st April everyone should have injected it. After that, Sir Thomas will take the serial numbers of the Tags sent to people and, using lists that the Hawks have drawn up, will match people with serial numbers and issue the command to the Tags. In essence, it is the largest eugenics experiment ever conducted."

I held my hand up to interrupt Gabriel's monologue.

"Hang on, why don't you just expose all of this? You know where the Tags are, you know about the wafer and the toxin, so why not just lay it all out there and wait for the response? I mean the whole thing, the Tag Law, the toxic tag, the lists, the Hawks – everything …" I trailed off as, while I was talking, I realized that what I was saying would be fruitless.

Gabriel smiled. "I don't need to probe your mind to know what you are thinking, and yes, you're right, it wouldn't work. All of our evidence to date is circumstantial. Everything is covered by extremely plausible denial, and we, or rather the information we supply, would simply be regarded as another crazy urban legend. The Tags would be swapped for genuine Tags, they'd be offered for inspection. The toxic Tags would vanish, probably get destroyed – it is easy enough to replace them in the future. We'd be discredited, arrested, and brain-wiped off the planet. And some time, one or two decades from now, the Hawks would suggest an upgrade, and then they'd kill another five hundred million just for good measure."

I nodded. It was true – the evidence without a toxic Tag was purely circumstantial, the claim so outrageous it would be aligned with the wildest conspiracy theories of the wildest crazies. It would be deemed as laughable to bring an action against Sir Thomas. There was no hard evidence, only conjecture, and worse, there was no one to bring any action against. That I believed it and understood it only made the task ahead of me the more impossible.

"So what is it you specifically need me to do?" I asked.

"We need you to go inside. You need to gain Sir Thomas's trust. You're an arbitrator. We want you to use being his 'nephew' to get inside the Hawks and find out what you can. In parallel, work out a case against the Tag Law, and at the same time build a stronger case for individual privacy laws. Just before the vote we'll go online, lay out the case, expose what we know and call for a full public investigation. If we're successful, we'll be heroes. If we're not, we'll probably be dead within the week.

"Of course, those arguments can be worked on under the pretext of building a strong case against any amendment to the Tag Law for the Hawks. The deeper you get, the more your uncle will trust you. He has to see you as a Hawk, and therefore you have to become a Hawk. That's not going to be easily achieved because your uncle views you as a smart liberal softie. We're going to have to change that, which means you have to quickly scale up into a ruthless person. We'll help with minor background alterations, but within a month you're going to have to do some pretty awful things to people to convince Sir Thomas you've got the makings of a Hawk. You won't be able to do this immediately, but the clock is ticking. We've got to be able to expose everything before the vote on 15th March next year. Your change in character must be seen as a reaction to an event. It must be explainable, for the deeper you get, the more your motive and desire will be tested."

I nodded. I understood exactly where Gabriel was coming from. My so-called uncle had at times tested my viewpoint on various subjects, from education to crime and related punisments. I realized that my arguments and position was that of 'a liberal softie', as Gabriel had put it.

Gabriel continued in the same soft, even tone.

"At some point, you will be asked to open your mind so that a telepath can examine you and report what they see. You must pass that inspection. You must appear to open your mind, but you must shield what you really know. It will be nearly impossible to do so, and discovery of, for example, this discussion, would mean either instant death or brain wipe. I have had over twenty years of practice with using my mind to probe others, and I find it difficult to resist, but there is a chance that we can train you well enough that you will survive. We will need to work on that next, but first I want to tell you about what we know."

Gabriel talked about the circumstantial evidence that they did have, and it was substantial. There was a lot of material that I was going to have to study at length later, as in my state and with the volume of the information, I was only able to grasp the highlights of what I was being told and shown.

"You look exhausted," Gabriel said, smiling. "Perhaps we should rest for a little while and recharge our batteries?"

"No," I said, shaking my head and looking at the time in the bottom corner of the Devscreen. "There isn't time. We must continue – you still have to teach me how to protect myself against a mind probe."

"All right, we'll move on to that now, then. I'm reasonably certain that when you return to Earth, and perhaps even before then, you will be requested to attend an interview. Take a look at your Devscreen."

On the Devscreen I could see myself as I exited my Env in Woodlands. The perspective of the images changed as different Devs played their role in tracking my progress from my Env, through the market where I had bought the beach clothes, and then all the way to the main Lev port at Changi. There I was with the violinist, with me sitting at the table. It seemed that the Dev capturing my image must have been somewhere behind my right shoulder and high up because it suddenly zoomed in on the table.

"That zoom in on the Devscreen set in the table was me," Gabriel said. "I manipulated the Dev because I wanted to be sure that you got the message I was sending. I couldn't send anything to your Devstick or the Dev in your Env – it would have been picked up too easily, so I hacked the suggestion feed into the Dev at your table in the café when I saw you take a seat. It was a risk, but I overlaid the suggestion to you on top of the regular feed. As far as anyone looking at that Dev would have seen, it was just the regular feed. But just in case someone did find it, we had to make it look like a suggestion. I had a back-up plan in case you did go to that resort in Tha Sala, but that would have been much riskier for me. Everything else, though, is picked up from normal observation Devs and CCTV cameras that are around New Singapore.

"The Nineveh itself is a construct. It didn't really exist. However, as far as UNPOL will be able to tell, it is real and has existed for over four years. We've put the design drawing permits into the local building commission's files, and anyone actually physically visiting it will find a third rate VacEnv with appropriately hot bubbling water. All of that took weeks to set up, just on the off-chance that someone else zoomed the Dev at the same time I sent the suggestion your way."

"How many of you? I mean, how many Doves are there?"

"Well, as with the Hawks, the Doves are a loose coalition of like-minded people, so exact numbers are hard to put together, and of course, like them, we operate in cells so that if some of us are caught, then the others have a chance to escape. In my immediate cell we are one hundred and twenty people, but as for how many of us there are, the number may well be over several million, all of whom are working actively to keep our universe a safe and free place to be.

"Again, we have no central command structure, but we do share information through channels that we have set up, and so we stay informed between the cells. We know that there are many more Doves than Hawks, especially if we count inactive participation and those possessing a fundamental belief in our ideals. In fact, the majority of the population can be considered Doves; however, getting those people to understand what is information and what is misinformation is problematic to say the least. The problem is in the demographics. Typically,

Hawks are by nature people with greater spheres of influence than your average Dove."

"You said when I get back, or possibly before, I will be interviewed. I agree, so how are we going to get around that? Especially if Cochran gets into the act, which I am sure she will."

"I'm going to hypnotize you and wipe everything to do with me and our conversation from your hippocampus, along with the one we had in the White Room and this one. The hippocampus is kind of like the index card holder of the brain. It knows where all the memories are stored in your brain. Your mind is a vast universe, and we only use about eight percent of its available capacity. That percentage varies from person to person, but it's roughly eight percent. I plan to hide these events in less than point zero zero zero one percent of the remaining ninety-two percent that you don't use. Cochran will not think to look there. Most telepaths wouldn't, simply because it's just white noise, but over the years I've learned to use that white noise quite efficiently."

"If they're hidden away in some white noise part of my mind, how am I going to remember any of this?"

"I'm going to create a trigger event. It will bring the memories back, but it will do it at a steady, even pace – a bit like receiving data over a datafeed, one block of information at a time. That way, you won't suddenly throw up as the reality hits you."

"Ooo-kay." I didn't sound too convinced, and my drawn out response was enough to cause Gabriel to let loose with one of his belly laughs again, slapping his thigh.

"It isn't as bad as it sounds. When the trigger event occurs, the memories will start to come back. At the beginning, you'll think that you're remembering a dream, but over the course of a couple of hours, the details of the dream will be filled in with ever-increasing clarity. Your mind will return again and again to the little reservoir of information that I'll plant, and the signals, traveling from the outback of your brain, will come in ever-larger memory chunks. Finally, you will reach the moment where this description will be relayed to you word for word, complete with the images of me and this room. I did it to you the first time we spoke using our minds. Do you recall a feeling that you were struggling to remember what we had voiced, but you clearly remembered what I had said to you through thought?"

"Yes, I remember that."

"I had to be sure that you would recognize the sign when you saw it, so I had to make sure you would remember every single word we thought together. I also put a little extra thought in there about how to deal with Cochran. That was to protect you. Do you remember thinking in the restroom, coming up with that plan, just before the interview with Cochran and your uncle? I inserted that idea telepathically about how you'd say how much you admired and wanted to be like Sir Thomas. Yes, that was me as well. And the same method will suffice for the interview you get when you return, with a twist. It dovetails nicely, forgive the pun, with our plans to install you into Sir Thomas's sphere of influence."

"I can see that."

"The worst probe that I have to prepare you for is the one that you will go through when you are considered as a candidate for entry into the Hawks. That will be far more dangerous and will be far more intense. In that interview, you might also call it a mind-scrape, they will go after the whole of your brain, and they will probe into all those little dark wells that the results of our existence give depth to."

"What is the trigger event?"

Gabriel smiled and, clasping his hands together across his stomach, lowered his chin to his chest and said, "If I tell you that now, we may set up a recursive loop. I'll do it when you're in the hypnotic state."

"What's a recursive loop?" I asked with a slight frown.

"It's where the eight percent travels to the point zero zero zero one place, finds the moment that I tell you the trigger event and then follows your time from that point on until the trigger event and then loops back to the beginning. If you create that loop, anyone looking inside your brain telepathically can retrace to where it is and release all the hidden memory. I'm also going to put all of the information we've gathered on your Devstick. It's a risk but less of a risk than me trying to send it to you later. I'll give you a code to enter in your Devstick and a reminder to make sure you're offline when you enter the code."

"Oh, right, good. Well, please keep the trigger event to yourself, then," I said with a smile and was rewarded with another of his belly laughs, this time slapping both hands on his knees and standing up. He walked over to the wall and sat down on the sleeper that was set against it.

Gabriel took out his Devstick and, thumbing it, said with a glance at me, "We have forty-five minutes before I have to start your hypnosis. I think we've given you enough information for you to work on after you get the trigger event.

Is there anything that you would like to ask me?"

I swiveled the Siteazy I was in to face him and pushed the Devscreen aside. The Devscreen folded itself back into the arm of the Siteazy and I, folding my hands across my stomach, asked the most important question.

"Who am I?"

Gabriel sat up straight on the sleeper. I got the sense that he had fully prepared what he was going to say, perhaps even rehearsed it.

"The name given to you by our father, Philip, is Mark Anthony, and our family name is Zumar. We are the last two surviving members of our family. I can tell you about our father, your mother and why you were taken. I can tell you about who we are descended from as far back as the fifteenth century. That's all I've been able to factually trace. Who you are – your character, role, purpose – I can't tell you that. It's up to you."

Suddenly tears came to my eyes as I thought of the warmth stolen from me with the loss of my natural parents. The sadness that I had at growing up having been told that my parents had been killed in a car accident when I was just a baby, suddenly replaced with grief for the murder of the father I hadn't known. The tears welled up and rolled down my face. I asked Gabriel, with a choke in my voice, "Please tell me about my father and mother, and tell me about you, my brother, and when we can be together again."

Gabriel leaned forward and rested his elbows on his knees, fixing me a with a look over the steeple that his hands had formed, almost as if in prayer, and said in a low voice, "It may be many weeks, perhaps even months, before we can meet again in person, and even then it may not be possible for us to have the time to talk about our family history. For now, let me tell you very quickly a little bit about our father and your mother and the circumstances that led up to you being stolen from me."

I got up from the Siteazy, walked over to the sleeper where Gabriel was sitting, and sat down beside him, wanting to be as close as possible. Gabriel smiled at me and, taking my hand, continued in his soft clear voice.

"Our father, Philip, was an intellectual who played a significant role in the formation of our Nation. It was he who wrote many of the speeches that propelled the Global Fellowship for Peace to prominence in the time following the Great War. The speeches that swept the people towards the world we are familiar with today may have been delivered by Bo Vinh, but they were crafted for the most part by our father.

"Once the nation had been formed, Philip remained an advisor to Bo Vinh and to the first Global Council that is the forefather of our General Assembly today. As the council expanded, he lost motivation, and in recognition of his contribution to humanity, Bo Vinh put forward and had granted by Popvote that Philip receive a grant for the development of ideas that would improve humanity. He was given the task of simply being among us as an observer, a commentator of humanity.

"Philip took to his new role with a passion. He wrote poetry, philosophy and produced papers that promoted different ways of realizing the value and potential of all levels of humanity. He looked a lot like you. His skin was a light tan, and he had a slim build and was tall at one hundred and eighty-six cent. Blue-green eyes, very similar to yours, and you share the same nose and chin. There's an image there on the Devscreen if you want to see." Gabriel pointed to the Devcockpit where he had been sitting earlier.

I looked at the full-length image of my father walking with his head bowed and his hands in the pockets of his outers as he talked with Bo Vinh. The two men suddenly stopped, and Philip waved and smiled in the direction of the camera. A little boy ran out to him and jumped up into his arms to be lifted high, but Philip protested, and I could tell he was laughing and telling the boy that he was too big to be lifted that high anymore. I knew without being told that the little boy was Gabriel.

"I'm ten in that image," Gabriel said, his voice almost a whisper, "but I can remember everything that happened at that time. The next two years were the happiest of our lives. My mother, Rebecca, had died of leukemia just after I was born, and I don't really remember her, so life with our father was all I knew. We had a happy life, but I sensed in him a sadness, maybe it was just loneliness. He tried to shield me from how he felt, I know that, but I would catch him when he wasn't aware my presence, staring off at nothing, and sometimes he would have a little sad smile to himself as though remembering a past event."

I put my hand on Gabriel's shoulder and gave it a light squeeze. Despite his self-control, I got the feeling that talking about the past was not easy for him. He put his hand over mine and, squeezing back, smiled slightly.

"Please go on," I said.

"We had just moved to the Geographic of Australia. Philip wanted to study the telepathic abilities of Aborigines, and it was there, in December of 2073, that Philip met Mariah. They met at a party held to celebrate the first manned landing on Mars. It had been broadcast at the Opera House. I remember how he looked when he came back that night to the hotel room we were staying in. I, too, had stayed up late to watch it, in the company of the hotel's childcare staffer. I hadn't seen our father that way. It was almost as if he had become younger in the time from when he had left me to the time that he had returned.

"Later, much later, after he was killed, and when I was already a man, I met a woman who had been at that party and was a close friend of our father's. She said that it was obvious to anyone within five meters of the couple that they had fallen in love at first sight. The normally reticent, and perhaps even shy, Philip and Mariah found in each other a place where they could simply be themselves and in being themselves were exactly what the other needed and wanted.

"I met her the next day, and when introduced I was shy, and I normally wasn't a shy child, but she was so beautiful that her beauty made me afraid to reach out and shake the hand that she offered me. I made a shield out of our father, but she knelt down to my level, and the warmth of her smile brought me into her arms. We went sailing that day out into Sydney harbor and then on beyond the Heads. We sailed for a long time, eating sandwiches that the hotel had prepared, and then we anchored off Scotland Island. I fell asleep in my bunk that evening, early as it had been a tiring day, to the sound of them talking in a low murmur and the occasional low laugh from one or the other. The last image I have of them for that day is them blowing me a kiss from their seat in the cockpit of the boat down to where I was looking up at them from my bunk in the cabin, our father with his arms around your mother.

"They never spoke of Sir Thomas in front of me, but once I heard half of a conversation between our father and Bo Vinh. What made me stop and listen was the serious expression on our father's face as he said he would be careful and that he understood that his affair with Mariah had caused him to become an enemy of Sir Thomas. They didn't discuss this in front of me, but I found out later, much later, that Mariah was Sir Thomas's wife when she met our father. Mariah left us for a short while, it was a week, as I found out later when I studied that time, and when she returned, we left the hotel in Sydney and moved to a place called Byron Bay. Here we rented a house next to the beach.

"My mother was Sir Thomas's wife?"

"Yes, and I think that played a part in your being stolen. Your mother became my wonderful stepmother. She wrapped me in her love and told me every day how much I meant to her and that her love for me was equal to her love for our father. The only time that I saw our father sad in that year was with the death of Bo Vinh. He went to the funeral, and the image of him at the funeral is the only one that exists in the public domain – all others have been deleted and purged by Sir Thomas. Wearing black, and I remember our mother packing the suit in his carry on, he is crying at the funeral of the man he helped to bring to prominence.

"Returning from the funeral, his mood stayed somber, but our mother drew him out, and within a month, the news that she was going to have his child, you, lifted his spirits, and we lived in a state of pure joy for that year. We took long walks on the beach and drives into the countryside, often eating on a rug spread out on a dune or a hill. We talked of everything. I was never denied an answer by either of them, they took the time to explain things to me.

"You were born at 2am on the morning of 23rd September 2075, and you weighed three point two kilogs and were fifty-three cents long. We stayed at the hospital for three more days after your birth, and then we moved back to the wooden house on the beach. What I didn't know at the time was that our father had been investigating the circumstances around the death of Bo Vinh and had begun documenting his findings in a report that clearly implicated Sir Thomas. That report disappeared after the events that followed. The evidence, much like the evidence we have today against Sir Thomas, was also largely circumstantial, and our father had kept it to himself.

"One evening in early October, the 6th, we had just come home after a walk on the beach. As we approached the house, we could see three men standing on the back of the deck that surrounded the house. Our father told Mariah, who was holding you, and I to wait, and we did as he walked up to the men and asked what they wanted. They went inside the house and that was the last time I saw him. When nothing had happened for over half an hour, Mariah with you in her arms and I approached the house. We heard nothing, and we went inside. Our father's study was a mess of papers strewn about, and the drawers had been tossed carelessly on the floor beside the desk. His Dev was gone and so was everyone. We were alone in the house.

"Mariah called UNPOL and told them what happened. They came and talked with us, and a woman stayed with us while the search for our father continued. After a week, Mariah called Sir Thomas to ask for his help, and he arrived half a day later. After their meeting, she told me that she was terrified of what Sir Thomas had told her and what he had done. She was crying and told me that we had to disappear, that we must run immediately and hide from Sir

Thomas. We packed some clothes into a carry on and fled on foot up the beach. The two of us walked for hours, stopping only to feed you and ourselves with the food we had brought from the house. It was a warm night, and as we walked up the beach where we had so many happy times, I cried, thinking about what we were doing. In a week everything that we had known was suddenly gone.

"We traveled north for four days, taking EVTours as far as Darwin, and it was there at a motel on Cavenagh Street that we stopped. The motel room had large air-conditioning ducts, and it was a good thing because the room was hideously hot. Too hot to be really cooled down – we were all uncomfortable and exhausted. You, however, slept and ate and smiled at us, and you gave us strength. You were less than a month old, but you gave us strength.

"It was in the motel, on the second day that we arrived there, where Mariah told me what it was that Sir Thomas had told her. He had told her that it was he that had ordered the death of Bo Vinh, and it was he who ordered the three men to come to the house that day to take Philip away. He told her of how he tortured our father until he cried for mercy and told him everything that he had found out. He told our mother that she was going back with him and that you were to be his child. If she did this, he said he would spare Philip his life. In his twisted way, Sir Thomas gave her time to think over what she would do, perhaps sure in the knowledge that she would come back to him. He gave her a day to think about it, and in this Sir Thomas had miscalculated. We can never be sure what would have happened because Mariah believed that Sir Thomas had already killed Philip, and so she explained why we had to run.

"I think she knew that they would find her because she unscrewed the cover off the air-conditioning duct and taught me how to crawl inside backwards. She would then hand me you, and I would pull the cover into place after us. She made me practice it a few times to be sure I could do it quickly and quietly, and on the fourth night we were there, a knock came at the door."

I am not a particularly tearful person, but I had to wipe the tears off my face. The understanding of what would come next was too sad to bear. I blinked to clear the tears from my eyes as Gabriel continued.

"I quickly climbed into the duct holding the cover in one hand, getting ready to take you in with me as we'd practised. But you were crying, and Mariah shook her head at me. I pulled the cover tight, hiding myself from sight. Mariah went to the door, but before she could open it, the door handle flew inwards with a great force, hitting her in the stomach. She fell to her knees, and it was all I could do to restrain myself with her last order in my ear. Don't move, no matter what, she had said. The door opened, and a man I know now as Sir Thomas came into the room. They argued, and he tried to pull her arm towards the door. She struck at him, and suddenly he pulled a long blade from within his outers. I saw it flash on the light from the outside of the door, and then he struck upwards with it, driving it into her stomach. He held it in her and twisted it; watching from my hide, I stared in horror as she died there on the floor of that motel. Sir Thomas leaned down and wiped the blade on her before he rose and walked slowly out of the room. A short while later, three men entered the room; putting her in a body bag and taking you with them, they left.

"I stayed in the hide for another hour, and then I left. There was nothing in the room or on me to indicate who I was or what life I had led up to that point. I was alone. I left at night without being seen. By lunch the next day, I had reached the outskirts of Darwin and just kept walking. I walked through the day and the night, into the country. The next morning a group of aborigines found me sleeping beside a tree. They talked to me, but I didn't say anything. I didn't talk to anyone for another five years."

Gabriel looked at the Devstick and, standing, said, "We will have to continue this discussion another time. We really should begin your training to defend yourself against a mind probe now."

I nodded and stood too, looking at him. He was slightly taller than me, and his hair was greying at the temples. I walked over to him, and we embraced. I hugged him harder and tighter than anyone I had ever hugged. I felt the loneliness of those years that he had been on the run, as I, too, had been lonely – shunted from one childcare institute to the next throughout my childhood.

It made sense to me now, that part of my life. I had wondered why there had been that coldness. It had always seemed as if Sir Thomas could not bear to be around me, and now I understood why. He wasn't my uncle. He was the murderer of both my mother and father.

Gabriel pulled a chair from the table and sat down. I sat down in the Siteazy again and waited for him to begin hypnotizing me. I took a long look at him, and he smiled. Once hypnotized, he was going to remove all my memories related to our conversations in the White Room and this chat on the Moon. After this he would become the runner again, and I wanted to savor my last memory of him as my brother.

In Hot Water

I woke up with a foul taste in my mouth, regretting my impetuous decision to come to the Moon. I could have been swimming in a beautiful tropical sea. Instead I was in a third rate VacEnv with uncomfortable sleepers, at least the one I slept in was, and my back hurt.

I stumbled out of the sleeper and read the suggestion on the Devscreen beside the sleeper. The hot springs seemed like a good idea to clear the stuffed nasal passages and ease my sore back, so putting on a pair of inners, I walked barefoot down through the carved rock tunnels outside of the room until I came to the hot spring. The corridors from the rooms were laid out like spokes on a wheel, with the hot spring as the hub.

Lying down in the pool, letting the low gravity float my body on the water, I laid my head back on the rock edge.

Crazy, I thought. Jonah James Oliver, you are completely crazy. You deserve to be recycled for this idiocy. Thinking that a word a runner had said in an interview is a clue as to his whereabouts and somehow you are going to track him down? What were you thinking? It's okay, I just won't tell anyone exactly where I've been. I'll tell them I just came to the Moon because I wanted to see what it was like to be in zero gravity. That's it.

Directly opposite the space that I was lying in, a woman emerged from one of the spokes. She laid a towel down beside the spring and, sitting down on the edge, put her feet in the water. Even at thirty meters away, I could see she was beautiful. She smiled and lifted a palm from the edge of the spring in greeting. I smiled back and raised my hand in return. She was tall, at least one hundred and seventy cents, and slim but not skinny. The white outer she was wearing showed off her long legs and was clinging tightly enough to her body that I could tell she wasn't wearing inners. Her long, black hair reached down to her waist, spanning out in a solid black wave over her tanned shoulders. I guessed Polynesian extraction or perhaps Indian.

Despite the beautiful woman sitting across from me, somehow my mood just didn't suit the pool, and after just ten minutes, still with stuffed nasal passages and a sore back, I headed up the spoke tunnel of unfinished rock and back to my room.

Leaving wet footprints on the blue matting that covered the distance to the room I had credded for the night, I checked my Devstick. I hadn't been able to use it when I arrived here from the Lev port, but it was back up now, with an explanation from the comms team at Peary that sun flares had knocked out the Satcom relays orbiting Shackleton. I did a find on ships leaving Shackleton or Peary for the Earth Orbiter. There was a ship leaving directly from Shackleton to the Orbiter in another twenty-five minutes – if I hurried I could make it. I noticed it was Friday the 13th.

I quickly threw the spare inners and outers and the 'Life's a Beach' bag I had brought with me into the Virgin Galactic carry on and headed out to the reception area. I thumbed my Devstick at the Dev on the reception counter and checked the cost had been deducted from my cred. They charged me full rate for the canceled night, but I wasn't going to stick around and argue with them.

I checked the map to the Lev on my Devstick and got the walkway lights going. I was short of time, and I didn't want to miss that ship back to Earth's Orbiter. With luck, I could be back in New Singapore by 9pm. The tunnel from the Nineveh to the main walkway tube was quite empty, but traffic in the main tube was busy with people headed towards their contributions.

Most of the people around me were wearing mining suits with the logos of their respective Ents emblazoned over their right breasts and writ large on their backs. I threaded my way through the crowd, my Virgin Galactic carry on marking me for the tourist that I was, and got to the Lev. There was a queue. The Levs were moving pretty quickly, but it was obviously a busy time. Standing in the queue waiting for my turn, I suddenly felt a tap on my shoulder and turned.

"Hi, it looks like you and I had the same idea," said the beautiful woman from the pool.

I noticed the envious looks from the other men standing around waiting for Levs as this gorgeous woman spoke to me. She, too, had a Virgin carry on, and I said, "Yes, I've only been here for a few hours, but the novelty's worn off."

That comment got me a few glares from the people around me, but I didn't care.

Deal with it, I thought.

The woman, too, noticed the looks and, smiling at me, said, "You think you've been having a hard time – the ratio of women to men on the Moon is one to twenty, and I'm getting zoned out by all these stares I've been getting."

As she said this, the Lev arrived, and we bustled in. I took advantage of the shuffle to move to an area that was reasonably far away from the people that had been standing around us while we were chatting. The woman followed me.

"I think we upset some people," I said to her as we stood waiting for the Lev door to close. It was standing room only, and her face was only thirty cents from mine. Smiling, she had white even teeth in a full mouth set in a strong jaw. Her cheekbones flared up and out in a slash under her green eyes. The green eyes crinkling now at the corners in a smile.

"I don't care what those freaks might think right now. I've been undressed in so many once-over looks this morning that I feel like I'm walking around naked."

"Where on Earth are you going?" I asked, making a very sincere effort not to glance at the breasts that I had admired in my brief glance at her in the pool – instead looking directly into her eyes.

"I'm on my way to my new contribution in New Singapore. I've just finished acquiring a new range of knowledge, and my transfer from Geneva came through. I thought I'd check out the Moon because I've never been here, and I'm glad I did because now it is off my list of 'Must Places to Visit'." She tossed the Virgin carry on over her shoulder.

"That's great. I live in New Singapore. I've been contributing there for about four years now. My name is Jonah, by the way," I said, giving her a wai.

She waied me back and said, "My name's Mariko. Pleased to connect with you," and flashed me another dazzling smile that gave rise to two little dimples in her cheeks.

"Do you …?"

"Do you …?"

We broke into laughter as we had said exactly the same thing at the same time, "You go first," she said.

"Do you want to travel together? I can brief you on New Singapore, or were you thinking of sleeping on the way back?"

"No, I mean yes, it would be great to travel with you, and no, I wasn't planning on sleeping. I feel like I've slept for a day, and I haven't really talked with anyone since I left Earth three days ago."

The Lev door opened onto the concourse of Shackleton Moonbase and right opposite the Lev doors was the cred deduct point for the JAS ship back to Earth's

Orbiter. We hurried over to the JAS point, and the man behind the waist-high Devscreen, which was suggesting flights and tours, said, "Good morning, and how can we at JAS help you today?"

"We'd like two normals back to Earth's Orbiter, please," I said and smiled at him.

"I'm sorry, sir, but all the normals are taken. We only have supers left."

"We'll take them," I began to say but was interrupted by Mariko.

"Uhm, I'm sorry, Jonah, but my budget doesn't stretch to the supers. It's okay, though – you go on ahead. I'll catch up with you when we get to New Singapore."

I turned back to the man. "How much is the upgrade from normal to super?"

"It's four hundred and fifty-six units with tax, baggage, alkys and nourishment included," he said and smiled a very smarmy kind of smile that said, 'Let's see if you'll cough up those creds, mister.'

I returned his smug smile and held up my Devstick. "Give me two Siteazys next to each other."

It was a bit extravagant, but there was no way I was going to let Mariko out of my sight until I had her complete profile in my Devstick. Turning to her, I said, "Okay, that's settled. This trip to the Moon has been pretty bad for me so far, but," I paused for effect, giving her my best dazzling smile as I gazed deep into those wide green eyes, "things are definitely looking up from my point of view."

She tilted her head to one side and studied my face.

"Are you flirting with me?" she said with a laugh hidden somewhere in her words.

"I most certainly am, Mariko."

"Could you make your way over to the spaceport immediately, please?" the JAS staffer said in a squirmy kind of a voice.

I ignored him and said to Mariko, "Think of it as a 'welcome to New Singapore' gift, and let's just get off this rock. We have six hours to talk through before we reach the Orbiter."

Taking her arm by the elbow, I thumbed my Devstick for the lights to the spaceport and led the way.

***

Agent Cochran froze frame on the image of Jonah's face smiling at Mariko, his lips slightly pouted as he had just finished saying Orbiter. It was 8:45am, and

Cochran was standing in the center of a Devcockpit in UNPOL's Trace center in New Singapore. She'd been woken by a call from a staffer in the Center at 7:15am, when Jonah's Devstick had been traced to a VacEnv on the third level of a place called the Nineveh Hot Springs Resort on Shackleton. At 7:29am she'd walked into the ten-thousand-square-meter-sized room, which was one of three primary tracing centers around the globe, and taken charge.

Either he's good enough to be starring in the Flicks or he's innocent, she thought. She'd reviewed the images from the time that Mariko had picked him up at the pool to now. Jonah showed no nerves whatsoever and seemed blissfully unaware of the strange coincidence of Mariko staying at the same resort and leaving for Earth at the same time. He'd even splurged the cred to have her upgraded, when he had the opportunity to dump her, which he would have if he had something to hide.

Could he be that good an actor? She looked harder at the screen. Her only contact with Jonah had been on the day that the runner had run. She'd heard about the brilliant nephew of the director, but they'd never met before. He didn't move in the usual social circles for one of his level, and that she found interesting, but put it down to a 'loner' type.

She stared hard at Jonah's smiling face, the angle of the image just catching Mariko's lower jaw, just the shadow of bottom of her chin seen occasionally brushing the edge of the image. She felt a little spike of ... what ... was it jealousy, as she saw the look in his eyes when he spoke to Mariko?

Well, Jonah, you and I are going to be having a most interesting chat over the next six hours, she thought, smiling to herself. Let's get to really know each other.

***

Settling into our seats, we were separated by a meter of space, which was currently occupied by the JAS Intrav staffer who was helping Mariko to buckle in. Take off and ascent from Shackleton out of the Moon's weak gravitational pull would be much less strenuous than it was on Earth.

I buckled in and was waiting for the staffer to get out of the way so that I could talk to Mariko. I didn't want to lose the warmth that we had seemed to generate this morning.

I looked at my Devstick and thumbed up my POS. Scrolling out on the image, I saw our path from the Moon to Earth. From the blue dot that was me, the craft would fly in a straight line to edge of the Moon's gravitational pull and then, turning right, would catapult itself around the Moon and head straight for the Orbiter. The ETA on the track display showed we'd reach the Orbiter around 2:15pm, and with luck, I could be back in my Env by 6pm. With even better luck, Mariko would be with me.

Out of the window on my right, I saw what looked like a heavy metal box about four meters long and six wide on large rubber wheels with a pole sticking out of the end of it and rapidly approaching the craft we were in. A clunk signaled its coupling with the craft, which jolted forward a little.

The staffer stumbled against my arm and, turning to me, said, "I am most sorry, sir, usually the drones are a bit more gentle than that."

I looked up at her. She was attractive, probably of Hispanic origin, I guessed by her features and her accent. She had large breasts and a generous cleavage, which the JAS Intrav suit was displaying to full effect. My eyes flicked from her cleavage to Mariko's, and I thought, I like hers better – not as big, but a really cute perky shape. I turned my eyes to find those of the staffer fixed on me, and I knew exactly what she was thinking. What she was thinking was she knew exactly what I was thinking, and I smiled at her. She was exactly right.

"Would you two like an alky before we take off?" she asked, returning the smile. I leaned around her also-generous backside and asked Mariko.

"What do you think? Do you want to go for an alky?"

She smiled back at me and, staring directly in my eyes, said, "Sure, why not? Order me something relaxing and smooth."

I looked up at the Intrav staffer and asked, "Would you happen to have the Endorpho 80?"

"Yes, I think I can find you a couple of those." And with another smile, she walked back to the prep area between Super and Normal.

I turned, continuing to look at Mariko. I couldn't get enough of looking at her. She was almost too attractive. She stopped doing what she was doing with her Devstick and glanced at me.

"What?" she said in a soft voice, and her eyes smiled at mine.

"I can't stop looking at you," I said and felt like an idiot the minute I'd said it.

She chuckled and said in a teasing way, "We're all beautiful, Jonah."

I laughed and said, "Okay, but perhaps I should have said, 'Your physical features are a perfect match to my aesthetic taste,'" and smiled back at her.

"I feel the same," she said, returning my smile. To my eye, her smile held a deeper promise. I wanted to kiss those wide lips. I knew that our mouths would match in size, and it would be a perfect kiss.

A Down to Earth Chat

Sharon Cochran knew that the Staffer Margarita Delgado had been an Intrav for six years. She'd qualified on the Hydroships traversing Earth's oceans and had qualified for space three years previously. She loved what she did. Her life was good – she met many nice men, and women, had a good balance of contribution and self-time, and had visited every major city on Earth and in space.

In all that time she had never received an UNPOL Blue Notice and had to think hard to recall her training as to what it meant, especially as her brain had sent a typical panic response to the unusual notice spelled out on the Devscreen in the galley. An UNPOL Blue Notice requests immediate assistance to gather more information about an individual who may or may not be about to cause themselves or others harm. The receiver, in their official capacity and acting on behalf of the state, is obliged to comply.

UNPOL BLUE NOTICE

Subject: Jonah James Oliver

Request Filed by: Special Agent Sharon Cochran

Requested authorized for Submission: Director of UNPOL: Thomas Bartholomew Oliver

Request Authorized: Judge Miriam Wu

Case #2109.

UNPOL requests immediate assistance by receiver of this Blue Notice, in accordance with UNPOL statute 34 B, D and E of UNPOL code of operations.

Intervention by actions to be performed by: Margarita Delgado. The intervention requested is for an immediate Truth Treatment to be applied to Jonah James Oliver. The truth treatment is to gather information related to Case #2109.

Agent Cochran had been extremely busy. Getting the Blue Notice on Jonah drafted and signed by the director had only taken a few minutes. Finding a recipe for an impromptu Truth Treatment in space had taken a few minutes longer. She

96

hit submit, sending the concoction of several parts of different alkys, which were all available on flight JAS1608 bound for Earth's Orbiter, to be mixed with the drink Jonah would be served.

Delgado bit her lower lip and pressed her finger on the Devscreen. Confirm.

At least they only want information, she thought. He must be one of those Ent scammers. Her opinion of Jonah had changed radically in the last few minutes. The prepare for take-off light flashed on her console, and she quickly sat down and buckled herself in.

***

The craft vibrated slightly as the roar of its rockets increased in pitch. Surging forward, the spaceport on Shackleton slid out of view as we moved off down the runway towards the ramp at its end. The craft picked up speed, occasionally bumping its passengers in their seats as it traveled down the runway, and then the steam catapult took up the pulling and punched us into our seats for the last two hundred meters of ramp – hurtling us into space at seven hundred and fifty kiloms per hour. The craft left the ramp with a slight drop, and then the rockets were pushed to their maximum as we climbed up at a steep angle.

A tanned hand reached over my shoulder, and a sealed container with the JAS logo on it was dangled in front of my face. Twisting in my seat, I reached up and collected it with my left hand.

"Thanks," I said, smiling. Intrav Delgado, as her name tag stated, didn't smile back but turned her attention to Mariko. Mariko took the alky and shared a look that puzzled me. It was as if they knew each other, but I shrugged the thought off, knowing how improbable that was.

Probably something to do with me checking out their breasts, I thought.

I forced myself not to look at Delgado's backside as she turned away, as I could see, out of the corner of my eye, that Mariko was looking at me. I smiled at her, and she raised the container with the spout first to toast me, then to her mouth and said, "Bottoms up." I copied her action and drained the Endorpho 80. It tasted a bit different than the one I had at the Polar Nights relax lounge, but that was probably due to the stuffiness I still had in my nasal passages as a result of the Moon sickness.

I sat back comfortably in the Siteazy and waited for the drink to kick in, anticipating the cool stillness that I remembered from the last time I had it. The muted roar from the craft's engine suddenly cut off, and the craft banked as the Devscreen in the headrest in front of me flashed a warning that we were now in zero grav. I looked across at Mariko and saw that she was also lying back with her eyes closed, giving me an opportunity to really take a good long look at her body. Her outers had the image of a dragon running down the right leg, the colors were bright green and red. Then the dragon's tail moved, but Mariko hadn't moved her leg.

I didn't remember that about the Endorpho. As it kicked quickly in with full force, I felt like I was in a Lev on steroids, dropping through one hundred levels faster than the speed of light. I panicked a little with the speed of the rush – it was nothing like what I remembered from my last Endorpho 80, and I might have gone too far with this one. Through wide eyes I looked at Mariko. She still had her eyes closed and seemed relaxed enough.

She turned her whole body toward me slightly, and I saw her left breast bulge out of the opening in the middle of her outers, the faint outline of her nipple clear through the material. She twisted fully onto her side and brought her hands up palms together, placing them under her cheek as though she was going to sleep.

I thought of her nipple in my mouth, and I felt myself reacting. Was this yet another side effect of the Endorpho? Obviously the Endorpho 80 was a whole different proposition in space, but as long as Mariko was okay, then I was determined just to go along for the ride. I struggled with my senses, trying to get a bit more control, taking several short sharp breaths. The assault calmed down, and the cabin took on a rose-tinted hue, my jaw ached a little: I had clenched my teeth too much. I wished I had some gum to chew.

Mariko opened her eyes slowly and gazed at me. I was still looking at her breast, but flicked my eyes back to hers, and she smiled. "So tell me, what did you get up to while you were on the Moon?" The softly spoken words seemed to journey to my ears one by one. Each traveling on its own, her lips putting each one out softly, slowly, and I could see them flying through the space that separated us until they went past my cheek and into my ear.

Cool, I thought, I can see speech, and then remembered that I was supposed to answer as I saw the question mark trailing the Moon.

My tongue felt thick and dry in my mouth. "Um, I didn't do anything, really. I wasn't there long," I replied. Thinking about it, I really didn't remember doing anything at all. I remembered leaving the Lev port at Shackleton and using the walkys to find the Nineveh, but then, well, nothing. I had been tired. It had been a long day's trav.

"I just wanted to go there, you know. It was a pure impulse thing. I saw a suggestion in the Lev port. I had actually been going to a small beach resort on the east coast of the Southern Thailand Geographic, but then I saw this suggestion that was the Nineveh Hot Springs Resort and thought since I'd never been to the Moon, I'd try it. It was stupid, really. I should have gone to the beach, but then again, I wouldn't have met you, would I?" I smiled at her, feeling tremendous tenderness and love for her. It welled up in me and almost made me want to cry.

She released one hand from under her cheek and held it out to me across the space between us, and I reached out with mine and held her hand for the first time. Her skin felt smooth and a little warm under my fingers. With my thumb on top of her hand, I could feel the slight texture of her skin pattern, and I stroked the inside of her palm with my fingers. She murmured and smiled, just lifting the corners of her mouth a little.

"Are you usually an impulsive person?" she asked, still holding my hand in the weightlessness. The words did their float through space. They seemed to be handling the zero grav environment just fine. I thought on that for a couple of secs before answering.

"No, I don't think I am, normally. In fact, you might think I am a very predictable person, boring even." I gave her a self-depreciative smile in return.

"Oh, somehow I doubt that," she said with a chuckle. "Did you meet anyone interesting on the Moon? All I met were sex-starved miners and comms geeks."

"Uhm." I struggled to think clearly but then gave up and just said what was in my mind instead. "No, not really. Actually, I didn't meet or speak to anyone, except you. Strange, isn't it? I mean, I was there for at least twelve hours, and I didn't speak to anyone at all. During the whole trip, I only spoke with three people. There was a guy on the flight to the Earth's Orbiter, a woman outside a relax lounge who offered me an orgasm in space and a relax lounge girl who had very saggy breasts with incredibly long nipples that waved around just below her eyes when she talked."

Mariko burst out laughing with a 'hah', and continued with, "Are you a breast man, Mr Oliver? From what I've seen, you seem quite fascinated by mine, for example."

"Yes, I think you could safely say that I am fascinated by your breasts, and your eyes, and your hand, and your voice, and your bum, and your mouth and –"

"Okay, okay, I get the image." She chuckled and gripped my hand a little tighter. A surge of warmth in my groin transmitted a signal through my spine, which registered in my brain as, 'We're going to sleep together.'

"Where do you live in New Singapore?" she asked, our bodies still connected through the tenuous senses of our fingers as we held each other's hands.

"I've got an Env in Woodlands, but I've been thinking of moving somewhere with a view. From my Env, practically everything I see has been made by someone or something. I've heard that they've just opened a new Lev port on Kuantan, and if you go about six kiloms east from there, you come to a place called Kampung Tanjung Sisik. It's on a white sandy beach, and the cred isn't too bad, lower than where I am now. I was thinking of getting an Env there. It means more trav time, but you can swim in the sea, and you have more sky to look at. And you? What are your plans? Have you found a place to be in New Singapore?"

"No, I've booked an Envdorm in Orchard. Thought I'd park near the city center so I don't have to trav too much, but this Sisik place sounds really good. By the way, what is your contribution?"

"I'm an arbitrator, both civil and criminal. The criminal stuff is mostly pro bono, and the civil stuff is mostly corporate, but either way, I sit in the middle of two opposing forces. I try to help them find the middle ground."

"When you're not contributing, what do you do? What do you do with your self-time?"

I thought, but again I couldn't seem to establish any coherent response – the images of my life associated with her question came to my brain unbidden, and the words associated with those images spilled out of my mouth. Perhaps it was just that I felt comfortable with her and wanted to tell her the unvarnished truth.

"I read a lot and spend a lot of time thinking about things. Flicks, backgammon, um, that's about it, really. Pretty sad, isn't it?"

"Do you trav much?"

'No, the trip to the Thai Geographic was the first trip out of New Singapore for over a year, and that trip was only to a resort on Langkawi, less than forty minutes by Lev. It's strange, but I seem to spend a lot of time by myself, but then again, that might not be so strange. One way or another I've spent most of my life alone. My earliest memory, I was four. My uncle had just sent me to an early learning camp in Scotland. It was freezing, and the first recollection I have is that I was crying because I was cold and nothing was familiar. I remember the matron telling me not to be such a baby and shutting and locking the door behind her as she said that."

"What happened to your parents?" she asked, her eyes wide and her voice low at the sadness of my first memory.

"I never knew them. They were killed in a car crash just after I was born, and my uncle – my father's brother – became my legal guardian."

"Are you close with your uncle?"

I snorted through my nose in a bitter laugh. "No, I don't think anyone's close to my uncle. He's always been sort of vague. I mean, I think he's only physically touched me maybe less than five times in my life, and three of those were handshakes at public gatherings where I'd won something."

"Were you a bright student?"

"I don't know if I was bright. Well, yes, I was, but it was more that studying was all I did. I went from one fast learning curve to another, and I'm lying here wondering if I've learnt anything at all in all those years."

I smiled at her. I was fully aware that this was the most I'd ever revealed about myself in a personal way and of my own free will to anyone in my life, but I didn't care. I'd known her for less than an hour and a half, but time didn't matter – her eyes told me that I could trust her. I felt sleepy, my eyelids drooped, but I kept my eyes open, barely.

"I'm twenty-six. How old are you?" Mariko said. She was still holding my hand, and now she stroked the inside of my palm with her fingers. I let my hand lie still in her touch.

"Thirty-four. I'll be thirty-five next July. When is your birthday?"

"September, September the 15th."

"You said earlier that you had just spent some time in Geneva. What knowledge were you acquiring there?"

I closed my eyes, the effort of holding them open was just too much. I heard her say something, but it was as if the sound in my ears was being turned down, slowly. Her voice faded until I felt a deep sense of ease and fell into a deep sleep.

***

Mariko kept holding his hand with hers, and with the other reached for her Devstick, lying beside her cheek where she had been able to keep an eye on it.

She said softly, "He's asleep."

Jonah grunted and moved, his hand slipping out of hers. She wanted to grasp it but was too late, and now it swung slowly towards the edge of the Siteazy Jonah was in.

A new data stream came through on to the Devstick at the top of a long stream of data from Agent Cochran, the UNPOL officer she was reporting to. She read the reply from Cochran.

"I'm surprised he lasted that long, but anyway, we found out what we needed. Thanks for your help. You can dump him as soon as you reach the Orbiter. He's not hiding anything."

Mariko looked across at Jonah. She felt relieved, and she felt dirty. Undercover was not her thing; she didn't like deceit, and although most of what she'd said to Jonah was the truth, the reason that she had met him was a lie. Yes, she could dump him now, and that is what she should do. Mariko lay back in her seat, staring at the ceiling of the spaceship. She didn't often feel confused, but now her thoughts ran in a jumbled mess of emotion.

Looking at Jonah, fast asleep, drugged, she thought about what to do. He's a really nice guy, and he is attractive. I don't want to dump him, and I don't want to have lied to him, but it's too late for that. How can I ever tell him? Well, maybe there'll be a way, when he's cleared and contributing again. I can take him out for a dinner and explain. Explain what? That you lied to him and interviewed him while under a Truth Treatment? That you arrived at the Nineveh three minutes after he'd entered the pool? She had no ready answers.

A mind that is clouded with feelings and one that has been touched by what she has heard is not a mind that will make rational decisions, and although she knew that the best thing for her career was to dump Jonah at the Orbiter, she also knew that she wouldn't.

At the End of the Day

Gabriel flipped back and forth between the image of Mark lying in the Siteazy, and the image of Sharon Cochran in the Trace Operations Center on Earth. The images were slightly delayed given the distance between them, but Gabriel had a complete dataset for the entire time that she had been logged in.

"And as for you, Cochran, I'm going to burn your mind out before this is over."

Gabriel was tired, he hadn't slept for over forty-eight hours, but still he refused himself the sleeper against the wall a short distance from the Devcockpit in the room where he and Mark had spoken. He was tired but satisfied. So far his plans were succeeding. Some things had gone awry, but for the most part everything had worked out. Mark, as Jonah, was primed. He hated putting his long-lost brother in this situation, but he really didn't have any choice.

At their last meeting Maloo had asked him, "Would you hesitate if it was not Mark, if it was another human so well fitted to this task?"

And Gabriel had known the answer before Maloo had opened his mouth, taking his indecision as doubt. There was no doubt in Gabriel's mind that Mark had to be the one, was in fact the only one who could get close enough to Sir Thomas and had the skills, whether he knew it or not, to survive the encounter and achieve the task. At least Mark had a slight chance: anyone else, including himself, would be a complete failure.

Mark's hypnosis had gone well. It had been exhausting for Gabriel, constantly checking on the Dev for the cues and memories that he had to erase for Mark to stand a chance with Cochran or Truth Treatments. Mark had to be a Hawk, and his memories had to be perfect. It had been a painful process and doing it had drained Gabriel.

Maloo had taken Mark to the Nineveh before they'd put the comms back online. He'd wiped the last remaining images of Mark being helped to his VacEnv through the lobby of the Nineveh, and then he had waited for Mark to leave. He needed Mark to leave quickly, didn't want him hanging around on the

103

Moon for two reasons. The first was that he had a flight to catch. With Mark on Far Side, UNPOL security would be tight – too tight to move – and it would greatly increase the risk of their capture. The second was for Mark. If he returned immediately, Gabriel would be able to at least keep an eye on the first part of the journey, and if required, could be in a position to intervene.

Maloo had been watching for anyone checking in to the Nineveh, and they'd picked up Mariko and her last transmission from Cochran before she'd created the encounter with Mark. They'd reacted quicker than he'd thought they would, and it showed the intensity with which Cochran was tracing him. To put a trace on the nephew of the director of UNPOL took guts and was an indication of a fierce attention to detail. The blocks he'd put in Mark's mind should be good enough to resist a Truth Treatment in the White Room, so anything they could do up here wasn't a concern. As far as Mark knew, he really was Jonah, so his truth was his safety.

He glanced at the time in the bottom left of his primary Devscreen. 10:20am. He still had a lot to do. Gabriel leaned forward in the Biosense in front of the Devcockpit and pressed his eyes shut with his fingertips, thinking back over the path that had brought him to this tiny room on the Moon.

Gabriel shook himself from his reverie. Thinking of Mark, his mood brightened. He was proud of what his brother had become, despite and against all the odds, he had made humanity's choice. Blood is blood, and the blood of a proud line of people ran in Mark's veins. Although it placed him in great danger, it didn't fail him when it had been called upon to do the right thing.

The Zumar blood ran strong in him, and Gabriel thought how much it must burn Sir Thomas to see the face of Philip Zumar as that of his own nephew. Or did he take some kind of perverse pleasure from knowing that the son of Philip Zumar and his wife, Mariah, lived the lie of being his nephew? Gabriel didn't know and really didn't care. Whatever Sir Thomas thought was only of interest in how it might be used to bring about his death.

His primary Dev pinged. "Gabriel?"

"Yes, Maloo," Gabriel said.

"How did it go?" The image of Maloo in the tunnel overhead talking to him on the Devstick came through with incredible clarity, but then, Gabriel had installed the Devs here himself and hadn't spared on the cred needed to get the best high-def Devs there were. The comms were on a local grid and not connected to anything. The two men were free to talk normally.

"Well, Cochran reacted faster than we thought she would, but other than that, it went as we planned, Maloo. He'll do it, and if he is really lucky, he'll succeed. What time are we leaving? Is everything under control?"

"We're on track. How long for you to pack? We've got to get to Peary before 3pm. I've set us up in a titanium freighter bound for the Congo. It's straight in, and it'll be a hot bumpy ride, totally hardcore, but we should survive."

Gabriel chuckled at Maloo's throwaway line about surviving re-entry, but knew they really were in for a ride they'd remember forever, if they survived it. He began packing some of the peripheral equipment around the cockpit.

After taking a long drink of water, he said in an even voice, "I'm more worried about being in a sealed box with you for eight hours. What did you eat for breakfast?"

Maloo, which means thunder in the Aboriginal language, lived up to the name he had been given by the tribal elders in response to his loud and long farts as a baby. The tribe was the one that Gabriel had joined on leaving Darwin as a boy, Maloo being his boyhood friend and blood brother. "Well, don't just stand there laughing, get over here as fast as you can, and help me get this stuff stowed away."

"I'm on my way. Couldn't you get anything faster than a golf cart?"

"Hey, don't knock the golf cart. It represents the only six hundred and fifty-four yard hole-in-one in recorded history, at least, according to the guy who sold it to me."

"Okay, I'll see you in about ten."

"Maloo?"

"Yes, Gaz?"

"What did you find out about Mariko?"

"Um, she's okay. She's just been manipulated into this by Cochran, but she's not evil, far from it."

"Okay, and make it eight. We've got a lot of work to do."

Gabriel took a look around the room. He'd been here on and off since he'd busted out of Level Ten. When they were done packing, he'd get Maloo to sanitize the room while he packed the buggy they'd use to drive to Peary. They'd bought a disused buggy and repaired it so that now it looked, complete with serial numbers, exactly like a BHP mining utility vehicle, one of thousands traversing the Moon's surface. The buggy would allow them to trav as far as Peary, and then they'd board the ore freighter to the Congo. A straight, long burn followed by a fast, hot re-entry. He hoped the suits they'd bought would hold up. The freighter wasn't designed to carry humans, but the box built into its guts and the titanium ore it was carrying should provide just enough protection from the heat.

He took a last look at Mark, his arm dangling by the side of his Siteazy in Super.

WHAT'S IN A NAME

Cochran called the meeting at 4:45pm with a soft voice command to the Dev.

The message from Cochran hit their Devscreens. "Full review of Case #JM-2109, 5:00pm, Conference Room 35."

Dominique 'just call me Dom' Signora couldn't believe it.

What a bitch, he thought and, with a scowl and shrug, turned to his colleague and fellow trace partner, Martine 'Marty' Shorne, and said, "Calling the meeting just when we're going back to our Envs. What are we going to do about Fatima's party?"

She just lifted her eyebrows in reply, and feet sprawled out in a huge vee in front of her, chin on her small chest, arms folded, she continued to scan the Devscreen. They'd been working together for over three months, him joining straight out of the Academy and her transferring into Trace Operations from Large Commercial Crimes Unit (LCCU).

She looked like she was asleep, but she was wide awake. It was just her style. In this team everybody had their own style – usually it only outed after you'd been in the team for a while – a style that would fit, that evolved into and synced with the other styles in the team. Marty came fully loaded with hers, and the team evolved and revolved around it.

Marty brought her knees up and her legs together and, pushing her hands into her spine, rolled onto her back in the Siteazy. She straightened her legs out and pushed back with her head until she was standing on her head, arms out straight and legs dead straight. She held the position for a count of fifteen and bringing her hands into play, slowly lowered herself in an arc over the back of the Siteazy.

"Let's go," she said and turned for the door.

The meeting would be held in the executive conference rooms on the two hundred and forty-second floor. Marty held out her hand to Fatima, who slowly walked from her Devcockpit in the southwest section of the room to the door where Marty was waiting. Taking Fatima's hand, she nodded at the others, and

107

with the door sliding open, they stepped out of the Cave. They all hated this part of their contribution.

Cochran stood at the head of the Clearfilm table, Marty sat opposite Cochran, with Dom and Fatima on her left and Stanislav on her right. She sat cross-legged on her Biosense, knowing it annoyed Cochran and knowing that Cochran wouldn't do anything about it.

Marty didn't like Cochran. She knew the type: ruthless and selfish, overachievers with no interest in morality. But there was no need to call a meeting at this time. They could do this tomorrow. Cochran called the meeting to show them what a dedicated contributor she was and how she was totally committed.

And she is, totally committed to herself, thought Marty as she sat listening to Cochran's intro. Now she'll pick on Stanislav with his stutter, knowing she freaks him out, she thought.

"Stanislav, can you give us a rundown on the illegals that our runner was running?" Cochran asked and sat down, swiveling sideways in the Biosense and crossing her legs. Stanislav stuttered under stress. He was brilliant at spotting something where there was nothing in the ether and being able to translate what it meant, but he was incapable of speaking to Cochran.

Marty didn't like what was going to happen, so she said, "Sharon, before coming into the meeting, the team and I have discussed what we think has happened here, and we'd like to present those ideas to you and then go and enjoy Fatima's birthday party, which is today. We can go over the objectives you set for us, of course. However, we believe that our time would be more productively employed if we focused on a new angle. Would that be acceptable?"

Cochran continued looking at Stanislav, who had gone bright red and was darting glances at Marty as if to ask her to come and rescue him, then she swiveled to face Marty, smiling. "Well, that would depend on the plausibility of your presentation and the credibility of your evidence, but I'd like to hear what your 'new angle' is, so please go ahead."

Marty pushed herself off from the table, and the Biosense rolled across the space behind her until she was facing the Devscreen. She called up a static image on the Devscreen that covered the far end of the room in huge quarter circle. The image started moving and showed two men walking together, one with his head bowed and his hands in the pockets of his outers as he talked with Bo Vinh. As he talked, the two men suddenly stopped, and the one with his hands in his pockets waved and smiled in the direction of the camera Dev. A little boy ran out to him and jumped up into his arms to be lifted high, but the man protested, laughing and telling the boy that he was too big to be lifted that high anymore. The little boy jumped up and down until the man picked him up, and standing together with Bo Vinh, they posed for the camera. The image stilled on the two men and the boy.

Marty said, "The little boy is your runner. He's ten in this image. The man walking with Bo Vinh is Philip Zumar, the boy's father. We know nothing more about the boy other than he disappeared and was presumed dead by authorities in Byron Bay in the Geographic of Australia. We have, however, found out a lot about the boy's father, Philip."

Cochran, turning her Devstick end-over-end on the table, her lips pursed together in a chaste kiss, said, "Go on."

Marty didn't turn around and sat cross-legged, her back silhouetted against the image of the three people on the Devscreen. She touched the Devstick clipped on her belt, and the image changed to another image of Philip Zumar, only as a much younger man.

"Philip Zumar was a firebrand activist in the early sixties." The Devscreen changed again, bringing up a slew of images, while Marty continued speaking in a soft voice telling the story of Philip Zumar. As each topic changed, the Devscreen enlarged one of the images and displayed it wall-length on the screen in front of them.

"He was married to a fellow activist Rebecca Oriata Hamilton. In 2063 she gave birth to a son, Gabriel Alexander Zumar. Gabriel was lucky to be born – his mother had already contracted leukemia as a result of her work supplying food to people on the edges of the nuclear-ravaged world. His poems about her death are particularly poignant. Philip kept his son by his side at all times after the death of his wife. He retreated from his activist life and instead focused on the child. This is when he really began to write. He was twenty-six going on twenty-seven at this time, and this is when he met Bo Vinh."

The Devscreen had enlarged an image of a list of writings by Philip Zumar. The titles ran from the floor to the ceiling.

Cochran felt a deep sense of unease settling into her stomach. This case had just taken an even more serious and complicated turn. Anything to do with Bo Vinh could potentially be linked to his assassination and that was a path that Cochran wanted nothing to do with.

"I see. Thank you. Please go on," Cochran said, the slightly crisp tone unavoidable with her increasing unease and irrational irritation at Marty's back.

"Bo Vinh and Philip Zumar met at one of Zumar's readings in New Paris in 2064. There were no cameras allowed. It was a condition of the reading. Philip Zumar was notoriously image-shy, so we don't have any image of the actual event. However, it is reported that when Zumar finished reading, Bo Vinh crossed the room and gave him a hug, the tears of their cheeks mingling. That last phrase is actually a quote from a later poem that Zumar wrote to Bo Vinh on his birthday, shortly before Bo Vinh was assassinated on the 1st of January, 2075."

The Devstick in Cochran's hand was turning ever more rapidly as she grew impatient with Marty's diatribe. Each time Marty referred to Bo Vinh, the weight of unease crept up a notch in Cochran's gut.

"Wait a minute, before you go on, just to appease my growing concern at the irrelevance of all of this, how do you make the connection between Jibril and this Gabriel boy, who disappeared thirty-six years ago?"

"Jibril is Arabic for Gabriel. Muraz is an anagram of Zumar. The house where Jibril Muraz was registered was 61 Sholle Street, Paddington, London. That was also an anagram for 16 Holles Street, Paddington, London, the birthplace of Lord Byron in –"

Cochran interrupted again, "Wait a sec, this Lord Byron, who's he? What does he have to do with this? Does he have something to do with Sir Thomas?"

With difficulty, Marty stifled an urge to laugh and said, "Uhm, no, Lord Byron was born in 1788. He has nothing to do with Sir Thomas; however, Byron Bay was the last known sighting of Gabriel Alexander Zumar." Marty waited to see if Cochran was going to interrupt her again. She cocked her head slightly to one side.

For some reason this little move made Cochran flare up inside with a hot flush of rage, but she suppressed it, saying in a tight, clipped voice, "Continue."

Marty waited. The room filled with silence. As the seconds went by, the silence increased in volume. Marty's head straightened, her body immobile. Cochran licked her lower lip. The three other members of the Gang of Four swapped furtive glances. None dared look at Cochran.

"Continue please, Marty."

"Philip Zumar and Bo Vinh became good friends. They collaborated heavily on Bo Vinh's masterpiece 'We are one tribe', which as you know became the foundation for the popular vote movement that swept the globe in the mid-sixties. Zumar insisted that his contribution to the work should remain unknown;

however, it was made known by Bo Vinh himself, who later said that actually the work was more Zumar's than his.

"With the popular vote accepted globally and countries abandoning their sovereignty for the sake of a single global nation, Bo Vinh stepped into the limelight, becoming our first Secretary General of the United Nation and remaining in that role until he was killed. Zumar faded out of the limelight. The only other image we have of him is this one taken at Bo Vinh's funeral. It's indistinct because he is so far back in the crowd. But it is him.

"Bo Vinh was assassinated on the 1st of January 2075. About ten months after Bo Vinh's funeral, Philip Zumar disappeared. This was the 6th of October 2075, according to Sir Thomas's case file. His partner called Sir Thomas for help in finding him. In the transcript of the call she says she thinks the disappearance is something to do with Bo Vinh's assassination."

"He has a new wife or has his old one suddenly cropped up from the dead as well?" Cochran asked with a bite in her voice.

Marty ignored the sarcasm and smiled to herself. She'd really gotten under Cochran's skin this time.

"He never married this woman. Her maiden name was Mariah Claire Foster, but she gave birth to a son on the 23rd of September 2075 at two in the morning. The birth was registered, and a PUI assigned to a Mark Anthony Zumar, father, Philip Zumar, mother, Mariah Claire Oliver."

"She was related to Sir Thomas?"

"Yes, she was his wife, or his estranged wife – by this time they had been separated for over a year, but by all accounts they were still on favorable terms."

"I see." Cochran's voice had lost its bite with Marty's latest revelation. "What happened to her and the baby?"

"Sir Thomas's report, he was director of Special Operations Executive at that time, stated that he found Philip Zumar's yacht floating forty-five kiloms off the coast of Byron Bay and there had been no indication of foul play, so 'death by suicide or accidental drowning' was recorded as the coroner's verdict. The report stated that during the time UNPOL was searching for Philip Zumar, the woman, boy, and baby disappeared. After investigating but finding no trace of them, Sir Thomas presumed his wife had also committed suicide and probably taken the children with her. Despite global alerts being put out, they weren't found and Sir Thomas's opinion became the recorded decision."

"And now you think this Gabriel, or someone using his identity, has transferred his anger at the death of his father to Sir Thomas? Is that it?"

"Yes, something like that – it really is the only explanation."

"But why go to all the trouble? Why didn't he just kill or have Sir Thomas killed?"

"Because he wants to make him suffer. In his talk with Jonah, he says, 'You probably think I am crazy.' This is transference – deep down he thinks he is crazy, but transfers that emotion to Jonah. There are other lines in the discussion between Gabriel and Jonah that give us an indication of his thoughts, which are 'Perhaps I shouldn't be asking such personal questions so early in our relationship, but then I feel as if I have known you for so many years' and 'Will you request God to strike me down for my sins, or having sought repentance of Him, shall I be saved as you were vomited from the great fish's mouth onto the shores of Nineveh?' The Devscreen had changed to the image of Jonah naked in the room with Gabriel. It switched focus from Gabriel to Jonah and back again. Something about the image made Cochran feel uncomfortable, but she couldn't put her finger on what it was.

"For someone who is supposedly crazy, the capture and escape was an extremely well put together plan and well executed. Hardly the mark of someone who is crazy."

"On the contrary, people who are obsessive can be extremely detailed in thought and action. Their lunacy is in the premise they are acting upon not in how they accomplish those actions."

"What is the significance of the meeting with Jonah Oliver?"

"It's a threat. Jonah Oliver is Sir Thomas's last surviving relative, so as Gabriel has lost his family he is telling Sir Thomas that he can touch Sir Thomas's family in the same way."

"I see. And is Jonah Oliver in immediate danger?"

"That is harder to predict, although we do think that he will be the first target, and he won't simply be killed – he will be made to disappear."

Marty spun around in the Biosense without otherwise moving and, still sitting cross-legged, faced Cochran.

How does she do that? Cochran thought, with a quick hot flush along her cheekbones, and said, deadpan, eyeballing Marty, "Well, I am sure you are on the right track, but we really aren't in any better position than we were a week and a half ago, are we?" Cochran pointed her Devstick at Marty.

"No, I wouldn't say that, Sharon. We have narrowed down the focus of this

WHAT'S IN A NAME

trace into a very specific area. We have identified the runner and identified the most likely target of his actions. We've also figured out how he escaped right from under your nose." Sitting in a perfect Lotus position, her face without expression, Marty's words hung in the air. Dom and Fatima cringed but didn't say anything and avoided looking at Cochran.

Her record until Gabriel had been perfect, and then the impossible had happened. Escape from the Deep. Until then it was thought to be impossible. That's why when the trembler alarm went off, the guard, under the command of Cochran, had ignored it as a malfunction.

The jagged hole in her reputation gagged in her consciousness. Frowning and turning her Devstick over end to end, Cochran said, "Supposing for a moment that this theory of yours is true, does Jonah's recent trip to the Moon have anything to do with this?"

"Yes. We think it's possible that Gabriel hypnotized Jonah in the White Room and planted the suggestion that he visit the Nineveh Resort."

The Devstick spun just a little faster. "So wouldn't this indicate an urgent need to provide UNPOL protection for Jonah Oliver?"

"No, that wouldn't be a good idea – I think you're missing the point."

Cochran's nostrils flared, the spin of the Devstick just a little harsher, and she said in a flat tone, "No, Martin, I think you're missing the point, but please go ahead, tell us. What is your point?"

Marty's posture straightened just that little bit more. Her gender re-assignment was common knowledge to the gang, but outside it wasn't, and no one inside or out called her Martin.

"Agent Cochran, my name is pronounced Mar-teen, not tin, and I'll thank you to remember that if you want one iota of contribution from me in the future – and that takes into account your likely promotion to director."

Stanislav said, "Ma, ma, ma, ma, me too."

Dom and Fatima nodded their heads in unison.

"Martine, please forgive me. That was uncalled for and unkind. Please accept my profound and sincere apology."

Dom's and Fatima's heads stopped nodding, and they turned in unison to look at Marty.

Marty felt the lie beneath the sincerity, but now was not the time to take this bitch down. There would come a time.

"I accept your apology, Sharon. Please let's forget this incident ever happened.

So to answer your question as to what is my point, I would say that the point was bait. We know that Gabriel is going to come after Jonah. The fact that he made it back from the Moon means that Gabriel wants Sir Thomas to suffer for a while before he makes his move. But if we shroud Jonah in protection, then he may pull back from Jonah and go straight for Sir Thomas."

"Bait?" The surprise in Cochran's voice was clear to them all. She hadn't expected this. She hadn't thought of using Jonah as bait.

"Yes, bait. Put a shield around Jonah, but make it invisible, and sooner or later Gabriel is going to try to penetrate that shield. If we're lucky, we'll be able to stop him."

"Lucky?"

"Sure. Gabriel might be crazy, but so far he's shown he is a brilliant operator, Sharon."

Cochran nodded her head, the casual use of her first name rankled her system somewhere and was stored away for future damage creation, but right now her systems were running on full, thinking about the possible scenarios that would involve Sir Thomas. She needed more information before she could go to him with this. What she had wasn't enough.

Cochran looked at Marty, her hands still on the table. "What next?"

"We have a gap of 36 years to fill in Gabriel's life. If we can get more detail on that, then we will have a better handle on predicting his moves. We plan to start in on that next."

"I see. Well, time is of the essence, so I suggest we call this review to an end and get working on this problem. I'd like to see a list of your proposed solutions to this investigation by midnight."

"Sharon, in our calculations for the time we require to come up with a solution, I've taken into account the fact that this is Fatima's birthday and we're taking the night off. We'll be back on by the midday shift tomorrow, but otherwise, I agree that this review is over. I just can't say exactly when you'll get our list."

I'm going to fry this little creet when this is over, Cochran thought, but smiled at the Gang of Four, one by one, as they waited for her answer.

"Of course, how silly of me. I completely forgot." She looked at Fatima, who flushed a deep red at being the object of the undercurrent of tension in the room. "It is, isn't it? Well, happy birthday to you. I hope it is a happy and" – looking hard at Marty – "a healthy year for you." She rose from the Biosense and walked

WHAT'S IN A NAME

out of the room.

The others looked at Marty and smiled. She raised one eyebrow with a flick and said, "Let's go."

Fifteen minutes later, they'd collected their belongings from the Cave and were back down at ground level outside the central Lev port on Jurong. Dom, Fatima and Stanislav shared an Envspace in Orchard Towers. The party they'd been planning for Fatima would start at 10pm.

Dom said to Marty, "Are you coming with us?"

With a brusque shake of her head, Marty said, "No, you guys go ahead. I need a shower after that meeting, and I've got a couple of things to do, but I'll be over there before ten. Okay?"

They split up: Dom, Fatima and Stanislav for their Env in Orchard while Marty walked north. She lived in an Env that was designated as Commspace – a warehouse on the northern shore of Jurong Island. From UNPOL Headquarters, it was about a three and a half kilom walk.

Marty competed professionally at race walking, and the walk to her Env was great practice. Before setting out, she stopped to stretch. She was tall at one hundred and seventy eight cent, for which she thanked the errant Y chromosome that had given her manhood. She called it gender realignment, not assignment. Her mind was not meant to be in a male body. She was female, had been for a thousand years, or at least that was her understanding. The surgery had taken twelve weeks from her life, lying in regen while the mistake was rectified.

When she'd come out of regen and first stood on wobbly knees in front of a mirror looking at her twenty-one-year-old female body, it was perfect. Everything had come out as she'd envisioned. The regen had been painful, frustrating and boring, the last being the worst she had to bear, but it had all been worth it and now, thirteen years later, she stretched out a long, smooth, tanned leg and eased her fingertips down to her toes. The pose stopped a few males and females in their tracks as her short outers tightened around her taut buttocks. It was an inviting sight, but one that was swiftly over as she tidied up her warm up exercises and, straightening, began walking at a furious pace.

Fifteen minutes later, she was moving at about eight kilos per hour on the home stretch along the wharf to her Env. The dockies yelled her in, chanting, "Go, go, go," as she hurled herself with full pelvis rotations at the imaginary finish line in front of the warehouse that housed her Env. Dropping her arms as she crossed the line to the cheers of the dockies on the deck of the ocean hauler tied up at the wharf, she shook off the walk and eyed her Dev. It unlocked her door, and she went in, turning to her left and striding to the far corner, she climbed the stairs to the second-story landing that fronted the space she had leased.

The space was huge, and after she entered the gap left by the double metal doors, each six meters high, she walked across the measured one-thousand-meter track that she had painted onto the floor around the circumference of the room. In the middle of this space, she had built a large single room that contained her Devcockpit, sleeper and hygiene facilities with outlet. She thought of this room as her cabin, soundproofed against the noise of the adjoining wharf. Outside, in the warehouse area, the room was filled with her hobbies. Plants grew in various stages all over the space under the nutritious light of grow lamps bought at a discount on e-cred. The cooking range and exhaust she'd built herself out of brick and metal, as a prelude to her sculptures, for which she had a following among those who liked their art large and meaningful.

It was 6pm. She went into the cabin and, stripping off, headed straight for the shower. The shower was a slate room of three meters squared. High above it in the rafters of the warehouse hung a huge shower head a meter across.

She said, "Shower," and the water dropped like a waterfall. Toweling herself off, she looked in the mirror, searching for any fat or wrinkles, knowing she wouldn't find any. Her short, black hair was spiky from the water. She stepped into the sanitizing drier unit and blew herself dry on full blast, the upwards draft of the slightly warm air blowing tenacious droplets off her.

Walking back into the main room of the cabin, she flopped down across her sleeper and reached for a Devstick on the side table. The Devstick looked like an ordinary one, but it would explode and fragment if the wrong key was entered. She keyed in a sixteen-digit code, and the Devstick came to life. She selected her mother's ID and, choosing message, typed:

Investigation now focused on known threats to TBO.

She waited, lying naked fully stretched out, looking at what she'd entered, the Devstick in both hands, and then she thumbed encrypt and submit. She paused, brushed a hand through her hair, and selecting another contact, typed 'I miss you', pressed encrypt and send.

LOVE

I walked into the Scuttles outer office area at 5:30pm and said, "Dora, is Bill in?" I knew he was, I could see his profile indicating contribution in my Devstick, but it was a matter of form that we allowed the assistants to interpret our mood for seeing or not seeing visitors.

"Hi, Jonah. Yes, he is. Would you like some tea? He's drinking a coffee and catching up on the feeds just now," she said and, reaching under her Clearfilm desk, pressed a button that opened the door to Bill's space.

"Er, no, thanks. This shouldn't take too long," I said as I walked past her into Bill's contribution space. The view out of the double windows of the converted Chinese shop house showed Clarke Quay with the Singapore river in the background, curving down to Bonham Place. Bill sat at the far end of the room on an easy chair. The room was white, but the furniture was black. It reminded me a little of the White Room. The heels of my shoes sounded loud on the painted white wooden floorboards as I walked the floor between us.

Bill's face registered a slight puzzled frown, quickly replaced by a smile, as he saw my casual attire. It wasn't what I normally wore to my contribution.

"Jonah, good to see you back – hope that business with UNPOL got resolved all right?" Bill said.

Bill Scuttle was the senior partner of Coughington and Scuttle, and a friend of Sir Thomas. It was my uncle who suggested that I contact Bill for a contribution when I first arrived in New Singapore back in July of 2105. At sixty-five years old, Bill still ran the New Singapore marathon every year and was always a serious contender in his age group. His shock of white hair off-set his ruddy, tanned face, showing off his preference for an outdoors lifestyle.

"Yes, thanks. It sort of resolved itself. Anyway, it's out of my scope of responsibility now," I said and stepped forward to sit down in the chair about two meters opposite to his. It was comfortable and deep, the arms were broad enough that you didn't have to worry about your elbow slipping off the edge while you talked.

"Bill, I'm going to resign my contribution here at Coughington and Scuttle. I wanted to tell you before anyone else."

Bill leant forward in his seat and put his elbows on his knees, steepling his hands in front of him. It was a posture I'd seen many times before. A delaying action while he gathered his thoughts – and usually those thoughts were very sharp.

"If this is about your share of the settlement of the Schilling vs. Bauer case, you know that I would happily talk to the board on your behalf."

I smiled and shook my head.

"No, it isn't about that. My share was more than generous, thank you very much. I'm just not happy doing this anymore, and I need a change."

"Well, this is very sudden. When were you planning on leaving us?"

"Today. Now," I said and looked him in the eye. He had sat in enough conferences with me to know that look. I had perfected it and trained its reputation for years. It was my 'this is my final offer' look, and I knew he got it when he smiled.

Bill stood up in front of me, and I rose immediately. He said, "It's been a pleasure contributing with you, Jonah. I wish you every success, and I am sure that whatever form of contribution you try your hand at next, you will be successful. I will miss having you here. Your insight and attitude have always been a source of inspiration for us all. Please keep in touch and tell us how you are now and then."

I gave Bill a deep wai, pressing my hands together, raising the fingertips to my lips, bowing my head and bending from the waist. Bill returned my wai and smiled. I said, "Can I leave the announcement of my departure to you?"

"Of course you can. Don't you worry about that – you go off and find happiness, Jonah," he said, clapping me on the back with his hand.

I turned and walked out of his space with tears in my eyes and strode swiftly past Dora and her enquiring glance so that she couldn't see them.

I felt really grateful to Bill for not making a fuss about my leaving. His parting words were kind, and I also felt a great sense of relief, like a huge weight had lifted from my shoulders. I clacked my way down the wooden stairs, too impatient to wait for the old-style elevator that ran up and down the four stories of the shop house, and burst out of the building on to North Boat Quay.

Mariko was sitting where I had left her fifteen mins ago, drinking a beer at a white cast-iron table on the Quay. I walked swiftly over to her. She looked great.

She must have changed at the UNPOL Complex before leaving, as the white cotton summer dress she had on was definitely not standard UNPOL issue.

She looked at me with those huge green eyes of hers and said, "How did it go?"

"Great. He took it like the true gentleman that he is and said some really nice things to me," I said, smiling at her, looking to see how much beer she had left in the bottle. She saw my look and picking up the bottle drained it with one long swallow.

She stood and, taking my hand, said, "Let's go."

We walked up North Boat Quay, through the gathering early evening drinks crowd settling themselves into bars around the quay. The evening sun reflected gold off the mirrored windows of the towers across the canal.

"Any regrets?" Mariko asked, smiling.

"No, none," I said, smiling in return. In the evening light her color looked stunning, a deep gold sheen to her skin, her long black hair flowing out behind her as she strode up the hill. Since returning from the Moon, we had spent all of our time together except for when she had to go to her contribution at UNPOL. That had surprised me, especially when she'd told me of contributing in the Special Operations Executive, the elite operational arm of UNPOL. I pushed a bit harder to keep pace with her.

"In a hurry?" I asked. She laughed. We had established a slight banter in the week we had been together, and this was a frequent question of mine. She slowed down, turning around, walking backwards.

"Well, the sooner we get there the better." She reached out with a hand for mine, her face scrunched up as she mimicked a show of pulling me along. A guy passing smiled at me. I sensed envy in his eyes and smiled back at him, trying to avoid feeling smug.

We reached the Lev port and joined the queue, standing close, our chests touching. She looked up at me, her hands around my waist. She bumped her waist against mine and gave me a cheeky grin that caused the dimples in her cheeks to show. I smiled down into her eyes and raised my eyebrows twice and grinned as if to say 'yeah, sure, let's do it', calling her teasing bluff. She pulled back immediately and gave me a mock glare, with a swift glance around to see if anyone in the queue had seen the exchange.

The queue in front of us cleared, and we were able to get into the Lev port door set into the wall of Citiplex, the Ent headquarters for Citibank. The harsh bright aluminum interior of the Lev contrasted with the soft evening light outside. Orange plastic molded seats ran down each side of the Lev with the hand bar and red straps running the length of the Lev down its middle for the standing passengers. We held onto the same red strap, my hand enfolding hers. The door beeped three times and sealed shut with a loud hiss, and then the Lev smoothly accelerated, giving us a good excuse to sway together. Again she ground her waist into mine, and this time to more effect as I widened my eyes to let her know what had happened. The grin wrinkled around her eyes in full knowledge of what she had achieved, and with an impish look, she swayed away and looked down. I smiled and, using my free arm, pulled her into me again, breathing deep the smell of her hair.

I lost track of the number of stops between the Quay and Changi, but it was at least four or five, and then she nudged me, and I opened my eyes. We stepped out on the level five platform at Changi, and I checked my Devstick.

"Come on, this way," Mariko said, pulling me by the hand again. We walked over to a walky that was going up to level two, the sign for Bangkok Line hanging above the entrance. The Bangkok Line is a Vactube that runs along the coast of the Geographic of Malaysia until it reaches the major concourse hub in Bangkok. I looked at the time on the Devstick, fifteen minutes since we'd left the Boat Quay, and put the Devstick back in the pocket of my white cotton bottom outers.

The walky zigzagged its way up to level two, and we walked out on to the platform. Mariko said, "Hey, not so busy. Less than three deep in most places – we won't have to wait for another Lev."

"No. I thought there would be more people traveling this line, but it doesn't look too bad, does it?"

"Let's walk up to the far end of the platform. It looks like the queue is only one deep there, and we may be able to get a seat."

We strolled along the bright cavern of a tube. The domed ceiling, painted white, gave a sense of height. Along the walls, the Lev doors every ten meters were sealed shut to contain the vacuum of the Vactubes. In between the doors, Devscreens displayed suggestions. The volume of the suggestions was muted but increased and then faded as we walked past each of them, reaching the end of the platform. A woman standing by the Lev door smiled at us as we stood next to her. She wore a pink scarf covering her hair in the fashion of Muslim women and was wearing blue overalls with a Hitachi logo over the left breast pocket.

The Devscreen next to the Lev door we were waiting at changed color to sky blue, and the words 'Breaking News' scrolled across the bottom of the screen from right to left. The image changed, and the woman with the scarf gasped and held her hand up to her mouth. On the Devscreen was an image of grey rubble, the remains of a building. At first I thought earthquake, and then I read the text scrolling along the bottom of the screen. I had a sense of déjà vu, but I often got that and didn't say anything to Mariko. Her eyes were glued to the screen. I turned back and continued reading, part of the word lost as it scrolled, "–rist attack on main Lev port in New Manhattan. Casualties feared high. Bomb ripped through main Vactube at peak trav ho–"

I squeezed Mariko's hand. This was the second terrorist attack in a week: the first had been the Paris bombing of the café. Still no one claimed responsibility, and the rumors gave no direction, only added to the confusion. We hadn't had this kind of violence for many years, and the shock of it was profound. In some deep part of me there was a fear, a fear that happiness could be ripped away. As I watched the Devscreen, I saw a stooped-over fireman walking, his face a white blur under his black helmet, his eyes wide, and his hands covered in blood and dust, held out at his sides, his yellow jacket open.

The Lev door opened, and we walked in, our mood somber with what we had just seen. Mariko held both my hands in hers, our knees touching as we sat on the bright yellow plastic seats nearest the doors and looked up at the Devscreen inside the Lev. It was showing the same images as outside. The doors beeped their warning and closed with a hiss. The Muslim woman sat on the opposite side of the Lev and stared at the wall of the Lev beside Mariko. Mariko held out her hand and patted the seat beside her. The woman got up from her seat and, taking Mariko's hand, sat down beside her. No one said anything.

At the Mersing stop, another eight minutes and a stop in between later, the Muslim woman, still holding on to Mariko's hand, raised it and pressed it against her cheek, smiling at us. She got up and, releasing Mariko's hand softly, walked out the door. We were alone in the Lev. I put my arms around Mariko, and she curled up into me. I held her tight.

The blipping white ball that signified the Lev moved closer to the next red square on the line that was displayed on the end wall indicating our progress. Kuantan, our stop, was next, and I patted Mariko on the back to let her know, rising at the same time. I stumbled as the rapid deceleration of the Lev caught me off balance, and Mariko, still sitting, steadied me. The Lev stopped, the doors beeped and hissed open, and we got off onto the platform. Directional lights, prompted by the map in my Devstick, led the way to a walky ten meters further down the platform. We got on the walky hand in hand and silently rode up to ground level.

As we reached ground level, Mariko said, shaking her head from side to side, "I can't understand the mentality of someone who could do such a thing. What could possibly be worth that kind of action? What do they want with this senseless killing? It's just barbaric. I don't understand it." Her voice choked as she said this, and I stopped, gathering her in a hug, pulling her tight to me.

Stroking her hair, I said, "They'll catch them, whoever they are, they'll catch them and life will return to normal. This is an aberration, a throwback. This isn't us."

"I hope you're right. I pray you are," she said into the cashmere outer top I was wearing. She pulled free of me and wiped her face with her hands. Forcing a smile, she shook her head and had to wipe away another tear. I smiled at her, trying to convey that I felt the same, and she sniffed loudly and said, "Come on. Let's go find this place."

The Kuantan Lev port exited onto a main pedestrian street, behind which a Travway ran. The town was spread out along this street with a pedestrian street on each side and two four-lane Travways in the middle. Taxis, private vehicles and EVTours waited on the Travway side. I took out my Devstick and highlighted my profile for Siti Merican, the Malaysian realtor we had contacted mid week. Across the street, a woman standing next to a white Toyota Terra Cruiser that had seen better days waved her arm at us, and we crossed the street to her.

Siti was about one hundred and sixty-five cents tall, slim and with a big smile showing off her white teeth. She gave us a wai, and we waied back, smiling.

"You guys made good time. Was the trip up smooth?"

I exchanged a quick glance with Mariko, and an understanding passed between us not to share the terrible news. I said, "Yes, it was fine," and smiled in return.

Siti pulled open the rear door, and we climbed into the back seat as she climbed into the front, saying, "I know it is a little warm, but I thought we'd drive with the top down. What do you think?"

"That would be great," Mariko said as she scooted her backside over the seat. I climbed in after her and pulled the door shut while the roof of the terra folded itself behind us. Siti pulled out into early evening traffic on the Travway. The inside lane that we were in was a snarled mess of traffic. Old long-haulers crawled by in the next lane as three-wheeled tuk-tuks, motorcycles and bicycles zipped in and out of the slow-moving traffic. There were no maglev tracks here, and the dust from the dirt roads leading off the main Travway hung heavy in the air. Siti drove confidently in the bustling evening traffic and soon took a left turn that, within fifty meters, dropped the noise level to the sound of the rubber tires of the Terra bumping over the dirt road we were traveling on. Siti talked over her shoulder the whole time, giving us a rundown on the locality.

"It takes about twenty minutes to reach Sisik from Kuantan – the road is just a dirt road, and the locals want it to stay that way. They're afraid that if the roads are better, then the area will see more development, and they like the old lifestyle. The schools are good, though, and even in Sisik we have a good online connection most of the time. There is only one shop in Sisik, but it has most of the basics that you would need. Most of us go to Kuantan or catch the Lev to New Singapore or Kuala Lumpur if we want to shop for anything other than food and toiletries."

The jungle closed in quickly as the sun dropped out of view behind the trees, and Siti turned on the lights of the Terra as we bumped our way east. Driving quickly and confidently, the fifteen kilom distance between the town of Kuantan and Sisik was covered quickly. The dirt road we were on narrowed to a track that was filled by the Terra and then turned sharply left as the jungle on our right-hand side was replaced with a view of the South China Sea at dusk.

Siti drove on for another couple of hundred meters and then pulled over beside a small, light blue building with a huge deck running around the outside covered by the roof. A white sign with red lettering written in Malay had an image of a fish and a shrimp on it. Hanging off the roof was what looked like an old brown parachute acting as an awning, billowing in the light breeze that came off the ocean fifty meters away. Underneath this awning were a mixture of blue and red metal tables and plastic chairs set in the sand.

Siti got down from the Terra, and we followed her as she walked up onto the deck surrounding the restaurant. It turned out to be the house of the owner of the land, and he approached us after swinging his legs off the hammock he had been lying in on the deck facing the sea.

"Welcome to Sisik. My name is Abdul Haqq," said the man, who was wearing a sarong and nothing else. He looked to be in his sixties, the grey hair on his head matching the few sparse grey hairs on his chest as he walked towards me, his hands lifted in a wai.

I waied him back, as did Mariko, and said, "Hi. My name's Jonah, and this is Mariko."

Mariko smiled at him.

"Come, come," Abdul said, moving his hand in a small downward wave to indicate that we should follow him. "We have to hurry because night falls very quickly, and we only have maybe twenty mins before it will be completely dark."

He walked around to the front of the deck and down the stairs that led to the beach, and we followed him down the shoreline, heading south. The beach was about fifty meters wide at its widest point and narrowed sometimes to just twenty as the jungle pushed its way towards the sea. The only sounds were our feet scuffling the sand, cicadas trilling their mating calls and the palms brushing softly against each other in the slight breeze. There wasn't a wave to be seen, and the ocean was devoid of life for all the movement it displayed.

As soon as I saw the house, I knew that I'd buy it. It had nothing to do with the house, it was the location. A bluff of steep-sided headland, dark in the rapidly failing light, rose in front us, and off to our right was the house. The building seemed to be losing the battle against the encroaching jungle, and one wall had tropical vegetation pressed up against it.

Abdul smiled at me and lifted his hand to show the way, saying, "Be careful as you come up the step. The wood has rotted, and I am afraid that I have been too busy to replace it yet."

I wondered if he meant too busy sleeping in the hammock and glanced at him. A twinkle in his eye and the wrinkles gathering made me suspect that he knew what I was thinking, but I just smiled and gingerly made my way up the steps to stand on the deck that surrounded the house.

The building was stand-alone and badly run down. It had no Travway leading to it and was only forty meters from the sea, white sand covering the distance between. The rear of the house faced the sea and had a large balcony running around the entire second floor. At the front was a garden full of flowers, reaching to the edge of a small patch of jungle through which was a path that led to the nearest Travway four hundred meters further on. I loved it.

As we walked back through the jungle towards the restaurant, a king cobra slithered across the path in front of us. Abdul placed a cautionary hand on my arm as with his other he pointed at it. Mariko knelt down to take an image of it with her Devstick. Siti and Abdul walked on ahead of us, to give us some privacy, and I turned to Mariko.

"So what do you think?"

"It's perfect. I mean it will take a massive amount of work to get it sorted, but it is such a great spot. What do you think?"

"I love it."

The word, love, hung on the humid air between us and brought me a serious look from Mariko. I took her hand, and we walked back to the restaurant. Abdul led us to a wobbly table set in the sand that was piled high with seafood, and a cooler sat beside the table with beer and soft drinks in it. Abdul pulled out a beer and twisted the top off, handing it to me. He reached in and did the same again, passing the beer to Mariko.

I lifted the beer in toast to Abdul, Siti and Mariko and said, "I think I'm going to like living here very much."

Abdul smiled, his teeth shining white in the darkness of his face and said, "Does that mean that you have decided to buy the house, Jonah?"

"Yes, and I'd like to talk to you about the adjoining land, too. Not for development, just so we can keep it unspoiled."

"You don't need to worry about that. All of this land belongs to my family, and in an agreement we made long ago, none of us may sell to another without approaching all that live here first. It took me three months to get everyone to agree to sell the old beach house, even though it is falling down. But finally when I explained that it was the only way that I was going to get customers for my seafood restaurant did the family agree." Abdul let out a loud laugh at his joke, and we all laughed with him.

"Siti, you will join us for dinner. Please call your father and tell him that you are entertaining me tonight."

"Ha, I do not think so, Abdul. It is you who should be entertaining me tonight. Is that not so?"

Abdul laughed out loud again and, turning to us, said, "Well, it is good that you will be my neighbors." He faced Mariko and took her hand. "You are a very beautiful woman. Please forgive an old man's forwardness, but at my age when we want to say something, we usually just say it. It is a privilege of simply having survived." And reaching over with his other hand, he took my hand in it, still facing Mariko he said, "I am a good judge of character, and I can feel the strength in this one. And in you, too. This is a good place for you to find the strength in each other." Smiling widely, he placed Mariko's hand in mine.

"Now I will leave you to sit and make romantic talk on the beach in the moonlight. Come, Siti, let us go inside tonight. It is semi-final of Malay Idol and Johan has an exemption." Abdul and Siti walked up the beach to the house and went inside.

Mariko and I remained under the old parachute awning strung out over the cool sand of the beach. The only light came from old oil lamps converted to solar, and they were set to emit an orange glow similar to the light cast by their forbears.

Mariko spoke quietly, her foot drawing circles in the sand. "I hadn't planned on this, our being together. Two weeks ago if you would have told me that I was going to be moving out of New Singapore to live with a man who I hardly know, I would have said you were crazy. But I guess that's love for you. And yes, Jonah, I do love you, but if we are going to be together, then we have to understand why we're together, and we have to always understand because if we forget, then we shouldn't be together."

"Yes, I agree totally," I said. I meant it, too. I understood what she was talking about because I had gone through the same emotional whirlwind.

She continued, "It would be nice, as Abdul said, if we can just talk sweet romantic things, but I feel like we're about to make a big commitment and it's suddenly rushed up on me. Yesterday this was just a dream and a fun thing to do. Today, now, it feels like I'm standing on the edge of … of … sheesh, I don't know, but it's … it's just different."

I closed my eyes and breathed in, drawing the salty air deep. The breath of a warm breeze rippled the cloth of my outers against my skin, and I breathed out slowly, emptying my mind. What I said now had to be right. If I got it wrong, she could be lost forever. I searched in my mind for the right words to say, feeling for her.

Suddenly a rush of thoughts entered my mind. The hairs on my neck stood up, and a shiver ran through me down to my toes scrunched in the white sand. They were her thoughts flying around, disorganized. I breathed in sharply and let out a soft gasp. The thoughts stopped. I was out of her mind. I felt shaken, shocked, maybe it was just the beer, but I thought for one crazy moment that I had actually entered her mind.

At my gasp, she turned to face me and placed her hand on my arm, a small smile upon her lips. I smiled back at her and put my hand on hers.

Speaking softly, I said, "I know you are scared of losing your freedom, but

I will never hold you back from what you want to do. All I can say is that everything that is happening feels right to me. I know it has only been a week since we met, but I also know that I will love you forever. If this feels too quick, we can stay in New Singapore. I confess I do love the peacefulness here, but I love you more."

She squeezed my arm and said, "No. I don't care about New Singapore, and I love you too. But when we get back to New Singapore, I will request a loan from my bank for half of the amount of the house. Our contract will say that as long as we are together here, then we will jointly own the property, but if we should split up –" and she held up her hand palm facing me to stop my interruption. "If we should split up, then we will sell the property and share the proceeds equally. I also want to continue contributing at UNPOL, and there are some things that I need to talk to you about that, but that can wait."

I interrupted her. "Look, I was surprised to learn that you were contributing at UNPOL, and doubly so at your being in the Special Operations Executive, but I understand and support your desire to keep contributing. My decision to quit from Coughington and Scuttle was my decision. Was it influenced by you? For sure, but only from the point of view that you've made me happy. Since I've never really been happy, I've never had anything to compare with what I thought was my happiness. Now that I have, I can see that I wasn't happy. But that's me, and I understand that you are in a different space with your contribution."

She nodded and smiled and turned slightly towards me.

"I've never lived with anyone else before. Well, of course I lived with my parents, but that's different. I've always been alone – even when I was in barracks in early UNPOL training I kept myself and my routine to myself. It's been great living with you this last week, but a week and a lifetime are totally different."

I kissed her hand and brushed my cheek against the top of it. "Mariko, if my life were to end next week, then I would have wanted to have spent that last week with you."

"That's another thing. I'm quite a traditionalist at heart, and although the subject hasn't come up yet, I want to get it out in the open now."

"Yes ..." I said doubtfully, wondering what was coming next, thinking maybe she wanted me to go and visit her parents, which was not something I was looking forward to yet.

"Sexual partners," she said and gave me a very direct look.

"Yes," I said confidently.

"Just you and me unless we agree otherwise, agreed?"

"Yes, agreed," I said and smiled.

Taking my face in her hands, she climbed out of her seat and straddled me, kissing me deeply with her tongue.

A Lunchtime Chat

I woke up lying face down on the sleeper in my Env in Woodlands. A shaft of sun streamed through the window. With one eye open, I saw the rose lying on the pillow next to me, and I smiled. I turned my head the other way and looked at the Dev beside the sleeper. 8:45am.

I turned over on my back and scooted my backside up so that I could rest against the wall of the Env. It had changed a lot in the last two weeks since being occupied by Mariko. Books, paper books, were piled in stacks around the room.

"Our library," she had said, as if it were obvious that we needed paper books when we could read them on a Devstick. "A Devscreen with all the titles of the books you have on your Devstick just doesn't have the same meaning as seeing the spines of real books," she'd continued as we returned from another visit to the second-hand book store on Orchard, near the Hyatt VacEnv. And she was right. I found myself absorbed in the feel of a book in my hands. So different from reading them on the Devstick. It is strange that although paper is such a low-tech medium, it allows for a far more random relationship with the data than a Devstick. What could be more random than laying books on the grass and allowing the breeze to select what you will read? You can't do that with a Devstick.

Apart from the rose, she had also bought croissants from the French bakery on ground level, three blocks down from my Env, and started the coffee pot. Another new vice that I'd acquired – but then I'd lost a couple as well so maybe I was ahead of the game. Thinking about her, I knew I was ahead of the game.

Since that day when we'd returned from the Lev port at Changi and she'd insisted on bringing me back to my Env, I was embarrassed at being that affected by the alky, and she had laughed it away, stripped my outers off me and pushed me into the outlet. I'd showered and felt clean, and when I came out of the outlet, she'd put new sheets on the sleeper and folded it back for me to crash on. She'd been sitting on the sleeper and patted the empty space exposed by the folded sheet. I'd walked over and laid down. She'd brushed the hair off my forehead and out of my eyes. No one had ever done that before. And it was a first of firsts. I'd fallen into a deep sleep, waking later to see her in the sleeper beside me, her arm over my stomach.

That was fourteen days ago now. I swung my legs out of the sleeper and walked across the padded floor of the Env to the outlet near the door. I took a seat on the recycler and tapped the Devscreen set into the wall opposite. Keeping myself on silent, I hit the menu for my data stream and, with my elbows on my knees and my chin resting on my knuckles, watched the screen. Mariko would be back at 2pm, and then we'd go. I rubbed my unshaven jaw. It was unfamiliar to feel the stubble against my fingers, but since I'd resigned from my contribution at Coughington and Scuttle, a lot of things felt unfamiliar to me. I liked the feeling. It felt like I had gotten off a treadmill.

Finished, I pressed a button on the side of the recycler and a blast of ice cold water hit me full force. I yelped and jumped up, the water immediately cutting off. Mariko, I thought and laughed. She had set the temp to manual and turned it to an icy three degrees Cel. She had a nasty sense of humor. I would have to think up something in return.

I reset the switch on the recycler to automatic and sat back down. A sec later the water, now warm, sprayed and cleaned me. I rose and entered the shower cubicle, but as I did so, a new direct datafeed on the Dev caught my eye. It was from my uncle. I hadn't told him of my decision to quit Coughington and Scuttle, nor of my decision to quit the pro bono work at UNPOL. I had just done it. I had acquired enough self-leave, and as a partner I could leave when I wanted, so I had quit within a week after returning to Earth. After that, I had spent all of my time with Mariko when she wasn't contributing. The rest of my time I'd spent reading and writing. I had never been happier.

I tapped the Dev and saw that my uncle had invited me to lunch at the UNPOL Executive Club located on the Topside of the UNPOL Complex. I thought about replying and then decided I'd take a shower first and shave. I checked that the switch of the shower was set on auto and that the temp was set at thirty cel. It was. She hadn't booby-trapped the shower as well as the recycler, and while I showered, I occupied my mind thinking of how I would pay her back for her prank.

Coming out of the shower, I stepped into the dryer, and the warm air blasted the water off my body, sanitizing at the same time. Once out of the dryer, I looked at myself in the mirror that ran above the counter of the outlet. A single wash basin occupied the counter along with my shaver. I ran a hand over my jaw. I hadn't planned on shaving today; however, I hadn't planned on the lunch with my uncle either, and now both were things I had to do.

I studied myself in the mirror. I hadn't really paid any attention to what I looked like before, but Mariko had touched me in so many little ways, and this was one of them. I wanted to look good for her. There were wrinkles at the corners of my blue-green eyes. I could have them disappear with a little regen, but I thought they suited the tanned face they were in. My light brown hair was long, longer than it had ever been. I hadn't had it cut or styled in over three months. Usually I'd had it done once a month, to a level above the collar on my outers.

I am of average height at one hundred and eighty-six cents and slim, weighing in at seventy-nine kilogs. My shoulders are slightly stooped, and I have to remind myself to stand up straight all the time. Mariko said that the rounded shoulders came from me thinking so much with my jaw resting in the palm of my hand. An image that conjured up another image, that of the runner who had called himself Jibril and who had disappeared. I picked up the shaver and ran it over my face, its wide laser removing my facial hair without a touch. The skin underneath was a slightly whiter shade than the rest of my face, but nothing that a casual observer would notice. Sir Thomas will notice, I thought, and I ran my hand again over my chin, leaning forward across the counter to be nearer the mirror, checking for any missed spots. I didn't find any and thought ruefully of how nervous meeting my uncle made me . That had never changed. My uncle still inspired a childish fear in me, the fear that I had done wrong and was now going to be held accountable.

I exited the outlet and went back into the main room, threading my way between the containers that held mine and Mariko's sparse belongings. Outers and inners mainly, but hers also held a collection of images of family and friends in image frames, plus objects gathered on her travels. When she had first moved into my Env, and we had collected her belongings from the EnvDorm on Orchard, I was surprised at the amount of baggage she had with her. Just as she was surprised when, the day after we'd returned from the Moon, she'd asked me how long I had been in the Env. When I'd told her four years, she had gone wide-eyed.

"Four years!" she'd exclaimed. "There's nothing in here at all. It looks like a VacEnv." And she was right. It did look like a VacEnv – there was nothing to show that the Env was mine, nothing except my Dev and my clothes.

There were two empty containers that sat on the floor nearest the shelves that contained our outers and inners. I was supposed to pack those, and then this afternoon when she returned from the UNPOL Complex, we would pack the car that was arriving at 3pm and set off for our new Env on the beach in Kampung Tanjung Sisik.

I walked across to the shelves that held my remaining unpacked inners and outers and, putting on my inners, leafed through the outers on the shelf. I decided to go and cred some new outers. I dressed quickly, poured myself a half cup of coffee from the pot that Mariko had put on earlier that morning, and took a gulp, putting the cup back down. Grabbing my Devstick off the sleeper side table, I walked to the door of my env and said, "Leaving."

I turned right, heading the sixty meters down the corridor to the Lev port. I'd been lucky to get the Env on the twentieth level, but now the plastic walls hemmed me in, and I couldn't wait for that moment when I informed the Env Dev that I was leaving permanently. The molded Env with its smooth one-piece cream interior just didn't seem like the place to be anymore, and I thought of the work that needed to be done on the beach house. I was looking forward to the work, it would be fun to do, and I hadn't had much fun in my life.

The Lev was on level eighty-two but descending rapidly, and I called up a map on my Devstick, saying, "Walkys to men's outers and clothing shops, Johor." The new shop space, 'Credabiliti' in Johor, featured as the address for over fifty of the top one hundred listings, so I decided I would go there. The Lev arrived, and I stepped in. It was just after nine, past the time for the half-morning shift to have already arrived at their contribution, and apart from a woman with a baby strapped to her chest, the Lev was empty.

The woman smiled at me. Smiling back, I said, "Ground level, please." You didn't have to be polite to a Dev, but it's a small thing to say please.

The woman with the baby got out on Level Ten, probably going to the mothers' and babies' center within the complex. The Lev door cut off the sounds of children's happy shouts and resumed its journey. It was one of the older models from Otis and hadn't been upgraded, but then that was one of reasons that the Env was a low-cred Envplex.

The Lev finally reached ground level. I stepped out into the ground floor of my Envplex. The door to outside was about one hundred meters straight ahead. I didn't bother with the directional lights in the rubberized walkway as I already knew the way. I had trod this path over fifteen hundred times in the past four years.

I strolled along a walkway lined with Angsana trees, each keeping the path in shade when it was sunny. Overcast as it was now, the trees still seemed to provide some respite from the humidity, and seeing the lights take a left turn over a grassy hill with a fountain on its crest, I followed the path into the shopping center named Credibiliti. It was here that I could find that shop to get some outers for the meeting with my uncle.

Credibiliti had only been completely finished six months ago, but it was already full and had a waiting list for retail shop space that ran into the hundreds. Even at this early hour it was packed, but then inside and under its roof, time had little meaning. It could be any time, day or night, and Credibiliti would be packed.

I stopped walking and took a look around to get my bearings. I had entered at the northern end of the shop space, and the clothier's shop that I wanted was in the middle.

I followed the lights and a short while later reached the shop I had selected on my Devstick, 'Smooth – finest men's clothing' said the sign above the door.

The door opened, and as I entered, the noise level from outside was immediately cut to a minimum. The shop was minimalist in design – white, dark grey with full-length image screens set into the walls in undulating curves, providing a chromium finish when not in use as now. The shop staffer rose from where she was sitting at a glass table with a black matte iDev positioned exactly in its center. It looked like it had never been used.

She took in my attire with a glance, looked like she had made her mind up about something, and said, "Good morning, sir. How can I help you?"

I smiled at her. She was an attractive woman of Chinese origin, slender and tall, perhaps as tall as one hundred and seventy-five cents. Her pale angular face was highlighted with a gold blush under her cheekbones and her lips accented with a lighter gold.

She looked good: sophisticated, expensive, much like the shop, I thought. I said, "I'd like to get some new outers, something for formal occasions, and a couple of others for smart-casual occasions."

Smiling, she walked over to where I was standing and took my arm. She led me to a black circle about a meter in diameter. "Please stand naturally as we take your measurements." Stepping back, she pressed a button on the Devstick in her right hand. My body was crisscrossed with thousands of thin beams of rose-colored light that turned off as quickly as they'd come on. Taking my arm again, she led me over to an unfinished but smooth stone bench and, indicating that I should sit with a gesture of her hand, sat down beside me on my left side.

A bench rose from the floor in front of us and then extended itself and opened in two. The top withdrew to reveal cloth of a myriad of colors made from natural fabrics inside. I reached out with my right hand, leaving my Devstick on the bench beside me and felt the cloth nearest me.

"That's Thai silk," she said. "Do you have a favorite color?"

"No," I said with a chuckle as I thought about it and realized I didn't, "but for the formal wear, I was thinking of something in a darker shade and more matte. This is a bit too shiny."

The woman looked quickly down the row of cloth, pressing a button on her Devstick, and the conveyor moved swiftly forward and stopped with a selection of dark cloth in front of me. A dark grey material with a very thin, almost invisible, line of scarlet red running through it caught my eye. I reached out to feel it with my thumb and forefinger, rubbing the cloth between them.

"This feels nice," I said.

She smiled and said, "Good choice. This particular cashmere comes from Gobi in Mongolia, and as you can see, it has this very thin silk thread running through it."

"How long does it take you to get everything together?"

Her eyes squinted slightly, and her forehead creased. "About forty-five minutes."

"Great, I'd like this cloth for the formal outers, and what about something really comfortable to relax in? Something that will keep me warm on a tropical night, but cool in the day. Do you have that sort of thing?"

She smiled and leaned over, taking out the bolt of cloth and putting it on the stone bench beside her. She sat straight-backed, and her movements were efficient. Turning to me, she said, "We've just got a new cloth in, and it is exactly what you are looking for." She reached and pressed the button on the cloth conveyor again, and the bolts moved in a quiet hum. "This is AC, short for ambient cloth. It takes on different thickness according to the ambient temperature. It's very expensive." As she said this, she arched an eyebrow and looked me straight in eye.

She's in her element, I thought and smiled in return. "Well," I said, leaning forward and feeling the cloth. I turned, put my elbow on my knee, and cupped my chin in my hand. "Well, even though I might be a pauper when I walk out of here, I simply must have it." I spoke in the voice of a young flick star, batting my eyelids at her at the same time.

"Can I ask you a personal question, and it has nothing to do with my selection?" she asked.

"Sure, go for it." I smiled, knowing what was coming.

"Are you in a committed relationship right now?"

I'd been right. "Yes, I am. Does it show?" I gave her an innocent grin, looking at her under hooded eyelids with the grin playing around my lips but not breaking out fully. "But you can be sure that should the day come when I am not in a committed relationship – and I have to say I hope that day never comes – but should it, then the first thing I am going to do is come back to see you and cred some new outers."

She burst out with a laugh and turned back to the input, concentrating hard on the Devscreen in front of her. The intensity of her look could have been professional focus, but I suspected it was more a shield to hide the sudden jolt of loneliness I had seen in her eyes.

I went and stood next to her and leaned in close, our arms touching. It was closer than socially acceptable for two people who did not know each other, but I reasoned that we had communicated more in the last five minutes than some people do in years. She stepped back from the Dev and swung her arm in an arc, the palm of her hand slightly tilted and pointing to the black circle where I had been measured. With a shake of her head, a little blink of her eyes, and a soft smile, she said, "There. What do you think?"

My image was facing me, wearing a combination of the cashmere and the AC.

"That's the formal – short collar, cuffed with five black pearl buttons on each cuff, and a single black-cut palladium button. More on that later, as you can see …" as she said this, the image spun around to show the back, "I have kept the single silk red threads in the back and one running down the inside of each sleeve. The AC inner outer is set for white, but you can change its ambience to a more subtle burgundy or a midnight blue, depending on the mood or occasion." The image changed. "For casual, I've gone with AC throughout, and as you can see, I've included inners for your extremities as well."

"And the palladium button?"

135

"Ah yes, sorry." She smiled, back in form now, in her element. "That controls the height of the collar and the width of the lapel. It allows for greater configuration of the top outers, say if you're going to a slightly less formal event. But if you still have a need to perform, then you can adjust."

"So am I going to be a pauper?"

She smiled wider, her nose scrunching up in a cute way, flicked her eyes down to the corner of the iDev sitting on the glass table, and said, "Most probably."

***

Two hours later, I walked slowly up the steps of the UNPOL Executive Club on the Topside of the UNPOL Complex. Security was discreet but heavy due to its patrons, and I guessed because of the recent terrorist attacks. A hard-looking young man gave me a nod as I passed through the entrance. Firearms were rarely seen, so it was a shock to see one riding casually on the right breast of the UNPOL staffer. Another rarely seen item, upon an old wooden desk next to the entrance to the club, was the sign-in book with a pen lying in the crease between the pages, guarded by an old Chinese man wearing a white outer top and black trousers. He bent slightly at the waist as I approached.

"Good afternoon, sir. You must be Jonah Oliver. Please follow me, sir – the director only arrived moments ago and informed me that you would be joining him for lunch." The man turned and walked through the three-meter-high double doors of dark varnished mahogany, across the black-and-white polished granite floor into the restaurant. The domed white interior of the ceiling soared above me, and belying the stern entrance, the interior was light, spacious and alive with green palm trees and other foliage. It had the essence of a summer park.

The maître d' led me to an alcove corner hidden from the main door by a golden palm in the shape of a fan. I saw my uncle sitting at a table next to the window, preparing to place the white linen napkin on his lap. Sir Thomas looked up, his head suddenly jerking back, and dropped the napkin on the floor as I, dressed in my new formal, walked around the palm. Sir Thomas rose, ignoring the fallen napkin, and came around the table to greet me, his hand held out in front of him. The Chinese maître d' recovered the napkin with a quick swoop as my uncle shook hands formally with me. The maître d' then peeled off and, with a smile and a little nod at me, walked backed to his guard post at the entrance.

"Jonah, so very good of you to come and join me. Sorry for the short notice, but I will be leaving New Singapore soon, and I wanted to catch up with you

136

before I left. Come, come, sit down and tell me all about what you have been up to."

Saying this, my uncle led me over to the table and, rejoining his seat, waved at the opposite one for me. I sat with my hands in my lap, straight-backed, and waited for my uncle to continue.

"Well, it's been quite some time since we had the chance to have a good chat, hasn't it? Why, I think the last time we met was over that troublesome mess with that runner, wasn't it?"

"Yes, Uncle," I said and smiled, but wondered inwardly if he was going to ask me about my trip to the Moon. Instead he picked up the menu and smiled at me. Everything in here was old-fashioned, I thought. Paper menus, wooden tables, even my uncle, it all creates an illusion of the past.

"So, Jonah, would you like an alky? As I understand that you have left your contribution, it shouldn't corrupt your thoughts too much, I hope?"

"No, Sir Thomas. I mean, yes, I would like an alky, and no, it won't corrupt my thoughts too much."

The Chinese maître d' appeared again, this time with a napkin folded over his arm, which was across his stomach.

"Charles, I'll have a single malt. Make it a double."

The maître d', who I now knew was called Charles, turned his head, his body remaining perfectly still. For a brief sec, I wondered if Charles was a Servbot and almost laughed out loud at the thought.

"I'll just have a beer, thanks."

"Would you like our draft or bottled beer, sir?"

"The draft would be fine, thank you."

Sir Thomas leaned forward in his chair and clasped his hands together with his forearms on the table, tilting his balding, short-cropped grey-haired head towards me, and softly chided in a voice that evoked a hundred memories, "You could have told me of your decision to quit your contribution. It was a little embarrassing finding out from Bill that you had decided to move on, hmm?"

"Yes, Sir Thomas, that was thoughtless of me. Please do accept my deepest apologies," I said, tilting my head forward in a slight formal bow.

Sir Thomas gave me straight, hard look, and then his eyes softened, and he smiled, "Apology accepted, and please accept mine for also not informing you of my resignation." Sir Thomas's smile turned into a grin, the horizontal slash set in the Moon-white round face turning up slightly as he registered the shock on my face.

"Resignation? Are you retiring, Uncle?"

Sir Thomas straightened fully in his seat, the grin disappearing to be replaced by his stone look. "Hah! Me retire? No, far from it – I will be busier than ever. The only time I'll retire is when my work is done, and that shall be after I expire."

"Yes, of course, Uncle. Forgive me for the foolish suggestion," I said with just a little trace of sarcasm in my voice. It brought a different kind of grin to my uncle's face. This one more competitive in nature and accompanied by another hard stare.

"So if you're not retiring, what are your plans?"

"I'm moving on from UNPOL, that's for sure. As for other plans? Well, I have a few irons in the fire, shall we say. And what are your plans, Jonah?"

I waited before answering as Charles came back with our alkys balanced on a silver tray. He placed the single malt within reach of Sir Thomas's left hand. Coming around the table, he set the tall, frosted schooner glass at my right hand . He also placed a menu on the white tablecloth in front of me and departed with a slight bow of the waist, his arm providing a fulcrum.

"I really don't have any plans. I was just not happy doing what I was doing. It wasn't my calling. You could say that it was an impulsive decision." On saying this, I picked up the frosted schooner and brought it to my lips. Sir Thomas raised his drink with his left hand in my direction, and I pushed the schooner out from my lips in response, toasting him. Forestalling the need to say anything more about my plans or the lack of them, I picked up the stiff white card menu and started reading. Sir Thomas gave me a look with a quirky uplift of one corner of his mouth and also picked up the menu.

Charles appeared back at the side of our table. He moved silently. I hadn't noticed him until he came into my peripheral vision. He must wear very soft-soled footwear, I thought, not looking up from the menu. Sir Thomas cleared his throat, a harsh rasping sound, and turned his head to Charles, passing him the menu at the same time.

"I'll have the chicken with the gruyere sauce, and the lobster bisque to start."

Charles turned to me.

"And I'll have the stuffed aubergine and the salmon." I also handed over my menu.

Sir Thomas sat back from the table with both of his hands resting on its edge and regarded me with an appraising eye. He brought his drink up and took a sip.

He didn't say anything, just looked at me with a slight smile twitching around the corner of his mouth. But his eyes, while not cold, were not warm either, and I felt compelled to add to my previous statement.

"Uncle, I do appreciate the support you gave me to achieve that contribution, and I believe that I contributed well in the four years I was there. I'm thirty-four. This feels like a good time to take stock and plan what I should do next. I'd like to start my next contribution when I'm ready, maybe after my thirty-fifth birthday. Give myself a good seven months of contemplation time."

Sir Thomas responded with a series of curt nods at each of my assertions. I wasn't sure if this meant that he had merely heard, understood or agreed with what I was saying but chose the last as the most preferable outcome. I took another long draught of my beer, inviting my uncle to fill the void between us with words. He'd already won the 'who would speak first' competition, and I didn't want a second round.

It seemed, however, that my uncle was in a good mood, and after another sip of his malt, he said, "Actually I think your resignation is a good thing, and your decision of taking time to plan your next move, a sound one. I have had very similar thoughts, but in a different context of course. I am seventy-five, well past the age that one usually continues to contribute, but as I pass the fitness, health and mental tests for my position each year, UNPOL has seen fit to allow me to retain a post of some significance and influence. But the time has come to pass that mantle to other hands. Unlike you, I have a concrete idea of what I will do next. However, I will take some self-time before I start to fully plan what that will be."

"What is it that you will be doing, Uncle?" My talks with Sir Thomas had always been formal. As long as I could remember, he had never encouraged familiarity. I was surprised that he was talking to me in this confidante way, and felt a little unease at the conversation.

Sir Thomas formed a steeple with his hands and spoke without expression. "In the last few years of my tenure at UNPOL, I have seen many changes in society. Some good and some, in my opinion, bad. You attain a certain perspective on what the world really needs when you reach my age. The question of life becomes less important than the question of death and what your legacy will be. Some are content to wind down, to hand over the reins and enter the receiving part of their contribution. Others of us feel that our experience and knowledge should be further contributed. In short, I have decided to devote my entire time to running the Oliver Foundation, hands on, providing guidance and direction for the orphans it sponsors."

"I see. Well, congratulations, Uncle. When will you officially resign your post at UNPOL?"

"Not until I've caught the terrorists that blasted Paris and New Manhattan." As he said this, he stabbed the air with his knife. I steered the conversation back to calmer waters.

"So, will you be returning to the England Geographic?" I asked. The headquarters of the Oliver Foundation had long been established in London.

"Good God, no. Miserable place, terrible weather and not a palm tree in sight. No, I'll be moving the foundation's headquarters to New Singapore. Already got a nice complex picked out in the SingCom Building."

"Congratulations," I said, raising my Schooner and smiling.

Sir Thomas raised his single malt again. Smacking his lips at the taste, he said, "I plan to announce my resignation on the global feeds next Tuesday and that I'll stay on until I've caught these terrorists. When I hand over the bridge, it will be when the ship is in smooth waters and safe seas."

"Tuesday evening is New Year's Eve," I said and turned to see Charles wheeling a silver trolley to our table.

An efficient disbursement of cutlery and food later, Sir Thomas, face tilted down, dipping a chunk of crusted bread into his lobster bisque, said in a much less formal tone, "Yes, New Year's Eve. My resignation is my New Year's gift to the children of the foundation."

My mind flashed an image of Sir Thomas making his resignation speech, under a spotlight, a redundant mic in front of him to tell the masses he was making a speech. A somber tone, humble, thanks for the years of civic duty, and then he would switch to 'good ole Uncle Tom'.

Sir Thomas leveled a spoon of bisque into his mouth, swallowed, and said casually, "After the announcement, I'll be having a small gathering of close friends and associates over to the Penthouse. I'd like it if you were there."

I sawed through a piece of stuffed aubergine and pesto sauce. It really was very tasty, so my concentration on cutting gave me a few seconds to formulate my reply.

"I'm sorry, Uncle. I've made plans for New Year, and I can't change them." I popped the piece of aubergine into my mouth so that I'd have time to think up a reply to whatever my uncle's response was going to be.

Sir Thomas didn't say anything. Sitting straight-backed in the comfortable chair, lifting the spoon to his mouth with almost mechanical precision, he ate his bisque without expression. He waited out my aubergine chewing.

I looked Sir Thomas directly in the eyes and placed my hands on the side of my plate, my knife and fork at the salute angle. "Uncle, I understand that this is a big occasion for you, but I've met a woman and it will be our first New Year's Eve. I had planned on making it a special one for her."

Sir Thomas set his spoon down into the now empty bowl and reached for the single malt with the same left hand. This method of eating always left his stabbing hand free to reach for the carbon fiber stiletto sheathed under his left armpit.

"By woman, I assume you mean Mariko?"

I was somewhat, but not really surprised that he knew of my relationship with Mariko. My uncle had often let me know in subtle ways that he kept tabs on what I was doing. Of course, this time he was hardly being subtle about it. Well, two can play at that game, I thought.

"Yes, Mariko. Does UNPOL have a problem with that?"

He deflected my barb at his prying with a tight grin, saying, "No, of course not, Jonah. Happy to see that you have found someone that you're happy with. Fine girl, our Mariko."

I felt a hot flush of anger, as he said, 'our girl', but held it down and didn't say anything. I didn't trust my voice not to betray my feelings. Sir Thomas continued.

"Look, never mind. Perhaps the two of you could visit me after the New Year, and I can have a good look at this young lady who has so charmed you, eh?"

"Yes, Uncle, that would be nice. Only it might be some time. You see, I'm moving out of New Singapore. I'm staying in the region, though, as I'm going to have to find some way to contribute, and New Singapore is the financial center of the region. But I am moving out to Sisik – I want to get out of the metropolis, and I've found a new Env in Sisik. Do you know it?"

Sir Thomas nodded and then glanced up at Charles, who was removing his soup bowl and substituting a plate of chicken smothered in a creamy mushroom sauce. "Yes. In the Malaysian Geographic about three hundred kiloms from here."

"Yes, that's right." I smiled – my uncle's photographic memory never ceased to amaze me. It wasn't a well-known fact and Sir Thomas did not broadcast his ability. But he could remember everything he'd read whether digital or not. "Well, I've found an Env out there that I can afford …"

"Hmph," Sir Thomas cut me off. "You can afford the best Topside Env in New Singapore with your inheritance."

"Yes, I know, but I prefer not to use that cred, as you know."

I had never touched the cred left to me by my parents, held at first in trust to Sir Thomas as the executor of the will and then later passing to me when I had demonstrated the ability to understand its value. Although that had happened when I was fourteen, I had never touched a single unit. The trust had stayed invested in the original Ents, and as they had prospered, so had the trust. It was by any accounts a large amount of cred – I could have bought all of Sisik had I wanted – but I preferred to think of myself as independent, and part of that was using what I had earned and saved. The trust was something I would have to do something about one day, but in the meantime I chose not to use it.

"Anyway, the place is a bit run down, and I plan to do some work to clean it up and also to spend some time writing."

"Writing?" Sir Thomas asked, pausing mid-chew. He had a speck of the creamy mushroom sauce on his upper lip.

"Yes, I've been doing quite a bit of reading lately, and the more I read, the more I get the urge to write about my own feelings and experiences."

"Hmm, I see, and do you think this writing about your feelings is going to earn the cred you need to exist?"

"Well, I don't know about that yet, but I plan to try."

Sir Thomas stopped eating for a moment and pointed his knife at me. He said, "Write for me, then. I'll cred you."

I looked at my uncle, my head jerking back in surprise. "Write what?"

"My memoir." Sir Thomas looked out at the view of thunderous black clouds. "You can keep whatever we sell it for, including the royalties. How's that?"

"I've never written anything other than legal briefs before. I'm not sure that I'm qualified to write your memoir."

"Neither am I," Sir Thomas said with a deadpan expression and the hint of a smile buried in his eyes, "and what's your point?"

I smiled a wry grin at my uncle and looked at him under lidded eyes. "All right, I can try."

"Good, that settles it, then. As soon as we've finished lunch, I'll set up my base Dev to provide you with a secure means of communication with me. I'll send you a brief of what we need to cover and provide you with my notes. You must be totally secret and discreet regarding what you write. I am trusting you with a great deal here, Jonah. The fact that you are related to me by blood is the reason behind my offer."

Saying this, Sir Thomas fixed me with a clenched jaw expression that defied any response other than that which he was looking for.

"Yes, Uncle, I understand, and please don't forget I am an arbitrator, even if an unemployed one at present. You are still protected by client relationship and disclosure of any sort would lead to me being struck off."

Sir Thomas relaxed his look, leaned back in his seat, and said, "Ah yes, of course. I had forgotten that."

My uncle never forgot anything. The Devstick in my inside pocket tickled my nipple, vibrating with an incoming call, but I ignored it. My uncle was a formal man, and answering a Devstick while having lunch would be frowned upon at best.

"Can I ask about your plans for the Foundation?"

"Hmph," Sir Thomas half grunted and snorted. "Simply put? Growth. For too long I've left a bunch of incompetent fools in management at the Foundation, and now is the time to change all of that. We have over fifty Oliver homes around the planet, but I intend to double that figure within a year or two. Children are the future, Jonah, and it disturbs me to see so many of our young wasted with a poor upbringing.

"I'm well aware of what I am, and I am not a charismatic man. I am not a Shaw, or Hei Lin, nor a Bo Vinh. What I am is a student of human nature, and human nature can be trained. I will lead the young children of the Oliver Foundation by example and teaching.

"I won't bore you with all the theory now. Suffice to say that nature is Darwinian, and we must prepare the youth of today to succeed. To take us forward in time in a way that will best prepare us as a race. My goal is to take the Oliver Foundation to new levels of support for the disadvantaged and appeal to the lowest echelon of humans with ambition: those people who wish to better themselves but do not have the means to do so."

I had the suspicion that Sir Thomas was practicing his speech on me but felt it would be ungracious to say so. I was somewhat surprised and gratified at the strength of his concern for the orphaned children of the Oliver Foundation. I had no idea he felt that deeply about them.

What shocked me more was that my uncle was being so frank with me about his plans. He seemed to be elevating our relationship to a new level. Perhaps it was my handling of the runner, or perhaps my uncle had been motivated by his retirement from UNPOL, but whatever the reason, he had never opened up to me like this before and that shocked me.

I nodded my head slowly and replied, "Well, those are extremely admirable goals. I wish you every success in achieving them."

Sir Thomas was picking at his teeth with his napkin, hiding the mining process. He put the napkin down, his tongue making his mouth bulge down near his chin, and then swallowed. With almost an exhalation, he said softly, "Oh, I'll achieve them," and smiled a quick smile.

I placed my knife and fork in the center of my plate and sat back, my hands on my thighs, resting on the white linen napkin with the UNPOL logo in the middle. Smiling at my uncle, I said, "Thank you for the lunch, Uncle, and for the opportunity to contribute to your future memoir."

Sir Thomas, rising, said, "My pleasure, Jonah."

I rose, bent at the waist, and gave my uncle a deep wai. He smiled and, coming around the table, took my arm. Leading me back through the scattered tables, he said, "When are you moving up the Coast?"

"I'm leaving today. I've got a car coming to the Woodlands Envplex at 4pm, and then I'll drive up there. I'm looking forward to it. I haven't really driven a car since I came here."

We walked out onto Topside. The sky had turned into a mass of churning grey, mustard and black, and sheets of rain could be seen in the east, hitting Orchard in great walls of water, and in the west just as dark a mass. "Well, we better be getting indoors. It looks as if there's going to be a thunderstorm. Drive safely, the long-haulers on that Travway are known to be faulty on occasion, and the results are always messy."

It's A Beautiful Lie

We parted, Sir Thomas striding away to the nearest Lev port and I walking along the edge of Topside. The UNPOL Complex was the highest, and the Topside landscape flowed down through a series of steps and arching walkys, each swooping down and rising as they reached the West Coast before rising again and topping out over the hill of Clementi's image-conscious Entplexs.

The green spaces of Topside hid their color in the midday darkness, but I walked with purpose in the direction of the West Coast. I didn't plan to walk all the way to the West Coast, but heading in that direction, nearer the center of Jurong Island, was a Lev port that was vertically over the part of the UNPOL Complex that Mariko was contributing in. If I hurried, I could catch her before she left for Woodlands.

Taking out my Devstick, I saw the missed call that I'd received when I was having lunch. I'd forgotten all about it in my haste. I saw it was from Mariko and hit reply. The Devstick held an image that I'd taken of her yesterday, sitting cross-legged, straight-backed, reading a paper book, with the book in her lap and her hands on her knees, her chin sharply angled downwards and her belly sucked in. She said it was a way for her to exercise her brain and her abs at the same time.

She came on, and I saw in the inset map on her image that she was at ground level at the Jurong island exit.

"Hi, I see you're Topside," she said and smiled. "What are you doing there? I thought you'd be back at the Env packing."

"I thought I'd come and collect my damsel in distress."

"In distress? Why, my knight in shining armor, you must be looking at some other damsel on your Devstick. I'm not distressed."

"You must be," I said. "You haven't seen me since last night." I grinned at the Devstick, walking faster.

"Oh please, spare me," she said, laughing.

"I'll be down to see you in about five mins. I was thinking I'd watch you eat and have an alky or two, and then we could head back to the Env and take off.

145

What do you think?"

"Sounds good. How has your day been? Did you enjoy my rose?"

"Day's been good, apart from the freezing jet of cold water this morning. Everything has been just great since then. Look, I'm at the Lev port, and it's a little crowded. I'll tell you my news over an alky."

"Great," she said and, waving with her left hand, signed off.

A few stops later, the Lev reached ground level, and I stepped a few paces out of it and looked around. The rain over Orchard had moved south, and now it was slashing down in the uncovered space in front of me, splashes reaching the new footwear I'd credded at Smooth. About thirty meters away I saw Mariko walking through the rain towards me. Even from this distance I could tell she was angry about something.

She looked around at something and then saw me, and with a last glance flung over her shoulder, she walked straight across, chin down against the rain.

I put my hand on her arm and said, "Hey, are you okay? What's the matter?"

She shook her head brusquely. "I'm okay. Let's just forget it for now. I'll tell you about it later. Can we just go? Skip the alkys and get on the trav? Would you mind?"

Shaking my head, I said, "No, of course not," and seeing how troubled she looked, I took her arm and steered her back to the Lev port.

Fifteen minutes and two Levs later, we were back at the Woodlands Envplex. I used my Devstick to tell the car to come earlier, and Mariko went to take a shower and get a change of clothes. She had hardly spoken since we left Jurong. I let her have her space – she'd said she would tell me later, and I was sure she would. Instead I focused on packing the remaining items and called up the Envplex's autotroll. The autotroll arrived with a beeping on my Devstick indicating that it was ready for use and waiting outside of my door.

I'd stacked the plastic boxes, each about a meter long and half that wide, on top of each other. Apart from the ones loaded with books, they hardly weighed a thing, and I loaded the autotroll in the time that Mariko was still in the shower. I flashed a note to her Devstick telling her that I was headed to the Envplex lobby to load the car. It had arrived in the same manner as the autotroll except that it was waiting for me at ground level just outside the southern Lev port entrance.

I walked to the entrance and looked back at the apartment. The last time I had done this I had walked out with a carry on and left the apartment practically empty. This time I was leaving a woman in the shower getting ready to join me and an autotroll full of clothes, images and books.

Progress, I thought and laughed to myself as I remembered the punk rap song, 'Progress is a Bitch', and decided not to tell that one to Mariko. I felt happy, but at the same time I was concerned about Mariko. She'd been on a kind of monosyllabic auto response mode since leaving Jurong, and I'd never seen this side of her. She was obviously working something really serious out, and I had to wait until she was ready to talk. I hoped with all my heart that she wasn't having second thoughts about moving to Sisik with me.

The Toyota Titan I'd rented was a mag/offroad hybrid. It was also all-terrain and ocean, which had pushed the cred up another thirty-five units a day, but I figured that we'd come in off the sea and drive up the beach to the house. It would save us lugging the boxes through the four hundred meters of jungle that separated us from civilization. I had no plans to change that amount of separation. In fact, I was already thinking about how it might be increased.

There were a few people standing around looking at the Titan, and I nonchalantly thumbed my Devstick while approaching with the autotrolly. The door slid open in the sixteen meter vehicle – to call it a car was a bit of a misnomer. It took up a lot of space in the lobby, and with its wheels set well inside the squat body shell, it looked like a very shiny, dark titanium box with a huge cockpit of swept-back glass floating on air. I saw the manual on the stairs leading to the top cockpit and picked it up.

One of the males standing looking at the Titan smiled at me reading the manual. It was pretty obvious this was my first time with this kind of rig. I smiled back and shrugged my shoulders.

A quick scan of the manual and I located the loader door panel button on the bracing column of the door. Pressing it caused a pneumatic hiss out of the belly of the beast that made me jump and then laugh at myself as I saw a side panel slide back in the hull. I loaded the plastic boxes into the cargo hold. The four lights that defined its corners were orange and cast a revolving glow in the dim of the lobby. Then I walked up the stairs and into the tan expanse of the primary cockpit. It had a high-end Devcockpit done in black with adjustable screens set into a dark grey interior with red piping. The twin drivers' seats allowed for observation or participation, meaning they were adjustable from extreme comfort to the pragmatic of reaching the controls. The steering column arced its way out from under the front shield in functional titanium, drilled out to reduce weight. Hanging off the end of the column, two thick black rubber grips with a face in between them of an array of multi-colored buttons.

Manual in hand, I sat down in the comfortable Siteazy behind the wheel. I looked at the black grips and opened the manual to find where the On switch was. My Devstick vibrated, and I dug it out of my lower outers pocket. It was the car rental company. I hit accept.

"Good afternoon, Mr Oliver, and thank you for making us your choice for vehicle trav. Welcome to the Titan. My name is Cindy, and I'll be taking you through the start-up routine. I am now turning on the interior systems – we recommend fully automatic trav out of New Singapore and collision avoidance systems will set to auto when you switch to manual."

The automated recording from the rental company played on as the Devcockpit came alive with color and images. I looked away from the little Chinese-looking girl reciting the Titan's features and systems on my Devstick. Instead I studied the Dev. I caught Mariko walking out of the Lev port, her Devstick to her mouth. I couldn't hear what she was saying, but while she didn't seem angry, she still seemed serious. She stopped when she saw me sitting up in the cockpit, waving at her. She had no idea I was going to rent something this huge. She probably thought we'd just go up in a standard cab, but I had gone with a trav liner and a top of the line one at that.

Mariko turned her face sideways but kept her eyes on me, now smiling. She took the Devstick from her ear and walked over to the door. I leaned forward so that I could see her face down the half-spiral stair. There she stood, her cloth bag over one shoulder, holding the Devstick in her hand.

She looked up at me and smiled. "Let's go." Grabbing the hand rail, she walked up the stairs and plonked down in the seat next to me. She pursed her lips together in a pout and made a sucking noise with her tongue.

The twin brother or maybe sister of my steering column rose out of the cockpit floor and extended from below the front shield, the extension of the twin grips easing its way towards a position above Mariko's lap. The black grips, Devpad and drilled out titanium column matched the matt black leg outers and chromed cloth outer tank top she had on. She stretched out her arms and flexed her muscles. I started to feel alarmed, hoping she wasn't thinking about driving the Titan out of here.

Mariko took hold of the steering grips and hit a button on the center Dev pad with her right thumb. The door slid shut with a quick hiss and metallic solid clunk. There was a slight whirring sound as Mariko adjusted her seat, going to a half recline with the steering grips still in her hands. Neither of us said anything – I wanted to see what she would do. She fiddled with the angle of her seat and then, appearing satisfied, reached up and pulled the rear and side view Devscreen down from the roof above her, the lobby behind us displayed in clear color and infrared. She took a last look at that and, reaching out with her left hand, tapped another button on the Devpad. She reached again and adjusted the black mic that coiled out of the roof above us like a dark snake about to strike.

She said, "Systems check – go."

A Devscreen in the wide expanse of dark grey carbon fiber came to life, and the liner's systems rolled up in a slow reading scroll. Mariko thumbed the Dev a couple of times, and the scroll speeded up. All the lights in the cockpit buttons blinked green three times, and she said, "Go manual, autocol on," and the Titan starting moving at a walking pace over the polished cement floor of the lobby. I thought about putting on the safety webbing but decided against it – she might not think that was funny, and at this speed I had nothing to worry about. We exited the Envplex and had to wait while the Travway cleared enough space for us to enter. The Travway radar came up on the Devscreen, replacing the systems check, and flashed green.

Mariko twisted the grip with what was almost a snarl of her lips, and the Titan leapt out of the on-ramp, thrusting me against my seat. She engaged the safety webbing for both of us as she accelerated through one hundred and forty kilos, taking us within two mins to the causeway. She had to drop our speed as we came to the causeway with the evening trav just starting, but she swiftly pulled over to the exit lane and took the exit ramp that lead to the wharf and warehousing area along the strait. Steering through a curving right corner and then cutting speed down to a crawl, she eased the Titan into a storm drain outlet that sloped down to the strait in between two warehouses.

I was sure the little Chinese girl from EasyRent didn't have this route in mind. There was a fairly strong stream of water flowing in the storm drain as New Singapore sluiced out the afternoon's rain, and Mariko edged the Titan down the ramp. A flashing red alarm button went off accompanied by a loud urgent repeated buzz. Mariko calmly reached over and hit the squawking button. The front end of the liner floated free on the water, and she gave the throttle a quick twist, pushing the back end of the craft into the water.

A schematic display on the center Dev showed the Titan's fat six wheels retracting into its belly and laying flat, as the current swept us sideways. The left-side Dev showed images of the hydro planes extending, and the Travway radar switched over to radar of the shipping and other craft that were traversing the strait. It was all big container ships with a few lighters and ferries scurrying about. The props fully extended and locked, Mariko twisted the throttle, and the nose of the Titan rose and then settled as she countered the sideways drift and then took us up in a series of smooth shudders on the small waves of the strait to hydroplane speed. The hull dragged itself up and clear of the sea beneath us.

She turned the craft gently, powering up all the way through the turn in a wide, right-hand arc, cutting underneath the stern of a huge anchored seahauler. I glanced at the rear Devscreen set into the roof and saw hardly a ripple behind us. The rain had stopped, and through the cloud cover, a dark golden sun tipping into scarlet found the center of the rear view Devscreen as we headed east out of the strait at ninety kilos.

I released myself from the safety webbing when our course straightened out and, steadying myself with a hand on Mariko's seat, walked down the steps behind into the cabin below.

I stepped over to the fridge and got out a couple of cold beers. I also checked to see that the food I'd ordered was in there, and it looked like EasyRent had done their job well. Then I turned and went back up the stairs to the cockpit. Ships' rusted sides gleamed gold with the sun at our backs as we flew down the strait. Mariko had both hands on the grips, so I twisted the top off her beer and fitted it into the holder on the side of her Siteazy.

She looked up with a smile and taking her left hand off the grip gave mine a squeeze. "Thanks for not asking," she said. She picked up her beer with an elbow bent back to reach it and raised the drink in salute. "Great choice – the Titan, I mean – I hope you don't mind me coming by sea."

"No, it's a great idea, but I had no idea you knew how to handle one of these things. Where did you learn to handle a rig this size?"

"There's a lot you don't know about me, Jonah. Let me get us out of here and tracking north up the coast in the open sea, and then we'll talk. Okay?"

I sat back down in my seat and swiveled to face her, kicking off my shoes. Curling my legs under me, I rested an elbow on a knee, the Tiger beer dangling from my fingers swaying to the motion of the craft's plunge through the darkening sea.

"Sure," I said and smiled softly at her, not understanding the look of sadness that haunted her green eyes. A cloud hastened the departure of the dying sun behind us as the craft pushed into the darkness in front, and the lights of the Devscreen and the buttons in the Dev consoles illuminated the inside of the cockpit, casting everything in a green light.

Mariko banked the craft left, and the GPS showed our track as running NNE at about fifteen degrees. She said, "Go to Autopilot at eighty kilos." The pitched whine coming from the engines behind us dropped a level as the craft seemed to raise its nose a fraction against a horizon now rapidly fading to black. She pushed the steering column out of her lap, and her seat rose to a sitting upright position. Then she hit a button on the side of the Siteazy, and her seat turned her to face me.

Holding the bottle with two fingers and a thumb and tilting her head right back to force the flow to full, Mariko took a long pull of her beer, looking at me all the time. She stopped gulping, removed the bottle from her lips, and exhaled forcefully.

"I've wanted to tell you what I am going to tell you since the first time I woke up with you in your Env. It's just that then I wasn't sure if it was legal for me to tell you, and when after I'd returned to my contribution, I knew it was, then everything was so perfect that I couldn't find a way to fit it in without spoiling that perfectness. This evening I've realized that there will never be a perfect time to tell you what I have to say, which makes the perfect time right now."

She put the beer back in its temporary home in the holder on the Siteazy, and reaching across, her arms fully extended, placed her hands on my leg. She looked at me from under her fringe and took a deep breath.

"I can't live a lie, no matter how convenient it may be and no matter how beautiful the circumstances. I can't do it, and right now I'm living a lie, and I've got to put it right. Are you ready for this?"

I was scared by the intensity of her words and my mind was reeling, tripping through possibilities of what she could have lied about. But I hid this and, with an inscrutable expression, said, "Yes, I'm ready."

She breathed out heavily again and straightened up, looking me in the eye, withdrawing her hands from my leg and placing them on her own knees again.

"I didn't meet you on the Moon by accident. I was flown to Shackleton to meet you and ordered to engage with you. On the flight home, I knew you'd been given a concocted Truth Treatment, and I questioned you under orders from Senior Agent Sharon Cochran. I am contributing in SOE as I have told you. The reason I was in such a bad mood this afternoon was that Cochran had just warned me before we met up that since you were no longer attached to UNPOL, I could not reveal any UNPOL-specific information to you. I told her that from a legal standpoint I could, since at the time I was cleared from the task of questioning you and you were cleared of the Blue Notice, you and I were both UNPOL-related and therefore both had access to the information.

"That's it. That's my lie. It's a beautiful lie because it led me to you, but I can't live with it and with you at the same time. One of you has to go. I hope it's the lie."

My mouth had fallen open while she was talking, and it remained that way as I looked at her, my head resting in the palm of my hand and the beer swaying gently to and fro. I didn't say anything, couldn't think of anything to say. All of a sudden I had no idea who she was.

"Is Mariko your real name?" I finally asked.

"Yes. Look, it was for those hours on the flight back from Shackleton only and my brief was to question you about your activities on the Moon. You set off an alarm in the trace center – it was the link between the Nineveh you booked and the Nineveh in the interview. The transcribe matched the two, but it wasn't spotted until you were already at Shackleton, and so they sent me up to intercept and question you. I didn't know about the Truth Treatment until we were on the craft, and then I received the order through my Devstick."

I tilted my head to stare at the ceiling, resting it on an arm folded behind me as I took a long pull of my beer. I breathed out heavily and let the bottle drop by my side. My voice flat, I turned to her and said, "Did the lie stop when we woke up together?"

Mariko looked at me as a tear rolled from her left eye. Her voice, caught on the edge of a sob, said, "The lie stopped at the Lev port on Changi."

After I replaced the beer in its holder, I reached out with the same hand and held it in the space between us, palm upward, little finger curled in. She took my hand, and I said, "Well, that's all right, then."

Mariko sobbed out loud and came out of her seat as if ejected from it, throwing herself lengthways on me, her arms encircling my neck as her tears fell on my throat. I pulled my hands from behind my head and placed them on the sides of her face, lifting her gently to look at me.

"Please don't lie to me ever again," I said, gazing deep into her tear-brimmed eyes.

Rising up on one elbow, she wiped tears away with her forearm, smiled at me, and sobbed at the same time. I leaned forward and kissed her. She opened her mouth and probed with her tongue into mine, holding the sides of my face now and pulling me into her hard as if trying to swallow me. She disengaged her mouth and sat up on me with a wild look in her eye, her hair in disarray as she reached down with her hands and yanked up the chrome tank top.

Auld Lang Syne

In the bedroom of his penthouse at the exclusive Marq V Envplex, Sir Thomas stood on the raised dais next to his enormous sleeper and looked out over the airships, ocean liners and private yachts tethered to spine-like piers and floating off moorings in the dark of the harbor.

There was very little traffic in the harbor now that the hour was approaching midnight. It wasn't raining for a change, and he told the door to the balcony to open, stepping out into the warm night and walking to the railing. The view was spectacular: looking out over the South China Sea; the ships with all their lights on in celebration of the New Year, lighting up the pitch-black sea; the Moon a sliver of silver. He took in a deep breath of the warm sea air, although at this height the taste of salt was minimal – it had to be imagined.

In another five minutes, his image would be broadcast for the world to see, and the culmination of a decade's worth of planning would be put into motion. The hole cards were dealt, the river down, and now the betting and bluffing would begin. He clenched his fists in anticipation, turned, and walked along the balcony until he had reached the door to the living room, which had been set up for the broadcast.

Dressed in a blue shirt with the collar open at the neck and an old-fashioned woolen jumper over khaki pants, complete with suede brogues on his feet and no socks, his ankles felt cool. He went indoors, sitting at the far end of a beige sofa. He checked his image in the Devscreen opposite him and rubbed his cheeks to put some color into them, a rosiness that led to the kind 'Uncle Tom' image that they wanted to portray.

He looked at the time on his Devstick and then put it away and faced the camera Dev, smiling. A timer in the camera Devscreen opposite him counted down to midnight, and a red light went on at top of the camera.

"Happy New Year, my fellow humans, and welcome to year 2110. I have chosen this time to announce my resignation from the post of director of UNPOL. I requested that my resignation be accepted by the Board of Governors, and they have graciously acceded to my wish. I have requested only that I may be allowed to perform one last task: that of catching and stopping the terrorists who have sought to cast our world back into darkness with their actions in Paris and New Manhattan. My promise to the family and friends of those who were lost in those cowardly attacks will be honored, and in this, too, the Board of Governors has been gracious in allowing me to achieve this last contribution to you, my fellow humans.

"My years at UNPOL have been happy ones for me, and I know that I will leave this fine organization in strong capable hands when the Board of Governors chooses its next director. It is traditional that the departing director offers words of advice for his replacement. I am going to break with that tradition. Instead, on behalf of the children of the Oliver Foundation, for their future, I am going to offer my advice to all of you out there on our beautiful planet.

"My advice is simple but heartfelt, and please think of it as the wish of an old man passing into the twilight of his years, with no motive other than to see his fellow humans prosper in perpetuity. My wish is that you embrace the new Personal Unique Identification Law. Embrace it as brothers and sisters who have nothing to fear from each other, as it will exclude those who wish to create terror and unbalance this beautiful society we have built.

"Thank you, my fellow humans, for allowing me to contribute as I have to UNPOL these many years. Thank you."

***

The clock on the Devscreen read 12:08am as I watched my uncle, my lips moving with the words he spoke.

I lay on a futon in the living room of the beach house, watching the Devscreen we had hung on the wall. Mariko lay with her head on my lap, yawning as she flipped the page of a book she was reading. She saw me and turned to look at the screen. She hadn't been watching, absorbed in her book, A Tail Of Two Zos by Nomis Elroy.

She sat up, slapped my thigh lightly, and said, "You wrote it?"

"Wrote what?"

"The speech he's giving. You wrote it, didn't you?" She waved the book at the Devscreen.

"Er, yes. But that has to be our secret. Okay?"

"Yes, of course, but how could you? I mean the Tag Law, you don't support that, do you?"

"No, not support, but then, I'm not against it either."

"Then how could you write that if you don't believe in it?"

"Well, Sir Thomas asked for my help, and I could hardly turn him down, could I? So I just imagined I was a slightly xenophobic conspiracy theory nut and went from there."

Mariko gave a full-throated laugh and then said, "That's kind of cynical, wouldn't you say?"

"I suppose it is, but they're really his words, not mine. I just made them sound better."

"Yes, but you're playing a pretty significant role in this. I mean, what if the Tag really gets voted in?"

"There's a good chance it will from what I've seen on the surveys so far. This is just Sir Thomas's last hurrah, another shining example of civic duty to be laid on the pyre when his time has come."

"Are you sure? He looks pretty serious about it."

"Oh, he's serious enough. I just think that it will happen irrespective of the speech. So writing it doesn't make a difference."

"Wow, that really is cynical. Of course writing makes a difference. What about Bo Vinh, then? Was he just another guy, or did his writing change the world?"

"No, you're right. He wasn't. He was a philosopher and a true leader, and without him there probably wouldn't be any humans left to fight over."

"But that's my point – by supporting something you don't believe in, then aren't you corrupting the very ideals that Bo Vinh espoused?"

I reached up and, stroking the back of her head, said, "Come on, let's not get into an argument about my uncle or politics in the first hour of the new year. How about we go for a swim instead?"

She smiled and said, "Okay, but allow me one last comment. A woman's prerogative, okay?" And she held her finger out in a parody of Sir Thomas.

I laughed and said, "Sure, go ahead."

Mariko leaned in close to stare into my eyes and said, "I don't care about your uncle or politics, I'm concerned about you, and that's why I'm a little upset. I like to think of you as my perfect hero, and thinking of you as cynical just doesn't fit that image."

She leaned her body forward and gave me a hug, pushing her chest against mine. As I held her, I smiled and thought to myself, I am the luckiest man alive.

She pulled back and reached down, stripping off her top outer. "Now let's go skinny dipping."

I stroked my hand up her leg and kissed her, my other hand coming up to support her as I shifted my thighs and laid her back onto the futon. I whispered in her ear, nuzzling it at the same time, "I've got a better idea," and brought my hand from her leg up to her breast, stroking the nipple with my thumb.

She pulled my face from her neck, slipping away a little and looking into my eyes, and batted her eyelashes at me. I smiled and suddenly found myself lying face down on the futon, with her knee in my back and my arm twisted up with her knee. Her lips teased the top of my ear, and she said, "No, I think your first idea was better, wouldn't you say?" giving my arm a little tug for emphasis.

"Yes, yes, it was a much better idea," I said, starting to laugh.

She released my arm and stood up, walking across the room to the open doors and out onto the deck that surrounded the beach house. She turned and looked at me lying on the futon, my head resting on one hand, gazing at her, smiling. She hooked her thumbs into her bottom outers and pulled down, stepping out one long leg at a time, straightening and hooking her thumbs into the tops of her inners. Turning to face me full frontal, she eased them down a few cents at a time. I rose, and she dashed for the stairs that led down to the beach as I came through the doors to the deck. I watched as she sprinted down the beach and into the surf, not slowing down but powering in until she had reached deep enough to swim. I saw her diving in, disappearing.

I stripped my outers off, watching where she had gone in. She still hadn't appeared. My heart beat faster and leaving my inners on I sprinted down the beach to where she had gone in and shouted her name.

"Mariko, Mariko!"

Suddenly my legs were taken from underneath me, and I went down into the meter-deep water. I put a hand out and felt her hair, as she twisted around me and, surfacing, pulled me up. I was angry.

"I thought you'd drowned."

She grasped my jaw, thrust her mouth against mine, driving a salty tongue in and grabbing my cock through my inners. She said, "I'm the most dangerous animal on this beach, baby, and don't you forget it."

Then she slipped out of my grasp and, twisting in front of me, pulled me off balance again. Taking me across her shoulders in a fireman's lift, she straightened her legs up and dropped to one knee, softly but firmly easing me onto the ground.

She tore my inners off with a single harsh swipe of her hand, fingers extended into talons. With the same hand she reached down and grabbed my cock at its base before lowering herself onto me. The sudden warmth surrounding my cock unleashed something inside me, and reaching back with one hand, I pushed myself, my knees straightening and lifting us both. We surged back into the sea as she molded herself to me, wrapping her legs around my buttocks. When the water came to my thighs, I held her close and toppled forward, taking my hands down to pull her waist into me. We twisted, joined together, in the sea, holding our breath, until kicking against the bottom I found purchase for us, and we surfaced. With her legs wrapped around my hips, and her arms around my neck, she pulled me into another long kiss, and together we swayed with the ocean.

"How does a Special Operations Executive feel about having children?" I asked her.

She clasped her hands behind my neck and, leaning back to look in my eyes, said, "Well, that would depend on who the father was going to be."

I ground against her and said, "I think I'd make a pretty good father."

"No, you'd make a great father. Now quit talking and get fathering, will you?"

Pulling herself up on my shoulders, she lightly bit my earlobe. I braced both feet in the sand, toes curled for extra purchase, as she plunged down with her pelvis, riding me hard.

Swimming With Sharks

Jonah and Mariko's Beach House,
Sisik Beach, Malaysian Geographic.
Wednesday, 1 January 2110, 11:40am +8 UTC

Sprawled in a tangle of limbs and blanket, I woke to the buzzing of my Devstick. I reached over, thumbed the Devstick to silent and, closing my eyes, tried to go back to sleep. But the Devstick had done its work.

Disentangling myself from Mariko, I got up and walked over to the shelves that we had put up on the wall facing the jungle. I pulled out one of her batik wraps and wrapped it around my waist, tying it into a knot below my belly button as I'd seen the locals do. I turned around and faced the sea. Our sleeper, large enough for four people, was against the wall to my left, positioned in the middle. Two windows flanking the bed were now shaded by the Clearfilm shading I'd put up as a temporary measure. Against the opposite wall was the railing guarding the stairs until they reached their zenith a meter up. The kitchen, shower and outlet were on the ground floor.

I went downstairs, treading lightly past Mariko, on the wooden floor that we had sanded together a couple of days ago, and walked over to the bench that we had put up that same day. It was temporary but served the purpose of holding the old-fashioned coffee percolator plus the other cooking machines. I filled the percolator with water and set it onto the electric heat pad. Searching the refrigerator, I found some grapes, and I ate those while waiting for the coffee aroma to hit. As soon as I smelled the coffee, I got out the cups and put them on a tray.

I dug the croissants out of the fridge. They weren't as good as those from the French bakery near our old Env, but they weren't bad. I put them under the heat and waited. The coffee percolated through, and the croissants' butter melted. I placed everything on a tray, added a tub of raspberry jam, and went back upstairs. Mariko was still sprawled out where I had left her, and I set the tray down on the floor beside the futon in front of the large Devscreen.

I thumbed the Dev on and leant back against the cushions. The late morning sun lent a hard reality to the light outside the windows, and I debated getting my eye shades. Laziness winning out, I let the daily data stream flush itself out

159

on the screen.

I flicked over to messages. There were several, mostly from acquaintances wishing me a happy New Year. But one stuck out: the subject was 'wake up'. I thumbed it, and the message read 'Jonah, Jonah, wake up'. I frowned and thought, that's weird, but then dismissed it as a joke or spam – the sender wasn't identified, which, given that it had reached my personal contact messaging, was a surprise but not unheard of.

I reached over and got the coffee off the tray. Coffee in the morning was a new taste, but I was already a committed devotee. The smell made me hungry, and the sweet dark taste made me flick data streams back to the daily feed, my brain kicking into action.

I frowned. Something bothered me, but I wasn't sure what it was. The feeling was like when you're sure you've forgotten something but cannot remember what, and I couldn't shake it. I spooned some raspberry jam onto a piece of croissant and popped it into my mouth. I felt fidgety. I picked up my Devstick to thumb the Dev again, keeping the volume down. The image changed, and I was watching a roundup of global news.

The restlessness grew, and suddenly an image of a stark room flashed in my mind. It felt like a dream, only I knew this wasn't a dream. With those, if I focused, I could recall the remnant images. With this, when I tried, the images hovered just out of reach. I flicked the Dev channel back to messages and scanned the received list again.

I opened it again, and it said the same thing. 'Jonah, Jonah, wake up'. That was it, the sender a series of numbers and an @ sign that made no sense. It was weird. Another flash hit me with searing clarity: throwing up into a recycler, a golf cart in a tube. I pressed my fingertips into my shut eyes and smoothed out over my eyebrows, pulling taut skin over my cheekbones and down my jaw, breathing deep. It wasn't from a dream. They were memories, recent memories. Mariko gave a little snore, bringing me back to the present.

I picked up the cup of coffee and walked silently to the sliding door to the deck. Knowing the right side opened with a loud squeak, I swapped my right hand for my left to hold the coffee cup and opened the left side of the clearfilm door. Closing the door behind me, I turned and went to the railing, leaning on it, looking out to sea. The midday sun beat harsh on the sand, turning observation into a squint, the blue-green of the sea easing the glare from the strip of white sand. The gap between the sea and the house was narrow with the morning tide fully risen. The sundial I'd made from a circle of wood found beside the house and mounted on driftwood showed the sun was at its zenith.

I pinched the bridge of my nose and shut my eyes to blackness, swarms of red, a new image. A white room. A naked man sitting on a Biosense. Jibril. Gabriel. The runner. My brother. The thought punched me in the stomach, and I threw up the coffee over the railing into the hot white sand. I stared at the spew of coffee as I wiped my mouth and sniffed. It wasn't a dream.

I turned to reenter the house but seeing Mariko lying on the floor, froze. The runner Gabriel was my brother. Somehow I knew that was true, and then another memory. A loud laugh, Gabriel sitting on a sleeper talking to me.

How will she react? I couldn't begin to guess. I hoped favorably – that is, she'd believe me and help me. Help me what? I couldn't trust my mind. What had seemed real was not, and reality was being displaced one chunk of memory at a time. One chunk of memory at a time, where had I heard that? Gabriel had said it, on the Moon. The sun beat viciously down on the top of my head. I walked across the deck and slid the door open; it protested with a loud squeak, and Mariko woke, coming upright, shielding her eyes from the glare and looking at me from under the shadow of her forearm.

I walked over to her and sat down, leaning my back against the edge of the sleeper.

She said, "What's wrong? You look like you've just seen a ghost."

I leaned my head onto the sleeper and, staring at the ceiling, groaned. My head hurt. It felt as if my brain had swollen and wouldn't fit in my skull, pressing against the sides. I brought my hands up to my temples and pushed in on both sides with knuckled fists, groaning again. Another memory came. Gabriel sitting on the sleeper opposite me, talking, and this time the images came with sound. Gabriel saying, 'It isn't as bad as it sounds. At the beginning you will think that you are remembering a dream, but over the course of a couple of hours, the details of the dream will be filled in with ever-increasing clarity. Your mind will return again and again to the little reservoir of information that I'll plant, and the signals, travelling from the outback of your brain, will come in ever-larger memory chunks, until you will reach the moment where this description will be relayed to you word for word, complete with the images of me and this room.'

"Jonah, Jonah, what's wrong? Talk to me."

The pain disappeared as quickly as it had come. I dropped my hands to the floor and looked at her.

"I'm okay. It's all right," I said and reached up with a hand to stroke her cheek. She made to kiss me, but I held her off with my hand dropping to her chest and pushing lightly. "No, no kiss, not unless you want to taste vomit."

"What, you threw up? Is it a hangover or what? You hardly had anything alky last night."

"It's not that. Look, we have to talk, but let's go for a swim. Okay?"

"What, now? It's midday and way too hot."

"Come on, trust me. It'll be fine. Just follow me. Okay?" I got up and, taking the wrap off, put on the swim outers that were lying on the bed. Without saying another word, I picked up a waterproof Devstick I had and headed outside, walking down the stairs and onto the beach. I strode quickly over the hot white sand, a glance over my shoulder showed Mariko following, and I dived into the sea.

I was stroking hard in a crawl for the cliff that marked the southern end of the bay. It was about two hundred meters away from me, and I had a good lead, but she was the stronger swimmer, and she caught me up as I was nearly at the cliff. The waves slapped against its base. She stopped and treaded water. I kept going, and then when nearly at the cliff, I dived.

In front of me, through the sunlight-filtered green water, I saw that the blunt, black edge of the cliff stopped short of the bottom. I dived for the gap that was about a meter wide. Coming up through the gap into a small cave, I climbed up onto a rock. I unfolded the Devstick in front of me, the white light from the screen guiding Mariko to me. She pulled herself up the dry rock face and sat down on the ledge, leaning against the smooth dry rock wall. Marks on the wall indicated that it was man-made or at least enlarged by someone.

"This place is amazing. When did you find this?"

I held up a hand while I caught my breath and panted out, "The first day we moved here, when I went for a walk. I wanted to see what was around the corner of the bluff. It was low tide. I saw the top of the gap and went to look. When the tide's low, you can just see the top of the entrance, but you have to be looking for it."

"Okay, so what's this all about?" Mariko asked, taking deep breaths from the exertion of the swim and holding on to the edge of the ledge. With both hands pushing down, she moved her bum further in.

"When we came up here, you told me what had happened on the Moon. You told me that you couldn't live a lie, not with me, right?"

"Yes, right, and so?" She said this with a defensive tone in her voice. She'd thought the subject closed and forgotten, and now here it was again, with all the insecurity attached reloading in pallets on her heart. I saw the look and reached out to take her hand, cutting through the light of the Devstick.

"No, this time it isn't about you. It's about me and what happened to me on the Moon, and it's about what that means to you. I came here because I am scared, and what I have to tell you places both of us in extreme danger, the kind of danger where you lose your life or get mind-wiped. Before I continue, let me ask you, do you really want to hear this?"

"Jonah, right now I could have your seed fertilizing me. Of course I want to hear it. Good or bad, in my world you come before everything."

I smiled at her statement and squeezed her hand. I took a deep breath and blew it out hard, drawing my legs up to sit cross-legged beside her, the Devscreen a block of white in between, a backdrop for my hand holding hers. "Okay, what happened on the Moon was caused by what happened on a Thursday in December on Earth. It was the 5th of December, in the morning."

***

It took me an hour, but I told her everything. Right up to the point that I'd been hypnotized by Gabriel and was thus able to avoid the consequences of the ad hoc Truth Treatment which she'd told me about.

She let out a deep breath, her cheeks ballooning for a moment, then she turned her face to me and said, "Wow, Jonah. You really know how to show a girl an exciting time, don't you."

"You believe me, then?"

"Yes, of course I do. I wish I didn't, but I think everything you've told me happened as you've said. I can see it, too, the planning, the execution. I was pulled off the Gabriel case after my meeting with you and when you were cleared of any involvement. Since then I've only seen the updates on the feed, but there's always some level of rumor within SOE, and the rumor was that the runner had gotten away clean, not traceable. But yes, I see your part and why they need you."

"Sir Thomas's move out of UNPOL, and the revised Tag Law – the things I penned for that eloquently delivered resignation speech – it's happening now. They're making their move."

"Yes, but from where I sit, Gabriel's made his move, too. Look, you're in, you're your uncle's writer and have a secure line into his base Dev. That puts you in his inner circle first degree, right?"

"Yes, it does. I've got no idea where to start."

"We can work that out. But I think the first thing we can do is to review the information that Gabriel put on your Devstick and tell Gabriel that you've remembered."

"Won't that be risky?"

"Not if we just reply that you're awake."

"Thanks for using 'we'. You've no idea how good that makes me feel right now."

She smiled and, leaning forward, kissed me. She said, "Look, we both know this is really serious, but we can work this out."

"You can't tell anyone at SOE about this. We have no idea who we can trust and who is a Hawk."

"No, I won't tell anyone. If Cochran and Sir Thomas are Hawks, you can bet that UNPOL and SOE are riddled with them. It wouldn't be hard to manipulate the selection boards. I'll have to stay clear of Cochran, though. With her telepathic ability, she could probe my mind and discover what we know."

"Gabriel said that telepathy works best when both subjects cooperate and are within a few meters of each other. That doesn't mean she couldn't probe you without your knowing. It just means that you'll have to try and avoid her and think innocent thoughts when she's around. When's your next security clearance check?"

"Not till March," she said, frowning, thinking hard. "And that's our deadline. The Popvote for the Tag law comes then. March the 15th, right? So that's the time frame. We've got at least two and a half months, and during that time I can be in SOE, working on the inside. After that and before my next security clearance check, I'll take leave."

"Won't that be suspicious?"

She smiled at me with a sideways look over her shoulder. "Not if I'm pregnant. I love your new, well, old, name, by the way. Mark Anthony Zumar. It's beautiful."

I smiled back. "You better keep calling me Jonah for now. If anyone heard you calling me Mark –"

She cut me off with a finger to my lips and a stern look on her face. "Don't worry, when we leave this cave, you're Jonah, but we're going to have to get you trained up in some of the basics of my craft, and we're going to have to get you fit. No more croissants for you."

"After today, okay. After today."

"Sure, we'll start tomorrow. And then I'll set you up with a routine to follow."

I nodded and said, "Okay. Come on, let's get out of here. I'm getting cold," and folding the Devstick, the cave plunged into darkness – a thin sliver of light coming from the underwater entrance to the sea. I heard her slip into the water with a small splash and slipped silently into the water next to her. We kicked off together and dived down, back into the light. Coming out of the cave, I almost swam into a black-tip reef shark, which quickly swam away, frightened of me. Swimming with sharks, I thought. We're swimming with the sharks.

A New Beginning

Cochran woke but didn't open her eyes or move. It was a trained habit of hers, the chance to observe through sound what was happening around her without changing what was happening around her. Once, when she was still a little girl, she had fallen ill with a high fever and had spent a few days in the infirmary at the dorm where she and other gifted orphans were housed when not engaged with the acquisition of knowledge or skills.

Two other girls had visited her. She could see the outline of their bodies through the transparent plastic oxygenated tent that she was kept in, but could not make out who they were. She was drugged and hallucinatory from the drugs and fever, but while she could not see clearly out, neither could the two girls see clearly in. Although they had told the matron that they were her friends and the matron had believed them, she did not have any friends, and the two girls, in the manner of little girls, who can be extremely cruel, had come to be mean to her in her moment of weakness.

She hadn't moved and had listened. The plastic tent muffled the sound of their voices at first, but she could gradually make out that they were gloating at her, joking about pulling out the oxygen tube to the tent. She was not concerned about that. If they did pull the tube out, she was sure an alarm would go off. What she was concerned with was finding out who these two were. She had strained and focused her hearing, as she had been taught, and narrowed down the choices by process of elimination. First there were the visual clues, height and size. She dismissed more than half of her class. Hair color eliminated half again, and then she had heard the name, Sally, and confirmed one of her choices. Knowing who Sally's friends were narrowed down the remaining teaser to one of two choices. The teasing girls finally left, bored with being mean, when the recipient didn't respond. As their heels had clacked across the floor of the infirmary, Cochran had opened her eyes. The girls left without ever being aware that she had, in fact, heard, and been hurt by, everything they had said, although she would have denied both vehemently.

She occupied the rest of her time in the infirmary planning how to exact revenge on the three girls. The fact that one of the three was innocent of doing her wrong didn't factor in. By the end of the year all three had gone. Two for cheating in knowledge retention tests, despite swearing their innocence, and the third paralyzed from the neck down and destined to spend a year in regen, when the uneven bars that she practiced on for hours in the gym alone strangely collapsed as she performed a Korbut flip.

This morning, Cochran sensed nothing other than the chirping and singing of birds outside, the metronomic tick-tock of the grandfather clock in the room and the steady breathing of Sunita next to her in the sleeper.

She cracked an eye open and saw that Sunita was still asleep. She rose and walked to the en-suite, stripping off the inners she had slept in and dumping them in the sanitization unit. She stepped into the shower and said, "Auto pulse stream." The hot water cascaded down, and she smoothed her hair with her hands, thinking that she must look her best today, for the images that would be broadcast would be of the new director of UNPOL.

Although the selection committee consisted of five, the outgoing director, Sir Thomas, had great influence and had assured her, before leaving, that he would support her nomination as his replacement. She would be the youngest person and first female ever to occupy the role in UNPOL and its predecessor Interpol. She jumped at the feel of hands on her back, lost in her thoughts and her hearing impaired by the stream of water splashing on her head.

Sunita's brown hands slipped from her back to her breasts, and the fingers brushed lightly over her nipples. She turned into Sunita's outstretched arms, and Sunita said, "Big day today."

Cochran placed her mouth next to her ear, her arms resting on her shoulders, "Yes, and it wouldn't have arrived but for you."

"Oh, I don't know. You're a very determined and highly intelligent woman. Somehow I have the feeling that you would have risen to the top of whatever contribution you had chosen."

"Perhaps, but I feel as if I was made not just for this contribution, but this moment. We're going to win, I can feel it." She kissed Sunita's ear and said, "I've got to get ready." Sunita released her and Cochran stepped out of the shower, her nipples grazing Sunita's shoulder, and into the body sanitizer, turning it on full blast for a quick dry.

She walked back into the sleeping room and sat down on the sleeper, turning on her Dev on the table beside her. She said, "Call Oche, voice only."

A few seconds later, not yet a minute, a male voice came on with a rush, "Good morning, darling, and how are we today? What can I do for you?"

"Oche, thanks for taking my call. I need you to style me – I've got a formal day ahead, and I need to look good for the feeds."

"But of course, darling. Now can you tell me a bit about the occasion and how you'd like to present?"

"I need to look sharp, official, styled within the current UNPOL uniform, but a superior cut, and hair should be blonde with a dark base, cut short and shaved at back, military-style. Footwear should be something unisex but classy."

"Okay, darling, I get the image. How about something between police and military, with a dash of Oche thrown in? And for the footwear, we'll go with jumpers, but I'll put some Oche touches on, very butch?"

"Sounds good. When can you be ready by?"

"Thirty-five mins, darling. That okay?"

"Perfect, but do the hair design now. Okay? I'll head over to the hair Dev."

"Okay, darling. I'll be waiting."

Cochran walked over to the hair Dev and lowered the dome over her face and down below the nape of her neck to just below where her hair stopped. On the Devscreen in front of her eyes, she saw Oche standing behind her. She smiled and changed the feed to the global newsfeed – the mix of all the different news brands scrolling with the latest news in real time. She scanned back with her thumb, scrolling through to the news of UNPOL announcements, and picked out Sir Thomas's resignation.

She felt the micro scissors and razors begin their work, as a light suction of air within the dome sucked up the remnants and sent them into recycling. She watched Sir Thomas deliver his speech again, six and a half hours after the speech had originally been delivered. She thumbed the console of the Dev and brought up the Tag survey numbers. Acceptance of Tag was up a staggering fifty-five percent and was across the board, in all Geographics. Using this Dev, she couldn't bring up the demographics and switched back to Sir Thomas's speech, but was interrupted before he finished by the flashing of a red light in the corner of the screen.

Oche appeared at the touch of her thumb, standing back from the chair she was in, with his hands on his hips.

She said, "Zoom and rotate on my head," and the image zoomed into her head in the Devscreen in front of her. She swung the image left and right, noting the highlights of blonde on top of the base of dark gold and the straight, razor look of the two cent of hair sweeping back in an arc to a sharp cut off at the base of her skull, and in a half circle around her ears. It looked sensational.

"That's great, Oche, thanks," she said, and checking how much he had deducted from her cred, gave him a tight smile. He smiled sweetly back, and she switched off the hair Dev.

An hour later, she walked out of the SingCom residence to her Bulgari T8. Getting in, she said, "Take me to UNPOL headquarters."

Everything was in motion now. Her promotion to this role had been ordained in the tempering of her youth – the hammer blows to her sensibilities, each a strike on the path to this point when she, by virtue of UN law, would become the de facto head of all armed forces within the world, including the colonies.

Cochran smiled to herself as she settled back in the plush leather seat of the Bulgari. Her thoughts moved ahead to the day when she would hold absolute power. Knowing that this contribution was one of the most transparent, regulated and scrutinized positions in the world, she also knew she could and would control those who were supposed to be scrutinizing. Due to the nature of command, the command cannot function unless there is a singular head. She remembered Sunita's words, spoken to her when she first left the Foundation, 'With singularity there is opportunity.' And later, when she had inducted her into the Hawks, 'With the right set of circumstances, it is possible to rule the world. It is also possible that the right set of circumstances could be set in motion through careful planning and a span of time that obscures the origins of the source of the action. Blended, adjusted, tweaked, until the right constituents have formed.' And that time was now. If their plans worked, within three months those circumstances would bear fruit.

As Cochran crossed the bridge from Sentosa, heading towards the West Coast Travway, the New Singapore skyline stood tall and proud. The sky was blue and dotted with white fluffy clouds, the outside temperature a hot thirty-one cel as the Devscreen on the console told her. Inside the Bulgari it was a cool nineteen cel. She wanted to feel cool, fresh. She turned to look at the traffic, the humanity around her in the auto-piloted family saloons, and thought of the Tag.

By this time next year most of you, perhaps all, by law will be wearing the Tag, and how many of you will be driving around? She thought it ironic that in New Singapore the Tag survival figure was pretty high. More than forty percent of the population would live. Hong Kong too would fare well with an even higher percentage surviving there, but then that was inevitable with the low population bases of these Geographics.

Her mind flashed back to the secret meetings held at the SingComm residence or Sir Thomas's Env at the Marque. The selection committee, they'd called it. Because of the high concentration of UNPOL officials and corporate telcos and finance, New Singapore had received a lot of attention. The list had more exceptions than other lists, and the number to be culled was less than three and a half million. They had debated long on what they called inclusions, people who should be included in the cull despite their passing the criteria for exclusion.

She pictured it in her mind, remembering with absolute clarity that moment at the Singcomm residence when Sunita had gone through the final agreed formula for the cull. Their 'algorithm', as it became known. After much debate, they had decided to keep it simple.

First, all known Doves who had injected the Tag.

Anyone who would lose a significant number of their family and who would then be alone. It was kinder to include them and certainly made for more predictable behavior on their part.

Everyone with an Intelligence Score of one hundred or less.

Cochran's time for direct action was just three months away, when the Tag Law would be accepted. Shortly after, once they had reached seventy-five percent global acceptance, injection, and acquisition, they would trigger the cull and declare martial law.

She imagined herself in her uniform as UNPOL director. Taking control as six point three billion people died within a week. Giving the orders to take control of the remaining humans: the brightest, the most intelligent, the quickest, a race unencumbered, a utopia, a true golden age of civilization for centuries to come.

The Bulgari swept down into the underground parking of the UNPOL Complex, and Cochran walked to the Lev port. "Governors' board room, offline travel," she told the Dev, and the Lev port confirmed and started to ascend.

The Lev port opened into a large foyer approximately fifty meters deep and two hundred wide, with a door at either wide end. The foyer was made of titanium and granite, interlaid except where they competed in the two straight paths that led to the doors. She strode to the intersection of the paths and turned right, her arms down her sides held still, thumbs facing forward as she marched the one hundred meters to the titanium door. She said, "Agent Cochran, open."

The door opened, and she entered. The five members of the Board of Governors of the office of the UNPOL directorship were already there and sitting in black-backed chairs, their backs to her, on an island in the middle of a dark pool. The path from where she was standing went right in a semi-circle. She followed it, walking at an even but swift pace, her three thousand cred Oche jumpers with metal studs up the back of the heel echoing in the hollow stillness of the room, until she was opposite the door she had entered. A path in front of her led to a solitary chair on its own island separated from the governors by the same dark liquid pool.

She walked to the chair and sat down facing the governors, looking up at them on their raised platform. The light in the room dimmed until everything except the governors and the spot she was on went into blackness.

At the center of the governors, Miles Tilling began to speak, with a slight forward inclination of his head, his hands folded over his stomach. He said, "Agent Cochran, it is the duty of this board to determine who among us is most capable of filling the role of director of UNPOL. In fulfilling that duty this morning, we assembled to vote on the choices we have been reviewing for the last week, and by a split vote we decided that this position would be best filled by Assistant Director Dietrich Flederson of the Large Commercial Crimes Unit. We further determined, by unanimous vote, that you would be offered the position of being his second in command. Do you accept?"

She was scarcely able to speak and felt that she might vomit the nourishment pills she had taken that morning.

"I accept," she said in a quiet voice.

Margarine Wu, sitting last on the left facing Cochran, said, "Sharon, the board made a further determination. We agreed that we would tell you the reason we chose Dietrich, and this is an exception to our common rule. However, we felt in the light of your continued and long dedicated contribution to UNPOL that you would be owed an explanation. The reason we settled on Dietrich, and it was a split vote, was purely experience. Dietrich is fifty-five to your twenty-eight, and that is the only reason we ultimately decided upon him. Under his guidance and with his full support, we further determined that the position of director would pass to you within three years."

Saying this, she smiled at Cochran, and Cochran smiled back. Aware of the biosensors in the room, she kept herself under control, coldly thinking, I'd like to pull your fucking face off – her mind spinning with the upset, thoughts racing.

She was furious but stayed mindful.

"I'd like to thank the Board of Governors for your faith in my abilities and in providing me with this opportunity to further my contribution to UNPOL. I will be honored to serve as assistant director to Director Flederson."

She stood up and saluted, the governors nodded, and she about-faced, stepping around the chair that she had just been insulted in. She marched, her outward emotions under control now, her body temperature slightly lower than normal, retracing the one hundred strides to the door. Previous life images flashed through her, wondering what they were thinking about her.

She turned at the door and gave a stiff bow to the governors, arms at her sides, bending low from the waist – her eyes fixed on their backs. She was thinking, Which of you three, or was it four, voted against me? I will find out. She thought about doing a quick mind probe, but decided it was too risky – one of them might be a telepath. And then she spun and walked out of the door.

She had planned on checking the results of the Gang of Four, but changed her mind as she was still too bitter and twisted to face anyone. Her failure was a lump in her throat, a heaviness in her stomach, with a center of acidic bile thrown in. She needed time to think, to get her thinking straight about what she was going to do about this problem. And that is it, she thought. This is just another test, a test that I will pass. It isn't failure, it's just another test – a problem to be solved.

She didn't remember returning to the underground parking, nor getting in the Bulgari, but her mind returned to the present when she was already on the West Coast Travway heading back to Sentosa, and she awoke to her surroundings and her current destination. She must have told the EV to take her home, but now she needed to get back to Sunita quick, and she told the EV to get up to the limit. She took out her Devstick from the pocket in the door of the Bulgari and said, "Sunita."

A few seconds later, her face appeared in the Devscreen, smiling, and before she could congratulate her, Cochran said, "I'm the new assistant director of UNPO." The hint of a frown, like a swiftly passing cloud casting a shadow on the Earth, crossed the face in the small screen.

"Congratulations, that's great to hear. Hurry home, and we'll celebrate."

"I'm on my way."

She thumbed off. Sunita had understood as she had known that she would. Understood her anger and her despair, and she would make it right.

The Bulgari T8 suddenly felt wrong to her. All that she had loved about it turned to hate within a single sweep of her eyes scanning its interior. It was too pretty. She wanted something harsher than this, something that looked and was lethal. It pulled up at the SingCom residence, and she got out without looking at it. She said, "Drive to Luxury vehicles and park there. Wipe the Dev once you have parked." Into her Devstick she said, "Give me a current list cred for a titanium Bulgari T8."

The Devstick flashed back two hundred and forty thousand creds. She said, "Send message to Arthur Ballyntyne. Put the Bulgari on the market for two hundred thousand." She looked at the Dev by the door and went up the steps as the door opened and Sunita Shido stood there, her hands on her hips.

"Get inside," Sunita said. It wasn't a request.

The door closed behind her as she walked past the stern-faced Sunita, and a brown hand flashed in the corner of her eye. She felt the thin whippy crop bite deep into her back and lifted her arms to protect her face as the blows rained down. The only sounds that could be heard were Sunita grunting as she laid the crop into Cochran's back and legs, and the noise of the birds in the cage by the door as they flew helter-skelter, excited by the physical activity near them.

She went down onto the floor and curled into a fetal position as the crop swung again and again on her back and thighs. Sunita, standing over Cochran, placed one latex boot in the middle of her back and, reaching down, grabbed the elegantly cut Oche UNPOL jacket and tore it along the gold etched seam that ran up its back, laying bare the skin that it covered.

Seeing Cochran's flesh like a canvas waiting to be painted, Sunita's flagging arm gained a reserve of power, and the crop slashed down with a manic frequency. The bloody crop, the thin stick of hardened bull pizzle thinned and twisted to over a meter in length, sprayed a fine line of droplets of blood over the pale blue walls and light cream ceiling of the entrance hall. The sprayed droplets fell in thicker drops and farther apart as Sunita tired, the drops painting their own story that no one would ever see.

Cochran curled in the fetal position, her head protected by her arms, and did not cry out or say anything. She just lay there as her skin was flayed off her back, her muscles gleaming white amid the bloody ragged mess.

Finally, as the corbacho, as it is called in Spain from where they had ordered it, dug deep into a muscle, she cried out as the pain cut into her senses. She had just been lashed over two hundred and fifty times and now and again had been

173

unconscious, but this pain was deep and to her core, and she cried out.

"Sorry! I am sorry!" It was their safe word, and immediately the whipping stopped.

She had only once ever used the safe word before, and that was when she was still a novice. Just as she slipped into unconsciousness again, she heard Sunita's footsteps receding down the hall and the sound of the corbacho being dropped onto a side table.

***

Later, she woke but kept her eyes shut without moving a muscle. She felt no pain. The room was silent except for the slow tick-tock of the grandfather clock in their sleeping room. She kept her eyes shut and tested her senses, reaching out with her mind. She found Sunita looking down at her, sitting cross-legged on their large sleeper. She deliberately let out a sigh, her presence miniscule, indistinct in Sunita's mind. The sigh a signal, Sunita laid a hand on Cochran's cheek and brushed the angular bone that lay there upwards to the hair she had styled just that morning. Cochran sensed the pressure of the regen bag.

She tested her own mind. She was purged of her guilt. Tomorrow, with new and perfect skin, was a new day, a new beginning. She reached out with her hand and took Sunita's lying between her crossed legs.

"Thank you," she whispered and lightly squeezed the hand she held, never opening her eyes as she slipped into the drugged sleep of deep regen.

Fact or Fiction

Being able to watch a sunrise every day is a luxury. I waited in the dark, standing on the deck. Still hurting, but feeling good from the morning's run. Ten kiloms of punishment, the last kilom run in the soft sand.

"Build those legs," Mariko had shouted, jogging backwards in front of me.

Looking out to sea, my legs still felt wobbly and my hand shook as I drank my first cup of coffee for the day.

Mariko had left for New Singapore an hour ago, carrying her newly acquired bicycle over her shoulder and walking up the beach to Abdul's restaurant, where the dirt road joined the beach. From there she rode the fourteen kiloms to Kuantan. Once at Changi she took a Lev up to Topside and biked the remaining sixteen kiloms to UNPOL headquarters.

We had spent the first day of the year reading and discussing Gabriel's information that I had unlocked on my Devstick while offline. When we'd returned to the beach house, the first thing she had done was to go to the kitchen on the ground floor and bring the heat pad up to the second floor. She placed it on a table, and then my folded-out Devstick on another table below it. The twin screens of the Devstick, the keypad and touchpad were all under the heat pad. Mariko explained that this way, infrared sat imaging could not be used – the movements of my hands and the Devscreen would be shielded by the heat signature from the pad.

Yesterday, after my run and after Mariko had left, I had sat down at the unfolded Devstick and started to plan. The root of any good plan is the outcome that you desire. I listed the outcomes I wanted:

- stop the Tag Law
- expose the existence of the Hawks and if possible their members
- justice for my parents, Gabriel and me. Or failing that
- get rid of Sir Thomas
- survive!

It was a daunting list, and I procrastinated in the task of forming plans, thinking instead in pointless speculation about who I was. At least I had a name for myself. Mark Anthony Zumar. The problem was that I knew nothing about him. But if now wasn't the time to spend thinking about that, it did cause me to think of something else.

Why hadn't my DNA matched Gabriel's? It was obvious to me that a DNA search would have been made on Gabriel, and it was obvious to me that we were related, but if we were related as closely as he said we were, then our DNA would have been matched. But it hadn't been. I was reasonably sure that if a search was done on my DNA, it would bear a closer resemblance to Sir Thomas's DNA than Gabriel's. Sir Thomas had fabricated a story around me and had substantiated those first lies with evidence in the online system. My fake DNA, no doubt, was planted along with my fake birth date, thirty-four years ago on the 29th of October, 2075. Gabriel had said that I was born on the 23rd of September, 2075, but Sir Thomas had changed that to the 29th of October, and there were fake medical records showing my birth at the Glasgow Memorial Hospital.

He had planned carefully. So must I. The best plans provide an action related to an issue. The action may well be a tactic to enable the next stage of the plan, or it might be an action that was the entire plan. With the Tag Law, I realized an immediate problem. If I suddenly started researching privacy laws, UNPOL or whoever was watching me would get suspicious. So either I had to find a way to do the research without causing suspicion, or I needed an accomplice. I immediately dismissed the idea of finding someone to help as too messy, with too many dynamics involved. It would be simpler to find a way to investigate the Tag Law without it being suspicious.

Exposing the Hawks and their members was a much more difficult task. To expose them meant getting in, and even then, with their insular behavior, it would be possible to expose only a few. Gabriel had described them as a tree. Roots, branches and leaves. From the original twelve heads, Gabriel had put together a list. Seven identified and eighteen maybes, all people who attended that first meeting. It is from them that the Hawks had grown. Over two hundred years of growth from twelve different roots. How many people is that? Assuming that the first twelve each had two children, and assuming that each of those children had two children – with thirty years between the generations – that was over fifteen hundred people. Allowing for deaths, the number of Hawks could be anywhere from one thousand to three thousand.

Gabriel had used Sir Thomas as the basis for analysis of the founding members tracing back from Francis Oliver, Sir Thomas's father, and through him to identify the first Hawks, or at least some them – the rest were conjecture based on their actions. The more I thought about this, the more impossible I realized it was to actually stop or identify them. If something is impossible, don't try to do it. The next best thing to stopping them was exposure. To make people aware of their existence and how they acted. This was not easy because there are always conspiracy theories, and theorists usually end up in the 'crackpot' category in most people's minds. For exposure to work, the evidence would have to be concrete and compelling.

Next to '- expose the existence of the Hawks and if possible their members' I wrote 'exposure - get concrete compelling evidence'. I ignored the last three things on my planning list. As much as I wanted to see a positive outcome for each of them, they were of secondary importance. Six point three billion people were going to lose their lives in about eighty days. Allowing eight days for the Tags to be delivered to their homes. Stopping that delivery had to be the primary goal.

The most difficult part of my plan was to gain the trust of Sir Thomas and use that trust to gain access to the Hawks. I had an in via his asking me to write his memoirs, but how to go beyond that I hadn't yet worked out. I had to come up with a way to push his buttons, to get him to accept my word as trustworthy and then … And that was it, I didn't really know what was going to happen. And Gabriel's advice in that area was noticeably vague.

I took a sip of my coffee as the sun peeked over the horizon then I turned and went into the house. The sun cast its warmth on my back when I returned to the unfolded Devstick under the table, under the heat pads. I called up Gabriel's file of information and pressed delete. I couldn't keep the information on the Devstick – it was too much of a risk – and anyway, I had what I needed in my head.

I folded the Devstick and pushed the clip over to lock it into its hand-held configuration and thumbed my contacts.

"Call Sir Thomas."

The stored image of Sir Thomas, sitting behind his battleship of a desk, annoyed me, so I flicked over to the global feeds. As the news of the planet filled in, the image was cut by that of Sir Thomas.

"Hello, Uncle. I hope I haven't caught you at a bad time?"

"No, Jonah, it's all right. I was just on my way to UNPOL." I could see the dawn sky of New Singapore bobbing around behind Sir Thomas's head as he walked and talked. He must be walking from his Penthouse to UNPOL across Topside, I thought.

"I saw your speech the other night. I thought that you came across really well. It looked good."

"Thank you, Jonah. And thank you for finding the right words for me as well. I think you may be on to something with this writing idea of yours," he said, smiling into the camera. I smiled back, forcing my eyes to smile as well.

"I was wondering when you would like to get together to discuss your memoir. I obviously don't have anything on yet, and I have some time on my hands so …"

"Yes, of course. Well, the sooner the better, really. Um, I tell you what. I was looking to get a round of golf in today at the UNPOL Officers' Course. Would you be free about, say 4:30pm for nine holes?"

"I haven't been on a golf course in years, Uncle. I'm afraid I won't give you much of a game."

"Nonsense, man, it's like riding a bike and fucking. Once you know how, you never forget!" Sir Thomas laughed loudly in the screen of my Devstick. I couldn't laugh, but somehow I managed a broader grin. My cheeks hurt.

"Right, well, okay then. I'll see you at 4:30, then. Please book a set of rental clubs for me, would you? I sold mine before I came out here."

Sir Thomas nodded, and then the screen reverted back to the global news feeds. No more bombs yet. That was the good news.

"Find me shops selling golf shoes in New Singapore," I said into the Devstick.

***

I strolled down the narrow, white-walled corridor to the entrance of the UNPOL Officers' Golf Course, near to UNPOL Headquarters on Topside. It was 4:25pm. Reaching the end of the corridor, I entered the lobby of the Clubhouse and walked up to the reception.

"Hi, my name's Jonah Oliver. Do you have some golf shoes behind there for me?" I said, smiling at the Indian-looking old man behind the counter. He grunted and reached under the counter, pulling out a cloth bag containing what I guessed were the new Nike golf shoes I'd credded that morning.

"Thanks, oh and, ah, where can I pick up rental clubs?"

He looked to his right. I followed his look. A large sign with white letters carved into dark brown wood said 'Rental Clubs' and had a long white arrow pointing past the reception counter. I gave him another smile. He picked his teeth with a toothpick and continued looking straight ahead to somewhere over my left shoulder.

I followed the direction the sign suggested and came out to a small paved area about a hundred meters away from the first tee. Ten golf bags on three-wheeled Dev caddies were standing around.

"Jonah Oliver," I said, and a Devcaddy with a black bag of newish looking clubs turned, came towards me, and stopped. Its camera rose until it was about the same height.

"Good afternoon, Jonah, I have your clubs ready here in the bag. I understand you're playing the back nine today. Would you like a quick rundown on the tenth and the weather conditions before we get there?"

"Sure, go ahead," I said and sat down on a white stone bench to put on my new golf shoes.

"Wind conditions are good. A slight eight to nine kilo breeze out of the northeast, humidity at a nice sixty-five percent, and the stimpmeter is at seven point five. The tenth is a par four, four hundred and twenty yards long, with two bunkers on the right at about two hundred and fifty yards, and a single small bunker on the left at two hundred yards. Best angle of approach is down the right side of the fairway to catch the slope."

It made me smile to listen to the word 'yards'. You hardly ever heard it anymore, only on a golf course, where golfers stubbornly refused to adopt the global metric system. I stood up and bounced on the soles of my feet to test the shoes. They felt good, a perfect fit, and walked out of the rental area towards the tenth tee, with the Devcaddy trundling along behind me.

Sir Thomas was standing on the green with a driver tucked behind his back and locked inside his elbows as he twisted back and forth. He was wearing a peaked cloth cap, white polo shirt, khaki long outers and white golf shoes. His eyes frowned slightly as he realized that the guy walking on to the tenth tee wearing green baggy surfer shorts and an orange batik shirt with fluorescent green golf shoes was me. I smiled and waved.

"Hello, Uncle. I'll be right there."

Sir Thomas nodded and smiled weakly back. "Good afternoon, Jonah. Taking this beach thing a bit seriously? Did you lose your clothes in the move?"

"No, not all. I just thought I'd bring a little sunshine into the grim, dark world of UNPOL."

"Hah, grim dark world indeed." And saying this, Sir Thomas flipped his tee into the air, spinning it. It landed point first towards him. Somehow I knew it would.

"What do you say, Jonah? Fifty creds a hole, and two hundred on the score? I'll give you two shots on the handicap."

I nodded and smiled, standing up on the tee. Looking down the fairway, I said, "Yes, that sounds all right. Are you still playing off twelve?"

"Yes, yes. Last time I checked." A small grin from my uncle made me think that he might not be telling me the truth, but I let it slide. It wasn't quite true that I hadn't played golf for a long time either. I played a lot of golf on the Dev, just not on a golf course. The world-famous UNPOL Officers' Course was one that I had played a lot. I knew every hole, bunker and green on the thirty-six-hole course, having played it hundreds of time on my Dev in Woodlands. Virtual golf is not the same as real golf, but it comes very close. I was looking forward to this.

Sir Thomas teed off with a respectable drive that faded right and put him on the fairway about two hundred and twenty yards from us. I selected the two wood and took a couple of practice swings, letting the muscle memory come back into my swing. I addressed the ball and swung, driving the ball low and out towards the right of the fairway, landing about ten yards beyond Sir Thomas's ball and rolling to a stop twenty yards farther on.

"Good shot," Sir Thomas said and started walking off up the fairway. Handing my club to the mechanical hand of the Devcaddy, I followed and caught up to him as we passed the ladies' tee.

"So have you had any further thoughts on how you would like this memoir to be constructed? I'm quite excited about the project. Your life has covered a very interesting time in our history, and perhaps I may have the chance to learn more about my parents, too."

Sir Thomas glanced across at me and nodded. "Well, yes, uhm, I think I have told you everything I know about your parents, but certainly there have been many changes in this world of ours these past seventy-five odd years. I think tying it into the big moments and movements that we've seen these past decades since the Great War of 2056 would be an excellent idea."

"You were in Europe during the Great War. Is that correct? I seem to remember you telling me that, or have I just picked that up along the way."

"Yes, I was in Europe. I was very lucky in a way because I was supposed to be in London, and if I had been where I was supposed to be, I would have been incinerated in the two bombs that hit London. Bit of overkill there, one bomb was more than enough. Anyway, I was supposed to join my regiment in London for the regimental dinner, but I got a call from battalion ordering me to replace a lieutenant who had been wounded in a firing range accident the day before. Of course I departed right away and joined the nuclear response command bunker the next day. At noon that day, the war started."

Sir Thomas stopped. We had reached his ball. Hands on hips and looking towards the hole, he said, "Three iron." He struck the ball cleanly, and it flew straight towards the hole, hitting the front edge of the green. But it had too much pace and, reaching the slope that begins in the middle of the green, rolled off into the bunker on the far side.

"Blast!" Sir Thomas exclaimed, and there was a loud thunk as he smacked the club into the Devcaddy's outstretched hand. I walked on without saying anything, thinking about the shot I had to play, and the moves I had to make with Sir Thomas to gain his trust. I was playing it by ear, probing with my questions, looking for an opening. My ball was sitting up nicely.

"How far to the pin?" I asked the Devcaddy.

"One hundred and sixty-two point three five yards to the front edge ..."

I laughed and interrupted, "Hey, what's your name? Sorry, I forgot to ask."

"Name, Jonah? No, I do not have a name. I am a Callaway Devcaddy from the UNPOL Officers' Course."

"All right, look. I'll call you Call, short for Callaway, and from now on, just give me the yards rounded down to the nearest five yards. Okay?"

"Certainly, Jonah. One hundred and sixty yards to the front edge, and the pin is one seventy-five from your current position."

"Seven iron, please, Call." On my practice swing, I saw out of the corner of my eye that Sir Thomas was standing, hands on hips, watching me. I swung and hit cleanly in the sweet spot. The ball soared high and landed just before the front edge of the green. Taking a single bounce, it then rolled to a stop about six feet from the pin.

Call, my new electronic buddy, said, "Good shot, Jonah." Sir Thomas marched off up the fairway, leaning slightly forward and swinging his arms briskly as he went.

At the green, I stood to one side, leaning on my putter, looking at Sir Thomas in the bunker. He swung, but all that came up over the lip of the bunker was sand and, "Blast." I didn't say anything. Another swing and the ball came out, landing on the green and rolling about three feet away from the hole. Normally, in a friendly game of golf, I'd just call that a 'gimme' and let the other player have the shot, but I wanted to get Sir Thomas off-balance.

I said nothing, walked over to my ball, and took a long look at the line of the putt. I dropped it.

"Nice putt," Call said, and I smiled. Call didn't have a mouth, but I am sure he would have smiled if he did. Sir Thomas sunk his three footer, and with a little glare at me as he bent down to pick up his ball, walked to the next tee without saying another word.

Despite the warm air, the silence was frosty and loud. The eleventh was a short par four just two hundred and fifty yards to the hole but with a narrow fairway with water running down both sides and a green surrounded by bunkers.

"Eight iron, please, Call." I cleared my mind and swung, putting the ball about one hundred and fifty down the fairway with a good approach to the green. Sir Thomas stepped up, and using his seven iron, landed his ball close to mine. He looked over at me with a tight grin.

"Good shot, Uncle," I said, and we turned and started walking up the fairway. "So, you were in the command bunker in … where was that actually?"

"Spain. Just outside of Barcelona in a mountain, in a place called Sant Vicen del Horts. I finally arrived, after a SNAFU, at 6pm on the 14th of May. I hadn't arranged accommodation yet as I wasn't sure how long I'd be there, so I just headed to the command bunker and slept there. In the morning we went on full alert and into lockdown. It was a terrible time, and the strain on the men, one in particular, was too much. That strain is now called Holt's Syndrome from that time."

"Halt's Syndrome? How do you spell that? H-A-L-T-S? What is it?"

"No, with an O. That's how you spell it. The extreme stress that comes with knowing that mass destruction is within your power. The man I was talking about cracked under that stress and killed everyone in the bunker except me. I was wounded but was the only other person aside from Holt – that was his name, Keith Holt – with a sidearm. I managed to shoot him before he got me. Terrible thing though. He launched the missile we were in command of. Nothing we could do of course. Flight time was only a few minutes, but he wiped out Bucharest just after the ceasefire was ordered globally."

We reached my ball. I had played for this spot, knowing that this green was bowl shaped with a funnel that would lead you off the bottom left side of it if you played the shot anywhere other than into the top right corner. One of the advantages of virtual golf is that you can take the same shot a hundred times and see exactly where you land on the green.

"Call, give me the sand wedge, please."

Call handed me the sand wedge, and I shook it a little to get the feel of the weight. I took a full swing and follow through, trying for as much backspin as I could get on the ball. I didn't need to see it land to know that it was perfect, and turned to Sir Thomas without looking at the green. He was still watching my shot.

"Wouldn't such an incident cause a blemish on your career?"

"Well, of course there was a court martial, but the evidence against Holt was strong. He had emailed his sister with crazy talk about how he could rule the world from where he was, God of the universe, that sort of thing, and I was completely exonerated." He looked up at me and smiled as he stood over his ball, "Gave me the DSO at the end of the court martial." Sir Thomas swung, and I saw that the line he had taken was wrong. It was a good shot, but he'd be left with at least a fifteen-foot putt.

"Good shot, Sir Thomas. What does DSO stand for?" I asked, and he beamed at me.

"Yes, not bad, eh? Well, let's go take a look, shall we? DSO stands for Distinguished Service Order." He turned to walk up the fairway. I joined him.

"And you were what, twenty-one, twenty-two at this time?"

"Twenty-one. I'd been in the army since one month after my sixteenth birthday, the absolute earliest age that one can join."

We reached the top of the slope at the edge of the green, and I saw that my ball was about four feet from the hole. Sir Thomas's ball was way off to the left of the green with at least a twenty footer. He grunted, and I walked down to mark my ball. I walked to the rear of the green and watched as Sir Thomas made his putt. His ball rolled by the hole by a good five feet, and I waited while he walked up, my arms across my chest, stroking my jaw and looking at the line of my putt. Sir Thomas putted. His ball rolled to within an inch of the cup and then stopped dead. He stayed bent over at the waist, shoving his putter at the hole as if willing the ball to go in, but to no effect. He looked at me, still bent over. I pretended not to notice, stroking my jaw. He straightened up with a glare at me and, stiff-legged, strode to the hole.

"Oh, that's okay. That's a gimme," I said, pretending to notice just before he was about to tap in. He bent down to pick up his ball, giving me an appraising look. I ignored his look and stepped over to my ball, kneeling down to line it up. Sir Thomas walked off the green and onto the small wooden bridge that went down to the twelfth. I sunk the putt. As I crossed the green, I had an idea.

"Call, can you record the game for me?"

Call's oval-shaped head with his camera lens eye turned to face me as I replaced the putter in the bag, taking out the driver at the same time.

"Oh yes, of course, Jonah. That is part of our better golf program. For twenty creds I can also provide you with an analysis of your swing."

"That sounds good, but if you could record everything that would be great. I mean us walking and talking – I'd like a memento of this game with my uncle. Is that possible, and can you upload the record to my Devstick?"

"Yes, I can do that. Shall I use the impression you gave me earlier at the clubhouse for the twenty cred?"

"Yes, use the earlier impression. Now the twelfth is five hundred and sixty yards, right?"

"Yes, Jonah, bunkers at two fifty on the right, water all the way down the left, and the first part of the fairway slopes up to the bunkers. If you can crunch a drive, then you'll catch the back slope and roll down, leaving a safe six iron short of the water before the green." Call said all this with the clubs clattering on his back as he rolled across the wooden bridge. We joined Sir Thomas on the twelfth tee. I walked straight up to the tee and crossed to the right side. Sir Thomas was directly behind me, standing by our Devcaddies. I put my ball on its tee, took two practice swipes and lined up to let one rip.

At the top of my backswing, just as I was about to unleash, Sir Thomas coughed.

I stopped the swing just in time, leaving the driver held high in the air behind my back. I didn't turn around or say anything, but slowly lowered the club to the ground and addressed the ball again. I cleared my mind and swung. I crunched it as Call wanted, easily clearing the bunkers on the right, the ball disappearing over the crest of the slope.

"So you joined the military at sixteen. Before that, what was life like for you? Do you have any material from that time, letters or images?"

"Yes, I do have some things. I will send them to you. I have had everything digitized. Life was difficult, with the death of my parents when I was twelve. I am sure you know what a loss that is to a person. But for you, not so much perhaps, as you never knew your parents. But for me, I lost them when I was twelve, and that was not so easy." Sir Thomas smiled at me, and I thought I could kill him there and then. The thought shocked me, and he saw something in my eyes because he spoke again. "Well, of course, I don't mean it was easy for you, Jonah, losing your parents – of course not. What I mean is that I knew my parents, and therefore I lost what I had known, and that is perhaps more painful."

I recovered myself and smiled at him.

For a man of seventy-five, Sir Thomas was still fit and strong, hitting his drive further than most golfers of thirty-five do, but he still didn't clear the hill.

"Nice drive," I said softly and fell in step with him as, driver in hand, he began to walk up the slightly sloping fairway.

"The military became my family, though, of course, I couldn't join straight away – I was too young. My brother, your father, well, he was busy with the estate and the family businesses, so most of the time I stayed with the cadets. As soon as I could, I joined up. Later of course, UNPOL became my family, but when your father died and the estates and the family businesses all passed to me, that is when I thought of creating the Oliver Foundation."

"Why gifted children only? Why doesn't the Oliver Foundation accept any child who has lost its parents?"

"Well, there's no shortage of care for orphaned children in our world. Indeed, the care given is superb. However, the opportunity for gifted children, or even just children with above average intelligence, to thrive in that environment is extremely limited, with the result that their potential is lost to the world. Over the years, Oliver children have risen to positions of great influence."

"Was the Oliver Foundation started because of the loss of your brother and because you were alone then?"

"Well, I wasn't quite alone, was I? I lost a brother but gained a nephew. But yes, losing my brother was the influence that led to the Oliver Foundation." He suddenly sidestepped towards me and, reaching out, put his arm nearly around my shoulders. He missed because he was quite a bit shorter than me and instead squeezed my elbows awkwardly. I stiffened involuntarily at his touch, and he stumbled away, withdrawing his arm and clearing his throat.

"We must do this more often, Jonah. It is one of the hopes of my having more self-time that I'll be able to spend more time with you."

"Yes, Uncle, we will. This memoir idea of yours is a great way for me to get to know and appreciate the life you have led. I don't believe that I have ever thanked you properly for the life that I have enjoyed, and you must allow me to make that up to you somehow."

He smiled at my words and kept walking. "Of course I will, Jonah, but raising you has been my pleasure. As you know, I had some regrets that you showed no interest in a military career, but you have made me very proud with your success in the legal field."

We walked on in silence for a bit. I glanced behind me to see how close Call was to me.

"Exactly where were you when I was born, Uncle?"

"Huh, let me see. You were born on the 29th of October, 2075. I was in Australia at the time – yes, that's right, official UNPOL business, top secret. But I returned to England the moment I heard the news of your birth."

Sir Thomas hit a good second shot but still had about one hundred sixty to the green. I took a six iron and played safe just short of the water, leaving me with an easy chip shot onto the rolling green.

"Thirty-four years ago and still top secret – that must have been quite some business you were on?"

"Yes, it was. Well, without giving away too much I can say that it had to do with the assassination of Bo Vinh."

"Really! But Bo Vinh died the 1st of January, 2075, and this was more than nine months later, right?"

"Yes, correct, but something came up that provided a lead in the case, and I had to follow that up personally. One of my great regrets, perhaps the greatest, is not finding the coward who killed Bo Vinh. I live in hope that one day we will uncover the truth behind the firing of that anti-tank weapon at Bo Vinh's convertible."

We walked in silence for a little while.

"And this lead, was it significant?"

"No. It turned out to be a dead end."

"I see. So getting back to when you were cleared in the court martial over the annihilation of Bucharest, what did you do next?"

We reached his ball. It wasn't in a good lie. Sir Thomas grunted and looked at the green ahead. An island green connected by a small wooden bridge with low railings and surrounded by a moat twenty yards wide. The sides of the green where they reached the water sloped sharply downhill, and anything landing five feet from the edge would roll into the moat.

Sir Thomas looked at me and grinned, "No guts, no glory, eh," and took out a seven iron. I smiled back at him, thinking how I could probe deeper.

Sir Thomas lined up his shot, and I stood waiting. He swung and hit it, the ball crisply rising up high, then sharply dipping as it passed the wooden bridge and hit the green. He'd hit the ball so cleanly it had lots of backspin on it, and Sir Thomas's proud grin vanished as the ball spun off the green, reached the sharply sloping edge and trickled down into the moat.

"Blast," Sir Thomas shouted and slashed the seven iron into the dirt in front of him.

We walked up another fifty yards to where my ball was lying. I had a short hundred-yard pitch shot – again I had played this shot a hundred times. Nine times out of ten I could shoot a birdie on this hole, with exactly the shots I'd used so far.

"Thanks, Call." I took the sand wedge that Call had already selected from the bag before I'd asked for it and, adopting a wide stance, lined up the shot. I cleared my head, getting ready for some distraction out of Sir Thomas, and took my backswing. Too late to stop this time, as I swung, Sir Thomas's Devcaddy reversed sharply, rattling the clubs in his bag. I was prepared this time and followed through, hitting the ball cleanly and dropping it past the pin by about twelve feet. It bounced once and spun back towards the hole, coming to a rest with a four-foot putt for me to make.

I held my follow-through, sand wedge high across, my right elbow pointed at the flag, and Call's voice rebuked Sir Thomas's Devcaddy. "Devcaddy violation, course rule Fifteen B. One more incident and you cost your player a stroke."

"Damned Devcaddy. Sorry about that, Jonah, must be something wrong with its circuit."

"That's okay, Sir Thomas. No guts, no glory, eh?" I smiled at him.

His apologetic smile froze on his face, and his eyes searched mine for guile, but I held his eyes with an innocent look that I'd had years to perfect. Finally he smiled, sure of my innocence, but suspecting that I might just be making a fool of him. I wanted him unbalanced, not thinking straight.

He dropped a new ball on the ground in front of him, and I waited while he chipped onto the green. He still had a long putt to make. I didn't say anything. When he'd finished his shot, we crossed over the bridge, me following him, and as we walked onto the green, I said, "So after Bucharest, what did you do?" and went and marked my ball.

"Yes, well, as you know, the immediate aftermath of the war was a troubled time. There was a great shake-up in how military forces were organized, and the UK along with most of NATO was deployed to manage the camps. Those were awful times, Jonah. People dying of secondary diseases caused by the fallout. People starving, begging for food. I was sent to the camps outside of Boston, in what was then the United States of America. At the time I must confess that I thought it ironic that a British army lieutenant would be put in charge of a camp in Boston, the birthplace of the American revolt against the British Empire. But it was a small camp, just three thousand people, and Boston was a wasteland."

He took his putt and missed. He was still outside my putt, so I stayed where I was and let him putt again, looking at his ball all the time. He putted and missed again, rolling past the hole by about a foot.

"Pick it up, Uncle," I said and walked over to place my ball on its mark. I cleared my mind. Just as I started my backswing, I heard the sound of Sir Thomas taking off his golf glove, the Velcro ripping loud as he pulled it off. I held the stroke steady and swung through the ball, following it with my putter as it rolled forward and dropped into the center of the cup.

"That's three in a row, Uncle. Would you like to go double or quits on the next hole?"

"Double or quits? Yes, all right. Why not? Your luck can't hold forever."

I laughed, and we walked up to the thirteenth, a short one hundred and thirty yard par three again with an island green.

Call held out the pitching wedge for me as I dropped my ball on the green and nudged it forward with my toe to find a slightly better lie.

I took a nice, steady, slow backswing and swung through the ball, hitting it crisply. The ball arced up and landed on the middle of the green, bouncing twice and stopping right next to the flag. I looked over and smiled at Sir Thomas.

"Just lucky, I guess."

He made a sound somewhere between a snort and a grunt and walked onto the tee. I waited until he'd finished setting up, and then just when he was about to take his backswing, I said, "What do you know about the death of my parents?"

He stood still with the club face at the ball and, not moving, said, "What do you mean?"

"Well, I know that they died in a car accident a month after I was born, but I mean, how did they die? What happened? I'd like to know the details."

His shoulders dropped a little, and he said, "It was a long time ago, Jonah. Those details are just useless bits of information now. Let it go. Your parents loved you. That's what matters. Hold on to that."

As he took his backswing, I let out a long breath loud enough for him to hear. He thinned the shot, sending the ball flying straight off the tee and landing in the water. I set off along the path beside the lake; the same lake that I'd walked past the first day I met Gabriel.

"I think the drop area is on the other side, Uncle."

He didn't say anything, but I heard the thunk as he slammed the club into his Devcaddy's hand.

As we walked along the path, Sir Thomas behind me, I said, "So how long were you in Boston?"

He didn't say anything. When I glanced behind, I saw that he was red-faced and muttering to himself.

We reached the thirteenth green, and Sir Thomas dropped another ball onto the ground. He looked at me with an expression I hadn't seen before, and I thought I knew all of his moods.

"I was there for eighteen months," he said and chipped his ball onto the green.

I walked over to my ball, waiting for him to say that I could pick it up, but he didn't. I walked past my ball and, using one hand, tapped the putter's face to the ball. It dropped in the cup.

Before the fourteenth was a drinks stop. A cylindrical cement block with a counter set into it and a couple of refrigerators behind the woman serving. She smiled as I approached. On the counter were hard-boiled eggs, bananas, and fried chicken legs.

"Chicken leg and a Tiger beer, please." I turned back to see my uncle coming up the path behind me and entering the seating area of the drinks stop. I said, "Uncle, would you like anything?"

"Just a beer, Jonah," he replied, and I held up two fingers as the woman collected the beers from the refrigerator. Sir Thomas took off his peak cap and laid it on the table in front of him, putting his glove and golf ball inside it. The Devcaddies took the path around the back of the drinks stop and trundled over to wait by the fourteenth tee, stopping under the branches of a large flame tree. I looked over at them and could see that Call's lens eye was still turned in the direction of Sir Thomas and me.

I collected the two beers and the chicken leg wrapped in a paper napkin and went to sit at the table where Sir Thomas was mopping his brow. The evening had turned muggy, and looking at the dark clouds gathered to the north somewhere around Changi, I thought we might be in for a thunderstorm later.

"Have you had any success in tracing the terrorists, Uncle? If it's confidential and you can't tell me, I understand …"

Sir Thomas sighed and laid the handkerchief balled up in his fist on the white iron trellis table. "Well, yes, it's confidential, but I know I can trust you. You're practically one of us after all. And the answer is that we have some leads but nothing solid yet."

I took a bite of chicken and washed it down with the ice-cold Tiger beer.

"Have you investigated the Ents who supply the Tags?"

Sir Thomas looked at me sharply and said, "What makes you ask that?"

"Well, they have motive. The Tag contract must be worth billions, and what better way of ensuring that the law gets through the Popvote than creating a little terror. That's, of course, if it survives its final passage through the Supreme Court – which I doubt it will."

"You don't think the Tag Law will make it through the National Supreme Court?"

"I doubt it. There's a ton of precedent case law around privacy, and the whole area of privacy and human rights is strewn with laws that have been formulated but never passed or passed and then immediately repealed. Since Bo Vinh's time, the Supreme Court has always voted on the side of the individual. I am pretty sure, for instance, that Annika Bardsdale will bring a case before the court within the month. Normal strategy is to wait until the last moment before filing, that way you leave the competition with little time to prepare a counter defense, and that would mean delay of the Tag Law, at the least."

Sir Thomas took a long swallow of his beer, looking at me around the bottle; draining it, he put the bottle softly on the table.

"Who's Annika Bardsdale?"

"Oh, Annika's the leader of the Social Responsibility Party. I was listening to her talk about Tag just the other day."

"Do you know her?"

"Not really, just acquaintances, you know, connections of connections, third degree of separation and all that."

"I see. And how do you feel about the Tag Law? Where do you sit?" he asked me, one arm leaning on the table, sitting back in his chair. His face was expressionless.

"Well, if I was asked at a party, I'd say I wanted it. But honestly, because you're my uncle, I'm a hypocrite on the issue. I don't want it for myself, but for the rest of the great unwashed I want it."

"Hah!" he exclaimed, and taking his hand off the table slapped his knee with it. "Great unwashed, hah! You know, Jonah … um, excuse me one moment, I must take this," he said, smiling his tight smile at me. Sir Thomas reached into his bottom khaki outers pocket and pulled out his Devstick, which was making a soft buzzing sound.

"Yes, Oliver here. What is it? I said I was playing golf."

His eyebrows raised, and he smiled that quick little smile of his, the corners of his lips flicking up once. Then his jaw clenched. "I see. When?" My one-sided hearing of the conversation led me to think that another bomb had gone off. A chill went through me as I thought about Mariko. I listened carefully to Sir Thomas. "No, no, that's quite all right. You were correct to notify me. All right then, yes."

He looked right at me, the Devstick held to his ear, his lips compressed. "All right, I'm on my way." Sir Thomas snapped his Devstick shut and smiled at me.

"We will have to finish this game another day, I'm afraid. Duty calls and all that."

I smiled back.

"We'll have to finish this up soon, heh. What, I'm four holes down? Well, I have to push off. I do think that this idea of yours, tying my memoirs to the great events of our time, is a good one. Sort of puts things in perspective."

"Yes, exactly. Your life as seen through the great events of our time. When do you think you will be able to find some more time for us to continue?"

"Soon, Jonah, soon."

Sir Thomas sat back in his chair and looked at me for a moment, then he licked his lips and stood. With a tight smile, he walked to his Devcaddy and, placing his feet on the pads next to the wheels, said, "Take me to the clubhouse."

I pulled out my Devstick, waving it at the Dev on the counter to pay for our drinks. I walked over to where Call was waiting.

"Looks like our game was cancelled, Call."

"Yes. Would you like to finish the round anyway?"

"No, thanks. I think we'll call it a day. You can finish recording now – please upload to my Devstick."

"Yes, Jonah. And congratulations on a great round."

A Hot Summer's
Night Walkabout

Lobby of Travelodge Mirambeena
VacEnv, Darwin, Australia Geographic.
Friday, 3 January 2110, 7:45pm +9.3 UTC

Marty was pissed off. She was pissed off with the heat. She was pissed off with the flies. And most all she was pissed off with waiting in this lobby. It had been her idea to come to the Australia Geographic. Cochran had quickly agreed, which had surprised Marty, and so she had gone on the trail of Mariah. It was a trail that was thirty-four years cold, but it was still a trail.

Not only was she pissed, she was also puzzled. It had taken her exactly five hours to find that a woman, a boy and a baby had taken an EVTour from a station in a place called Coolangatta, at 2am in the morning on the 14th of October, 2075. She'd been lucky with that because that is what had stuck in the mind of the ticket seller. Why was a woman with a very young baby and a young boy traveling at that time of night? That and because she'd asked for any EVTour leaving immediately. At the time, he'd put it down to a broken marriage and no business of his anyway. But it had stuck in his memory, waiting for Marty to find a use for it thirty-four years later.

And that's what puzzled her. If she could find this evidence after so many years had passed, why hadn't Sir Thomas when he'd investigated at the time? Marty thought that Mariah, with the two children, had been smart. She'd avoided the major EVTour stations and walked for a long time and a long way. Reaching Coolangatta, Marty presumed, by walking most of the way along the beach, fifty-five kiloms north of Byron Bay, the EVTour then took her as far as Andergrove about one thousand kiloms farther north. Again she'd been smart, but Marty did what she always did and asked herself the question: If I was Mariah, what would I do? If I was a mother, scared for the life of my children, running from someone who had killed my husband, what would I do?

She tried to put herself into Mariah's mind, a scared woman with a young boy and a newborn. Long EVTour rides give the chance to rest and hide, and I can buy food along the way. I have to feed the boy, Gabriel, and myself for the baby and to stay strong. I have to stay out of sight and use cred chips. Not my Devstick. And I have to get as far away as possible, quickly.

Thinking as Mariah, Marty closed her eyes and felt herself slip into the role of the woman running scared from the murderer. Two choices. Head for the most populated part of the Australian Geographic or the least – the Northern Territories. Go for least cameras. I need to start thinking about how to get out of the Australian Geographic without going through a security zone. Cape York, the northernmost point on the continent and close to the Geographic of Papua New Guinea. No, there's nothing and no one there. I'd stand out too much.

Darwin, sitting between the PNG and the East Timor Geographics is a better choice. And I am a smart woman. I'm tired. I'm stressed. I reach my destination. I'm in Darwin. What do I do? It's 9:30am on the 18th of October, 2075. I'm hot and tired and want to get off the street as fast as possible. The first thing is to walk. Two hundred and fifty meters from where I had disembarked from the EVTour is the Travelodge Mirambeena VacEnv.

It had taken three hours and an UNPOL Blue Notice to get the VacEnv to cooperate in releasing details of staff who had contributed back then, but they had located one who still lived in Darwin. An aboriginal desk clerk by the name of Billy Boy Malangi. He'd agreed to talk with Marty and said he would pick her up at the Mirambeena at 7:30. She'd drunk too much coffee and was about to head back to the Darwin Lev port, when a battered ancient vehicle rolled to a stop opposite the window of the VacEnv's lobby where she had been waiting. A man stepped out of the vehicle, wearing a checked shirt and jeans. His hair and beard were long and totally white, and he held a bushman's hat in his hand. He took a long look at the entrance of the VacEnv and then walked up the stairs and into the lobby.

Marty rose and intercepted the man before he reached the Dev on the check-in counter.

"Mr. Malangi," she said, walking over to him. An EVTour pulled up with a loud hiss of its brakes just outside, and the door opened.

The man's face broke into a huge smile as he saw her.

"Yeah, that's me. UNPOL makes 'em good looking dese days. If I'd known you were a looker, I'd a come sooner."

The automatic doors of the lobby opened and a stream of people barged in, milling around them.

"Come on, missy, Billy Boy'll take you for a ride." Saying this with a wave of his hand, Billy turned around, skirting the edge of the tour group, and went out through the lobby doors. Marty followed and climbed into Billy's ancient vehicle.

"Is this thing safe?"

"Hey now, missy, be nice to Matilda. She's a sensitive old girl," Billy said as he pressed a red button on the dashboard between them. The vehicle's starter motor kicked over and over before finally the engine coughed. Marty had never heard anything like it before and was sure the vehicle wouldn't pass environmental inspection. Billy drove out of the forecourt of the VacEnv and onto Cavenagh street.

"What does this thing run on?"

"Bit of everything, really. Right now, she's running on coconut oil," he said this with a smile, and Marty wasn't sure if he was pulling her leg or telling the truth. She decided she didn't want to know.

"So, Billy, do you mind if I ask you a few questions about the woman and the boy?"

"Not now, okay. I don' like to talk and drive."

Marty nodded, telling herself to be patient and go with the flow. She sat quietly looking out of the window as they drove out of Darwin heading east. Reaching the Arnhem Travway, Billy guided them on to the inside slow lane, and their speed rose as he connected to the maglev track. About half an hour later, Billy pulled off the main Travway and on to a normal tarmac road. They headed north until he turned right, this time onto a dusty track that made Marty close the window she'd opened. About five kiloms down the track, Billy pulled to a stop in front of a small white house, its windows dark in the night. Marty looked at the time on her Devstick, noticing that out here she was offline. 8:10pm. It had been a long day in a string of long days, and it wasn't over yet.

She followed Billy through the iron meshed gate that he unlocked with a key from his chain, and walked up to a porch. "Hang on a mo', I'll get some light on," Billy said, and he disappeared into the house.

Solar lamps lit up the porch, then Billy came out of the house with a bottle of red wine in an ice bucket and two glasses in his hands. He put the ice bucket on a small table set between two rocking chairs made from the branches of dead trees and indicated that Marty should take a seat.

Marty sat down, and Billy, twisting the top off the wine bottle, poured them each a glass. Putting the wine bottle back into the ice bucket, he picked up her glass and gave it to her.

"Thank you."

"No worries, missy," Billy said, taking the seat next to hers. He offered his glass to hers in a toast.

"Now we can talk like civilized humans, eh?" He smiled at her.

She took a sip of the wine. "Mmm, this is delicious. By the way, please call me Marty or Martine if you prefer."

"Glad you like it, Marty. Mob down south sends 'em up for us. We send 'em de bark paintings and the yirdaki."

"What's a yirdaki?"

"You fellas call it a didgeridoo. We call it a yirdaki. Born here it was, Arn'em. Anyways we trade 'em for the wine. Dead euca for live grape – good business, eh?"

"Very good," Marty said, taking another sip of the delicious wine. "So what can you tell me about the woman and the boy?"

"Damn sorry business dat. I did not see nothing."

"That means you saw something, right?"

"Yeah, I works dere maybe for a week or two dat time. Come down from me camp to Darwin and fella at Mirambeena give me a go. Do de desk, Billy, and I done it. And dat Chinaman and Balanda coming next day, tell me dey's check out and pays de cred."

"Sorry, Billy, what's a Balanda?"

"You, youse is a Balanda, a white man or woman."

"Right, okay. So what happened? The woman checked in with the boy and the baby. How long was she there? Did you talk to her?"

"Just to say g'day, you know, how you do? Dey was dere 'bout three day. The next night, the fourth night, dey was gone. I was on early morning shift, three to eleven, you know, and fellas come to me at five. I was sleepin'. Nothing going on about. And then fellas wake me. Say dey come to take the woman and de babe home. Pays the cred and up and left. By 'n by, I checks the room, and that me make think strange."

"What was strange?"

"Room clean as a whistle. Nothing dere. Only cover on de duct off see, lying on de floor."

"But you didn't see the woman or the boy leave?"

"Nah, just de babe. Fella was carrying 'im in 'is arms, when 'e cred the room. Cute little fella, de babe, I mean."

Marty took a long sip of her wine and looked out into the warm dark night.

What Billy had told her was significant. To her it meant that the baby was taken alive and could still be alive. Whoever had the baby or had brought him up, could lead back to the people who had killed Philip Zumar and his wife, Mariah. Mariah had hidden Gabriel in the air-conditioning duct, and he had crawled out of it after whoever came for them had left. Otherwise they'd have replaced the cover on the duct. She'd saved her children at the expense of her own life. A tear rolled down Marty's cheek. She let it roll. For Mariah, she thought.

"Would you be willing to sign a statement about what you've told me and, if required, repeat what you have told me in a court?"

"Yeah, no worries, Marty. Never like bad business. Making wrong right is okay by Billy."

Martine sniffed and, with an embarrassed glance at Billy, smiled. She wasn't pissed off anymore. She and Billy rocked on in silence.

***

The Lev ride up the Australasia Vactube took forty-five minutes to go from Darwin to Changi Lev port. Darwin time being three hours ahead of Asian Time, Marty had left Darwin at 10:35pm and, with the Friday traffic delays in getting a Lev, had arrived back in New Singapore at 8:05pm. Tired, and with the strange feeling of having gone back in time, which traveling on the high-speed Vactubes always left her with, Marty was glad to arrive back in front of her Env.

She glanced at the time on the Dev by her Env door. 8:20pm, Friday the 3rd of January, 2110. The Dev scanned her eye, and she went in, walking across the running track and swiftly to her cabin. What she needed badly now was a clean and a good, long sleep. She entered her room, and the hairs on her neck rose, and she froze. Something was off.

She went into a crouch, reaching into her canvas backpack side pocket. With her left hand she pulled out the black market fight gloves that she'd bought in Pattaya. Still crouching, she turned a full three hundred and sixty degrees and saw nothing out of the ordinary in the room. But something had set her on edge. Her heart was thumping in her chest. She controlled it, forcing a steadiness into her veins. She put the fight gloves on and turned them on, the sleeve of mesh running up and around her arm to her shoulder. The mesh from fingertip to shoulder couldn't be cut, and its power lent a deadly speed and force to any blow commanded by tapping her fingers in their glove tips.

Still in a crouch, she silently stole to the light control Dev in the room. In the bottom drawer of the stand it was on was a night vision helmet. She took that out and put it on. The oiled drawer slid back in its place without a sound. She reached up and killed the master switch. Counting to two with her eyes shut, she opened them to see the fully lit room through the visor of the helmet. She silently walked to the shower room and, reaching out with her hand, pushed a button set into the granite wall of the shower cubicle. The meter-wide shower head descended into the cubicle, stopping ten cents from the floor.

Marty climbed onto the shower head, hooking a long, lithe leg around the steel pole in the rear of the shower head and rising three meters above her. She pressed a green button set into the top of the shower head, and it started to swiftly rise. The noise of the wires running on the rollers to the counterweights was all that could be heard in the warehouse. She came to a stop in the center of the ceiling, nestled among the steel ceiling beams that held the roof of the warehouse.

She looked over the warehouse from her perch high in the rafters. There was nothing out of the ordinary. There was no one here. Lowering herself to the ground, she took the helmet off and said loudly, "Lights." She rolled her shoulders, shaking the adrenalin out of her limbs. Lifting her arms and beginning a springy, bouncy walk, she walked out of the door of her cabin and across to her fight bag. Before she reached it, she tapped out a sequence with her fingers in the fight gloves, and without halting her stride, her fists lashed out, two lightening fast jabs from her left, two fast solid punches from her right, and then she went in with the elbow. The bag swung violently on its hook. The warehouse echoed with the sound of its chain rattling. She stood back from the bag and, taking a deep breath, shut her eyes and turned off the gloves. The mesh uncoiled itself from around her arms, and she shook the gloves off, holding them in her hand as she went back into the cabin.

She walked over to her sleeper and looked at the table beside it. The Devstick that she used to call Mother was gone.

Perfect Timing

Assistant Director Cochran and Director Flederson walked out of the Lev together onto the red carpet that had been laid specially for them. The traditional New Year Board of Governors Dinner at the UNPOL Executive Club on Topside was made special by their inauguration. Flederson was wearing the full dress uniform of an UNPOL director with its single gold star denoting the highest rank achievable by an UNPOL officer. On his hands, white gloves contrasted with the dark blue of the rest of his uniform. Cochran, walking slightly behind him, was dressed similarly – the difference only in the silver star on her cap and epaulettes.

Reaching the entrance, the Devstick in Cochran's hand lit up. Looking at it, she said to Flederson, "Director, I must take this. Please go ahead. I'll be there in just a moment."

Flederson smiled at her and said, "Don't be too long, Sharon, the Board of Governors is not known for patience." He turned, tugged at the bottom of his jacket to straighten it, straightened his back, stuck his chin out, and walked into the club.

Cochran smiled into the Devstick, saying, "Yes, it's happening now – I'm sorry, I've really got to go. The governors are waiting for me." She turned with the Devstick at her ear and looked at the entrance to the club. The guard by the door stood at full attention, practically quivering with tension waiting for her.

"A few hours, but I should be home before midnight. Yes, me too, bye. I'll call you when I'm finished." She looked at the time, 8:30pm, and folded the Devstick to its smallest. She put it into the pocket of her bottom outers. Like Flederson, she straightened her jacket, both hands tugging sharply down, and in the same motion strode forward. She walked through the tall dark mahogany doors and saw the single large round table where the governors and Flederson, with his back to her, sat waiting.

The next thing she knew she was lying face down on the granite floor with a loud ringing coming from one ear, blood dropping onto the floor near her eye.

She twitched her arms and legs to check if she was all there. She couldn't hear anything. She reached up and touched her forehead with her hand. It stung, and when she looked at her hand, the blood spread in the white material of the gloves. She became aware that a pair of boots was in her line of vision and looked up into the face of the guard she had passed moments ago.

He was shouting, but all she could see was his mouth moving. He pulled her by the arm, and she stumbled up into a crouch as he led her back out of the entrance and sat her on the red carpet, her legs splayed out in front of her. She saw that her bottom outers had been blown off and her legs were naked. The guard left her and ran back into the Club. Sitting on the carpet, she wanted to lie down, but resisted the temptation and pulled her legs up under her so that she was kneeling on the carpet. The blood dripped from her forehead as she slumped forward, and she still couldn't hear anything. She knew that a bomb had gone off.

Out of the corner of her eye, she saw the Lev door open and a full team of SOE come out running. The glare of the light above the door hurt her eyes. Two of the SOE team ran to her and crouched down. The rest went running by into the club. The SOE officer was saying something, but still she couldn't hear anything. Watching their lips, she understood what they were asking, and rather than attempting to speak, she took out her Devstick. She quickly unfolded it to be a Devscreen with a keyboard, then she typed, 'I am all right. See to the others inside. Please hurry.'

The SOE team member nearest her took out a bandage from a pouch on their belt and pressed it against Cochran's forehead, wrapping the bandage around. Looking into the helmeted mask that the SOE officer wore, she saw with a shock that it was Mariko. Mariko's eyes smiled at her through the visor of the helmet as she reached into another pouch, pulled out a regen bag and gently placed it over Cochran's head. Supporting her back, Mariko then pushed Cochran's chest softly, laying her down on the carpet.

Cochran let herself go and laid down, keeping her eyes wide open and fixed on the entrance to the club. The Lev door opened again, and a team of regular UNPOL officers ran to the Topside railing. Taking out a crime scene tape, they taped it to the top of the railing and ran backwards towards the club. Medical teams rushed past her, a stamp of feet that she felt rather than heard. Carrying foldable wheeled stretchers on their backs, they disappeared into the club. Two of the medicals stopped and knelt down beside her. One unslung the folded stretcher and turned on the Dev attached to it. The stretcher quickly unfolded and slid itself under her; thin straps closed around her to hold her firmly against the stretcher. Suddenly she was rising and reaching the waist height of the medicals. She twisted her head on the stretcher, watching the door space to the club, but nothing came out. Cochran closed her eyes as the two med staff rushed her into the Lev.

***

Sir Thomas sat in a lounge chair on the balcony of his penthouse, holding a scope to his eyes. He pressed zoom, and the Dev in the scope focused in so that he could see the threads in the bandage on Cochran's head. He felt the Devstick in his inside breast pocket vibrate, but held the zoom on Cochran's face as she lay on the carpet until the clearfilm edge of the stretcher blocked his view, and he set the binoculars onto the low teak table beside him. He took out the vibrating Devstick.

"Yes?"

"Sir, there has been an explosion at the UNPOL Executive Club."

"Casualties?"

"Five dead, two wounded. One of those wounded is in a life-threatening condition, and the other has minor injuries. Sir, it was the –"

"I know. The governors' dinner. Who are the dead?"

"The governors, sir. Director Flederson is seriously wounded, but the med staff say he may make it. It depends on the brain damage, sir."

"I see, and so Assistant Director Cochran has only minor wounds?"

"Yes, sir. They have taken her and Director Flederson to the UNPOL Intensive Care Unit."

"All right. By UNPOL Code 23 A, of the UNPOL Regulations Statute, I will assume command of UNPOL until Director Flederson or Assistant Director Cochran is able. I want UNPOL ICU to be put under the tightest security, no one in or out without my explicit authority. Next, close all security zones in or out of New Singapore. There will be no cross-Geographic travel at this time. Cite UNPOL Code 82. Is that understood?"

"Yes, sir."

"Good. Execute those orders. I will be at the scene in ten minutes."

The UNPOL staffer nodded on the Devstick screen, and Sir Thomas cut the connection. Rising from the lounge chair, he picked up the scope and walked to the edge of the balcony. He raised the scope to his eyes, it quickly zeroing in and steadying against the tremble of his hands as he watched the scene outside the Club. He heard a cough behind him, and he turned, holding the scope to his chest.

"Five dead, Charles, and Flederson and Cochran wounded."

"Yes, Sir Thomas. Is Assistant Director Cochran all right?"

"Yes, only minor wounds, but Flederson is serious, perhaps brain damage. I will be leaving immediately. Please prepare my operations uniform."

"Yes, sir, I will attend to it immediately." Charles, the former maître d' of the UNPOL Executive Club, had retired with Sir Thomas to be his butler. He backed out of the sliding clearfilm doors and walked across the living room and down the hall, decorated with old regimental battle flags, to Sir Thomas's bedroom. There, he opened the large walnut wardrobe opposite to Sir Thomas's sleeper, and selected the operational uniform.

He lifted out the uniform by the hook of its hanger and turned, then he walked with it held away from his body and, smoothing out the back with his arm, laid it gently on the sleeper. He reached forward with both hands and grasped the sanitizer sheet that covered it. With a quick tug, he tore the sealed strip down the middle. Taking the bottom corner, he pulled it out from under the uniform and balled it up in his hand. He walked over to the recycler and there, stooping, put it in. Straightening, he looked at the image on the wall hanging above the recycler. It was of Sir Thomas and him in Boston just after the war. Sir Thomas stood in the doorway. Charles was a dark shadowy image in the background, standing behind Sir Thomas in the hallway of their hut.

He turned back to the suit and looked over it for any wrinkles. Reaching across, he smoothed the dark blue cloth where the breast pockets were, then he stood back and let out a long, soft sigh.

Sir Thomas stepped into the room. Charles turned and walked to a trunk against the wall next to the walnut wardrobe. Pulling the heavy metal clasp upwards, he lifted the lid of the trunk and gently laid it against the wall. Arms spread wide to match the width of the trunk, he reached in and lifted out the top layer fitted out with medals and insignia, and balanced it gently on the chair beside the trunk. Underneath was Sir Thomas's footwear, mostly shoes, but also boots. He took out the operation uniform boots and placed them on the floor. Set into the lid of the trunk was a wire frame and attached to this frame were Sir Thomas's weapons. Guns, explosive devices, knives and assorted hand weapons were clipped to the wire frame.

"Will you be requiring a weapon, sir?"

Sir Thomas paused in his dressing. He skewed his mouth to one side as he thought.

"Yes. That would be good for image. Let them know we mean business." He turned and stared at the lid. He didn't need to turn to know what was in there, but he enjoyed looking at them.

"The Colt 12-mil automatic, I think, with the UNPOL webbing shoulder holster."

"Yes, sir."

Sir Thomas stood in front of the full-length mirror, straightening his dark blue UNPOL tie. Satisfied, he stood ramrod straight, arms by his sides as if a private on a parade ground. He looked his image over head to toe. Then he straightened his Special Operations Executive red beret.

You shouldn't have tried to put your freak spy on me, Flederson. That was a big mistake. He angled the beret down slightly on his forehead. Using Cochran to snuff out the trail the runner had laid to him, and eliminate the entire UNPOL oversight committee in one single act, was a stroke of genius, he thought and smiled to himself. With a smart about-turn, he marched to the door held open by Charles.

The Heliocopter on the roof of The Marque, blades turning, door open, was for him. The two UNPOL staffers standing next to it saluted smartly. Sir Thomas returned the salute and climbed into the belly of the craft. He took out his devstick and started issuing commands. He would be at the scene of the attack in three minutes.

Sir Thomas strode out of the Lev into the forecourt of the UNPOL Executive Club. The Lev's access had been limited to authorized personnel only and the forecourt cordoned off with crime scene red and white striped barriers on the Topside path in front of the club. He paused, hands on hips and looked around. A barrage of flashes hit him from the news people jostling for position behind the barriers and holding their cameras high to get an image. Despite his operational uniform not bearing any badge of rank, they all knew he was director of UNPOL.

He walked over the red carpet, noting the darker patches where Cochran's blood had stained it, and entered the club, his feet crunching on the broken glass and debris on the floor. The room was covered in foam, blood, shards of glass and scattered broken tables and chairs. He looked over to his normal table and saw that it was untouched. A bomb disposal team member walked up to him and saluted.

"It was a shaped charge, sir. Placed behind the curtain in the rear of the room. The governors didn't stand a chance, and by rights, Director Flederson shouldn't be with us."

"Yes. Have you found any evidence, any trace?"

"Nothing yet, sir, but we've only just started. Unfortunately, the fire crew contaminated the area when putting out the secondary fires, but we've identified their trace, and it just means that sorting out the forensics will take a little longer, sir."

"Very good. Carry on."

The BDU officer saluted.

But you will find evidence, thought Sir Thomas. Once you sift through the pieces, something won't fit, and that thing that doesn't fit will do away with the spy who's trying to bring me down.

Sir Thomas walked out of the club and over to the crime scene barriers where the news teams were waiting. They all started shouting and asking questions at once. He held his hands up and patted his hands in the air, signaling for them to quiet down. The noise settled, and Sir Thomas cleared his throat.

"There will be a full news conference at —" he paused and looked at the watch on his wrist, "10pm at the UNPOL press center. Other than that, I have no comments at this time." The news peoples' shouting of questions immediately resumed, but he ignored them and turned and walked back to the Lev port. Entering it, he took out his Devstick and said, "Call the secretary general."

Meet The Press

Filled to standing space only, the press room at UNPOL's headquarters was silent. Sir Thomas and the secretary general of the United Nation, Lin Deng Chui, sat at a raised stage at one end of the room. Behind them were the twin flags of the United Nation and UNPOL. Deng took a sip of water. He could not see any floor from where he was sitting, the room was too packed. The 10pm broadcast out of New Singapore was global. It was 2pm in London, 9am in New York and 1am Saturday in Sydney, and the datafeeds showed almost global attention. Six and a half billion people were watching.

"My fellow humans. It is with great sadness that I address you tonight in my capacity as the secretary general of the United Nation." Deng spoke looking straight out at the crowd in front of him.

"In the wake of this latest attack, I have requested that the acting director of UNPOL, Sir Thomas Oliver, briefs us in UNPOL's progress in putting a stop to this violent madness. We ask this, not in criticism of UNPOL's efforts, let us be clear on that, but rather in pursuit of transparency, and simply because we know that humans everywhere are shocked by these outrages against humanity. I will ask Sir Thomas Oliver to continue."

Sir Thomas adjusted his round rimless glasses and shifted in his seat, leaning slightly forward with a straight back. He cleared his throat, preparing to read the words that Jonah had crafted and sent to him thirty minutes earlier.

"Thank you, Mr Secretary General and my fellow humans. We at UNPOL appreciate your kind words on behalf of our contribution to solving these heinous crimes." Sir Thomas's eyes flicked to the Devscreen on the table beside him as he read the next line in his prepared speech.

"I asked Secretary General Deng for the opportunity to talk with you here tonight because it is time that we share with you what we know about these crimes in order that you can help us to stop this vicious violence. The attacks are related to the coming Tag Law. A powerful, criminal organization called the Hawks is acting now to intimidate us to not go forward with the Tag Law. This

205

flagrant attempt to obstruct the law of the Nation, the law decided by the people, is something that we at UNPOL will not allow. Freedom of choice is the basis of civilized society, and I promise that we will maintain that freedom for you.

"I have spent my life protecting the freedom of the individual, but in that time I and my colleagues in UNPOL have fought a constant foe. That is the criminal gangs that still persist in our society. Operating at the highest levels, on the fringes and within the respected organs of state, these criminal gangs are now desperate with the thought of the coming Tag Law and seek to derail or delay it. The simple reason for this is that the Tag Law will make it impossible for them to continue with their criminal activities.

"I am sorry to say that the institution of UNPOL has also been penetrated by these criminal subversive elements. We have made much progress in identifying the global nature of this gang called the Hawks, and in identifying their leaders and members. Arrests are imminent. My fellow humans, while operations against the Hawks are in process, we must ask that you be ever-vigilant against any suspicious behavior and report such as immediately as you can. These people are desperate now that their criminal empire is in mortal danger, and desperate people do desperate things.

"I have requested of Secretary Deng that UNPOL is provided with the opportunity to attend to our internal problems immediately. To this end, all of Jurong island and the sea around Jurong for a distance of three kiloms will be accessible by UNPOL-authorized personnel only. Travel in and out of New Singapore will be done through UNPOL checkpoints at all entry and exit points. These measures will also be enacted in any and all locations where a terrorist bomb is exploded.

"The secretary general has received the approval of the UN Security Council to take these measures, and these measures have been deemed lawful under the Law of the Nation by the National Court of Justice.

"I would stress that these measures are temporary and will go before a global Popvote within a week or two; however, we ask for your cooperation and understanding of the necessity of these measures in the meantime. Thank you."

UNPOL press relations officer, Stephanie Goodson, walked to the middle of the room in front of the stage and said, "We will take questions now." The room immediately burst into sound with hundreds of voices clamoring for attention. Stephanie, a silver haired and elegantly groomed lady dressed in smart outers but not wearing a uniform, stood silently, her arms by her side until the noise died down. She pointed at a woman sitting in the front row of Biosense and, smiling, said, "Yes, Joan?"

"Joan Johnson, CNNI. Sir Thomas, can you tell us how many of these Hawks are out there, and how long have they been in existence?"

Sir Thomas nodded, his almost bald head shining bright with sweat under the lights in the room, even though the temperature of the room was ambient for all.

"The Hawks originated in the traditional criminal gangs that existed in the early twentieth century and in some cases before that. We believe their number to be in the tens of thousands; however, the leadership is only a couple of thousand at most. They operate in distributed cells so that it is hard to trace one gang of Hawks to another. The leaders are also a cell, and recently we contained one of the ringleaders. It was his escape that provided us with the ability to track down these other ringleaders and once we cut the head off the snake, the body will die."

This comment caused a flurry of hands to go up, but Stephanie calmly picked her choices.

"Andy?"

"Yes. Andy McDowel, GNC. The criminal that escaped from New Singapore, has he been arrested yet?"

Sir Thomas smiled his tight little smile, with his hands clasped together on the table. The smile disappeared, and he said, "I am not at liberty to discuss the current operations against the Hawks, as that would endanger UNPOL personnel in the field. We are making solid progress in the case and have identified a number of individuals that we would like to interview. However, our initial focus will be the elements inside UNPOL that have been obstructing the course of justice. What I can disclose to you is that the criminal who escaped was not called Jibril Muraz. His real name is Gabriel Zumar, and he is a high-level Hawk. As such, he is extremely dangerous and believed to be armed at all times. If you are a member of the public, do not attempt to approach this man but do inform an UNPOL officer as soon as possible without placing yourself at risk."

Stephanie stood up on her toes and pointed to a man at the rear of the room with his hand up waving at her. "Yes, sir. What is your question?"

"Mr Secretary General, I, er, sorry, Malcom Nkose of the New African Centinal. Mr Secretary General, martial law has not been imposed since the post-war food riots. Isn't this response too extreme?"

"No. Martial law will be restricted to any area where a bomb goes off. This

207

is simply to control the movement of people in that area who are performing the acts of terror. Each is a localized incident but orchestrated on a global level, therefore our response is to treat it as such. The measure of martial law is only imposed on a relatively small local area, while our efforts to track and identify the Hawks are global."

"Marjorie?"

"Majorie Hemmings, New Washington Post. Sir Thomas, I gather from your statement that you have subversive elements within UNPOL that are Hawks. Have you identified who these UNPOL staff are?"

Sir Thomas cleared his throat, took a swallow of water, and pulled his chair closer to the table until his stomach was pressed against it. Leaning forward, he spoke. "Again, I am not at liberty to discuss current operations; however, what I can say is that progress is ongoing, and we are confident that with this latest bombing, the forensics will provide us with the final evidence we need to expose the most senior subversive elements."

Stephanie brought her hands together as if in prayer and said, "One last question and we must allow the honorable gentlemen to get back to their contribution. Yes, Steven."

"Steven Haines, GNBC. Sir Thomas, did UNPOL allow Gabriel Zumar to escape so that you could track his movements?"

Sir Thomas glared at the journalist with a blank expression and shook his head from side to side. "No, we did not. Gabriel Zumar is an enterprising and utterly ruthless criminal who will stop at nothing to maintain his freedom in order to continue his criminal activities."

"Sorry, Sir Thomas, one last question. Is Gabriel Zumar any relation to Philip Zumar, Bo Vinh's confidant and friend?"

Sir Thomas lowered his head slightly and shook it softly then, looking across at Deng, turned to face the journalist from GNBC. Sir Thomas brought his clasped hands up from the table and placed them under his chin, looking down at the journalist.

"We believe, sadly, that he is Philip Zumar's son. Our information is that his father was murdered by those criminal elements responsible for Bo Vinh's assassination and that they kidnapped and brought up this Gabriel Zumar in their criminal ways."

Sir Thomas turned in his seat and smiled at Deng. The two men rose together to walk off the stage and through the door that was opened by an UNPOL guard standing at attention beside it.

***

Marty, lying on her sleeper with her arms crossed behind her bed, said, "Devscreen off." She had watched as Sir Thomas had left the room with Deng. She sighed. Tomorrow, perhaps even this morning, the stolen Devstick would be found among the debris in the club, and she would be identified and contained as a Hawk. She looked at the time on the Devstick on the table beside her sleeper. 10:20pm. She had to go rogue. She was bone tired but knew that she had to move. Do it now, or it was over. Move and there's a chance. A slim chance, but a chance.

Her mind went back to the meeting that had led to this moment. Governor Tilling, Flederson and her, just over three months ago, after the seminar 'Enterprise Level Commercial Crime'. Governor Tilling saying that an eyewitness to a murder allegedly committed by Sir Thomas had come forward but there was no evidence. Flederson – 'Mother' – asking her to go undercover and dig for evidence. And now he was in a coma, and Tilling was dead. Sir Thomas had outsmarted them all and acted swiftly and ruthlessly. She was sure of it, but she couldn't prove it. Or was it Cochran? She didn't know, and now was not the time to spend brooding about it.

She puffed her cheeks and blew out her breath, unfolding her hands from behind her head and swinging her legs over the side of the sleeper. She rubbed her face vigorously with her fingers, trying to coax energy out of her body. Fuck it, she thought and reached to the handle of the table drawer beside the sleeper. Pulling it open, she took out a small capsule that looked like a tube of lipstick. She lifted her bum and pulled her bottom outers down, spreading her knees. Taking the capsule in one hand, she pressed one end against her inner thigh. A little green light flashed several times, and she pressed the top of the capsule. Marty hated stimulants, but she just didn't have the energy to run. While she sat waiting for the drug to hit her system, she took a deep breath in and held it. The stimulant hit. She felt it coursing through her veins.

She put the capsule in her pocket and pulled her outers over her bum again. Time to run.

THE NAKED TRUTH

I felt hopelessly out of my depth.

The sun climbing over the horizon seemed to be moving faster than usual, forcing its influence on the colors in front of me. The news over the weekend had shown me that I was outnumbered, outwitted and had little chance of success. The odds were stacked too high. How could I possibly convince people that a man sitting with the secretary general of the United Nation could be a murderer and genocidal?

Although I had crafted Sir Thomas's speech at the UNPOL press conference, Sir Thomas had told me to include the Hawks' name. That puzzled me at first. Why bring them into the spotlight? But then the more I thought about it, the more it made sense. Pre-emptively naming the Hawks as the terrorists was a smart move. Now, if anyone claimed that the real Hawks were a small cadre of highly placed officials in positions of power, the claim would automatically be rejected as propaganda from the terrorists. The opinion polls focusing on the Tag Law told its own story. The number of those for adoption of the Tag had increased to over sixty-five percent. Gabriel's image was everywhere. On every feed and broadcast Devscreen in every city around the globe.

Where are you my brother? I sighed.

"Hey, why so solemn?"

I jumped and spilled my coffee on the railing of the deck. Mariko laughed.

"Sorry, I didn't mean to startle you."

"Yes, you did," I said, smiling back at her and reaching out with my arm, pulling her in close to me. I put my mouth close to her ear. "I don't think we can stop them," I whispered.

Mariko pulled my head down and put her mouth next to my ear. "Let's go for a swim. Bring your Devstick," she whispered.

It was high tide, and the underwater cave entrance would be hidden. I smiled at her and went inside to get my swimmers and the Devstick. When I came back out onto the deck, she was already stroking hard for the point off the headland

210

where the cave was. I ran down the beach, putting the Devstick in a side pocket of my swimmers, running into the surf as far I could before diving in.

The tide was still coming in, and I had to swim hard through a choppy swell. I didn't hurt as much from the running now, and my times had improved every day. I was thankful for the training – if I'd had to swim in this swell a week ago, I would have been exhausted by now. About fifteen meters from the headland, I dived and swum down till my eardrums hurt with the pressure and then aimed for the mouth of the cave. I surfaced in the darkness and swam to the wall with the ledge where we had sat before, reaching out my hand, feeling for it in the dark.

My hand touched Mariko's leg, and I felt her grab my wrist and pull me up onto the ledge. I skirted my bum over and got a firm seat, taking the Devstick out of my pocket. I opened it and folded it out onto the ledge in between us. The light from the screen of the Devstick lit the cave. Mariko was squeezing the water out of her black hair, twisting it into a thick rope that reached to her belly button. She turned to look at me.

I sat back a bit farther on the ledge. All the warmth that she had shown on the deck had gone from her eyes. She looked the same as when she'd come out of my Env in Woodlands that day when we'd left to come to Sisik. I scrambled to think who she could have argued with.

"Mark. You can stop this defeatist bullshit right now."

I started to speak, but she sharply held up the palm of her hand right in front of my nose. "No, not yet. I am going to say this once and once only because we don't have time for another one of these kinds of talks. I called you Mark because that is your real name. That is what your parents named you. Your brother has not been captured, and so far he's run rings around Sir Thomas and his friends. And now he needs your help. Our help. This was never going to be easy, and it was always for high stakes. The minute you opened that file on your Devstick, you accepted this role. Let's run our conversation from this morning in a different way. Let's start with the premise that defeat is not an option. Now what do you have to say?"

I looked at her, feeling pretty low about myself. I looked into her eyes. They held no compromise. There was no easy way out there. I sucked power from those big green eyes of hers. Sucked it in deep. Deep in my belly, down by the base of my spine, the feeling grew. I breathed out heavily and drank in deep the salt air of the cave.

"All right. Defeat is not an option. However, it appears to me that the chance of success in stopping the Tag has been greatly diminished."

"Agreed. Now what are we going to do to counter that?"

"The only thing I can see possible is to somehow figure out a way to block the Tag Law legally, but I haven't come up with anything yet."

"Have you been researching that online?" she spat out with a horrified look on her face.

"Yes, but it's okay. I sort of cleared it with Sir Thomas when we played golf. At least if I get asked why I am researching the law, I can say it is to help him."

Mariko blew out her cheeks. "Sheesh, don't do that to me, please. Tell me more about this game of golf. What happened when you talked about the Tag Law?"

"I can do better than that. I can show you."

"You recorded it?"

"No, Call did."

"Who's Call?"

"Call was the Devcaddy that Sir Thomas rented for me when we played golf. They can record your game so that you can study it later for improvement. I just asked him to keep recording at all times. Here, look." I flipped the screen of the Devstick over so that she wouldn't have to view it upside down.

She watched intently as I talked with Sir Thomas, the two of us sitting at the drinks stand. We were suddenly treated to a close up of the back of the wall of the stand until Call had emerged from the other side and refocused on Sir Thomas and I. The image zoomed in on the two of us, and the sound was clear. Mariko nodded at me, and I hit pause.

"Who's this Annika Bardsdale?"

"I saw her on a newsfeed some time ago. She was arguing, not very successfully, against the Tag Law on a panel discussion."

"So you don't know her at all?"

"No."

"Perhaps you should. How about this for a short-term plan? You get together with your uncle again, as soon as possible, on the memoir. You've planted the seed of Annika Bardsdale so use that. What if you tell him that you're planning to offer your services to her and you wanted to prepare him for the inevitable media fallout that will cause?"

"Why would I do that? I've already told him that I'm for the Tag Law."

"So that you can betray their efforts at the last moment. You show Sir Thomas that you're capable of doing that and he might just invite you into the Hawks."

"Okay, so that gets me next to someone who wants to stop the Tag Law but cannot, and into the Hawks. The only action that I can think of so far to discredit Sir Thomas is to expose myself as Mark Zumar. Suppose I had an independent DNA analysis done and requested, under a court order, that Sir Thomas had the same done, to compare. Even allowing for the fact that might take up to two years to get through the courts. He could easily corrupt the process somehow."

"Yes, but Sir Thomas is an evil man. No matter how clever he might be, that fact pervades and touches everything he does. The fact is that your birth is registered in a hospital and your DNA is registered at that hospital. Gabriel substantiated that."

"But that's all we have. The birth register in Byron Bay shows Mark Anthony Zumar on the 23rd of September, 2075, and then there's Sir Thomas's registering of my birth in Glasgow which shows my birth as being registered on the 29th of October, 2075, thirty-six days later. Then there's my entire upbringing within the auspices of the Oliver Foundation. Wait a minute. That is one possible avenue. The Oliver Foundation. What if I'm not the only one? What if Sir Thomas has killed the parents of other children?"

Mariko pursed her lips together and nodded her head. "Go on."

"The Oliver Foundation was started with me. I mean he founded it the year of my birth and the year of the death of my fictional parents, his brother and stepsister. But it has spread. They are on every continent except the poles and in every major metropolis. What if there are other Jonahs? And what is he really doing with the Oliver Foundation? It's for gifted children only, so doesn't that define them as Hawks, or at least a breeding ground for potential Hawks. Hawks started with families, right? Passing it down from one generation to the next, father to son and daughter. Sir Thomas has no family but he has the Oliver Foundation, right. What if he's using children from there as his branch of the family?"

"Cochran was Oliver Foundation, you know."

"No. I didn't know that. How do you know that?"

"Just SOE gossip. I was talking with a colleague about her being wounded in the bomb, and he mentioned it."

"I could visit the foundation under the guise of doing the memoir. I mean the home where I was raised, it was the first of the orphanages. I could dig around in my birth records and try to identify other ex-Oliverans."

Mariko shook her head. "No, it would take too long, and what if you do identify others like you? You have no way of knowing if they're Hawks or not. Stick with Bardsdale. That seems like the best course of action for now."

It made sense. We were running out of time and to try to convince others without knowing where their loyalties lay was too dangerous. At least if I got close enough to Bardsdale, it could lead me to being more trusted by Sir Thomas and hopefully induction into the Hawks. At least it was a direction to move forward in. I nodded.

"Agreed."

"I'll get closer to Cochran. You know I helped her the night of the bombing?"

I shook my head. I had no idea.

"I was the first team member to get to her. Patched her up. Anyway, I'll also ask her to assign me as your personal bodyguard. In light of the bombing, she might agree."

"Be very careful, okay. She's telepathic. When you're with her, don't think about anything other than what you want her to know. Best would be to think about impressing her and what a brave woman she is. What do you think about that? Was she seriously wounded?"

"No, minor wounds only and the rumor mill has it that a call to her Devstick from her partner Sunita Shido saved her life."

"Do you think that was coincidence?"

"No, not for a sec. I think the whole thing was intricately planned and perfectly timed, but it still takes a special kind of woman to walk into a bomb."

"What about this Martine Shorne, the high-level UNPOL officer who is now on the Most Wanted list right under Gabriel? They're saying she's a high-level subversive and used a booby-trapped Devstick as the bomb?"

"They found her prints on fragments of a Devstick. She's disappeared, and they've charged her with being absent from her post for now. Nothing more than that. She used to work with Flederson. The rumor is that he approved and supported her transfer from Large Commercial Crimes unit into Deep Trace. In there she'd have had access to everything. I suspect we just found out who our allies were."

"You mean Shorne and Flederson?"

"Yes, but they're no use to us now. One's in a coma in deep regen. He's a complete wreck of a human. Lost both legs, burst ear drums, collapsed lungs, ruptured intestines and over fifty fragment wounds. It's amazing he's still alive, but he isn't going anywhere for at least a year. Shorne has gone to ground. No sign. Her team were questioned, and one of my guys was the guard. They haven't got a clue what's going on. Of course, it's possible that she's already dead."

I looked down into the dark of the pool. My reflection shimmered in the water. Mariko's danced and twisted beside mine, the light of the Devstick between us, a wavy shaft of white.

"There's something else that we haven't explored, but I can't think of a way to do it without arousing suspicion."

"What?"

"Bo Vinh and my father had friends. They must have. Some of those friends may still be alive. Sir Thomas couldn't have killed them all."

"Yes, and?"

"Well, we might find support there, that's all. Some of those friends may be in positions of influence and power. Considering the two men, we could say that it is likely that their friends would be their peers and as such share their sentiments. If we could find out who they were, they may be willing to help us."

"Have you started work on it yet?"

"What?"

"The memoir. I mean he's going to ask to see what you've done at some point."

"You're right. No, I haven't, but he hasn't put a timeframe on it yet either."

"Why don't you suggest one – the Tag Law, March the 15th. What more suitable date to gain maximum exposure for his memoirs could there be than that. But if you suggest such an early date, then you'll need to convince him you're making rapid progress. How many words is a memoir?"

"Varies but commonly between eighty and one hundred thousand."

"That's a lot of words to put together in a short time."

"Yes, it is. Moving up the timeframe is a good idea, though. It'll make my immediately poking around his past more acceptable if we're on a tight timeline. Give me more freedom to move. I'll just have to get on with it and start drafting the memoir. Show that to Sir Thomas, and hope he sees the need for me to go and see the first orphanage."

"That's our plan, then. Agreed?"

"Agreed."

Mariko held a clenched fist out in front of me. I put my lips to her fist and kissed it softly.

"Not like that. You're supposed to thump the top of it with your fist. It's what we do in SOE each time before we go into action."

"Oh please, I prefer my way. Yours is just a bit too rah rah for me."

"Rah rah. All right, have it your own way, but out there you're going to need a clenched fist not a soft kiss. Okay?" She fixed me with a stern look made hard by the harsh light and softened by the smile stalking around the corners of her mouth.

"Yes, ma'am."

***

I looked at the time on Devscreen. It was 10:30am. Since coming back from our swim, I'd worked steadily on the outline and had what I thought was a passable concept. As I'd discussed with Sir Thomas, I planned to tie his life into the most significant major global events that had shaped it. Or perhaps that he had shaped? A quick search online of EarthLog, the major online database of factual events, gave me a list of the major events that had occurred in the last seventy-five years. 2035 to the present day. I noticed there was already an entry for the bombing of the UNPOL Executive Club.

Within each of these ten-year periods, I filled in major events. There wasn't much to write about the early years but perhaps that could focus on his parents. He was the second child and born when his mother was in her early forties. His father fifty. The next decade dealt primarily with the war and its aftermath. His court martial, exoneration and later posting to New Boston to manage a refugee camp.

From 2066, we have the rise of One Nation and the global Popvote comes into full existence, TBO transfers from the military to UNPOL. In the early years, he is inducted as a Senior Officer Grade 3, equivalent to his rank of captain in the military. And at the very end of the decade, we have his rise through the ranks and the assassination of Bo Vinh on the 1st of January, 2075.

The latter years were a bit sparse for major events, but I pulled in things like the Australasian Travway and Vactubes being built. These could be tied into greater movement of peoples and the whole 'we are a village' concept that Bo Vinh espoused through his book, One Nation. I could link that back into the present day and Sir Thomas needing to close off the village to protect its inhabitants.

The whole time I was working on this I was also thinking about what kind of alternate history Sir Thomas really had. For instance, in 2075 I knew he had killed my parents, stolen me and formed the Oliver Foundation, but what else had he really done. Was it possible that he was responsible for killing Bo Vinh? Was Bo Vinh's replacement, Ted Hughes, really a puppet of Sir Thomas? Was it possible to manipulate the secretary general of the UN? I sat back in my chair, thinking about that one. Was it possible? Sure everything's possible, but was it likely that Bo Vinh's replacement as secretary general could be manipulated? Possible. Suppose Sir Thomas or other Hawks had incriminating evidence used to blackmail and corrupt him. Anyway, useless to speculate but worth the time to take a look at the lineage of secretary generals since Bo Vinh's time.

I chopped, changed and added to what I had until I was satisfied with it. It looked real. The three hours of effort that I'd put into it was worth it. I picked up my Devstick.

"Get me Sir Thomas, please."

Sir Thomas's image came up. I studied his face for signs of the evil that I knew was there. His eyes were small, his head nearly bald, kept close shaven. Once more it struck me how unlike my uncle I looked. Why hadn't I ever questioned that?

The Devstick said, "I'm sorry, but Sir Thomas is offline at this time. Please send your message to his inbox, and he will get to it in due course."

I went back to the Dev on the table and began to package up more coherently what I had written and collected as the outline for his memoir. If I was going to send it to him, it had to be in a format that would pass inspection. I got into it, and the document was taking shape well when the Devstick on the table buzzed and vibrated nearer to my hand. I picked it up and saw that it was a call from Sir Thomas.

"Jonah, sorry I couldn't take your call. Things are little bit hectic at the moment, what with one thing and another."

"Yes, Uncle, no problem. I was just wondering when we might get together. I've been working away on the outline to your memoir since we played golf, and I'd like you to review it for direction before I go any further."

"Oh yes. I see. Well, all right, uhm, perhaps we could get together this evening. Would that be convenient?"

"Well, actually, I was thinking of taking a trip, and I was hoping to get going today so that I can be back in time for the weekend with Mariko."

"I see. Where are you planning on going?"

"I want to travel to the locations where the major events in your life occurred. I've finished quite a detailed overview of all the significant events tied into a timeline of your life. Beginning with your birth – in fact, going back beyond that to the latter lives of your parents, Sir Humphrey and Lady Oliver – and up to the present day. Perhaps I could just send it to you, and if you feel it's the right direction, I'll start visiting the places I mention in the outline."

"Right. That makes sense. It isn't too long, is it? I'm awfully busy at the moment."

"No, Uncle, it isn't long, and it's pretty straightforward. What you'd expect. The war, the forming of the nation, Bo Vinh's assassination, Oliver Foundation, your rise in UNPOL and then for the last part I want to focus on the Tag Law."

"Yes, that sounds all right. Send it over, and I'll have a look over it."

"I just sent it to you."

"Yes, I've got it. Hold on a moment and let me quickly scan it."

I waited while he read the file that I'd sent him. I could see that he was reading something – his lips were moving. I kept my silence. He turned and looked out of my Devscreen face on again.

"Yes, that seems fine. Good job. I'm looking forward to reading it. That's quite a trip you're planning there, Jonah. London, Paris, New Boston."

"Yes, well, I was hoping that you'd like the outline. I should be back before the weekend."

Sir Thomas smiled at me through the Devscreen. I smiled back.

"Good. Well, safe travels, then."

"There was one other thing I wanted to clear with you?"

"Yes."

"I was thinking about meeting with Annika Bardsdale. It might help. You know, get a feel for the strength of their case."

"Will she meet with you? She must be aware that you are my nephew, and of my support for Tag."

"Well, she knows I'm an arbitrator, and if I pitch it that you and I are not totally in agreement on the Tag Law, then I think she might be intrigued enough to at least meet me."

Sir Thomas leaned back in his Siteazy, his hands folded over his stomach. He looked directly at the camera. I thought I might have pushed it too far. My thoughts scrambled for something to say that would convince him, but he interrupted.

"Yes, that might be useful. But are you sure you want to do that?"

"It's worth a try, isn't it? If they've got something in the wings, she might give it away."

"You feel pretty strongly about this Tag Law, then?"

"I know how important it is to you, and as I told you on the golf course, I'm for it, although I haven't broadcast that fact."

Sir Thomas smiled at my words. I thought I might have overdone it, but he seemed convinced. I smiled back.

"Goodbye, then, Uncle. I'll be in touch as soon as I return."

"Goodbye, Jonah. Safe travels." And his image disappeared from the screen of my Devstick.

***

The Lev to London had been tiring, crowded and noisy, when travelers had joined the Express Lev at the stop in Paris for the last fifteen minutes. The final leg of the trip to London.

Tossing my beach bag on an overstuffed ancient chair next to the large double sleeper, I sat down and thought about the call I had to make. Annika Bardsdale, head of the Social Responsibility Party. Not a major party but still with significant numbers. More of a leverage player in large Popvotes, able to swing their followers' voting to one cause or another and thereby keeping themselves as a fulcrum in politics. They mostly campaigned on green issues and civil rights.

I picked up my Devstick and called the SRP office. The Interactive Voice Receptionist led me smoothly through a list of options, but the one I wanted wasn't there. I could register with them, donate, complain, recommend a cause, join a march, but I couldn't speak to them. I didn't have her direct contact details, so I decided that the only other thing to do was to walk down to her offices. I had hoped that I could call in advance and make the meeting a bit more normal than me just walking in off the street, but it seemed that this was the only option. I clicked through to their site.

I must be tired, I thought. All the pressure from those Lev tubes had squeezed my brain so it wasn't functioning. Right there on the front page was a huge banner suggestion to send a message to Annika: Go Here.

I thumbed Go Here, and with a quick glance in the wall-length glass mirror opposite the sleeper to check my appearance, set my Devstick on the table next to the sleeper and, looking directly into it, said, "Hi, Annika. I am Arbitrator Jonah Oliver – Sir Thomas Bartholomew Oliver's nephew. I am in London on my way to New Boston. I hoped we might have a chance to sit down together and talk. I believe that I may be able to help you with your goal to stop the Tag Law. I'm attaching my contact details with this message. Hope to hear from you. Thanks, Jonah." And with what I hoped was a convincing smile, I reached over and thumbed End Message.

I needed a shower, and I needed some clothes. I spent the next ten minutes ordering clothes and asked for them to be sent to the hotel. Stripping off, I walked through to the outlet and was surprised to find that unlike the building and the room, the outlet was modern, with a sanitizer dryer and shower unit with a mirror running the length of the room. I took out my shaver and got rid of the stubble that had formed over the day. The Dev in the outlet read 11:45am, so 5:30pm in New Singapore. I wasn't that tired, but I was hoping that I could get some sleep before meeting with Annika. If she wanted to meet, I guessed it would be after leaving her contribution, which typically means 6pm. I wouldn't be at my sharpest after going for seventeen hours without sleep. I stepped into the shower, and my Devstick in the room buzzed.

I wrapped a towel around my waist and went back out into the room, feeling a bit cool, the room's temp was set too low. I picked up the Devstick – it was Annika. I thumbed 'show my face only' for the transmission and answered.

"Hello, Annika." I smiled at the beautiful Annika Bardsdale. Prior to becoming involved in politics Annika had been a model and a flick star. To say star is a bit of an understatement, though. She was a mega star, until she quit, saying that the flicks had given her enough of a platform to be of use, and she entered politics. That had been twenty years ago, but she was still an extremely beautiful woman.

"Hello, Jonah. I must say having the nephew of Sir Thomas, my most vocal opponent, call me to say he thinks he can stop the Tag Law was not what I was expecting when I got out of my sleeper this morning."

An image of Annika in her sleeper popped into my head. I was glad I'd said face only, otherwise this conversation could have got very embarrassing.

"Yes, I imagine that would be a surprise. I have to tell you that I have already informed my uncle of my decision in this matter, and while of course he's not happy about it, he accepts it as my personal choice."

"I see. And how do you think you may be able to help?"

"I'd prefer if we talked about that offline, face to face. Would that be possible?"

"Sure, when and where would you like to meet?"

"Whenever's good for you. I can travel anywhere."

"Okay, come over to the offices. You know where they are, right?"

"Yes. What time?"

"About six would be fine. We can meet here and then go get something to eat if you'd like?"

"Sure, that sounds fine. I'll see you at six." I smiled, and she smiled back. Putting the Devstick on the side table, I remembered my promise to Mariko about sexual partners. I fell on the sleeper and shut my eyes. I could shower later.

"Hold all calls, and wake me up at 5:30pm," I said to my Devstick.

Five and half hours of deep sleep had restored my energy. It felt good to be doing something. Anything was better than inaction. Mariko's talk with me in the morning had given me confidence and renewed my faith in our cause. I felt a sharp spike of a 'sense of her' within me. I missed her: thinking how lovely it would be to walk these streets with her, without a care in the world.

The Social Responsibility Party headquarters was in an old brick building on the border of the city where fire and shockwave had not reached. Much of Richmond had survived and had remained largely unchanged over the years, with many buildings being declared national treasures for the architecture and style of a time gone by. I was dressed in a long coat, wearing thick woolen leg outers and a silk top outer with a light woolen outer over that. The colors I had chosen were differing shades of grey. I had a scarf wrapped around my neck, defending it from a temperature that had now dropped to one cel.

I walked up the steps and pressed the intercom. It was 6pm, midnight in New Singapore, but I had slept for a few hours and was rested. I was also hungry and looking forward to having dinner with this beautiful woman. The door buzzed open, and I went in. Annika was waiting in the entrance hall. She looked even more beautiful in person, standing perhaps at one hundred and seventy two cents tall, with dark brown hair sweeping off her high forehead down across her breasts. Her cheekbones were pronounced, and she had the largest blue eyes I've ever seen. She smiled, and her full lips stretched out wide, putting a dimple in her cheeks.

I paused and gave her a polite wai, which she returned, bowing at the same height to indicate that she thought we were equals.

"Come with me," she said, turning. She was wearing a long black dress open at the back in a vee that went to her buttocks. I followed her down a flight of stairs, and we turned left into a room that had a fire. Small windows just at ground level would provide light in the day, but it was dark, and the only light came from the fire.

"Isn't that a bit environmentally unsound," I said, nodding at the fire as she sat down in a large comfy looking Siteazy next to the fire.

"No, the carbon is recycled, as is the material burning. In fact we need a bit more carbon than we're getting in this part of the world."

"Oh, I confess I don't know much about the environment. I sort of assumed that since the raft of green laws most of that battle had been won."

"It has, but there's never a time when we can relax. The Ents are always looking to lower costs, cut corners, and before you know it, you've got a mess on your hands."

"Yes, sure, that I do know."

"Jonah, you don't mind me calling you Jonah, do you? And please do call me Annika."

"No, not all, Annika."

"Good. Could you please lay your Devstick on the table and strip. When you're done, please place your devstick and clothes into the box next to the fire," she said and nodded at a small black box with an open lid to the left of the fire.

"I'm sorry," I said. I wasn't sure I had heard her correctly.

"Please turn your Devstick off and strip. I want to make sure that it is just us having this conversation."

I looked at her for a moment and then took off my scarf and put it on the arm of the Siteazy opposite hers. She was sitting less than a meter away from me. I stripped off the tops outers. The room was warm, but still I got goose bumps. Annika sat with her hand under her chin, watching me with a slight smirk on that wide mouth of hers. I thought to hell with it and undid the catch on the bottom outers, pulling them off one leg at a time, remaining facing her and looking into her eyes. Her expression didn't change except for a slight lift of one eyebrow like she sensed my change in attitude.

I put a thumb into the top of the inners and pulled them to my knees, then stepped out of them with my hands by my sides, standing in front of her, looking into her eyes. She looked right back, smiled and said, "Not bad."

"What about you? How do I know that you're not recording?"

Her eyes flashed and narrowed. "You were the one who asked for the meeting. Not me. And I could have this whole room wired for sound for that matter." Her eyes changed, widening . Then, arching her back in the Siteazy, she said, "However, if it will make you feel better, and in the interests of fair play."

She stood up and with her hand released something on the side of her dress. Grasping it, she pulled it aside to reveal that she was naked underneath. A thin, half-inch strip of dark pubic hair acted like a runway for my eyes landing there, and I quickly lifted them to look across the flat stomach, with what looked like a large diamond nestled in her belly button, and up to her generous but perfectly shaped breasts. She was stunning, and my cock knew it.

She looked down, and I smiled at her. She smiled back.

"I must say that standing naked with Annika Bardsdale was not what I was expecting when I got out of my sleeper this evening," I said with a smile.

She burst out laughing and, still naked, sat back down in the Siteazy, crossing her legs and waving at the opposite Siteazy with her hand. I scooped my clothes and Devstick up and placed them in the box as she'd requested and then sat in the Siteazy and faced her.

"So, Jonah, what do you have in mind?"

"Is this room really safe for a confidential conversation?"

"Yes. It might look old-fashioned – I like it that way – but it has white noise filters surrounding it. Nothing gets in or out."

"Good, because what I am going to tell you could cost us our lives if it becomes known to anyone other than us. I need your help, and while it is about the Tag Law, it is also about me. Before I begin, I feel compelled to offer you the chance not to hear what I have to say. Once I have told it, your life will be in danger."

Annika's face remained calm and expressionless. She regarded me with those huge eyes, but her eyes didn't move. They remained fixed on mine. She suddenly leant forward, her breasts swinging out a little, and placed her elbows on knees – her face a few cents from mine. She said, "After a build-up like that, do you really think that I could not hear what you have to say?" And she smiled. I couldn't see her lips as her eyes were too close to mine, but I saw the set of fine wrinkles around her eyes crinkle up. She sat back in her seat, and her breasts wobbled deliciously on her chest.

I let out a soft sigh. I thought about calling Mariko and asking her permission to fuck Annika, but just as swiftly dismissed that idea. Our first night separated, and I call her to ask if it is okay to fuck one of the hottest women on the planet? No, Mariko, I said in my mind. If our roles were reversed, I couldn't say yes. I don't want to share you with anyone else.

Annika broke into my thoughts of not fucking her.

"Do you want an alky? I find that serious chats always go smoother with a glass of wine in your hand." Saying this, she reached over and picked up a bottle of red wine and poured two glasses, handing me mine. Her breasts swung forward again. Puffy pink nipples.

I switched my glance to her face to find her with that same wry grin she had when I was stripping.

"Do you want to have sex?" she asked softly.

"Yes, but I can't. Or at least if I was going to, I would have to call a woman in New Singapore, where it's midnight now, and I doubt that she'd give me permission. So ... as much as I want to, I can't."

Annika took a big swallow of her wine and, holding it in her closed mouth, ballooned out her cheeks, swirling it around. She turned her head in profile to me, and the cheek facing me ballooned in and out rapidly. She swallowed loudly and dripping her finger back in the glass ran it dripping with red wine down her throat between her breasts and around the diamond in her belly button, coming to rest on that little landing strip.

"Annika, you're killing me. Please stop it. I know I am going to regret this decision for the rest of my life, but I can't change it. Please!"

I wasn't quite begging, but my resolve was crumbling fast. She laughed while she was taking a sip of her wine, and it went down the wrong way. She coughed and spluttered as the wine she had spat out was sizzling in the fireplace. I reached over and gently patted her back. She held up a hand, recovering.

"I'm sorry. I'll be a good girl. It's not nice to tease you like that, even if it is fun. And I seem to have at least one supporter." She nodded at my cock, which was poking straight up.

"No, honestly, you've got two supporters. Even I think I'm idiot, but a promise is a promise."

She reached over and, smiling, patted my leg. "I think I would have enjoyed sex with you very much, but I think also that I am going to enjoy the man even more."

I took her hand in mine and raised it to my lips, kissing it softly, looking it her eyes as I did so and swirling the tip of my tongue ever so slightly on the taut skin of her knuckles.

"Ooh, look, you made the hairs stand up on my arm," she said, chuckling.

I sat back, releasing her hand.

Her face was open and honest, as beautiful inside as out. I knew I could trust this woman. We needed friends for this cause of ours, and I chose to trust her.

"My name is not Jonah James Oliver. My real name is Mark Anthony Zumar. My father and mother were murdered by Sir Thomas just after I was born. I never knew them. My brother, Gabriel, is now the most wanted man on the planet, and he's trying to stop six billion people from being killed. And I need your help."

A Bond is Forged

I had just left San Francisco, a beautiful old city full of charm and a vibrant society. Another city lucky to have escaped the bomb. Nearby in Sacramento, where I had dinner, they were not so fortunate. Everything there had been built in the last thirty years.

The speed of the Lev and the time difference between San Francisco and New Singapore made me feel as if I was in some kind of time machine. After traveling the sixteen and a half thousand kiloms in two hours, the fifteen hours' time difference was what was really throwing me. I had left San Francisco at noon on Thursday and now, as we sped along the coast of Indonesia Geographic, it was 5:15am on Friday. The light inside the Lev never changed. Day or night, it was the same.

After the meeting with Annika in London, I went to Paris and New Boston, and both had been a waste of time. I'd cut both trips short. Instead, I spent more time with the publisher I met in San Francisco.

In San Francisco, the editor for HarperCollins had invited me to his Env in Sacramento for dinner. When I offered him Sir Thomas's memoirs for publication, he jumped at the chance. Strictly speaking, Sir Thomas didn't need a publisher. At his last public appearance, over six billion people had watched him on a datafeed. I could have hired a publicity and production company to get the book out, but I was concerned about how much time I'd have to do that properly. The book would need editing and formatting, and I wanted to include moving as well as static images. So I had decided to go to Harpers. It was slightly out of my remit to do this, but I hadn't made any firm commitments, just dangled the project and gave them a first refusal. We'd talk details about the cred and rights later. They'd assigned an editorial team to the project, and we'd parted company just before lunch on Thursday.

The blinking white dot was rapidly approaching the big red dot. I had to make my mind up. I could change at Changi and head back to Sisik, or I could meet Mariko. I yawned. I was tired and felt like I was still on London time. The

Lev was empty, the air smelt stale. I thought of Annika Bardsdale and guiltily switched my thoughts to Mariko. My Devstick vibrated in my pocket. It was Mariko.

"Where are you?"

"I should be at Changi in about three minutes."

"Great. Come straight home. I've taken self-time today."

"Good, I'll see you soon."

She smiled at me and cut the connection. I was looking forward to telling her how I had resisted sleeping with one of the biggest flick stars ever.

***

Gabriel read what he had typed one more time.

Earth, 10 January 2110

My Fellow Humans,

It is with great humility that I write this letter to you. I am asking you to get involved in stopping what is currently happening. I ask this not for my sake, but for humanity's sake. I had hoped to provide you with hard evidence relating to the crimes of Sir Thomas Bartholomew Oliver; however, recent events require that I act now to tell you what I know. Because I have yet to find the hard evidence that would prove guilt beyond doubt, I am asking merely for your time to consider that what Sir Thomas is telling you may not be true.

I understand fully that many of you will read this letter and ignore it as a plea from a wanted 'crazy' man, which is how it will be portrayed by those that wish me dead or worse. Be assured it is not. I am safe and perfectly sane. Ignore the contents of this letter at your peril. No one can find me without my wishing them to, so consider: how do I benefit from telling you this? I benefit only if you believe what I say and take immediate action to demand our government acts with transparency and in our true interest.

When I was nine years old, in November of 2074, I shared a dinner with Bo Vinh and my father, Philip Zumar. At that dinner, Bo Vinh told my father that he had discovered evidence of a secret society called the Hawks. He told my father that the Hawks were increasingly frustrated at the equality that was being achieved on

227

Earth and that they planned something to change that equality. Just over a month later, on the 1st of January, 2075, Bo Vinh was assassinated.

My father spent the rest of his short life trying to find evidence of who had murdered his friend. Before he could disclose his evidence, he was killed for learning it. Shortly after that, so was my stepmother. On the 26th of October, 2075, I watched as Sir Thomas stabbed my stepmother, Mariah Claire Oliver, in the stomach and thrust a dagger into her heart, killing her. I was witness to this event, and that is why I am being persecuted.

There is a conspiracy and a secret society called the Hawks. Some of their members are criminals, but some of their members, like Sir Thomas, are also in positions of high legal authority. The bombings that have been happening are not my work, nor is it the work of anyone I know. What has been broadcast about a gang of criminals called the Hawks is pure fabrication by Sir Thomas Oliver. Sir Thomas and his nephew, Jonah James Oliver, represent the worst that humanity can be. Selfish, ruthless and without morals, they prey on the weak, and corrupt all that they touch. If they cannot corrupt, they exterminate.

The tragedy of what has happened in my life could happen to you. It is what happens when those in power are corrupt and when there is no higher power to hold that corruption in check.

In the interests of transparency and for the sake of humanity, we must

- suspend Sir Thomas from duty, and
- ask for a full disclosure and investigation into Sir Thomas's actions since the bombings began.

Use your voice. Ask.

Your Fellow Human,

Gabriel Alexander Zumar

He pressed submit. The code left his Dev and traveled to the Sydney Stock Exchange as a buy order on the Ent Broken Hills Mining. Two seconds later, a broker picked it up, accepted the price offered by the bank in Kinshasa, Gabriel's front for the order. Gabriel confirmed the buy, completing the transaction. The code was now buried in the broker's contacts list on his Dev. As soon as the broker contacted someone on his list, the code would go with the contact. Within five minutes, the code would be untraceable, and within an hour, at 10:25am Sydney time, those who had it on their Devs would send out Gabriel's letter to everyone in their contact lists.

Gabriel swiveled his Siteazy to face the sea. He had purchased this land when he returned to Australia in his early thirties. Aboriginal money and contacts had made it possible for him to build an identity that he had been living for the past sixteen years in plain sight and yet out of sight. The sea and his yacht gave him access to travel without passing through security zones, and he seldom visited cities.

When he needed to travel, he went under fake identities and had accumulated hundreds of those over the years. But now his image was broadcast everywhere so he remained at home. The reclusive owner of Vanishing Point Vineyards. Gabriele Esposito, never interviewed, never appeared in public, but produced the famous Pinot Noir of Vanishing Point, South Australia. The organically managed vineyard grew fifty tonnes of grapes a year and sold all of its wine before the growing season had ended.

Gabriel stood up and walked out to the large deck that faced the sea, leaning on the railing. The letter was a risk, he knew, but they were running out of time. He would have preferred to wait until he had solid evidence against Sir Thomas, but he couldn't wait. It was out there somewhere, of that he was certain, but Sir Thomas was a wily old survivor who would stop at nothing to gain his ends. The announcement after the last bombing, the maiming and taking out of action his only contacts within UNPOL had meant that time had run out. The killing of the Board of Governors had removed any of the governance that might have held Sir Thomas back. Given the free hand he now had, as verified by Secretary General Deng's appearance with him, Sir Thomas was too close to gaining total control and forcing the Tag.

Yes, it was a risk. But it was a calculated risk. He'd been thinking about it for a week, and now the time had come to act. If nothing else, the bombing might stop – but even that was a long shot. What was more important was to get the message out so that the billions of bloggers and members of online communities could begin to focus on Sir Thomas.

When it did, he reckoned Sir Thomas would come up with more lies about criminal gangs, perhaps even with evidence that he would fabricate. But then Gabriel would respond with another letter.

The one piece of evidence that Gabriel had, he couldn't use yet. That evidence was Jonah James Oliver, who existed as a result of Sir Thomas's actions in Darwin. He had deliberately left Mark out of the letter. It would have been his brother's death warrant if he spilled that Mark was Jonah. No. Better let that one play out. There was still time. Sir Thomas might play safe and kill Jonah. That was a very real risk. But if he thought that Gabriel remained ignorant of who Jonah was, then Mark would survive and be in a better position to gain the trust of Sir Thomas.

At the crucial moment, they could reveal that Mark was Jonah. Prove it beyond doubt with a DNA test. His DNA and Mark's would match, proving they were brothers. With this irrefutable evidence, Sir Thomas could be brought down. But that wasn't enough. Even with Sir Thomas out of the picture, there was still a risk that the Tag Law could be voted in. That was the biggest risk of them all.

Gabriel looked at the time and picked up the imaging scope. He pointed it at the horizon opposite the house and waited for his yacht to appear. The swell crashing into the shore told the story of the weather out in the Bass Strait. They'd be flying with this wind, he thought. A sail appeared on the horizon. He zoomed in the scope. It was them, and they were flying. His yacht, the main hull out of the water and with its wings extended. The scope detailed the plume of water rising from the twin wings where they touched the water. It was doing at least eighty kilos.

Leaving the scope hanging on the railing, he walked to the path that led to the beach. The deck of his house was two hundred meters above sea level, and as he descended the steep path to the beach, he knew the yacht was fifty kiloms away, approaching fast. Ten minutes later, he stepped onto the white sand of the beach, warm in the morning's sun. He couldn't see the yacht now, as it had dropped below his horizon, and he walked out to where the surf rolled in to the shore. Shielding his eyes from the glare of the sun to the east, he faced south and waited for it to reappear.

The wind tore at his white cotton outers. The surf was high, perhaps two meter swells, and a few surfers were out testing their skills on the waves. The yacht's high mast and distinctive sail came into view, and within minutes, it had rounded up into the wind on his mooring. The mooring was three hundred meters off the beach. He saw the crew of two climbing into the dinghy slung underneath the wings and releasing into the sea. It turned and pointed its lifted

A Bond is Forged

nose to the right of him, and he waved. The crew waved back, and the inflatable dinghy paused its run to catch a wave and then came in fast, powering through the surf. The roar of the throttle reached him through the wind.

He walked down into the surf to catch the dinghy's nose, and the crew of two jumped out into the surf. The three of them pulled the dinghy until it was out of the reach of the sea and then laid it down in the sand. Panting with the effort, Gabriel looked across at Martine Shorne and said, "I missed you, too." He turned to Maloo and stepped to him, giving him a bear hug and lifting him off the ground. He said, "Great job, brother. Thanks for getting her out."

"Ah, no worries, mate. It was a piece of cake."

With his left arm around Maloo, he held his right arm out, and Marty came under it. Hugging her close, he kissed her temple and said, "Come on. Let's go up to the house. We've got a lot to talk about."

Showered and with a white towel wrapped around her head and a gold sarong wrapped around her body, Marty walked into the large living room. Gabriel, who was sitting on a large white cloth sofa, rose to greet her. The walls were decorated with a bark paintings and other aboriginal art. A huge yirdaki hung on the wall nearest Gabriel. It made Marty think of her conversation with Billy.

Folded out on low wooden table in front of the sofa was Gabriel's Devstick. Next to that stood a bottle of wine and two glasses. He gestured at it with his hand.

"Will you join me in a glass?"

"It's a bit early, isn't it?"

"Well, my internal clock is a little out of whack. I've been working nights and sleeping days. So for me, this is around about when I normally have dinner and then head off to sleep."

An uneasy silence settled. The brief but wild romance that they shared when they had met was now a memory trying to find a foothold in the present. It had been a little over three months since their two days of bliss in Tahiti, and Marty wondered if he still felt the same.

Gabriel smiled a little and walked across the room, holding out both hands palm upwards. She took his hands, and he pulled her close into him as she wrapped her arms around his back. Gabriel, a head taller than her, placed his hand on her neck and pulled her head into his neck.

He whispered, "I've missed you every day since we parted. I know this is

231

difficult being here with me like this, but there's no pressure. If your feelings towards me have changed, I will understand."

She turned her head and, reaching up with her hands, pulled his head down to kiss him. She finally broke the long kiss and leaned back to look at him. "I feel the same. I didn't want to leave you in Tahiti, and if I'd been there on my own accord, I wouldn't have. But I was there because Flederson sent me to meet you, and I had to report back."

"I know. We each have our duty. Speaking of which, come and have a look at this, and tell me what you think."

"Sure, and I'll have a glass of that wine, too. I've been awake since midnight. That yacht of yours is something else. We topped a hundred kilos per hour coming into the Bass Strait with that southerly behind us. It kept us busy, but that water ballast system, which Maloo told me you put in, works great."

"Yes, she's a beauty – but nothing compared to you."

"Compliments and wine in the morning – are you trying to get me drunk?" she said playfully, taking his hand and being led over to the sofa. Gabriel looked at the time on the Devstick. 10:14am. He turned the folded-out Devstick toward her and gestured at the letter on the screen.

"In one minute this is going to be all over the planet." Her blue eyes flicked back and forth as she read Gabriel's letter. Finished reading, she reached over for the glass of wine that Gabriel had poured for her. Her eyes flicked to the bottle.

"I shared a bottle of this with a very interesting man in Darwin recently," she said and gestured with her hand at the bark paintings and the yirdaki on the walls around the room. "You wouldn't happen to know him, by any chance?"

"Billy. Yes, he told me about your visit. I'm sorry we couldn't get you there earlier. I wasn't, and I am not playing you. Okay? I agreed with Flederson, before I met you, that I would provide you with the reason to do your own investigation. And that I wouldn't interfere with the collection of evidence. That was the trade off. He wanted me to come in and testify. I didn't think I'd survive that. I was sure Sir Thomas would see me dead a long time before I got to any kind of a court. About a month before I let myself get arrested in Bangkok, Flederson contacted me and told me that you weren't making any progress. I got the sense that he was getting impatient, so I acted. I didn't know that Sir Thomas would react so swiftly in shutting you down. I thought you'd have time to follow the evidence and build a case, but he moved too fast."

"How is Flederson? Do you know?"

"Well, the news reports say he's undergoing regen and still in a coma. From what I can gather, he's under twenty-four-hour guard in UNPOL ICU. You can bet that the guard is made up of Sir Thomas's people and that Flederson, if he comes out of his coma, will be in serious danger. What I haven't been able to figure out is how Sir Thomas found out about Flederson and you."

"He might not have found out. Cochran was passed over for the director's role by the Board of Governors. It was probably her."

"But she was injured in the explosion. Two or three days in regen, and apparently only narrowly missed losing an eye."

"Her wounds were minor. She timed it perfectly, I think, and I know she's crazy enough to do it. Think about it. What better defense can there be than being present and wounded when the bomb went off. No one will believe that she's insanely clever enough to walk into a bomb. She kills five people, cripples Flederson, gets rid of me – who she hates – and gets the top job in UNPOL. There was only one time when she could do that without having to go after them individually, and that was at that dinner."

She tilted the wine glass at the letter on the screen. "What are you hoping to achieve?"

"I'm hoping it'll get Jonah in. He's our best and perhaps only chance at stopping this." Gabriel sat cross-legged, facing her with his arm along the back of the sofa, a wine glass in his hand and the other hand resting on his ankle. "To expose Tag now is too big a risk. We don't have any solid evidence. We don't even know how the toxin will be hidden, and it has to be hidden, doesn't it?"

"We talked about it. Flederson and I, I mean. Flederson believed your story about your mother's murder and you being a witness. But then you sent the message about the Tag being poisoned and that you thought it was going to be used to kill sixty-five percent or more of the population. You started us on the trail of Sir Thomas for killing your stepmother and father but to then claim that Tag was his plot to, well, take over the world, was a stretch for us both. You've got to understand that Flederson is a thorough, calm, logical policeman. He doesn't make leaps of faith, that's why initially I was surprised at his request. When he asked me to go undercover and find out what I could of Sir Thomas's operation, I thought it was part of an internal audit. But then when he explained your story to me, I was surprised because I had never seen him make that kind of decision, purely based on trust, before. But after I met you in Papeete, I understood. But he wasn't convinced of the Tag being a device to commit mass genocide."

Gabriel looked grim at her words. "And you? What do you think?"

"At first I leaned more towards his way of thinking, but then, after your escape, the bombings started, and I believed you. It fit. It made sense. Flederson still wasn't convinced, but he had swung sharply away from being certain and urged me to get down to Darwin and begin the investigation as fast as possible. I had to wait a reasonable time to make it look like we discovered the evidence about you through process, and I was about to file my report when Flederson and Tilling were blown up. It's hard to believe it is a coincidence."

"What?"

"The bombing of Flederson and Tilling. I keep trying to convince myself that it was Cochran, but it could just as easily have been Sir Thomas. Maybe I'm letting my dislike for her cloud my judgment."

"Maybe. But whether coincidence or not, the end result is the same. We've lost our support in UNPOL, and we're at the top of UNPOL's most wanted list."

Marty placed her glass on the table and. taking his glass from his hand, put it beside hers. Turning to face him, she crawled up onto the sofa and brought her legs under her, kneeling in between his legs. She started to unbutton his shirt.

"Right now you're on top of my most wanted list."

He laughed out loud and reached for the knot that held the sarong in place. A single tug and the knot unraveled, the sarong slipping down her body. He leaned forward and took one of her nipples in his mouth, his hand squeezing her perky uplifted breast softly. She moaned from deep in her throat. Easing her back down on the sofa, he pulled the sarong down her long, toned legs, then ran both hands up the inside of her legs from her calves until he came to her inner thighs. He licked at her opening and ran his tongue through the wetness that had pooled there. A taste better and rarer than any wine filled his mouth, and he flicked his tongue up and around her clit. Her hands clawed in his hair, pulling him closer. He shifted his nose to one side so that he could still breathe and –

"Hey, Gabe, I … Oh, sorry."

Gabriel looked up from between Marty's legs at Maloo, who smiled and, with a raise of his eyebrows and a thumbs-up, backed out of the room. Gabriel looked at Marty over her smooth-shaven pussy to see her reaction. She was smiling. He started chuckling, and she joined in.

"I'm sorry. I forgot to lock the door."

"Don't be. It isn't me with my arse stuck up in the air and my face covered in juice."

His head went back, and he laughed out loud, crawling up the sofa to stretch out beside her his face level with hers. She kissed him and smacked her lips. "Hmm, yummy," she said and smiled.

***

We lay on the bed, Mariko's left hand playing with my spent cock, her head resting on my stomach. I was twirling a strand of her hair around my finger.

"I had a chance to have sex with Annika Bardsdale while I was in London."

She lifted her head from my stomach and looked at me with a frown. "And?"

I grinned at her, proud of what I was about to say. "And nothing. I turned her down because of our promise to each other."

She smiled. "You're crazy. You had a chance to have sex with perhaps the most beautiful woman in the world and you turned her down because of me? You didn't even call to check if I'd mind?"

"It was midnight. I didn't think you'd appreciate it if I woke you up and asked if I could sleep with another woman on the first night that we were parted."

"If it had been evening, would you have called?" She still had a smile on her lips, but I felt like I was walking on ice – very thin ice. I thought honesty was the best way to go.

"No."

"So how did this happen?"

"She asked me to strip so that she could see I wasn't wearing any kind of recording device, and then, well, one thing led to another."

"You're crazy. I'd have called," she said with a broad grin on her face.

"Really? You mean if you were with, say, Anthony Gibson, you'd have called at midnight and asked me if you could have sex with him?"

She laid her head back down. "I'm not sure. I might have called."

Our Devsticks started buzzing and vibrating at the same time. 'There's been another bomb,' went through my mind. I reached over behind me and picked up the two Devsticks from the side table and handed Mariko hers. I looked at the time, 7:30am. My message inbox showed thirty-four messages. Since leaving my contribution, I usually got about four or five a day. I'd just received thirty-four in five minutes, and they were still coming in. The small screen of the folded Devstick didn't give me enough information. I quickly unsnapped the Devstick and folded it out to its full configuration of keyboard, screen and touchpad. Scanning the inbox list, it seemed that everyone who knew me was messaging me. And then my heart stopped, and I looked at the name. Gabriel Zumar. I sat

235

back from the Devstick, pulling my hands off the keyboard, my pulse racing.

Mariko, sitting cross-legged on the sleeper, spun her Devstick to face me. Her inbox was the same, even more messages and there, one from Gabriel Zumar. She opened the message and read aloud, "Subject: A Letter from a fellow human." When she finished reading, she looked at me, her lips pursed together. She shook her head slowly from side to side and put a finger to her lips.

"Let's have a shower and go for a walk along the beach," she said softy, slightly nodding her head. Rising, she held out her hand. The number of messages in her inbox was now over one hundred and twenty, and mine over fifty-five.

A Hawk For Life

On the table between us sat a crystal bottle of one-hundred-and-fifty-five-year-old Macallan Lalique Scotch whisky. It was half empty. The remainder was in our stomachs. We sat side by side, looking out over the Topside of New Singapore. The evening was warm and humid. Dark clouds moved level with our view as we sat. Each of us silent with our own thoughts. I picked up the whisky and took another sip. I was not really a whisky drinker, but Sir Thomas was an aficionado and had told me the rare whisky cost one hundred and twenty thousand cred. I calculated that I had thirty thousand creds' worth rolling around in my stomach. But I focused, fighting not to let the whisky take control of my senses. I had to stay sharp.

We had dined together at the now refurbished UNPOL Executive Club. Sir Thomas had eaten there every night since it had been blown up. In defiance of the terrorists, the newsfeeds reported. I had spent a lot of time with Sir Thomas these last few weeks. I'd defended his name, as he had mine, against the crazy, libelous, terroristic. Annika Bardsdale had come out in support of me and announced my decision to work with her and the Social Responsibility Party in stopping the Tag Law. Sir Thomas had used my appointment as Annika's arbitrator as further proof of his tolerance for difference of opinion and opposition to his view.

Over dinner, in public, we had discussed his memoir. I had fleshed it out since that first draft outline, and it now had some meat on its bones. Another fifteen thousand words or so and it'd be ready for sending to Harpers.

Sir Thomas had agreed to go with Harpers as publishers, and we'd signed a deal with them for a single book to be released on 15 March 2010, the day of the Tag Law Popvote.

It was hard writing the memoir because my heart wasn't in it. I struggled to get a flow. I had sent the first few chapters to Harper's editor, and it came back covered in red changes. They obviously didn't think much of my writing, and if it had been anything less than Sir Thomas's memoirs, I doubt that they'd have kept me on as the ghostwriter. I told Sir Thomas that the writing was my gift to him, that the memoir would be published under his name.

Initially he had protested. "Nonsense, boy. You have to take the credit." But after just a little persuasion, he accepted.

Gabriel's letter was dismissed as the desperate ramblings of a wanted man. Slurring two of society's finest individuals, Gabriel had found little sympathy with his fellow humans. Sir Thomas pointed to the evidence of how he tried to help Gabriel's mother before she committed suicide and that this had deranged the boy who became an insane driven man. It had also drawn us closer together, in Sir Thomas's eyes.

I was surprised at some of the vitriol that came forth as a result of the newsfeeds' interest in me, digging up people I could hardly remember from my student days. These old classmates delivered stinging character slurs. More news portraits were drawn by opponents in court cases, especially from my early days, painting me as arrogant and ruthless. I realized this was Gabriel at work. Supporting me with Sir Thomas, making it appear as if I were 'a chip off the old block' as he often said lately.

I had gotten into a routine. Up at 4:30am. Fifteen minutes for dressing, stretching and warming up. Then the ten kilom run on the beach. Mariko running beside me. She'd been assigned as my bodyguard, after I asked Sir Thomas if he could arrange it. We ran to Kampung Bugis and back. We had the run down to forty-nine minutes, which on the sand was a fast time. After the cool down, we'd have a swim and sometimes a chat in the cave to catch up on our plans. Then I'd have a coffee and, by 6:30am, get to work writing. I wrote solidly until noon. A light lunch of fish and vegetables and I'd go back and edit what I'd written, taking as my examples the chapters heavily revised by Harper's editor. By 4pm, I'd be done editing, and we'd go to a spot we had worn clear in the jungle and spar. Gloves and headgear on, I was still no match for Mariko as we shadow-fought. Getting as close as we could to hitting one another without actually making contact. It taught control, timing and focus.

An hour of sparring and we'd return. Shower and have dinner. Then at 6:30pm, I would sit down and turn to the legal case, sometimes writing until midnight. Most nights I stopped before 11pm and got some sleep. I broke the routine, three days in seven, going down to New Singapore with Mariko discreetly armed and by my side. She would leave me alone with Sir Thomas while he recounted his past to me. How much was fiction and how much was truth I had no idea and no way to know. It didn't matter. The point was to make him trust me. To bond.

The dinner tonight had been his idea. When we'd finished, he had taken my elbow in his bony hand and steered me away from the Lev port and back across Topside to his penthouse. His bodyguards in front and Mariko trailing us, we came up to his penthouse to 'have a drink and a chat'. Charles had let us in.

The bodyguards and Mariko stayed in the living room while Sir Thomas grabbed the whisky and two heavy lead crystal glasses and led me out onto the balcony.

We sat in darkness, the lights from the city providing enough light to see our shapes but not much else.

He sighed a long, drawn out sigh.

"This has been a messy business getting the Tag Law in place. What have you learned from Bardsdale?"

"She's planning on using the Rape Law to prevent the Tag Law. The Rape Law states no person may be violated without their permission. It's possible to argue that the injection qualifies as a violation of one's body."

"Whose idea was this?"

"Mine."

"And is it a solid case?"

"Yes, it is. There are actually some precedents, which I have shown Annika, that support the position."

"I see, and —"

"And it's solid, but not watertight," I said and smiled a low grin at him.

He smiled back. "Go on."

"The precedents I chose were all individual against individual or corporation, i.e., a private entity against another private entity. And if that were the case, then they would hold up. The problem with the position is that this is not a private entity. It is the will of the people and therefore cannot constitute violation of an individual because an individual is the people."

Sir Thomas chuckled and took a belt of his whisky, looking at me over the rim of the glass. He glanced inside the living room of his penthouse to see if the guards and Mariko were still sitting in the same place, then he leant closer to me.

"How are you going to disengage from her and the party?"

"I'll have a change of heart just before the final presentations of the differing sides of the argument. That should be on March 14. Without me, they'll use their party arbitrator, and your lawyer can tear him to shreds."

He chuckled and poured us each another shot. Then he launched into a soft-voiced rambling discourse, intermittently pouring us double, then triple shots from the bottle, talking about the Tag Law and the control it would bring. From the Tag Law somehow he segued into Darwin and the natural law of selection. Leaning back in his lounge chair and saying softly, almost a whisper, "Technology has betrayed Darwin's natural law. Nature needs help."

His words sent a shiver through me in the warm night air. And then he fell silent, and we sat side by side, the half-empty bottle of Macallan's between us. I waited, alert, but feigning a sluggish drowsiness.

His voice came out of the darkness. I had to strain to hear what he was saying.

"It took me a long time to be sure that you were ready, but this work you've done for me, with Bardsdale, tells me you are. Are you ready, Jonah?"

Clearing my throat heavily and sitting up slowly in the lounge chair, I said, "Ready for what, Uncle?"

"Are you ready for power, Jonah. Pure power. The power of life and death. The power to change people's lives. The power to do anything you want. Are you ready for that?"

I turned my head slowly to look at him. I smelt his excitement, and I could see, in the shadow outline, a tremor in his jowls. His eyes caught a glint of the light from the living room, giving them a yellowish glow. The hatred I felt for him put an edge in my voice. I hissed a sharp, cold-voiced, urgent, "Yes, I'm ready."

"Are you sure? I have had my doubts in the past, but lately you've shown me a side of you that I hadn't appreciated. Perhaps because I wasn't paying close enough attention. But now I feel you've become the man I wanted you to be. You're like me in so many ways, but you are your own man, and you'll make your own destiny. This is no trivial matter. If you are ready, truly ready, and remember what I said about the power of life and death, then tell me so. But think hard before you answer because there is no turning back. If you say yes, you will be asked to take a test of loyalty to me, to us, and failure to pass that test is death. You say yes and then you are one of us for life."

"Who is us?"

"Are you ready? Life and death, Jonah. Are you capable of that kind of decision? Are you sure you are ready?"

I felt spittle hit my hand as he spoke, and used the darkness to hide wiping the back of my hand on my outer leggings. I sat silent, my brain hurtling at maniacal speed with the thought that this was it. This was the moment we'd been working towards since my trip to the Moon. He was asking me to join the Hawks.

Using my hatred for him, I said in an even, soft voice, "Yes, I am capable of a life or death decision. I am sure I am ready. I was trained for this moment, wasn't I? You trained me. All those special schools, the exercise and mental regimes I went through. This is my destiny, is it not?"

"It is, Jonah. It is, and it gives me great pleasure to hear your words. 'Us' is the Hawks, Jonah. Not everything in that runner's letter was a lie. The Hawks are very real, and I am a very senior Hawk. Now that I have told you this simple truth, you will die a Hawk. There is no going back now."

A quiet panic spread through me as his words sunk in. Survival was never a priority, but his words squashed that hope with the finality and certainty of their tone. 'You will die a Hawk.'

He stood up, supporting himself on my armrest as he rose. He said, "Wait here. I have a gift for you." And he walked around me down the length of the balcony, past the living room, and stopped at the large windows of his sleeping room, tapping softly on the clearfilm windows. Someone, I guessed Charles, opened the door from within, and he stepped out of sight.

I dared not show any reaction. My mind was racing. I sat up straighter, then I reached down and picked up my glass of whisky, taking a long swallow.

Sir Thomas came back out onto the balcony, his silhouette blocking the blood red light of the SingCom sign behind him. He walked over and knelt by the side of my lounge chair, obscuring the view of those inside the living room. I turned to face him. I could smell the whisky on his breath. I could see a bubble of spittle on his lip.

"Here, take this. You're going to need it," his voice rasped, and he slid something out of his sleeve. Holding the armrest of my chair and feeling for my arm, he slipped his hand down until he felt mine and placed there something cold and heavy. He pushed my hand away until it was in my lap. He took out his Devstick and used the glow from its screen to show me the dagger in its scabbard.

It was about thirty-six cents long with a silver chain hanging from the cross guard. An SS sign and an Eagle with its wings spread were inset into the handle. I was shocked that I was holding something from that evil time. The shadows cast from the light of his Devstick made him look ghoulish as he reached over and, taking the dagger by its handle, slowly withdrew the blade from its scabbard. There were German words written on it. 'Meine Ehre heisst Treue.'

"What does it mean?" I whispered.

He cleared his throat and spat into a plant pot next to my chair, groaning as he stood up, with one hand supporting his back. "'My Honor is Loyalty.' On the reverse side it says, 'With Cordial Comradeship from Heinrich Himmler.' He was a German officer and leader of the SS before and during the Second World War. I was born on the same date – the 7th of October – as him. Over a hundred years apart, of course, but I have always admired his strength of purpose. His ideas were extremely advanced for his time. He gave 200 of these daggers to the men who helped him achieve his masterplan. A plan that began with a night called, 'The Night of the Long Knives.'"

He walked around me and sat back down in the lounge chair next to mine. The thought came to me that he made no sound when he walked. The dagger felt heavy in my hands. Another thought arrived. I felt it come from the dagger. This was the dagger that killed my mother. I was sure of it. I pulled the blade fully out of its scabbard and looked across in the dark at the outline of Sir Thomas. After a moment, I pushed the dagger back into its scabbard and reached for the whisky on the table. Taking a huge swallow, feeling the burn of it down my throat, I slowed my breathing and my thoughts. I could hear him breathing next to me. Another surge of hot hatred came. I took another swallow of the whisky.

The crystal glass suddenly shattered in my hand. I had squeezed too tight. The top half had collapsed into the bottom, and I felt blood seeping from my hand. Sir Thomas didn't seem to have noticed. I put my broken glass back on the table, with a thump.

"Oh, damn. Sorry, I've just broken your glass."

"Don't worry about that. Get yourself another from the cabinet. We have things that we have to talk about urgently."

I got up from the chair and, putting the dagger on it, crossed to the sliding doors. Opening the clearfilm doors to the living room, I went inside. A single lamp near the door lit the room in a soft yellow light. Mariko, still in UNPOL uniform, didn't say anything but looked questioningly at my hand. I shook my head softly with a glance to the bodyguards, who watched me when I came in, and then professionally looked away.

I got a new glass from the cabinet and, wrapping a tissue around the bleeding wound, went back out to the balcony. Sir Thomas hadn't moved. His dark shape stared forward, his back hard up against the chair, arms on the armrests, the glint of a glass in his left hand. I picked up the dagger as I sat down, placing it back in my lap, then I twisted over to take the top off the whisky bottle and poured myself another shot. The little walk had done me good – I was back in control and focused again. The alcohol and my emotions had got the better of me. For a while back there, I had come close, too close, to plunging the dagger into his chest. The whisky sat like a smoldering fire in my belly, waiting for the winds of my emotions to fan it. Be cool, Jonah. Stay cool, stay calm, learn and think.

"Jonah," Sir Thomas hissed.

I jumped in my seat, startled. "Yes, Uncle."

"I want you to do something for me. It is a test of your loyalty to me and to us as Hawks. Will you do it?"

"Yes. What is it you want me to do?"

"I want you," his voice changed, and he turned and leaned very close, putting his mouth next to my ear, almost a lover's kiss, "to kill someone for me."

I sat dead still. His words running through my brain. I felt stone-cold sober. I cleared my throat, to be sure that there wasn't a quaver in my voice, and didn't turn to face him.

"Who is it that you want me to kill?" As I said this, my brain was running through the list of people it could be. For a panicked sec I thought he might order me to kill Mariko in the living room. I sucked in air sharply. If he did that, I'd kill him, and we'd just have to take our chances with the bodyguards and Charles.

"Someone. Anyone. It doesn't matter. What matters is the commitment. Kill and bring me evidence of your kill. Then I'll believe that you can make life or death decisions. The greatest generals all cared for their men, and didn't hesitate to spend them to attain their goals. This is no different."

I exhaled slowly. We've already committed a crime together, I thought. This. Talking like this is conspiracy to murder. Enough to have both of us put in containment for years. I have to kill someone. Or I will die.

"When?"

"Within two weeks. You have until Friday week. Do it. Don't get caught, and don't tell anyone what you are going to do. Especially not her." He tilted his head and rolled his eyes in the direction of the living room. "If we decide later to bring her in, she'll have to go through the same test of loyalty. But until then.

243

Not a word."

A test of loyalty or a tool for blackmail? I thought.

Sir Thomas continued with the same breathy quality to his voice: sexy in a woman, scary coming from the mouth of a seventy-five-year-old lunatic. "Events are moving fast. I need you to get through the test and join me. I want you to be by my side as these events unfold. He paused and leaned closer; reaching out with his hand, he turned my face to his. He's going to kiss me, I thought, shrinking back in the seat. But instead he spoke softly, his sweaty hand tenderly cupping my cheek. "If you can't do this thing for me, then this will be our last two weeks on Earth together." His eyelids lowered, and he squinted through them, looking directly into mine.

"What do I get when I do this?" I said, staring at him hard.

He smiled. "When you do this thing for me, I promise you power like you could never imagine."

He patted my cheek lightly before standing up with a grunt. I looked up at him, my hands folded in my lap over the dagger. My sight impaired by a stray hair falling down over my eyes. I reached up and swept the hair out of the way, not taking my eyes off him. The reason for the two bodyguards became clear as I saw him shake his head slightly while facing the clearfilm windows of the living room. If I had refused, I had no doubt my death would have been a dual suicide with Mariko, off Sir Thomas's balcony. Or perhaps a staged crash on the Travway. Either way, we wouldn't have survived the night.

He seemed smaller in the dark, and his shoulders were slumped. He turned sharply almost as if on a parade ground. And then stopped and turned to me. "You better hide that," he said, nodding at the dagger. I rose from the seat and slipped the dagger into the back of my bottom outers and lifted my jacket over it. I rolled my shoulders and shook my hands. He looked me up and down and then sniffed in loudly and tugged at his jacket. Straightening, his shoulders square and with his chest puffed out, he chuckled and clasped my arm.

"Come on. Let's sally forth, eh?" he said, chuckling again as he opened the door and walked inside. The guards and Mariko came to attention sharply when Sir Thomas and I entered the room.

"At ease. At ease everyone. Relax. No need to be formal. It's late, and we've all had a long day. Mark ..." I jumped at hearing the name, but realized he was talking to one of his bodyguards, "... please escort Jonah and Operative Mariko to their vehicle."

"Sir!" The bodyguard, who I now knew was called Mark, saluted Sir Thomas and went to the door. He opened it, stepped outside, and closed it after himself. I turned to Mariko and smiled. She didn't smile back but stood with her legs apart and her hands behind her back in an informal 'at ease' position.

"Shall we?" I said and held out my hand to her. She smiled at me then and, ignoring my hand, walked towards the door. Sir Thomas put his arm out in front of her and clasped her arm as she passed him. Taking her hand in his, he brought it to his lips and said, "My dear, I do apologize for being such a terrible host this evening, but in my defense, Jonah and I had some very serious matters to discuss. I look forward to having the opportunity to address my failure as a host in short order."

Mariko smiled at him and left her hand in his. "Oh, please don't apologize, Sir Thomas. I think it's wonderful how you and Jonah get on so well."

Sir Thomas patted her hand and released it, smiling at her. His eyes were puffy and bloodshot in the rimless round glasses. I crossed to Mariko and put my hand in the small of her back as we walked to the door. She put a hand out behind her to hold me back and pulled the door swiftly open, stepping through, her head moving from side to side. I saw through the gap of the door that Mark stood in the foyer next to the Lev port. The Lev door was open, and a soft chiming noise came from it.

Mark left us only when we had climbed into our Titan, and Mariko had given him the thumbs-up from the cockpit. I had bought the Titan in the week after Gabriel's letter, worried about Mariko traveling on Levs. I slumped in the co-pilot's Siteazy, too tired to even think about driving. Mariko took over, and I looked out of the window at the world going by. Soon we were clear of the city and traveling up the Intracoastal Travway towards Sisik, still about two hundred and sixty kiloms away, according to the Dev on the console.

Mariko was driving fast as we passed long-haulers transporting goods north to the markets of the Thai and China Geographics. My thoughts swayed from 'how do I get out of this?' to 'how do I choose who to kill?'

"Can you pull over?" I said with some urgency.

Mariko glanced at me, her focus on the Travway, and suddenly my weight shifted sharply right as she swung through five lanes of traffic and took the off-ramp, rapidly decelerating. About two hundred meters farther down the road from the off-ramp, she pulled over at the side of the road. I went down the stairs, opened the door, and got out into the cool night air. Here, without the heat of the city, the air was about twenty-three cel. I breathed in deeply, the hum of wheels on the Travway loud in the still night. My feet crunched the gravel on the side of the road. The jungle was dark in front of me.

Who to kill?

The heat in my stomach boiled up and a surge of liquid rose in my chest. I fought it, but my brain took a dive like an out of control Lev heading down into blackness. The heat surged again, and I threw up. The dinner and about sixty thousand creds' worth of whisky lay on the gravel in front of me. Some of the puke had splashed on my footwear. My stomach heaved again as my stomach muscles twisted and squeezed everything out.

I felt a hand on my back. Mariko. I was bent over, my hands on my knees. I breathed in deeply, my brain swooshed again, but I felt better and breathed deeply again and again. I straightened up and tilted my head back. Big mistake. My brain did the swooshing thing, and I stumbled, losing my balance. Mariko caught me, and I found my feet. Gazing up at her, I smiled weakly.

"You okay?" she said with an even look.

I breathed heavily, puffing my cheeks out as I expelled the air in my lungs. My mouth tasted foul.

"Yeah, I'm fine. It's just the rest of me that's alked."

She laughed at the look of chagrin on my face. "This is the second time I've had to carry you home. I don't want you making a habit of this, Jonah." Her teasing smile laid false the rebuke, and I took her arm as we walked around to the door of the Titan.

"Come on, let's get back home, get you cleaned up and into the sleeper."

***

I woke up to the sound of my Devstick beeping at me and the light of the sun streaming through the windows. My brain felt like it was too big for my skull. I pushed the heels of both hands against my temples to try and force it back in, but it didn't work. Mariko stood by the sleeper with a container of something orange and green in her hand. It looked like the vomit on the roadside.

"What's that?" I said between clenched teeth.

"Does it matter? Just drink it!"

I reached out for the horrible-looking drink and, staring at it down my nose, hesitated. The Devstick's beeping was getting louder.

"Just drink, and you better answer that. It's from Annika Bardsdale. It's the fifth time she's called you."

I drank. It didn't taste too bad, a bit earthy, and I really didn't want to know what was in it. Well, not now anyway, but it went down okay and most importantly stayed down. I sat with my arms around my knees and the sheet pulled up to my waist.

"Hi, Annika."

"Jonah, I've been trying to get hold of you for hours. Have you just woken up?"

"Yes, sorry, Annika. Had a bit of a late night last night and a few too many alkys. Anyway, what's the urgency?"

"You haven't heard, then?"

"No. Haven't heard what?"

"As a result of the bombings, they've moved the Popvote day for Tag up."

"Why? The bombings were a few weeks ago. Why didn't they move the date forward, then?"

"No. There were new bombings yesterday. Geneva, New Berlin, London, Houston, Sao Paulo. All within an hour of each other."

"Oh shit. I went to sleep at about one in the morning New Singapore time. When did all this happen. Many dead?"

"It started in Geneva, about 7pm European time, and by 8pm all of the cities had been hit. Over two hundred and fifty dead and over a thousand wounded."

"What date?"

"Feb 15th, Friday week. The General Assembly voted yesterday at 4:30 in urgent session, and in view of the bombings, they moved it forward."

"What percentage was for?"

"Nearly eighty percent. How's the case going? Will you be ready in time?"

"I'll have to be, won't I? Okay. Let me catch up with the news. Have a think, and then I'll get back to you with a plan, all right? We may need to meet. What's your schedule like early next week?"

"It's a mess. There's a climate conference that I have to be at till Wednesday. After that, I'm booked to speak in Melbourne on GMD."

"What's GMD?"

"Global Mother's Day, Jonah. You should know that. Oh ... sorry. That was stupid of me."

"It's okay. Forget it. I do know it, just never heard it called GMD before. Where's the conference being held?"

"That's the thing. It's being held in New Zealand Geographic. No Levs there yet. Takes four hours just to fly there from Australia. No sub orbs either. They're very protective of their ozone down there."

"Well. Okay. Where's this GMD speech you're doing?"

"Melbourne, Thursday evening. And then I'm on a sub orb back to London."

"All right. How about we meet in Melbourne after your speech? Will that work?"

"Sure, that would be okay, but it means we lose three, nearly four days."

"I'll need at least that much to sort out a response anyway. What we've got now is just case history and a law. I've still got to construct the argument."

"Okay. Thursday evening, Melbourne. It's a date."

"Bye, Annika. See you Thursday."

The concoction that Mariko had given me really had made me feel better. My headache was gone, and my stomach didn't feel as if someone had been beating on it all night. And then I remembered. How could I forget? I had to kill someone. The reality of the thought consumed everything I'd been thinking and squashed them with its weight. I had no idea where to begin to even think about how to do it. Selecting someone to kill seemed worse than killing, but then again, I didn't have to do that yet. But I did have to choose someone. Who to kill to become a Hawk?

"Come on. We haven't had any exercise. Let's go for a swim around the headland," Mariko said, stripping off her bottom outers. Even the sight of her naked didn't change the thought. I climbed out of the sleeper and went to get my swimmers. I walked out to the deck and down to the beach and realized that I had forgotten the Devstick. After I went back and got it and returned to the deck, Mariko was gone. I couldn't see her in the water, but then, she'd probably already reached the cave.

I jogged down the beach a little to reduce the distance I'd have to swim. Then I cut in to the edge of the surf and dived in. The water felt good, cool and alive against my skin. Pulling against it, I made up for missing the run this morning and went for it, striking hard, hands cupped to get maximum pull. Dipping my body through the larger waves, I was at the headland and took a dive. Going deep, using the breathing technique Mariko had taught me, I aimed for the cave, swimming along the bottom of the ocean three meters deep and pulling strong for the opening of the cave. I was through the entrance, and my world went black.

The sound of my breathing echoed with the slop slosh of the water in the cave. I swam to our ledge and felt. Nothing. I reached along the ledge further and further until I came to the wall. Nothing.

"Mariko!" I shouted, although it didn't matter. All I got was my echo. My heart raced, and my breathing was more like fast sips of air as I pulled myself up onto the ledge and fumbled for the Devstick in my pocket. Don't drop it – slow down, I told myself. Finally I got it open, and the weak white light from its screen washed into the cave. What I knew became true. She wasn't here.

I dropped off the ledge, taking a deep breath as I went, and hit the water with my knees tucked under me, diving immediately for the entrance. As soon as I was through, I came up and swam as fast as I could back around the headland to where I could see the beach. Hope and panic. Oh no. Oh no. These were the thoughts that came the strongest.

I stopped and scanned the beach. Far down toward Abdul's restaurant there was a person, but it was a man. A fisherman by the look of his outers.

I swam. The Devstick a hindrance, I dropped it. I had two more back at the house, and now I just swam as fast as I could thinking, It'll be all right. She changed her mind. We passed each other swimming. While my logical brain dismissed my hope with ease: you would've seen her. No, I ran down the beach. I cheated. I've never done that before. You still would have seen her. No! Suddenly my hands were scraping sand. I lurched to my feet, lost my balance, and hit the water again.

I got up and started running for the house, powering through the powdery white sand. I hit the deck running and shouting, "Mariko, Mariko." I went inside and said, "Mariko," in a slightly softer voice. I went down the stairs to the ground floor, but she wasn't there. I went out the door facing the jungle, and only the Titan was there.

I ran back around the side of the house and out onto the beach again. I stopped. Footprints in sand are easy to spot, and usually the only footprints on the beach in front of the house were ours, and usually they were made with bare feet. These were footprints made with a boot of some kind. Thick zigzag tread evenly spaced down to the heel. I followed them. It looked like there were two people, maybe three, but it was hard to tell as in some places they were scuffed and hard to see clearly; the sand was deep and soft. They led to the deck of our house.

My heart racing, I searched for other signs, but there were none. That was it. I looked down the beach and walked out of the line of the jungle to see more clearly. It was empty. I turned back to the house, walking and then running. Back up to the steps through the open doors. It was the same as I'd left it moments ago. No. No. No. Think. Do not panic. Think. Call Sir Thomas. I went to the sleeper side table and grabbed the Devstick that was lying there. Turning it on and thumbing for contacts. 10:35am.

"Get me Sir Thomas!"

The Devstick's screen changed to the image of Sir Thomas sitting by his desk, and I noticed that I had a message from him received at 10:31am. While waiting for him to pick up, I opened the message.

Jonah,

Good morning. Hope you're feeling all right after all that whisky we consumed last night. I'm off traveling on official business for a few days. Attached you'll find a file with images and archive footage of me when I was younger. Please discuss with Harpers whether they can handle the new launch date. I expect they'll need at least a week to take care of things, but at least they can get the packing done in advance. Good luck with getting the memoir finished – at least you won't have any distractions to tempt you away from your duty. Mariko sends her love, says she's fine and will see you as soon as you've done what you have to do.

My Honour is my Loyalty.

Your Uncle,

TBO

Cancel request.

I sat on the sleeper. Oh fuck. What have I done?

Just When I Needed You Most

It took an hour and fifteen minutes to go from Sisik to Melbourne with stops at Changi, Darwin and Sydney on the way. I'd booked a direct Lev, and I was lucky as all the seats were taken. I felt strange that normal life was going on around me. People were traveling to their contributions, taking vacs, and just doing what people do. I moved among them with my relentless thoughts and acted normal while my life was in chaos.

I'd achieved what I had set out to achieve. I was in the Hawks, but Sir Thomas had outsmarted me or at least upped the stakes. I didn't know if he was setting me up, or if he just wanted insurance, but either way, he had outplayed me. In the time that Mariko had been gone, I had tried to keep my routine. I needed to be strong to get her back, and so I ran where we had run and ate what we had eaten. I was strong. I was a wreck. I had no choice.

If before I had been playing a high-level game, Sir Thomas taking Mariko had just made it very personal and very real. Until then, it was all talk. Even what Gabriel had told me hadn't really sunk in. I suppose it was too long ago and somewhat removed from me. It was almost as if I had an evil image of Sir Thomas that hadn't meshed with my reality of him. But now the image and the reality had become one, and I understood just what an evil sick fuck he really was. I also knew now that I was capable of killing. He had taught me that.

I hadn't been stopped yet, so I could only assume he hadn't put Mariko through Truth Treatment or had Cochran probe her mind. I wondered about that. It could be that he had put Mariko through Truth Treatment and was having me followed to see who else I could lead him to.

I wanted more than ever to get in touch with Gabriel. I was sure that I was under very tight surveillance, tagged, and my every move analyzed. I wasn't one hundred percent sure that Sir Thomas didn't already know of my association with Gabriel, and that my killing someone was just his way of getting rid of me, but it didn't really matter. If I sent any strange messages anywhere, I was sure they would be traced. So that ruled out getting in touch with Gabriel.

For the past five and half days, I'd written practically non-stop and slept four hours a day. This morning I'd fired off the memoir manuscript to Harpers with instructions that they had to get it together for February the 15th no matter what. I copied Sir Thomas on the message and told them that I was traveling and would be unavailable. I'd done what I could, but I had a feeling I wouldn't be winning any Pulitzers for the writing.

The final debate papers for the Tag Popvote were done. There was the fake 'rape' position that Annika would not use, but that I would give to Sir Thomas as her debating position. There was also the real paper for Sir Thomas or his nominees to use in their position together with counter-arguments against the rape case. Finally, there was the real paper for Annika's lawyers to present once I resigned and joined Sir Thomas. I had all of these on my Devstick, but I wondered if I would show them or continue with Annika. It would mean Mariko's death if Sir Thomas believed I had betrayed him. At the least he would think me incompetent, and that could get us both killed just as quickly. Or should I betray Annika? Would Mariko even be with me if I managed to save her life under those circumstances? I knew the answer to that, and I didn't like it. I banished the question from my mind.

The Lev decelerated swiftly. I shook myself from my thoughts and looked around. There wasn't a face I recognized, but then I wouldn't. The Lev doors opened, and we all filed out, those nearest the doors rushing to get to the walky ahead of the others. Take it easy, I thought, there's nothing so important that a few extra secs will hurt. Move slower, enjoy life. What, like you're enjoying life? Are you enjoying this ever-present panic in your gut? Taking pills to sleep and living on fumes?

I waited until I got on the walky and then took out my Devstick to find the way to the Hilton on the Park. Being in the Australia Geographic always made me feel as if I had gone back in time. Australia had resisted population growth and high-rises with equal ferocity. Boasting a population of forty million, it was the least densely populated developed Geographic on Earth.

I came out of the Lev port and headed over to the taxi rank. As I reached the railings that zigzagged back and forth to control the queue, a black guy wearing a bush hat cut in front of me. The guy behind shouted, "Hey, mate, there's a queue back here." But the black guy just ignored him and looked forward.

He was shorter than me, and I felt angry that he'd jumped in front, but I kept my tongue. No point getting in a row and making news of myself. He was also very well muscled with broad shoulders. I wasn't sure that I could beat him even with the moves that Mariko had taught me. I shook my head. A week ago I had never entertained a violent thought against another human, and here I was contemplating attacking this guy for jumping ahead of me in a queue.

The taxis were arriving quickly and regularly, and soon I was at the open end of the railing next to the Travway. A fat woman wearing a yellow jacket with STAFF written across its front and back in big black letters pointed at the black guy in front of me and at a taxi at the front of the queue.

Without looking at me, the big black guy in front of me said, "Gabriel sent me to get you. Don't ask questions. Follow me and stay under the cover of the taxi rank. Follow me now."

He started walking away, and shocked as I was, I followed him. He got in the taxi, leaving the door open, and I climbed in headfirst after him. I heard him say something to the Dev in the cab but didn't catch what it was.

"You got a Devstick on you?"

"Yes."

"Give it 'ere, lie low in the seat, and strip off," he said in a low voice, smiling. I blew out my cheeks in a sigh and rolled my eyes. Does everybody I meet have to see me strip? I undressed, lying low in the seat, and as I did so, he picked up my discarded outers and inners and tossed them in a bag. The taxi had pulled out of the airport. All I could see from my position were the lights lining the Travway. Naked as the day I was born, I turned to him, spreading my hands.

He raised a finger to his lips and shook his head. Then he reached into a backpack that I hadn't noticed and pulled out a pair of shorts and a T-shirt with an 'I', a big heart and 'Pussy' written on it. I put them on, but when I started to rise from my low position, he shook his head again. He smiled, his huge white teeth gleaming in the dark of his face, indicating with his hands that I should lower my head. I did. I felt his hands smoothing over the top of my head, down around my ears and then around my neck. He gave me a thumbs-up and pulled a large floppy white hat out of the backpack and jammed it on my head. He patted his hand, palm downwards, to indicate I should lay low. I lay and watched the travlights and blue sky go by.

Wondering if this was an elaborate ruse by my uncle, I decided I was giving him too much credit, but also wondered why he would go to all of this trouble. With Mariko under his control, he could simply ask me and I'd tell him what I knew. Or would I? I didn't know the answer to that and didn't really want to. I was cramped, squatting on the floor of the cab below window level, but I stayed where I was. Suddenly the taxi picked up pace, and I felt myself pushed against the edge of the back seat.

About five mins later, we slowed. All I saw was a ceiling and then lights on a wall as we turned and then descended. I knew this because I was thrust forward sharply against the back of the seat in front of me. And then we stopped, and the doors opened. I looked at my companion, but he was already climbing out of the cab, so I followed suit. The cab turned around and pulled out of what I now could see was an underground parking lot.

The black guy walked over to a large tanker. Written in gold on the white tank was 'Vanishing Point Vineyards'. He continued to the rear of the tanker and pulled a handle while pushing another button. The whole rear end of the tanker swung free. He smiled at me and shifted his eyes to the inside of the tank and then raised his eyebrows at me.

I walked around him and looked inside. It had a compartment built into its mid section about two-thirds inside the tank. The compartment had another small door in that with a big round handle set in it. I jumped in and went to the door. I turned the circular handle until the door swung free, and then, once sitting inside what was probably roomy enough for cramped four adults, I closed the door and locked it shut again.

I was now inside a tin box, inside another tin box, and being driven somewhere. I should count to keep track of the time, I thought, and began counting. Wait a minute, this is pointless. You have no control over where you are going or what time it will take to get there. So what is the point of knowing the time? Right, think of something else. Mariko. Images of her. At the Nineveh sitting across from me in that pool. In the book shop in Orchard. On the beach in Sisik. Naked under me on the floor in the house. I've got to get you out of this, babe, and I will. Or die trying. So this is why people believe in God? So they can have someone to ask to help save someone they love.

I slid forward on the seat. We'd stopped. I heard three raps on the tank. Opening the door of the compartment, the rear of the tanker was already open, and I could see we were in some kind of building.

I jumped out of the tanker, and the black guy hugged me. "Oh, mate, it's so good to see you. When we heard Gabe's bro' was still alive, we were all so happy for him, and now to meet you. Just a beauty, mate. Eh, let me look at you." With this, he pushed me away from him with his hands clasping my shoulders.

I realized with his push just how strong he was. "You look like yer old man," he said, smiling even broader. I smiled back, it was impossible not to, his face was so warm.

"My name's Maloo, mate. It means 'Thunder' in English, but you can call me me Loo if you wants."

I waied him. And he grabbed me again. "No, mate, no wais, just hugs. I wanna feel you."

I smiled, and he threw a massive arm around my neck and pulled me towards a huge stack of barrels. There was a Porsche Diablo and a couple of white BMW Airbikes that looked very close to what UNPOL use but without the lights and sirens.

Maloo did something on his Devstick, and the stack of barrels moved across the floor of the warehouse. Underneath them, in the floor, a metal plate slid sideways. Steps led down into a passage. Maloo pushed me in front of him, and I went down the steps. It was a thin passage, just wide and tall enough to walk slightly hunched over. If another person came the other way, you'd have to turn back or climb over each other.

There was a single line of strip lights leading the way around a curve up ahead. The curve kept going, and the tunnel looked the same.

"About two hundred and fifty meters down, we'll come to another set of steps, but there's a fork up ahead. Take the left fork. Okay?"

His voice echoed in the tunnel. The only other sound was our footsteps on the concrete floor. I took the fork and, after walking another fifty meters, saw the steps. I went up these and came to another door, which opened just as I approached the top of the stairs. Standing in the light of the doorframe was Gabriel. I recognized his shape.

He smiled and held his arms out wide. I realized in that instant how alone and lost I had been these past few days. A hard lump hit the bottom of my throat, and my eyes teared. We hugged, and I held him tight. I sniffed and breathed out loud, still hugging him tightly.

"He's got Mariko."

"I know. I read the message he sent you. It's going to be okay, my brother. We're going to get her back." He squeezed me hard and then, with his arm around my shoulder, led me into the room, which was another warehouse, but this one was all flying vehicles and a rubber dinghy on a motorized trailer.

"Come on. There's someone I want you to meet, and we have a lot of work to do in a short amount of time, as usual. But let's get to the house, and we can talk there."

We crossed the warehouse, and this time a workbench moved sideways, and a flight of stairs appeared. It was obvious that this wasn't set up as a temporary place.

"Is this where you've been living?" I asked Gabriel as we walked down the flight of stairs, which was wide enough to fit both of us side by side.

"Yes. I've lived here for about twenty years. I trav a lot but always under assumed identities. I've never used my real identity. I knew that Sir Thomas was just waiting, and that would have been the end of me."

We came to a set of doors that looked like they were sealed with fat black rubber-like bands on either side of them. Inside was a four-seated pod.

"You've got your own Lev tube!" I exclaimed. I had never heard of anyone having a private Lev tube, but of course, buildings had them.

"Yes, the house is about ten kiloms away, and this is the quickest and most discreet way of getting there."

We all took a seat, and with a command to his Devstick, Gabriel shut the doors. We took off fast – I slid over on the seat to Maloo, who was sitting next to me. He laughed.

"Not quite as smooth as commercial Levs, but it's safe. Don't worry about that," Gabriel said this, and I realized he'd braced himself against the sides of the pod, as had Maloo. I nodded and smiled at my brother. It was great to see him. Just when I needed him most.

The Lev rapidly decelerated, but I was ready and braced for it, coming to a stop with a thump against something that gave. We rocked back a bit before locking into place. The doors opened, and there was another small platform with concrete steps leading upwards. I followed Gabriel out, and we went up the steps to a door at the top.

The door opened into a small room with another door. When Gabriel opened that one inwards, I saw that it had various kinds of cleaning equipment hanging off it, and then he opened another door, and I realized the access to the Lev was hidden in a cleaning equipment storage closet. What a life he must have had to live like this, I thought.

The cleaning closet emptied us out onto a wooden floor passageway with white doors at both ends. Gabriel walked to the one on the left and opened it to a beautiful sunny room that looked out over dunes to the ocean below. I followed him into the room and saw, on two matching white sofas, Annika Bardsdale and a woman I recognized as Martine Shorne, sitting opposite each other with a bottle of wine between them. Annika had been saying something, but when she saw me, she stopped and rose from the sofa. I smiled at her, and she walked over and gave me a hug and a kiss on the cheek. She held the back of my head and looked into my eyes.

"Gabriel told me about what's happened to Mariko. I'm so sorry, but you must know that we'll do everything in our power to bring her home safely."

I smiled back at her, returning her hug. "Thanks. I know."

Martine stood up and came over to us. She waied, and Gabriel walked to her side, putting his arm around her.

"Mark, this is Martine, or Marty as she likes to be called. She's the love of my life." When he said this, she looked up at him and with a hand steered his head so that she could kiss his cheek.

I stepped over to her and held my arms out. "That makes you my sister, Marty." She smiled and hugged me. I was struck by how beautiful she was compared to the image that UNPOL had issued of her. We stopped hugging, and Marty sat down on the sofa with Gabriel. I sat on the opposite one with Annika on one side and Maloo on the other side of me.

"I'm sorry I couldn't move sooner to bring this meeting around, but we needed you away from the heavy surveillance you were under. Sir Thomas is watching you like a Hawk, if you'll forgive the pun, and we couldn't move. When I saw that you were meeting Annika in Melbourne, I thought it better just to wait. This is home ground. We have a lot of resources we can call upon here and practically none up in New Singapore. Anyway, I'm sorry, this last week must have been hell for you."

"Don't apologize. I understand. And yes, it's been rough. What about this meeting, though, won't UNPOL have picked up on my disappearance?"

Gabriel poured me a glass of wine. I took a gulp to wash away the lump in my throat. He smiled at me, like he knew what I was thinking.

Elbows on his knees, Gabriel leant forward on the sofa.

"No. Right now you're in the Hilton on the Park with Annika, and you'll be in her room ordering room service tonight after the two of you have spent all evening talking. Then you'll spend all of tomorrow making love, after which Annika will return to London. As for you, that will depend upon what we decide to do. Sir Thomas kidnapping Mariko, is that because he's blackmailing you to do something?"

"No. Not exactly. The night before he kidnapped Mariko, I joined the Hawks. He asked, and I accepted. But right after I accepted, he said I had to prove my loyalty to him by killing someone. I asked him who. And he said just anyone – it doesn't matter."

Annika gasped. "This is incredible. This man is the UNPOL director! What kind of a world are we living in?" Shaking her head, she got up and walked to the windows facing the ocean.

"I take it you said you would kill someone?" Gabriel asked me in a low voice.

"Sure, what choice did I have? He had two bodyguards in the living room with Mariko. If I had said no after what he'd just told me, I'm pretty sure we would have been killed right then."

Gabriel nodded. "I'm sure, too. No, you did the right thing. Does he suspect anything about us?"

"I don't think so. I think he thinks that he's training me by doing this. Or maybe I'm just being hopeful, but I think he's showing me how to be ruthless. It fits with ways in which he has interacted with me in the past. Anyway, I doubt that he's harmed Mariko, that is if he still believes that I know nothing about you other than what he has told me. I am worried about Cochran doing a mind probe on Mariko or Truth Treatment."

"Cochran's not in New Singapore. She's been visiting each of the bomb sites. Every city where a bomb attack has taken place is now under martial law. UNPOL Special Ops teams have been placed in force at each location. They're getting ready to make their move, and Cochran's not due back in New Singapore until next Monday."

I nodded, relieved. One less thing to worry about.

Gabriel went on, "When do you have to kill someone by?"

"By Valentine's Day. Ironic, isn't it? I wonder if he didn't choose the date deliberately."

With a wry smile, Gabriel said, "He might have done. He's certainly sadistic enough to take pleasure in such details."

Which increased my worries. "So, what about the chances of Sir Thomas putting Mariko through Truth Treatment?"

"There was a chance that he might have used it straight away, but we're sure you would have been picked up or killed if he had done so. As you haven't, it's probably because loyalty, trust and honor are crucial qualities between Hawks.

It's a matter of honor for him to trust you now until you prove otherwise. It would certainly risk your loyalty to him if he questioned your lover behind your back without a valid reason."

"What about Cochran next week? I doubt she has any scruples about doing a mind probe. Though I have coached Mariko in how to avoid dangerous thoughts."

"Now you're a Hawk, you are a rival to Cochran," Gabriel said. "I think Sir Thomas would prefer to play those cards close to his chest as yet, so I doubt he'll give Cochran access to Mariko. Either way, we have a bit of time to work with."

Giving a shrug, Gabriel glanced at the other conspirators and changed tack. "All right, let's sum up where we are. Sir Thomas doesn't yet suspect you know the truth about me, Mark. He doesn't know where we are or who we all are, so those are things in our favor. Against us is we still don't know anything about how to prevent the toxin from killing people and how they're hiding it in the tags. And it looks like we're not going to find out until the Tag Law is passed. We don't know where Mariko is being held, and if Mark doesn't kill someone within eight days, then Mariko will probably be killed. We also have to consider that Cochran may attempt a mind probe on Mariko within the week, and that might lead to her and Mark being killed. Would you agree with that summary of where we are now?"

Gabriel sat back on the sofa and looked around the room at each of us in turn. I exhaled heavily, and Maloo put his arm around my shoulder.

"Don't ya worry, mate. Gabe's gotta tell it like it is, but we'll fix this fucka for ya, don't ya worry." He looked over at Annika and said, "Pardon my French, Ms Bardsdale."

Annika flashed a grin at Maloo. "I don't think that was French, Maloo, and I agree. We will fix this fucker."

Maloo burst out with a bark of a laugh, and I had to grin, too.

"I'm serious," Annika said, smiling. "I know some pretty high-level people, and they would be horrified to find out this is going on. They'd move fast to stop it, too."

I looked at her and said, "I'm pretty sure that Sir Thomas has got Secretary General Deng, either with him or being manipulated by him. That's high-level. Without evidence, rock-solid evidence, anyone going up against Sir Thomas at this point would just be putting themselves on a list for execution."

Gabriel leant forward and picked up his wine glass. He said, "We'll have to use every resource we've got in an orchestrated plan if we're going to succeed. I think the big question we have to ask ourselves is, do we have enough to stop the Tag being voted in?"

"I don't think that we do. Even if we exposed Sir Thomas and all of the conjecture that we have about Tag, even if Sir Thomas was out of action, Tag would still go ahead. Once the cull is completed, they'd just release Sir Thomas. The question isn't about whether we can legally stop Tag, because let's assume we can't. The real question is how do we stop the cull happening and at the same time make sure it can't ever happen? Once we've done that, we can then work on getting rid of Sir Thomas. Or maybe if we're lucky, we can kill two birds with one stone."

Gabriel raised his eyebrows and shrugged at me. Maloo rolled his eyes.

"Okay, okay, enough with the bad puns." Gabriel's moment of levity passed, and he shook his head. "Seriously, this guy is dangerous and clever, but he's not infallible – no one is. Enough things start going wrong and he'll make a mistake. We just have to be there when it happens. He'll be at his weakest when the Tag has been distributed. Once released, we can get a hold of it and set Maloo to work on it."

I looked at Maloo. Gabriel said, "Maloo's got a PhD in bio-engineering from Sydney uni."

I tried to mask the surprise I felt, but Maloo saw right through me. With a big grin, he said, "Had ya fooled, didn't I, mate?"

Gabriel laughed, but then his look turned somber again. "The problem with this approach is that it means we have to wait until the Tag is distributed. Which means that you and Mariko are exposed. Essentially, you have to choose whether you want Mariko or someone else to die. Unless, of course, we can locate and extract her before the 14th, which will be our primary focus."

"I can't put Mariko's nor my life in front of six billion deaths. She wouldn't want me to. I detest the thought of having to kill an innocent human to save her. I know I can do that. I'm sad to admit it, but I do. That's just love, but what worries me is that in doing it, she will hate me forever."

"What if the person you killed wasn't innocent?"

The question from Marty turned the room to silence. I looked at her. She held my look and sat calmly next to Gabriel. Her legs together, leaning forward with her arms on her thighs, she stared at me under her blonde fringe. Her eyes bored into mine.

"I mean a really nasty person. Unfit to call themselves a human. That kind of non-innocent. Could you kill such a person?"

"It doesn't matter whether the person is a bad or a good person. Under the law I believe in, they are both due the same rights as humans under the Nation's Law. If we have failed to stop this person from committing illegal or just plain evil acts, then that is a failure of the Law and its processes, not the individual. Any other understanding leads to anarchy or vigilante mob justice."

"That doesn't answer my question. I'm not talking about theories, I'm talking about right now. A particular person and whether you want to save Mariko or not."

Gabriel put a hand on her arm. "Maybe we'll come back to that question later. I have an idea that I'd like to run by you. Something I've been toying with for a while now, and I'd like to get your opinion on it. Okay, here goes. What if we delete all identity records? Everyone's PUI. Gone in an instant?"

Marty shook her head and said, "Shrouded in the heaviest of security, and even if you get through that, there are backups in several different places."

"Yes, I know, but suppose we could do it. What do you think of the effect?" Gabriel sat back in the chair.

Annika walked to the table and held her glass out for Gabriel to refill. Once filled, she emptied half of it in a huge swallow. "You'd destroy personal wealth, contribution would cease to have a reason, and the world would sink into anarchy overnight. But apart from that, I don't see a problem with it," she said, smacking her lips. Hand on hip, she raised her glass, giving us her profile. We all burst out laughing.

"Okay, to be a little less extreme," Gabriel said. "The Tag has to be controlled with a command that would be uploaded to it. This would release the toxin. To do that selectively, you have to match serial numbers of Tags distributed with names of people distributed to. Makes sense, right?" He wasn't expecting an answer. "Right. So we need to find those two lists, and once the product has been released, destroy the lists of serial numbers or randomize it. Because if we can't do that, then our last recourse is to delete everyone's identity. And Annika, I agree with your evaluation of what would happen, but that's still better than six billion dead. Right?"

"Yes, you're right," I responded. "How much time do you think we have after the Tag Law has been passed?"

"I'd estimate no more than two weeks. By that time I reckon they'll come up with something to force the issue. It looks to me like the Hawks have achieved enough insiders in the UN and in the Security Council to manipulate a crisis and get people to inject the Tag quickly. So yes, about ten to fourteen days tops."

"So no later than the end of month?"

"No. I reckon he'll order the cull once he gets seventy to seventy-five percent adoption. If what we know about the toxin is correct, and we think it is, then it takes about a week before it kills. Which means that he can kill the ones who haven't injected before the ones who have start to die."

"So the key is the list of Tag serial numbers, and to get it, I have to kill someone. There's no getting around that, is there?"

"No. Unfortunately not." Gabriel looked straight at me and spread his hands.

Leaning forward in her seat, Marty spoke softly. "I know who you can kill."

I looked at her, struggling to match the beautiful woman with the words. She continued in the same soft tone. "His name is Jonathan Wigley. We called him 'Wriggly Wigley' because we couldn't get any evidence on him even though he practically boasted about his crimes in a few online forums. He lives in Bangkok and on the surface is a –"

"I know him. He was lead counsel for Bauer."

"Yes. That's why he's perfect because you do know him. And you had some serious arguments with him too, right? We got that tracing some of his communications with his people back in Bangkok."

"Yes, that's right. During the settlement negotiations, he was obstructive without being constructive. He was just wasting time, I suspected, so that he could charge more for his contribution. Finally I accused him directly in a meeting, and the Bauer team replaced him with David Chalmers. After that, we reached settlement quickly."

Marty nodded. "Mr Wigley spends his cred and self-time getting young boys and girls from all around Asia and having sex with them. They're always under ten years of age. We haven't been able to get a witness or evidence to point the finger at him, but we know he's doing it. It is only a matter of time before he slips up and we get him, but who knows how many more young lives will be corrupted by his touch before then."

Gabriel leaned close to me. "I can do this if you want. We'll rig it to make it look like you did, but I'll actually take care of it."

"No. I will take care of it. As much as I hate the thought, it's possible that the deception would be found out, and then all this would be for nothing. I'll kill him unless we can figure out a way to get that list before the 14th."

"So you want to leave it until the final day?"

"I know it's risky, but yes."

"All right. I think you should stay with me until then. What do you think?"

"Won't that raise all kinds of alarm bells?"

"We'll come up with a good reason for your absence. I think it will also unsettle him and Cochran."

"Cochran?"

"Sure Cochran. She's in deep with this thing."

"I should go back the day after tomorrow when Annika leaves. Being here is nice, and I feel safe. A part of me, a big part, wants to stay here, but I've got to get back into it."

Gabriel nodded and smiled at me. "I've got to provide you with some protection against any mind probes or truth treatments. We can't take the chance of those being successful, for all our sakes, and we need at least twelve hours to do that. It isn't a pleasant process either, and at the end of it you'll be too messed up to trav. So I think that you will need to stay until Sunday morning."

"Annika?"

"Yes, Gabriel."

"I need you to continue your affair with Jonah through till Sunday morning. Can you do that?"

"I think it'll probably make my popularity ratings increase," Annika said with a smile and blew a kiss at me.

A Change of Pace

Cochran stared intently at the image of Jonah standing on the platform waiting for the Bangkok Lev. The platform was virtually deserted. She panned the camera down its length and zoomed on each of the people, picking up the PUIs broadcast from their Devsticks. She switched back to Jonah. He looked relaxed and tanned. But there was something different about him. She couldn't put her finger on what, and so she stared intently at his image on the screen.

"Contact Sir Thomas," she said in a curt tone to the Dev she was sitting in front of. The Devscreen in front of her popped up a box showing Sir Thomas's image. 'Available' was on, and the image changed to Sir Thomas sitting at his desk in a room in his penthouse. He was dressed in what looked like a civilian version of an UNPOL uniform, except that instead of light blue, it was all black. She thought it looked good, and her mind immediately flashed to herself in a black UNPOL uniform with that distinctive 'Oche' edge.

"I'm sorry to disturb you, Sir Thomas, but I wanted you to know that Jonah has surfaced."

"You did well, Sharon. Thank you. And where is Jonah now?"

"He's still in Melbourne. I'll patch you in, Sir Thomas."

He smiled at her in his tight-lipped manner and then resumed a blank expression while he waited. Secs later he was watching Jonah on the Lev platform in Melbourne.

"Where is he headed?"

"He's on the Bangkok line, but that might mean he is headed to his Env in Sisik."

"What did the Hilton say?"

"Same as before. That Jonah was in the room with Annika Bardsdale for three days."

"Did we get trace from the room?"

"Unfortunately, we didn't. The room was sanitized before we got a chance to get in. In itself that would be suspicious, but it is standard policy at all Hiltons

– I checked."

"I see." Sir Thomas's expression made Cochran feel uneasy. It hadn't changed, but with the abrupt comment, she felt she had done wrong.

Sir Thomas caught the doubt that had crept into her face. The pink scar that she had as a result of the bombing turned a slightly darker shade as he waited for her to say more.

"The feeds are full of the affair between Jonah and Bardsdale."

"Yes. I know. Quite out of character for Jonah, wouldn't you say?"

"Not if my meeting with him was anything to judge by, Sir Thomas. He is an attractive man, and in my meeting with him, I got the distinct impression that he wanted to have sex with me."

"Yes, well, be that as it may. I feel something is not quite right. Have you made any progress on tracing the source of the letter?"

"No, sir. We can trace it to the Sydney stock exchange, but we cannot home in on its origin."

"I see. Well, keep an eye on our boy, and let me know if he does anything out of the ordinary."

"Yes, sir."

She cut the connection. It burned her that even now as the youngest director and with more power than any of her predecessors, she still felt like a little insecure girl in front of him. She returned to the image of Jonah standing on the platform. There was something wrong, but she couldn't place it. She stared harder at him. It was something to do with how he looked, but she saw nothing out of the ordinary.

Shrugging it off with a frown, she said, "Turn all lights off between here and the Lev." The room went black.

***

Marty checked the time on the Devstick laying on the table next to the Devscreen. 5:15am. Gabriel was in another room. They had quickly decided that they worked best when they worked alone. They had also decided that they played best when together. Marty was working. She sat in one of Gabriel's Devcockpits and was hacking the account files of 'Utopia'. Utopia was regarded as what the world might become, a virtual reality where Stanislav spent large amounts of his self-time. She needed the Gang of Four, and Stanislav was the best way to get in touch.

She took another glance at Mark on the platform just getting into the Lev.

265

Some space in the bottom of her stomach felt heavy at seeing him alone, going into the Lev. She thought of Mariah, his mother. She refocused – no time to think about that now – and Gabriel was watching over him. Maloo had left to take up station in Bangkok in advance of Jonah's trip to 'get eyes' on Mr Wigley.

It was 2:15am in new Singapore, and the odds on Stanislav being in Utopia were high. She chose an account. ID Pagan Moon. 23, single, here for relationships, dating, sex, chat buddy, and exotic vacations. Perfect, she thought. She took a look at Pagan Moon's digital image and cringed. Ouch. Resolving to send Moon a message about her dress sense, she hacked the image into something less catastrophic and entered the environment.

Marty's avatar, Pagan Moon, landed in Utopia through its main doorway. The usual touts hung around there offering software upgrades to the avatars and accessories. Pagan Moon ignored them all and walked rather stiffly, Marty thought, as she sent out a stream of code looking for a sexier motion for her avatar. She strode over to Utopia's map. It was large: over one and a half billion inhabitants, an alternative world with people contributing full-time within it. Her code had picked up a smoother motion than the one the default supplied.

She turned and saw that three of the touts had taken an interest in her. She ignored them and hit New Singapore on the map. It took her twenty secs to find him. Sitting on a Ferarri V9 SuperAirBike, a SAB, as they were known, in front of Newton's Circus, he was tanned and muscled.

Pagan Moon didn't waste any time. She walked over to him, spreading her legs apart as she stood in front of him. She said, "Can we have a chat in private? I mean, really private?"

He looked at her and leered.

She leered back and said, "I don't think I can wait much longer. I mean, you know. Let's go. Okay?"

He swung his leg over the handlebars of the SAB. Marty laughed aloud, her avatar Pagan Moon swooned and put her hand on his stomach as she swung up onto the seat behind him. She pulled her body tight against his back and mashed her breasts against it. Dropping her hands into his crotch, she whispered in his ear, "How's Fatima?" The bulge being fed by his plugged-in biosensors shrank as quickly as it had arisen, and he twisted awkwardly on the seat to look at her. He had a guilty look on his face.

"Is that you, Fatima?"

"No. It's the other female on the team. Don't name talk, okay. You know who this is. All right. Get it together and quick. I haven't got all day."

The avatar that was Stanislav's grinned at her. She saw that his programming was flawless. The avatar looked and moved as a real person would. It was hard to tell the difference. He gunned the SAB and took off heading south.

One of the Devscreens in her cockpit changed. Sitting up in his sleeper in his Env in New Singapore, wearing a plain white T-shirt and white boxer shorts, was Stanislav. He looked more imaginary than his avatar, but it was Stanislav. In Utopia, Stanislav didn't have a stammer.

"Wh-wh-wh-where have you been? I've been looking everywhere for you. Fatima has been going nuts, and Dom thinks that he is the cause that you've not got in touch with us. Where are you, and did you blow up the ga-ga-ga-governors like they said?"

"Are you sure this is secure?"

"Ye-ye-ye-yes. We're still back in Utopia riding around on the bike. Well?"

"Can't tell you where I am. That's too risky right now, and no, of course I didn't blow up the governors. That was Cochran getting even with me and the governors. Just goes to show how looks can deceive, right? Stanislav, I need your help. I need you to take care of Dom and Fatima, okay? That's the first thing, but there are some other tasks that I need your help on. Can you help me? It's going to be very dangerous, life-threatening perhaps, but if we succeed, we'll save the planet from destruction. Now before we go on, remember what I said about stuttering. Slow down."

"Okay, Marty. Is this real, or are you in the character of some cartoon? I knew you hadn't blown up the governors – I told Dom and Fatima that you'd been framed."

"Stanislav, there's a plot to kill billions of people. Will you help me stop it?"

"Are you kidding? Save the planet from destruction. That'd like make me a superhero type of stuff. Of course I'm in. What do you want?"

"First, I need you to tell Dom and Fatima about this chat. We'll need their help. Second, we –"

"Who's we?"

"I can't tell you right now. Honestly, the reason is that with what I am going to ask you to do, you stand a high chance of being captured and tortured. So everything I will tell you is strictly on a need-to-know basis. Getting out of this alive will depend entirely on your skill."

Speaking very slowly with his hands on his hips and his head to one side,

Stanislav said, "Oh please, Marty, I may be a virgin, but I'm not dumb. I already said that I would do this. No need to make it more exciting for me. Okay?"

Marty laughed. "It's great to see you. How are you guys holding it together?"

Stanislav sat down, and his face loomed large in the screen as he leaned forward nearer the camera. "Not good, but okay."

His comment made Marty feel guilty. It was irrational she knew, but they were her team, and they were struggling without her. She couldn't do anything about that now but made a mental reminder to try to stay in touch with them as much as the chaos to come would allow.

"What's Cochran got you guys tracing?"

"We're still on the runner. We got given other stuff after you left, but then when his letter came out, she put us back on him."

"Okay, here's what I need."

Stanislav had leaned back from the camera, and it looked like he was watching something else as he wasn't looking at her.

"Stanislav?"

"Yeah, sorry, just checking to see that nothing is on to our chat here, but we're cool. Okay, go ahead."

"Has Cochran got you guys looking for me?"

"No, but she did order us to report any contact from you on pain of instant containment for aiding and abetting a fugitive if we didn't." He grinned at her. "Looks like I'm back in the crime business."

"No, you're not. Very much the opposite. Okay then, what I need you to do is build an ironclad story around finding my location and then report that location to Cochran. Build up some trace around it, and be aware that with the embarrassments the runner and I have given her lately, she will want to be absolutely sure that you are right. So be sure. Can you do that?"

"Yeah." Stanislav put on his bored expression – his 'this is too easy' look.

"When she is ready to come and get me, let me know. Now, we need to set up a link between us. Can I leave that with you. It must be secure and easy to check."

"Utopia's best. I'll set up a dead drop and message you from there."

"That sounds fine. I'll leave my hooks in their member base, then, and wait for your message. There's one more thing, and this is the skillful part. You have to wait for my signal before you get Cochran to make her move on me. You'll only have a very small window, perhaps no more than fifteen or twenty mins to convince her to move." Stanislav straightened from his slouch and flashed her a quick, cocky grin.

"Na-na-na-no problem."

"All right then. I have to go. Give my love to Fatima and Dom and take care of each other and be very careful. Okay? Cochran is a very dangerous person."

Stanislav grinned at her again, and a twinge of conscience hit the pit of her stomach. He's so young. Is it right for me to do this? Put him in this danger? The stakes are so high that the end justifies the means. Oh boy, what a slippery slope this is, she thought. His image disappeared from her Devscreen, and she placed her palm where his face had been, just for a sec. She coughed and cleared her throat.

Sitting in the room next door, Gabriel heard the murmur of Marty talking as background noise. It was there, but he didn't pay it any attention. He was focused on his code. A Dev runs on code. The code he was writing had to be small, very small, and therefore it had to be elegant. The idea for hiding the code was simple. Make it very small. The problem with that is that the code has to do a lot. It has to find and destroy the list. Failing that it has to destroy the databases holding the PUI records of all humans. He also needed to figure out a way to get it into Sir Thomas's Dev without any alarms going off.

A borrower, he thought. That's what it can be. I can string together a sequence that when activated borrows the code from other code in the Dev. Then it's just a wait for start sequence code and a sequence code. That would keep it small.

He reclined in the Siteazy and, using both hands, brushed his hair back and sucked in a long breath. And held it. He closed his eyes and cast thoughts aside as they came. Clearing his mind. He pictured himself with an old-fashioned broom sweeping dry leaves off a bare cement floor. Slowly, he exhaled through his nose. More thoughts snuck in. The broom went back and forth, back and forth. Let it go. He opened his eyes and stretched his fingers onto the input tablet in front of him. He began to type.

***

Mariko lay on the molded plastic sleeper. The room that she was in was two meters long and three wide. It was colored white. It reminded her of the White Room in UNPOL. She'd had a tour when that room was first built. This room had none of the special effects of the White Room, but it was still a long time. All she knew was that she had been stupid. How could she not have been more aware? Dumb. She suspected that it must have been Sir Thomas who had grabbed her, but she didn't know. She hadn't seen anyone. She idly wondered how long it would take for her to go insane if she was stuck in here for a long time. Don't think like that. Basic crisis training, stay positive and look for a solution. She assumed she was being watched. The meals gave some clue – she knew from her biological clock when she was hungry, but as they had drugged the food, she had no real idea of time.

She had expected to be questioned. But it never happened. A positive sign, she thought and fought against the despair that the reason they didn't need to question her was because she had been eliminated. Pushed into a hole and forgotten. No, they still feed you. Stay positive and in control of yourself. She hadn't said anything. Hadn't asked why she was being kept captive. She was following training. Do not provide any unnecessary information unless you really have to. Asking why she was here was irrelevant.

She'd adopted her 'hard face' for the benefit of whoever might be watching and tried not to think about Jonah and how he would be feeling with her gone. She knew he would blame himself for not being able to protect her. She knew that and smiled. Him protect her – it was a funny thought that distracted her from her surroundings for a sec. She felt guilty for not being there to protect him. For exposing him to the dangers of her captivity. Don't. Pointless exercise. Guilt is negative. Use the time you have.

She closed her eyes to the light in the room and continued to write the poem she had been working on. It was in her head. She carefully thought of each new word before adding it to the ones already there. By her count she'd spent about three hours on the last word, and she smiled again. It had been worth it. Torpor. Euphoria in Torpor. A whole new line to think about. The luxury of having an entire day to think of a single word to describe something. Captivity. Bring it on.

***

Maloo had left Melbourne traveling in the same Levtube but leaving fifteen mins before Jonah's. He shifted his bulk on the seat and stared at the little white dot progressing its way down a line of connected white dots. He formed an image in his mind. A future bark painting or maybe rock. Yeah, rock.

Maloo was going to Bangkok to set up the Wigley kill. Jonah would be the one to do it, but Maloo would prepare the ground. He shifted the backpack containing his clothes to a more comfortable position on his lap and leant his elbows on top, his chin cupped in his hands. His massive shoulders and the look on his face gave him the appearance of a bull about to charge. Yet he hated violence in all of its aspects. It was the only thing he did hate.

A while later, he took a hand off the backpack and felt in the pocket of his bottom outers. The diamonds were still there. All two million creds' worth. Easily enough to get what he needed in Bangkok and pay so well that no one would say a thing for fear of losing the rich life ahead of them. He glanced around the Lev. None of the other five passengers had noticed his surreptitious feel of the stones.

The painting continued to develop in his mind. Connected white dots, large to small diameter. Two lines next to each other. A white rectangle. A sorry business, he thought in Waalpiri, using the term they use for a funeral. To represent six billion, the stars in the sky as people. He wondered how this painting would unfold.

***

Cochran landed her new Bell 400 VTOL (Vertical Take Off and Landing) Turbo-charged Heliocopter on the lawn in front of the SingCom residence. The copter's blades retracted with a whir and clunked into the space behind the pilot's seat where she sat. She exhaled steadily and softly. Red-lining it all the way in, in a straight line, she'd covered the distance from UNPOL in 1:59 min. Her mind flicked back to Jonah getting into the Lev in Melbourne. An intuitive sense of unease rose in her gut. Something was wrong with him being out of sight for three days with Annika Bardsdale.

She climbed out of the angular nose of the Bell's cockpit and stood beside the machine. The warm New Singapore night quiet on the dark lawn. Tomorrow, no today, she thought with a glance at her Devstick – it's 2:18am – I'll get the little fat Arab girl, Fatima, to run a scenario on Bardsdale and Jonah. Thinking of Fatima made her think of Marty. She looked at the mansion in front of her, biting her lip. Bitch. She felt bested by Marty and hadn't forgotten any of the slights or her arrogance. But I got you, she thought. I got you good.

No, you didn't. She escaped. You don't have her. You didn't think she'd get away. You thought you would pick her up the next day. You failed. Again.

She didn't like this voice. And it was speaking up more often. The more she succeeded, the more the voice had to say about her failings. She wanted to stop it, but she didn't know how. It seemed it was never satisfied.

You lost. You lost Martine Shorne, and you lost Gabriel Zumar. You had them both –

Wait. Shut up. That's it. That's where I've seen him before. Walking with Bo

271

Vinh. The images that Shorne presented. Jonah James Oliver is Philip Zumar's son. Gabriel, the runner, is his brother. And Sir Thomas made him his nephew. But why? She chewed her lower lip and folded her arms across her chest. Then, twisting her upper lip between a thumb and a forefinger, she contemplated her revelation.

Cochran strolled slowly across the lawn to the door of the mansion, thinking it would be hard to sleep now, wondering if Sunita would be awake.

TIME TO KILL

The cicadas sang loud enough to cover the sounds of me climbing over the wall. I felt an urgent need to urinate. A mosquito buzzed around my ear. I felt it land and, a moment later, took a hand off the ladder that went up the wall in front of me to rub the bite.

I needed to urinate badly. I knew it was nerves, but I still needed to pee. I couldn't. It would leave too much trace. I thought about getting off the ladder and retracing my steps along the bottom of the wall to the Titan parked half a kilom away but dismissed the thought. I brought my bladder under control and took out one of the small sealable bags that Maloo had given me. I took out my cock and put it in the bag. Closing the seal around my cock, not too tightly, I relaxed.

My pee sounded loud to me as I scrunched over, crouching and hanging off the bottom rung of the ladder that went up Wigley's wall. I changed angle so the splash would hit the side of the bag. It was quieter. I squeezed out the last drop and shook off, taking the bag off my cock, sealing it and placing it in a zipped pocket. On my way to kill someone with a bag of my own pee in my pocket.

Focus. I softly breathed out. I was hidden from view by the trunk and branches of a tree. I started to climb, one hand over the other. As I climbed, the sound of my heart thumping in my chest beat out the cicadas. I stopped, listened. The cicadas came back. In the far distance, a dog barking, music playing, jazz.

Reaching the top, I extended the ladder. I had to control my breathing. There was a light in a downstairs window. I looked around. Nothing. Nobody moving. No one in sight. I started out to cover the gap. It was about three meters. Moving forward in a crawl, hands and feet on the pipes of the ladder, I crossed the gap between the wall and his balcony. I crouched below the railing, hidden from the street by the pillars of the Greco-Roman style mansion. If Gabriel was right, this was Wigley's room.

I reached into the black coveralls and felt for the handle of the dagger. I had to move. Move. The panic came on slow but strong. A light in the room went

273

on, illuminating the back of the curtain. I realized that the light was turned on by Wigley, turned on by the man I was here to kill. I kept my breathing as shallow as possible, but it seemed to speed up each time I tried to keep it quiet. No, I can't do this. I can't kill. I swallowed and licked my lips. My tongue was so dry that it stuck to them. I crawled back over the bridge to the wall, looking around me again. No one saw me. I went back over the wall and down the ladder to crouch behind the tree.

I slowed my breathing. My brain cleared. I heard the cicadas again.

My thighs ached from crouching. I cleared my thinking. Far off I heard a fight erupt among a pack of dogs. It's not a choice. You have to do it. There is no other way of getting past Sir Thomas. None. If you don't do this, you die, Mariko dies and maybe six point three billion people die. Or he dies. It's either all of them or just Wigley.

I took my Devstick part way out of my inside pocket, shielding its light with my coveralls. 10:29pm. All of that happened in four minutes. It had to be done.

I swallowed. My throat was too dry. I opened the coveralls again and took a sip of water from the bottle that Maloo had provided. Don't get dehydrated. I went up the ladder swiftly. I slowly raised my head over the wall and took another look around. Still nothing. I noticed that the cicadas had stopped. The night was still. The faint scuffling of rubber shoes on the rungs of the ladder was all that I could hear as I made my way to Wigley's balcony. I went into a crouch against the railing and waited.

The light went off inside. I put on the gas mask and waited.

My thighs burned with the energy of being in a crouch and when I could stand it no more I went over the railing and laid flat on the floor of the balcony. The sound around me stayed the same. Nothing. In the distance I could hear the hum of a Travway. But nothing where I was. I swiveled until my face was mins from the clearfilm sliding doors.

I needed to cut a hole in the door so that I could pump in the gas that would knock Wigley out while I broke in. Maloo had given me a small circular disc, one side covered in tape to stick on to the door, the other a handle to pull out the plug. Far down on the right of the door I placed the disc and pressed hard to stick it to the door. I gave it a tug to make sure it was firmly attached to the clearfilm and then pulled the small cord that would cause the disc to burn through it. The edges of the disc started smoking. Tendrils of the smoke, the fried remains of the clearfilm door, floated up to be caught by the breeze over the balcony. The plug came free in my hand. I put it, and the circle of clearfilm attached to it, into my pocket.

I felt the cool air inside the room hit the end of my fingers in their thin-tipped gloves. I inserted the nozzle of the canister and turned the valve open full. In thirty seconds, six cubic liters of gas vented into Wigley's room. I took out the magnet and placed it near the handle, holding it lightly against the door. With my thumb I turned it on and felt the pull of the metal bolts. I pulled it downwards, and the doors unlocked. Maloo had obviously invaded property before as everything he had told me was working.

I slowly slid the door open. The seal squeaked once as it came free from its partner. I stopped and listened. Nothing. I could hear Wigley breathing. I slid the door open fully and stepped into the room. I could feel carpet under my feet, and I felt down the curtains with my hands until I found the manual button on the wall. The curtains slid open quietly and light from the Moon let me see in the room. I stayed low and went over to the edge of the sleeper. Wigley was on the other side. In a crouch, I crossed his room and checked his door. There was no bolt to lock.

I crouched my way back across the carpet to where Wigley lay sleeping with his head on his arm, curled up in the fetal position. The gas was enough to knock him out for five minutes, long enough for what I had to do.

I took out the injection Maloo had prepared and lifted the cover of the sleeper to one side. I grabbed the little toe of his left foot and carefully inserted the micro needle of the injector. It looked like it was in. I swallowed hard and pressed the button. The injector made a soft hissing noise and ended with a click. I pressed the red button, and the micro needle withdrew. I put the injector, disarmed, back into my pocket and took out the mobile biosensor. I placed it against his throat, leaning over him. Wigley was dead.

I steeled myself and reached over with thumb and forefinger. His eyelids suddenly opened, and his eyes stared into mine. Why? I screamed in my mind. Why didn't the injection work? Safety. The safety-catch on the injector. Maloo had stressed it three times. You have to twist up and around to release the safety catch. I hadn't done it.

His eyes were just cents from mine and shocked. I dropped on top of him with my upper body, my hands grasping his upper arms and my legs pinning his thighs to the sleeper. His eyes were glazed. I waited. I could hear my heart in my eardrums. His pupils narrowed, and he tried to sit up. Then he realized what was happening and pushed.

"Who, why, who are you?" he strangled out as he strained against my hold. I saw in his eyes that he was going to shout out, and I dropped on him, forcing my gloved hand over his mouth. He got his left arm free and flailed at my back, but it didn't hurt. His eyes were wide and staring at me behind my gloved fingers.

"Did you do it?" I said in a low hiss in his ear. "Did you?"

He shook his head violently from side to side. His eyes bright, white and wild in the dark.

I looked in his eyes and threw my weight on him again, focusing my mind using what Gabriel had taught me.

"Terror, panic, disbelief, it's a nightmare, no it's real." His feelings came first. No coherent thoughts, just raw fear. I recognized it from the beach when I had lost Mariko. I pushed that thought away and went behind his fear.

I cast the thought. "Open your memories to me." I felt his mind react to my presence in it. "Do it. Do it now. There is nowhere for you to hide. I am in you. It will be all right, just open your mind. Open."

His mind opened. "My safe, he's come to rob my safe." He was thinking of his safe behind the image on the wall behind me. An image of a small sack of diamonds and bars of gold. I pushed further, his eyes widening. Sweat poured off me, dripping onto his upper lip. I looked down into his eyes. Going deeper.

My mind turned red and black. With an animal snarl, I released his arms and sat up, kneeling on him. My hand went into my coveralls' inner pocket and found the dagger. The cross bar on the hilt snagged as I started to pull it out. I heard the scream form through the red and black and lifted the dagger high in the air with both hands.

"No, no, please wait, no I –"

Using both hands, thumbs locked over the hilt, I plunged the dagger into his chest using all my strength.

He shook his head from side to side, silently mouthing no. I leaned into the hilt of the dagger with my chest, putting all my weight behind it, and twisted the handle.

"No, no, no."

The final no came out gurgled, and with a last-ditch effort, his chest heaved upwards, and he coughed blood over my face. The breath wheezed out of him in a groaned sigh. I sat back, my chest heaving as I sucked in air, my temples throbbing. I watched his eyes realize their death. He would never see again what had caused me to want to kill him.

Taking out my Devstick, I thumbed for Sir Thomas and sent the message that I had drafted earlier.

I need to transmit in confidence.

I waited. Looking at the dark grey screen of my Devstick, I could hear my own breathing. I avoided looking at Wigley.

Go ahead.

I sent the next pre-drafted message.

It's done.

I held the camera of my Devstick pointed at the body of Wigley, his eyes wide open and his tongue hanging out of his mouth. The hilt of the dagger in his chest surrounded by a pool of blood spreading over the thick white cotton of the sleeper. The Devstick shook in my hand, the small digital Wigley in the shaking screen as dead as the real one on the sleeper. I cut the image and sent the next message.

I best hurry home. I expect Mariko will be waiting for me.

Yes. I expect she shall. See you soon.

I took small comfort from Sir Thomas's reply. Mariko will be waiting for me. She must be okay. She must be. I closed my Devstick. Folded it and put it back in a pocket, noticing that it was smeared in blood from my gloves. I went back to Wigley, grabbed the dagger by the handle and pulled. It didn't come out. I leaned over him and, using both hands, heaved up. A sucking noise and the blade came free. The smell hit me then. He had soiled himself.

I replaced the dagger in the coverall pocket and looked around. Have I forgotten anything? No. Calmer now and feeling detached, I stopped and listened. I couldn't hear anything, only the slight hum of the air-conditioning unit. I pulled off the bloodied gloves and put them in a side pocket and, taking out a fresh pair, crossed to the image hanging on the wall. The image swung free on a hinge. A small metal box, a keypad and a handle. I entered the code that I had read from his mind and opened the door to his safe.

Tag You're It

I stepped softly into the sand from the door of the Titan. The second floor of the house was lit, the light spilling out onto the beach in front. I stood on the edge of the light, trying to see in. All I could make out was the top half of the inside of the house, but I hadn't left the lights on. I hoped it was Mariko, but what if it was Sir Thomas, or worse, Cochran? I reached into my backpack and pulled out the gun that Maloo had bought in Bangkok. And then I slowly put it back in the backpack.

I stepped into the light and walked to the steps that led up to the deck. I climbed them with a steady tread, my eyes focused on the steps, waiting for the interior of the house to be revealed. And there she was. Mariko. A wave of blissful relief passed over me. Lying on the sleeper, her back to me. And then a wave of pure terror swept down my spine. Opening the sliding doors, I crossed to the sleeper and sat down beside her. I held my emotions in check and put my hand against her neck. She was only sleeping.

Something wrenched free inside of me, and I nearly lost it, but I held on. I didn't want those watching to get anything from me. I put the backpack on the floor next to the sleeper and lay down beside her. I reached over to the Devstick and turned off the light.

I shut my eyes. And saw Wigley. I wondered if I would ever sleep again.

***

Gabriel shook his head softly, his fingers stroking the three-day stubble on his chin. The Tag was being voted in. He looked at the time in the lower right hand corner of the Devscreen, 5:14am, and voting had started in Auckland at one sec past midnight – six hours ago with the time difference between the two places. Another eighteen hours to go before the poll would be closed. Midnight in Samoa. Already the vote in favor was ahead by more than eight percent.

As Gabriele Esposito, Gabriel voted no and went back to reviewing the code he had been working on for a week. It was perfect. The code that had already been planted in Sir Thomas's base Dev by his messages would grab the code he was looking at and together form a Dev code virus that would find and scramble the list of serial numbers. At least that was the plan.

He sighed, thinking about what Mark had done, or perhaps more correctly for what he, Gabriel, had done to Mark. Sorry for the lost innocence. Sorry there was no choice. Looking out to sea, he saw that Maloo was back and getting the yacht ready for the trip. At this time of year, with the wind where it was, they could expect to average fifty kilos an hour on the trip back to New Singapore. Covering about seven thousand five hundred kiloms of ocean in about six and a half days.

Gabriel's strategy was simple. Sail to New Singapore, make sure the Tag serial numbers get scrambled, and kill Sir Thomas. The only part of the plan that he thought was at risk was scrambling the Tag serial numbers. He expected to kill Sir Thomas because the plan didn't allow either of them to survive. He wasn't sure if Marty had worked this out yet, but Maloo had, and was furious with Gabriel for even thinking of it. Gabriel closed the code page and opened a document. His will. He smiled.

***

I woke up. She was staring at me, a small smile on her lips and the palm of her hand on my cheek. She stroked down my face with a single finger until she pressed it against my lips. I blinked my eyes, and her smile twitched up a fraction. I turned around and, picking up the Devstick on the table next to the sleeper, saw that it was 5:15am. I'd slept for four hours. I immediately flashed back to what I had done yesterday. Could she see it? Could she see that I had murdered a man? Could she see that I had done it for her? I hesitated to turn back to face her, but I turned and looked again into her eyes.

I desperately wanted to talk to her, to explain, but I couldn't. I assumed that we would be under intense scrutiny. That even the slightest whisper would be recorded and analyzed for its meaning. Gazing into her eyes, I had a thought. My thoughts belong to me. I reached out with my mind as gently as possible. "Mariko, Mariko, can you hear me? Please don't be scared. It is me, Mark."

She smiled again and looked intensely into my eyes, bringing her face closer to mine.

"Mariko, can you –" she blinked, and her mind shouted "YES" at me. I blinked, and my head jerked back slightly as I was startled. Her answer was so clear and loud in my mind. She licked her upper lip, and her forehead creased in a slight frown.

I thought, "We can't say anything in this room. I think it will have been bugged by Sir Thomas or Cochran."

Her thoughts weren't coherent to me. I was getting mixed-up in images of me and her emotion at seeing me. Her thoughts seemed to be in a constant flow of noise. I focused and reached out with my hand to cup her cheek.

Finally, I caught it.

"Yes, I know. What day is it?"

"It's Saturday the 15th of February. 5:15 in the morning."

She smiled, her teeth showing white in the dark room. Her thoughts and emotion, hitting me in a blast of happy noise, overwhelmed my untrained mind. I shut my eyes and forced the threads to sort themselves out. "Pregnant. Baby. I am pregnant." Another wave of happiness and I opened my eyes. I smiled back and sent back the wave of happiness that spread through me. A thought flashed. Killing Wigley was worth it. I quickly pushed it away, but a frown crossed her face.

I willed happiness into my thoughts and, pushing everything else away, reached out for her mind again, smiling. The frown passed, and she smiled back, but I saw the lingering question in her eyes.

"Not now," I thought. "We can't talk about it now, and I am too happy at our news to spoil it with bad thoughts now. We can deal with them later. Okay?"

Her mind seemed to have cooled, and the thought threads came distinctly.

"Yes, all right. We have to get out of here. This place is unbearable."

"Yes, I agree," I thought. "I have a plan. We can wake up naturally in a minute. Don't talk about the baby. Let's keep that news to ourselves. Let's get cleaned up, eat and chat normally, and then later this morning, we'll go for a swim."

She blinked, and her hand fell from my cheek to my chest. Stroking the hair there, she opened the outer top I was still wearing and with her hand sliding down inside opened it fully. I reached out and pulled her tight to me in a hug, her long black hair tickling my stomach. Her belly against mine. Our child in her belly, against mine. I stared at the ceiling, stroking her head, her breath warm upon my neck.

I waited until she dropped off to sleep again and then slipped out of the sleeper. Crossing the room, I went out to the deck. The sea breeze felt good against my skin. The white sand in front of me appeared dark grey in the dark before dawn, the sea black, white waves curling, flashing briefly and disappearing.

I'm not going to tell her about killing Wigley. Not while the baby is growing in her. Maybe after. And then maybe not. And Gabriel was right. I can live with it. I don't like it, but I can live with it. I let my thoughts drift aimlessly on the breeze.

The sun rose, a blood red orange revealed by the revolution of the land I was standing on. Red sky in morning, sailors take warning. I thought back over the last couple of months. It was only the 5th of December when I had met Gabriel. It seemed like another life. It was another life. Life before Gabriel. Life before Mariko. Life before my baby.

I sensed her behind me and turned. She was trying to quietly open the sliding doors. I grinned, and she smiled shyly back, caught. I looked at her through the Clearfilm. No one was ever going to take her away from me again. The door slid open with a loud squeak. She walked out to where I was standing at the railing and looked out to sea. Her hair wafted up on the breeze.

"You ready for a swim?" she said and turned to me. I smiled.

"Race you there."

***

Later that evening we ate at Abdul's restaurant. He had been a bit cold with me since Gabriel's letter had been broadcast, but he thawed out as the evening wore on. We had a few beers and ate a lot of seafood cooked on a small fire on the beach. Abdul shrugged off our offer of help to clean up.

Grinning, he said, "How could I charge you for the meal if you clean up. Go, go."

We walked back along the beach, the breeze absent now, just the lap-slosh sound of the sea keeping us company as we headed for home. I stiffened. Sir Thomas and Charles were on the deck, looking in our direction. We changed angle away from the edge of the surf and walked towards them across the white sand.

I could hear the sound of the sand shifting beneath our feet as we approached.

"Splendid place you have here, Jonah," Sir Thomas called out, standing against the railing, spreading his arms wide to take in the beach. Charles was behind him near the sliding doors. I walked up the steps from the beach, looking up at him. I held the look until I was on the deck and looking down at him. I didn't say anything. Mariko was behind me. I turned and smiled at her.

"Could you get my uncle and me a beer?"

"Sure, Jonah."

Sir Thomas, with his hands clasped behind his back, said, "Terrible thing that Gabriel kidnapping you, my girl. Terrible. Just glad that we were able to get you out of there safe and sound. Eh. And how are you holding up, my dear?"

Mariko smiled at Sir Thomas and didn't say anything. She walked past Charles, who stepped back to let her pass into the house. I'd put the gun in the cool box before we had left for Abdul's. I had told her in the cave that Gabriel had given it to me for protection and that we'd put it in the cool box – where we kept the beers.

I watched her disappear down the stairs and listened carefully, feeling uneasy at her being out of sight. Then I turned to Sir Thomas, leaned my forearms on the railing of the deck, and looked sideways at him. He smiled.

"Don't ever lay a finger on her again. She's mine. All right?"

The smile disappeared off Sir Thomas's face, and I heard Charles shift his stance.

"Now, there's no need to get upset, Jonah. It was a simple precautionary measure. I know how much you feel for the girl, and I just wanted to make sure you wouldn't talk about our, um, arrangement before it was consummated."

"I'm not upset, Sir Thomas. I fully understood your intentions. Now you understand mine. Are we clear?" I saw Mariko's head moving up the stairs. "Well?"

Sir Thomas looked at me and smiled. That horrible little upwards twist of the corners of his wet lips. He brought a fist out from behind his back and softly banged it on the railing. He nodded his head.

"Oh, and one other thing?"

His eyes went wide, the smile disappearing again.

"What?" Sir Thomas's eyes flicked to Mariko, who was shifting the beers to one hand so that she could open the sliding doors. Charles didn't move. I saw out of the corner of my eye that his gaze was fixed firmly upon me. Sir Thomas's eyes flicked back to me. Mariko got the door open.

"What?" he said in a low urgent hiss. Charles's hand crept into his jacket.

"You owe me eleven hundred cred from the golf."

Sir Thomas blinked, his mouth opened, I thought he was going to say something. His mouth opened wider. And then his loud barked laugh ripped through the quiet of the night. Mariko handed a beer to me and offered one to Sir Thomas.

"No, thank you, my dear. I must be going. I just wanted to personally drop off this invitation." Sir Thomas reached inside his jacket. I stiffened, but his hand came out holding a small piece of white card. He passed it to me and said, smiling, "Don't leave this laying about, will you, and do bring Mariko? And now I must be off."

Sir Thomas walked down the steps onto the beach, followed by Charles. They disappeared out of sight around the edge of the house. I listened, and Mariko went back inside the house to the windows opposite the deck. She came back out.

"They've gone," she said and came to stand beside me.

I held up the card in the light from the house and read, "Sir Thomas Bartholomew Oliver requests the pleasure of your company at A Cull Party, Marq V, Penthouse, New Singapore, at 10:30pm, 28 February 2110."

In the bottom corner it said, Dress Code: Formal. There was no RSVP.

A Cull Party

"This is a very cool party, no?"

The play on words came from the tanned young man with a French accent and smug grin, standing in our little group of six. I smiled and glanced at Mariko, who also smiled politely. The man to my left laughed out loud and said too loudly, "A cool party. Oh, very good, excellent." His wife patted him on the arm and, glancing at the alky in his hand, quickly looked over her shoulder to see if any of the other guests had noticed.

There were perhaps fifty or so people gathered in Sir Thomas's large living room, broken up into small groups, standing and sitting around. I saw Cochran with her partner Sunita Shido, who I recognized from the newsfeeds. So she's a Hawk, too, I realized and quickly shielded my thought as Cochran looked in my direction. I turned to Mariko.

"Will you excuse me for a moment? There's someone I must talk with."

Mariko nodded. "Of course, darling. You go ahead, and I'll let these charming gentlemen amuse me in your absence." The tanned young man looked alert and smiled a competitive little smile at me. I ignored him and turned away, giving Mariko's hand a squeeze.

I walked across the room towards Cochran. The last time I had seen her was in the small conference room at UNPOL on the day that had started the journey that would end here, tonight. Weaving my way between French perfume and testosterone mixed in the charged atmosphere, the forced laughter and stiff poses, I sat down close beside her on the sofa. Our legs almost touching. She looked down her nose at the distance between our legs and sat back slightly, shifting away. Sunita hesitated in what she was saying to Secretary Deng, but with a quick once-over at me, carried on.

"Good evening, Sharon. You're looking stunning as usual."

"Thank you, Jonah," Cochran said, watching me with slightly raised eyebrows.

"And congratulations on your promotion. The youngest ever director of

UNPOL – that's quite an achievement." Cochran smiled demurely, and I thrust the crudely prepared thought into her mind. "I want to fuck you."

She spilt her drink as she jolted forward, her mouth open, staring at me. She ignored the spilt drink, so I took out a handkerchief and dabbed at the liquid splash on her bare leg. This earned me another harder look from Sunita, but Deng was talking to her now, so she turned away again.

Cochran lashed herself into my mind with a feral leap. "Take your hands off me. So the young Oliver has learnt a new trick, has he? And he wants to play silly little boy games with his new toy." Her thoughts crackled with venom.

I stopped dabbing at her thigh and put the handkerchief back in my pocket. I forced my thoughts through the noise in her mind. "Not games, Sharon. I'm serious. The Cull is tonight, and bloodlines are being drawn."

I switched my line of thought to the second phase of my unbalancing act.

"You've never had a man before, have you? It's always been her. You're still a virgin. Perhaps fuck was too strong a word, although I think we would enjoy it. Perhaps breed is better in the context of tonight. Think about it. Matriarch of a dynasty. Can she do that for you?"

And rising from the sofa, I smiled and said, "Well, lovely to see you again, Sharon," and I turned and walked slowly back to Mariko. Cochran was incoherent.

***

Stanislav stared at the Devscreen. There was only one word on it.

Now.

He turned to glance at Fatima on his right and, sitting next to her, Dom. They had pulled their Devcockpits together for this one. This one was special. Dom and Fatima looked at him, and he said, "Re-re-re-"

"Ready," Fatima and Dom said in unison as they both smiled at him and then turned back to focus on their Devscreens. The three Devcockpits were pushed up against the door to the Cave.

Stanislav pressed submit, and the level one security alert that he had prepared for Cochran was transmitted. Now they were committed.

***

Cochran was having a mental argument with herself. She wavered between walking over to Jonah and telling him he was Philip Zumar's son and no relation of Sir Thomas, or asking him if he was serious about his offer. In her confusion, an uncomfortable and unfamiliar feeling, there was a thrill. The thrill of the unknown. What would it be like? The little voice, which had been silent for a couple of weeks, decided it had been silent too long. There are two ways to interpret 'I want to fuck you'. A hot flash of anger spiked through her, and then her Devstick, resting on the black leather seat of the sofa, flashed red. For a crazy moment she thought she had caused it. She swallowed the alky in her hand in a single gulp and used her other to pick up the Devstick.

Level 1 Security Alert.

Positive trace identification: Gabriel Alexander Zumar

Location: Wharf Three, Warehouse 21, Jurong Island, New Singapore

She paled. He's been here all along? On Jurong Island. Within four kiloms of her the whole time. She had scoured the Earth and the Moon for him. Her breathing became shallow. Sunita laid a hand on her forearm, but Cochran ignored it and, getting up from the sofa, walked across to Sir Thomas. He was talking to a stately looking woman well into her eighties and wearing a dress from her thirties. Cochran waited.

"Yes. Tonight at midnight," he was saying to the woman. "It will be released by Harper's to the global feeds. I must say that I am very pleased with the effort they've put behind it. It will be going into print as well – hardcover."

Cochran hovered just behind the elderly woman's elbow and out of her sight.

"Yes, Sharon?"

She took a step forward. "May I have a word, Sir Thomas? In private. It's UNPOL business."

Sir Thomas turned to his companion and, grasping her softly by the elbow, said, "Francesca, I hope you will not be offended if I take this young lady up on her offer of a private tête-à-tête with me." He winked at her upturned smile and, releasing her arm, said, "Unfortunately, I fear that all she will want to talk about is business."

***

I watched as Sir Thomas left the old lady and walked out onto the balcony through the sliding doors with Cochran in tow. I could see them through the clearfilm, Cochran's head bent low, talking fast and gesturing with her Devstick. Sir Thomas nodded. She came back inside and walked swiftly through the room. She bumped shoulders with one lady who had stepped back suddenly but ignored her and continued straight to the door where Charles was standing. He opened the door for her, and she strode out, her Devstick like a baton in her hand.

I looked back to where she had come from. Sir Thomas was standing, watching me looking at him. He stroked his chin, glanced at his watch and then, looking up again, motioned for me to join him.

"What do you think?" The young man with the French accent had said something to me, but I had missed it, focused on Sir Thomas.

"Excuse me for a moment. My uncle needs to talk with us." I inclined my head in a slight bow and took Mariko by the hand. We walked a little way, and then I stopped her and looked in her eyes, smiling, holding her by the shoulders. "Cochran has just left, and Sir Thomas wants to talk. Let's stick together," I thought. She smiled and nodded back. We walked over to Sir Thomas.

He frowned when he saw that Mariko was with me. I looked evenly at him, ignoring his frown. As Hawk heir apparent, I took my role seriously, glad of the imperviousness it afforded by its nature.

Sir Thomas went out onto the balcony, and I followed, swooping two alkys off a table set against the sliding doors. Sir Thomas was leaning with his arms resting on the railing of the balcony, looking out over Topside to the UNPOL Complex. The thump-whoop-whir of a Heliocopter startled me as it passed overhead, and I glanced up to see the black underside a mere ten meters above me, speeding away toward the warehouse district. Cochran has taken the bait, I thought.

I passed one of the alkys to Sir Thomas. He took it and raised his glass to mine.

"Cheers, Jonah, salute."

"Cheers, Uncle. What are we raising our glasses to?"

"To tonight. To this moment. Victory. And to you, Jonah. I must confess I wasn't sure you had it in you, but you've made me proud."

I clinked my glass against his to forestall any more talk of what had made him so proud of me. Conscious of Mariko standing by the door, her arms loosely by her sides, I glanced across at her. Sir Thomas read my glance and nodded his bald head minutely in understanding.

"Have you worked it out yet?"

"With a name like the Cull Party, it didn't leave much for the imagination. Yes, I think so. You're going to cull a portion of the population using the Tag somehow."

He turned and smiled at me. "You were always a bright boy, Jonah.

Sometimes I wondered if you were too bright. Too much thought and no action. Well, tonight is about action . Tonight we're going to change the world and make it a better place. Not just a portion of the population, Jonah. That is thinking too small. No. A large portion. Six point three billion people will die at midnight tonight, and an hour from now we will own the world and everything in it."

I looked out over Topside and, not trusting myself to say anything, slowly sipped the alky.

***

Cochran, sitting in the Heliocopter, hovered silently in position, two hundred meters from warehouse twenty-one. She was waiting for the SOE teams she'd called to get in position. A dark blue helo assault craft slid in beside her. She couldn't see it and wouldn't have noticed except for it showing up on her Devscreen. Her eyes were on the next Devscreen, showing the infra-red satimage of the three bodies in the warehouse. She thumbed her comms switch on the secure channel.

"All teams report in."

One by one the five teams reported in. One team to cover each wall and she would lead the entry team through the roof.

She steeled herself and checked her weapon – a Glock 45 loaded with fragmentation shells.

"On my mark." Mark? Why did that word jar with her – Mark Zumar, of course. She thought back to the mind conversation at the party and shook her head. Focus.

"On my signal, three, two, one. Go."

Stanislav and Dom had split the tasks evenly. Stanislav had taken all comms into and out of Cochran's Devstick and her Heliocopter. It had taken him all week to set up, but Cochran had no idea that she was talking to him and him alone and that the satimages she was looking at were false. Dom had taken the comms role for the four other teams that didn't exist, and Fatima had taken the UNPOL operations center pretending to be Cochran. There was no getting around the one team that they had allowed to be dispatched: Cochran would be too suspicious if there was no one on the roof with her. The other four teams were digital illusions on Cochran's Devscreen. To all intents and purposes she was about to enter the warehouse without back up and with no one aware of what she was doing except Sir Thomas.

***

The explosive tape wrapped around the skylight was ready to blow. Cochran looked over to the team around the other skylight. She raised her fist, her stake for the rappelling rope in her other hand primed to fire into the roof. The signal came. Electricity cut, and she pumped her fist downwards. Twin spirals of smoke blasted up, and the skylight in front of her dropped in as she pulled the trigger on the stake. Heaving on the rope to make sure it was tight in the ratchet, she turned on the night vision helmet and tossed her coil of rope through the black charred edge of what remained of the skylight. She walked to the edge and dropped into the hole.

When she reached the floor and cast free of the rope in a crouch, her team spread out around her. The warehouse was empty except for two huge round disks leaning against the walls. She thought, Wha –

The light hit her as her brain computed what the disks were, a fraction too late. Lunar lights used by mining Ents on the Moon. Turn night into day. With her night vision helmet on and her wide open pupils, the light blinded her instantly. Her retinas burnt away. Blackness now, a red kind of blackness. She heard a clicking sound and turned towards it and heard the bodies of her team hit the floor. Something rolled along the floor. It rolled and rolled and then stopped. Devstick, she thought, and reached for it in its holster across her chest. The teams outside will get me, she thought.

She still hadn't figured out that her Devstick had been hijacked.

"Sharon."

She froze. That thought had been in her mind, but it didn't belong to her. Her grip tightened on the Glock. She thought a tentative, "Yes."

"Sharon. Put the weapon down on the floor and put your arms out to your sides. No one knows you are here. No one's coming to help."

She hesitated. Perhaps if she removed the helmet, her eyesight would come back.

"Sharon. If you don't put down the weapon, I will be forced to cut off the hand that is holding it. Put the gun down now."

Cochran quickly knelt and laid the Glock on the floor and straightened, holding her arms out to her sides. She heard footsteps approaching across the floor, getting nearer. Steady footsteps. She thought, I can reach it.

"Sharon. Don't even think about it. Just stay calm, and everything will turn out all right. Do something stupid now and you'll be dead or worse."

She thought and heard her little voice say. Did you hear? He said or worse.

Yes, I heard it.

The footsteps stopped, and a hand gently took hers and calmly pulled it behind her back, doing the same with the other and putting a restraint on her wrists. The hands took the helmet off. She kept her eyes open. Darkness, no more red, a deepest, darkest blue, almost black. A hand took her by her upper arm and pulled, indicating she should walk. She went, following the pull of the hand. After thirty steps, she'd counted, the hand stopped her. Two hands now held her by her upper arms and pushed down. She sat, resisting the urge to ask what was happening to her. She tried not to think.

***

"There is no list," Sir Thomas said in response to my question and looked at his watch.

Well, that's it, then. Plan B, I thought and glanced over my shoulder into the room. It had been twenty minutes since Cochran left, and any moment now Shido would be getting the call. I looked at my Devstick. 11:45pm. In the fifteen minutes we'd been talking, he'd told me everything about the Tag. The Ents that made it, the toxin from South America, and the last most shocking information, that there was no list.

"How do you select, then?" I said, turning to face him, one arm on the railing.

"It's a simple algorithm based on simple parameters. Find, inject, move on to the next. When It reaches six point three billion confirmations, it will stop. Simplicity is always best."

Sunita Shido yanked the sliding doors open and, brushing past Mariko, barged in between Sir Thomas and me, a Devstick in her hand.

"They've got her."

"Calm down, my dear, calm down. Who has her, and who is she?"

Shido jerked her head back, and for a sec I thought she would hit Sir Thomas. So did he because he took a step backwards, and his hand dropped inside his jacket.

"We have to delay. We can't do it tonight. He has Sharon, and he says he will kill her if we relay the command."

I moved behind Shido so that I was closer to Mariko – Shido and Sir Thomas in front of me.

Sir Thomas, with one hand slid into the lapel of his jacket, said, "Who has her, Sunita? Who is he?"

She stepped backwards towards the railing and seemed to notice me for the first time. Her look hardened, and she raised her hand, a finger pointing straight in my face. If I reached out with my mouth, I could have bitten it.

"His brother. That's who. It's my satellite, and we are going to cancel this ri —"

Sir Thomas moved so fast that I didn't realize what was happening until he was shielding the stabbed body of Shido with his own. Her eyes stared, panicked, above the hand that covered her mouth. It reminded me of Wigley. Her legs kicked stiffly and then bowed.

"Quick, don't just stand there. Help me drag her over to the lounge chairs quickly now. Yes, that's it," Sir Thomas said and panted with exertion as, blanking the scene from inside with our bodies, we heaved Shido onto the lounge chair. Sir Thomas reached down and gathered her legs up, swinging them up onto the chair.

He brushed his jacket with his hands. His face was flushed and sweaty. "How do I look? Any blood?"

"You look all right. No blood that I can see."

"Right, let's get back inside and keep the guests entertained, shall we?" He left Shido with the dagger's handle sticking out of her chest.

"True friends you stab in the front," he said, noticing my look, and then taking me by the arm we walked back into the living room with Mariko following us. I glanced at Mariko, her face hard and serious, and I knew she was furious but keeping her emotions masked. Sir Thomas closed and, I noticed, locked the sliding doors behind us. I also caught his look and nod to Charles across the room by the hallway to the outer door.

"I must go and attend to business now. Please enjoy yourselves. This is our night." Sir Thomas squeezed my elbow and, grinning, walked off through the room, speaking to Charles before going into his study. I glanced at my Devstick – it was 11:50pm. Suddenly the lights in the room dimmed, and on the far wall a huge Devscreen displayed a spinning globe. Earth. The crowd in front nearest the wall moved back as others moved forward. I walked with Mariko over to the edge of the crowd near the hallway exit.

THROUGH MY EYES

Gabriel leaned forward in his seat and put his hands on Cochran's shoulders.

"I'm sorry you had to listen to that. I didn't think he would kill her," he said. "But now you know what kind of man Sir Thomas is. There is no loyalty in him. Just self, an evil self. You can let him get away with this, or you can help us destroy him. Which will it be?"

Cochran's sightless eyes stared wide. Tears flowed down her cheeks. She sniffed loudly and breathed out. Sunita had died for her. Sir Thomas had killed her.

"What do you want?" she said in a voice that was almost a whisper.

"Call UNPOL and take the Blue Notice off Martine Shorne and me. Explain we were working undercover for Flederson and are now working for you. And get us clearance to fly the assault craft to the roof of the Marq."

A sob wracked through Cochran.

Gabriel looked at her. The hatred he felt turned to pity. He couldn't avoid the emotion.

Cochran snarled a savage cry from deep back in her throat, but it ended in another body-wracking sob, her mind screaming. "Don't pity me. Don't."

Gabriel, his hands on her shoulders, pulled her into his embrace, holding her tight. She stiffened at the contact and then went limp. "You're right," he thought as clearly as he could, projecting the thought into her anguished mind. "Pity is wrong. Really, it's sorry I feel. Sorrow for the pain you've suffered. You're as much Sir Thomas's victim as the rest of us. Sharon, come with us. Look into my mind now. It's open to you. Look and see that I am your friend not your enemy."

Sharon heard the word 'friend' and latched on to it, like a person sinking in quicksand stretching for a branch. She tentatively reached out and entered Gabriel's open mind. It was a vast universe of warmth, golden, and its intensity made her gasp. She sobbed, and he hugged her tightly to him. Tears flowed from her blind eyes.

"How can I go with you? I'm blind," but even as she thought it, she knew she could and would. The walks in the dark she took every night were no different than this. She could see with her mind.

"Sharon, if you trust me, then stay with me and look at the world through my eyes."

His words spurring hope, she searched and saw herself as he straightened away from her, his hands still on her shoulders. He smiled at her – she felt rather than saw it – and through his eyes looked at herself in a way she never had before.

11:55pm, his watch said, before it was covered by a sharp tug of his cuff.

Sir Thomas poured himself a cognac and, taking the snifter in hand, walked over to his desk and sat down on the leather Siteazy behind it. It was a large desk with a single-shaded light bulb hanging over the middle. In this light, Sir Thomas stretched his arms to his Dev console and thumbed his Dev. The spinning Globe was replaced by Tag uptake numbers displayed over a color-coded world map with the Moon and Mars insets spinning in the top right corner, the Moon on top of Mars. The twin of this image was displayed in the living room next door. But this was a moment he didn't want to share with anyone.

The number was half a percentage point lower than their minimum requirement. Soon, very soon, he thought. He let out a long breath, almost a sigh of satisfaction, and leaned back in the seat, crossing his legs, the cognac snifter in his left hand. A voice command or press submit, he thought. Press submit – by my own hand is better. But wait, wait until we reach seventy-five percent. By the time the sickness strikes, the figure will be eighty-five, perhaps even ninety percent, and the rest can be taken care of later.

He sniffed, taking in the odor of the cognac mixed with the scent of the leather Siteazy, a strangely comforting smell. Restless for the point zero four percent remaining to complete, he rose, a hand on his hip as he levered himself up, and walked over to the window.

It was a clear, cloudless night, stars were visible, and only the light hanging above the Dev on the desk behind him gave rise to his reflection in the armor glass. He looked out, off to his right, over the New Singapore skyline to the EntPlex of SingCom, where the signal would go out from, its red branding casting a rosy glow over the lesser Ents it dwarfed. Sunita was a fool.

He looked at his watch again. Just two minutes had passed. Can't look yet, he thought. Be patient. A quick thrill ran through him: the moment was so near, he savored it, and he waited, like leaving the strawberry off the cake until last – the sweet delay of anticipation. He took another draught of his cognac and saw that his Tag suggestions were running simultaneously across the three newsfeeds

A NECESSARY EVIL

security. He snorted back a laugh, his cognac splashing on the cuff of his outers. He dabbed at it with his fingers and looked again at his watch. 11:59pm. It was time. He thumbed his console, and the screen switched back to the color-coded map. He reached out with a pudgy, sweaty finger and pressed submit, leaving a smear on the Devscreen where he touched.

***

I watched in horror, squeezing Mariko's hand tightly, as the submit button went a darker shade. Sir Thomas had submitted the cull command. The floor-to-ceiling Devscreen lighting the room with the billions of white light tags showing the whole of civilization online suddenly started to go black. In seconds, and from one corner of the screen to the other, the tiny little lights winked out one by one, and then the screen went black.

The room lit up again as the screen changed into a document. White background with black type streaming down the Devscreen, coming to a stop just off the floor. The title at the top said, 'A Necessary Evil'. My eyes scanned through from top to bottom, a smile slowly spreading across my lips.

I read.

'My fellow humans,

By now most of you living in the European and the American Geographics have realized that your Personal Unique Identifier, your PUI, has been deleted. Those waking up tomorrow morning in Asia will realize the same. This event happened at midnight, New Singapore time, and is a global event. That means that you are not alone. Everyone's identity has been deleted from all population databases on Earth, the Moon and Mars. There are no backups – it was necessary to delete those, too.

This had to be done because over 75% of you have injected the Tag, and the Tag contains a toxin that was going to be released at midnight by Sir Thomas Bartholomew Oliver. The only way to stop this crime against humanity was to destroy all PUIs.

We are now at a crossroads in the history of humankind. We are nameless, and being nameless, we have no past. We have no property. We have no cred. This would be an easy time for humanity to slip into chaos and anarchy. And if we do, then we have no future.

There is an alternative to anarchy and chaos. Write in your Devsticks who you are and include all the members of your family and where they are. Share this with the first person you can. You should each then give a copy of what you have written to the other person. As you meet others, do the same. This is the only way of collectively establishing who we are. In another 24 hours we will set up sites where you may register yourselves and your families.

Respect your neighbor's property. Respect and defend their property as if it was your own.

Take care of the young and the old, the young especially. If you see a young person looking lost, ask them who they are and where their parents are. If they do not know, give them shelter but do not take them out of the area that they are in. If you do need to do that, then leave trace of where you are going. Register them if they can tell you their name. If not, provide a clear description and register that.

Parents: if your child is not with you, you should go to them immediately.

There is no cred, therefore the monetary system that we have relied on for so long has gone. If you were wealthy, now you are not. If you were poor, now you are not. Some of you will think of this as an opportunity to grab a disproportionate share of the resources that are currently available. This will lead to chaos. Share what you have with your neighbor and teach them to do the same. In sharing what we have, and respecting what others have, lies a golden future. This statement applies to material and non-material properties.

The future of humanity depends on what we do over the next few days, weeks and months. Think of this as the final triumph of good over evil and humanity will have a glorious future. Think of this as a way to gain advantage over your fellow humans and we will have no future.

Further instructions will follow.

With great respect and humility,

Gabriel Alexander Zumar. New Singapore, 1st March 2110, 12:01am.

Elder brother to Mark Anthony Zumar.

Husband to Martine Shorne Zumar.

PRESS HERE to see the evidence against Sir Thomas and the reason we had to delete the PUIs.'

Gabriel's virus had succeeded in preceding the cull command – the virus attached to the messages I sent from Wigley's house. The letter we had worked on was proof that the cull command had failed. Our virus had deleted all PUIs in existence. Now none of us had a name.

As the document scrolled large on the living room wall, the icon hovered over the 'PRESS HERE' in the last sentence of the letter. The crowd was silent.

"Let's get out of here," I said to Mariko, softly whispering in her ear, my eyes flicking to the hallway. As we walked down the hall, the door to Sir Thomas's study opened, and Charles, seeing us, ran the few steps to block the door to the outside. He stood on the balls of his feet, his hands by his sides. I pulled up, and Mariko stepped in front of me, smiling and holding out her hand to Charles. I thrust my thoughts into his brain; his eyes shifted, and he smiled at me. Thinking in Mandarin.

The loss of focus was enough, and Mariko fired the Maloo-modified Devstick, twin darts appearing in Charles's chest. He looked down at the darts as if offended and fell to the floor. Two pools of blood marked the spot where the carbon fiber bolts had entered. His legs started shaking, twitching, and then they stopped, and he fell slumping against the door, his dead eyes staring at me, still offended.

Sir Thomas appeared in the study doorway as Mariko hit the button and the outer door opened. She went through.

"Take care of yourself and our child," I urged as I shut the door on her and locked it.

Glancing down, I saw the butt of a gun sticking up from Charles's armpit.

I quickly knelt, grabbing it and pulling. But it didn't come free. I looked up, fumbling with the catch of the holster over the hammer of the gun, as Sir Thomas advanced, his hand going into his jacket and pulling free the dagger he had used to kill Shido, which he or Charles must have retrieved.

I was too slow, and Sir Thomas was on me before I could free the gun. His arm swept back for the blow, but I reached out with my mind and screamed, "Stop!" throwing the thought into his mind. He reeled back as if I had struck him. I held the thought and wrenched at the gun butt. It came free. But the effort caused me to lose my grip on Sir Thomas's mind. His arm swung up, and I twisted sideways. The dagger cut through my outers and blazed a trail of pain across the left side of my stomach.

Sir Thomas saw the gun as I rose from my knees. He turned, running for the door of the study. I brought the gun to bear, scrambling to my feet, but I slipped on Charles's jacket, the cloth sliding my foot out from under me. I went down hard. Seeing Sir Thomas disappear through his study door, I scrambled up again, ignoring the searing pain from the knee I'd twisted in my fall. In three strides I was at his study door.

He wasn't in the room. The clearfilm doors to the balcony were open, curtains billowing in with the breeze. Gun extended, I limped, dragging my left leg behind me as fast as I could, across the room to the balcony and edged my way around the door. The curtains blew in my face, tangling with my vision. Pushing them aside with my left hand, I stepped out onto the balcony, quickly turning left and right. He wasn't there. He's gone back inside, I thought, but a glance at the doors to the living room and his bedroom confirmed they were shut.

Then I saw it. A black rope tied to the railing of the balcony. I limped over to it and looked down. It ended just above the floor of Topside. I peered out and saw him, running, surprisingly fast for his age, towards the walky that led to the golf course. He disappeared from view under the trees that shaded the walky. I looked down the rope: it was a good fifteen meters to the floor below me. With my damaged knee, I wasn't sure if I could make it and turned to go back inside and get the Lev.

I heard the savage thumping of a copter's blades and turned as it came into view in the red glow of the SingCom sign. It flew in closer, and I could make out Marty in the pilot's seat. She gave me a thumbs-up and then made a sign with her thumb and little finger extended from a fist held up to her ear. Devstick, I thought and pulled the Devstick from my jacket pocket.

"Mark, where is he?"

It was Gabriel. He was in the copter – I could hear the blades in the background, Gabriel shouting over their noise.

"He's run out onto Topside, headed for the golf course. I'm going after him. Can you track him for me?"

"Yes, but hold on for a sec. We're going to drop Maloo off to take care of the other Hawks. Don't worry about Mariko, she's signaling us. She's on the roof."

The copter swept over my head, and I could only see the tail, then Maloo, as he swung out and dropped down on a hoist. Looking at me, with a machine gun strapped over his shoulder, he grinned. He dropped but swung in and on top of the roof of the penthouse, disappearing from my view. I plugged in my earpiece and shoved the Devstick back in my pocket and the gun in my trousers. I grabbed the rope.

I held tight as I swung over the balcony. Though I had never done this before, I had watched a film of people abseiling down buildings. I stretched my legs out straight and held the rope tightly. Then my body twisted in the gust of wind blown downwards by the copter as it circled away from the roof. I banged against the wall, the pain from my knee shooting through me and almost causing me to lose my grip. But I held on. The gun slipped out of my waist and went down my bottom outer leg. I heard it clatter on the floor below. I looked up, but my hands slipped on the smooth rope. And I slid. Bumping the wall, sending spikes of pain from my knee, I held on as tightly as I could despite the rope burning my hands.

I held on just enough to slow my descent and hit the ground, my good leg taking the strain. A glance at the palms of my hands showed me they were marked by a solid raw red stripe of blood and burning.

I got up and stumbled over to where the gun lay, picked it up, checked it over, and though I knew nothing about guns, it looked okay – the magazine was still in place. I got my bearings. The walky was twenty meters away. I started towards it and collapsed. My leg wouldn't take the weight.

There. Off to the right of me, less than five meters away, was a Devcaddy. Sir Thomas's Devcaddy – I recognized it from our game. I pulled myself up onto my good leg and hopped over to it. Each hop jarred with pain, and I nearly fainted before I got my hand on the handle of the Devcaddy. I stood on the platform by the wheel with my good leg. The other I swung around with my right hand and pulled onto the platform by the other wheel.

I pressed the on button, and the Devcaddy said, "Good morning, Sir Thomas." I hit silent on the Devscreen and twisted the throttle set into the handle, taking the gun in my left hand as the Devcaddy surged along the path and bumped up the ramp onto the walky.

"We've got him on infrared. He's on the golf course. We'll fly ahead and cut him off," Gabriel's voice came through loud into my earpiece. I had forgotten it and was surprised it had stayed in during the fall. I focused on staying on the DevCaddy, my palms burning where they grabbed the handles.

I saw the sign on the walky for the UNPOL Executive Course and swerved hard left. Fifty meters farther on the left, a sign said 'ninth hole' and the walky had a gap leading to a path. I took the gap and Gabriel's voice came over the earpiece again.

"He's somewhere around the first green, but we've lost him. There's some kind of heat flare there, and we can't see through it. We'll track up to first tee and work our way back to you."

We hadn't got to play the first, but I remembered the layout from the virtual game. Trees, forest really, all the way down to the green and surrounding the green as well. I turned the Devcaddy and twisted the throttle as hard as I could, the pain screeching through me fueling my anger. I flew down the path and slowed the Devcaddy to cut the noise from its tires on the surface.

I stopped. Far off I heard the Heliocopter's turbines wind down and stop. Gabriel and Marty had landed. The night was quiet. I was panting loudly and struggled to get my breathing under control, to make less sound.

"Can you see him?" I said as quietly as possible. The mic in my earpiece muted, and Gabriel came on.

"He's in there somewhere, but I don't know where. Towards the back of the green, I think. Wait for me. I'm coming." Gabriel was obviously running, his words were ragged breaths jolting in time with his strides.

I could hear a loud humming off to my right and saw two large circular exhaust vents, used for sucking stale air out of the roof of New Singapore. They weren't in the virtual game, I thought. Hopping as quietly as I could, I made my way around the edge of the wood, the gun back in my right hand. I edged around to get closer to the vents.

I stopped again and listened. Nothing. No sounds except the loud whirring hum of the vents. My back against a large tree, I edged around it, gun extended, and thought "Where are you?" reaching out with my mind, feeling for him.

My mind was noisy, the hum of the vents and the pain in my knee dominating, but I focused hard, seeking out the pulse of Sir Thomas's mind.

Oh no, he's behind me! I thought as I found him, and he came crashing into me. The dagger flashed in the dark. I twisted, and my leg gave way, the gun flying out of my hand. We both went over backwards, the top of his head butting my jaw, and we tumbled backwards into the bunker on the side of the green.

We rolled to the floor of the bunker, him on top of me, smashing his fist into my chest as he rose, kneeling on me. This is how Wigley died, flashed through my mind. Sir Thomas reached up, grasping his dagger with both hands above his head. I shouted the thought, "Look out!" into his mind. He hesitated, and I twisted as hard as I could, just as he struck, and rolled away in the sand, his blade slicing into my back. I rolled over again and pulled my own dagger from behind my back where it was wedged into the waistband of my bottom outers.

He turned just as I lunged at him, his left hand thrown out as if warding me off, sand flying into my face, blinding me. I surged forward and brought the dagger up as hard as I could. It hit something solid, and then it gave, sliding in as far as the hilt, a liquid warmth covering my hand. I twisted the dagger's handle and, shaking my head, opened my eyes.

His face was cents from mine, eyes bulging. Staring at me. He sighed and went limp, squatting down on his haunches. I followed him with my hand still on the dagger, still pushing it in. My good knee slipped in the sand, but I grabbed his shirt and held on, dragging myself through the loose sand to kneel in front of him.

"You could have had it all," he said in a whisper, shaking his head, blood welling out of the corner of his mouth.

A white hot rage surged through me, pure white hot hatred, and I yanked the dagger from his stomach.

"I had it all, and you stole it."

He smiled. I swung as hard as I could, the dagger a blur as I cut his throat, slashing through. His hand went to the gaping wound – he tried to say something, his mouth opening, but no words came. He gasped and grunted, blood spurting between his fingers, and fell face-first past me into the sand.

THE EYES OF A HAWK

Sharon looked at the time on the Devscreen. The ceremony was at 5pm. And they needed at least an hour and a half to get there. With New Singapore time being three hours behind Melbourne, that meant they had two hours before it was due to begin. Enough, she thought. Fifteen minutes to get ready and an hour to get over there. It was enough.

She walked to the Devcockpit stationed in the corner of the room, next to the balcony that looked out over the Bass Strait. For a moment, she just sat and stared through the window. She focused her eyes and zoomed in on a yacht beating to windward. It was thirteen kiloms away. Her built-in rangefinder gave her the distance as a small number tucked into the top right corner of her vision.

She forced her mind to think clearly. Commanding the software to do its work, the image sharpened on the face of the man at the helm. At times fifty power, her new eyes could make out the grey in his beard. She smiled to herself, remembering Gabriel's comment the first time she had tried her new eyes. 'Now you have the eyes of a Hawk, but the soul of a Dove.' She turned her attention to the Dev and went through her contacts. Selecting and then calling Oche.

He answered immediately. "Sharon, darling, how can I be of service today?"

"Have you finished and sent the gown?" Sharon didn't have time to waste on Oche pleasantries today, but Oche missed that.

"Yes, all done, and it looks beautiful if I say so myself. But isn't it a bit small for you, darling?"

"Oche, stick to fashion design – comedy's not your strong point. Have you sent it?"

Oche, a hot flush spreading up from his neck to his receding hairline, nodded.

"Good."

Sharon smiled at him, gave a little wave with the fingers of one hand at the Devscreen, and cut the connection. She walked across to the mirror, smoothed her dress over her thighs, and sat down on the cushioned seat in front of it. With

301

her hands in her lap, she looked at herself in the mirror.

Her blonde hair had grown out and was shoulder length, cut evenly, with a long curl on both sides that almost met under her chin. She reached for the soft brush on the table and began brushing her hair. Smooth steady strokes. When she was blind, Marty would do this for her, soothing her senses. When she first opened her eyes and saw again, sitting at this table and looking in this mirror, it was Marty standing behind her. The first person she saw with her new eyes.

She smiled. If Sunita could see her now. A tear escaped from one eye, and she ruefully wiped it away. The pain was still there, and the anger, yes. The anger at what their relationship had been versus what it could have been. Mostly now there was just the sadness at the lonely, frantic way in which Sunita had spent her last living moments. The life ending she had listened to with Gabriel, unable to intervene or prevent and now thankful that she couldn't.

Speaking to the dead Sunita in her head, she thought, It's not that I wanted you to die. It's just that since I have been away from you, I have discovered so much more of what life means. The way we were living was wrong. Too much pain and fear. All really unnecessary. I hope you understand. I hope you are at peace.

She wiped away another tear and laid the brush back onto the table in front of the mirror. A knock at the door to her room caused her to twist in the seat.

"It's open," she said, in a clear, light voice.

The doorknob turned, and a hand appeared, pushing the door open. Marty stuck her head in the crack around the door.

"You ready?" Then she smiled. "Oh, you look gorgeous!" She walked into the room to stand in front of Sharon. "Up you get. Let me see."

Sharon smiled and stood, smoothing the pale blue dress with her fingers. This was the first time she could ever remember having worn a dress. It was a simple dress, pale blue with two thin straps over her bare shoulders.

"Turn around," Marty said, still smiling. The dress had no back, just the two straps that descended to the cloth that covered her hips and ended in a short skirt well above her knees. Her back was completely exposed except for the two straps. There wasn't a blemish on it. Sharon turned to face Marty.

The material of the front of the dress was thin enough to see her skin, except at her breasts and hips where the cloth wasn't transparent. A deep V was cut into the middle of the top, ending below her navel, the two pieces held together by a gold chain at her neck.

"It's time to get moving. We can't be late," Marty said, taking Sharon's hand. Lifting it, she pulled her lightly towards the door. Sharon picked up her dark blue, thick canvas shoulder bag from the table and slung it over her shoulder, following Marty out of the room.

They descended the spiral staircase from the second floor and, passing through the corridor, walked into the living room, where Gabriel was sitting on the sofa. Though talking on his Devstick, he looked up at them as they came into the room. He was wearing a white cotton shirt and light white canvas trousers. He studied the two women for a moment and smiled.

"Annika, I've got to go. Your news is great. I'm very happy for you, although I wonder about that old phrase – be careful what you wish for." He paused, nodding. "Yes, I'll talk to him, I'm sure he'll accept. Take care, and we'll talk soon. Okay? Yes, bye for now."

He closed the Devstick and turned to them, still smiling.

"Why are you two armed?" He could tell from the way their bags were hanging off their shoulders that they were carrying more than cosmetics.

Sharon looked at Marty. Marty looked at Sharon.

Marty spoke. "Gabriel, there are a lot of people out there who are pretty upset over losing everything they had, including their names. Family ceremony or not, neither of us is ever going to let harm come to anyone in this family if we can prevent it. Right, Sharon?"

Sharon nodded and turned to Gabriel. "This is not an option, nor is it for debate." She smiled sweetly at him.

Gabriel returned her smile and rose from the sofa. "You both look gorgeous. Come on, let's go."

"Where's Maloo?" Sharon asked.

"Oh, he went on ahead. He'll be there by now. He had quite a few things to do to get ready for the ceremony. He looked great, though, dressed and painted in the tribal way. But come on, let's get moving."

Marty stopped him, moving with a hand on his arm and a slightly troubled expression on her face. "What did Annika want?"

"Annika's just been elected secretary general of the United Nation. Mainly for her work in getting the identity crisis sorted out but also because she's a dammed good politician. She's asked me to help her by becoming her chief intelligence officer."

"And?"

Gabriel smiled at her and stroked her hair. "And I accepted, on the condition that I didn't have to wear a uniform or nametag."

***

Maloo sat in front of the shallow pit he had dug in the beach and carefully laid the dry conkerberry wood over the bottom of the pit, stacking it so it would light easily. Then it was time to light the fire. The eldest elder of the Waalpiri tribe, the tribe that had sheltered Gabriel on his run from Darwin as a boy, carried the dry grass that they had brought with them that morning. The grass had been twisted into hard chords resembling thick rope. Maloo took the chords and, lighting them, pushed them into the bottom of the pit. The dried wood caught quickly. Good, Maloo thought. It needed at least another forty-five minutes to burn to that state where it could smoke properly.

Kneeling in front of the fire, he sat back on his haunches and took in the sight on the beach in front of him. Starting from the steps of the deck of Mark and Mariko's house, a path of large white stones had been laid to curve down to the edge of the sea. Maloo was about five meters from the shore and beyond the fire. Opposite him, were nine Tibetan monks, sitting cross-legged. A large white sail stretched above them, keeping them out of the direct sun.

One of the monks giggled, whispering something in the ear of the monk sitting next to him. Talking about us no doubt, Maloo thought. He glanced over his shoulder at the rest of the mob he'd brought up with him from the Tanami desert. Twenty of them had come: ten males and ten females. The elders and the young 'uns. The young were off playing on the beach, in front of the cool breeze provided by the huge Sea Breeze air-conditioning unit placed there that morning by Abdul.

To his right another sail stretched out across the white sand reaching to the deck of the house. Forty white chairs were laid out, evenly spaced, with a gap in between them for the white stones that ran down to the beach. The fire burned in earnest now.

The path through the jungle flittered with shafts of light from the sun, highlighting the lush green foliage with tints of lime. They walked single file. The noise of the party filtered back as snatches of laughter and the murmuring of voices. Gabriel in front, Marty behind, and Sharon bringing up the rear. Gabriel emerged from the jungle onto the lawn in front of the house.

A table covered in white cloth was next to a hoop wreathed in white flowers. On it was a book open to a blank page. Siti stood up from her seat behind

304

the table, recognizing Gabriel from the image she'd seen on the shelf in Mark's house. Gabriel smiled at her and stopped at the table.

"Hi. My name is Siti."

Gabriel recognized the name as the realtor who had helped Mark and Mariko find the house. "Yes, Mark talks of you often. I think it's great that they have friends such as you."

Siti smiled a huge smile.

"Would you please sign the guestbook?" she said, before turning the guest book around and lifting it gently. Her thumbs were a golden brown on the startling white of the paper.

Gabriel wrote 'The happiest day of my life – GAZ' and turned and gave the pen to Marty.

Marty wrote underneath Gabriel's words 'Me 2 – MSZ'. She turned and gave the pen to Sharon, as she stepped up to the table. She thought for a long while, the pen hovering above the paper. Its gold nib was perfectly still as she thought. Gabriel, Marty and Siti waited, all eyes on the pen in Sharon's hand. Finally she smiled and wrote underneath Marty's words.

'Me 3 – Sharon.'

They passed under the hoop, each accepting and slipping over their wrist a bracelet made with jasmine and tied with a red rose. The lawn was crowded with people standing and chatting in the soft early evening light. The sun hung low now. A glance at his Devstick confirmed that it was nearly five. Avoiding the table laid out with alkys and non-alky drinks, in deference to the Tibetan monks who he had asked to be here today, Gabriel slid through the people, with Marty and Sharon in tow.

He walked around the house until they reached the edge of the beach and the jungle. The sight on the beach brought a smile to his eyes. He kicked off his canvas shoes and turned to Marty and Sharon.

"You should go and see Mariko. She's upstairs in the house. I have to take care of things down there." And he nodded down at the beach. They nodded in unison and turned to the steps leading up to the deck of the house.

Walking around the back of the people in the chairs to the water's edge, Gabriel angled back until he stopped short of the large carpet that the monks were sitting on, and knelt down. The hubbub of noise from the crowd hushed within a few murmurs to a silence. Gabriel bowed his head to the carpet in front of the monks.

A gong sounded. Its clear metal tone spread over the silence on the beach. Gabriel, his hands on his thighs, sitting with a straight back, looked over to where the white stones met the deck of the house. The gong sounded again, each minute representing a year.

Mark appeared on the deck by the top of the stairs. Gabriel knew it was him only by the black trousers and the stick that he still used to walk with. One step at a time, his brother came into view, limping and using his stick but smiling. In his other hand he held a gold framed image on a stand clutched tightly to his breast.

The gong sounded twice more before Mark knelt down slightly behind Gabriel.

***

I knelt before the monks and placed my forehead on the ground. Bringing my hands together under the tip of my nose, I pushed my hands back through either side of my head then placed them on my thighs.

Gabriel shuffled forward on his knees. My damaged knee was beginning to really hurt so I slipped sideways, taking the weight off it, and slid my folded legs behind me. Gabriel placed the image of our parents in front of us. He had discovered it in an old archive in an aboriginal community center. An image of Philip and Mariah, his arm around her, smiling at the camera, a gum tree in the background. In the image, Mariah was clearly pregnant. With me. They looked young, happy and at peace.

The head monk handed Gabriel a lotus bud, a large yellow candle and a single stick of incense. A wooden bowl filled with water was placed in front of the image. Gabriel laid the lotus bud on the edge of the bowl. Using the taper of flame provided by the monk, he heated the wax on the bottom of the candle until it was soft. With the same taper, he lit the candle and stuck it so that it angled out over the water in the bowl. The hot wax dripped into the cool water.

Reaching over, one hand on the carpet, he lit the stick of incense. Gabriel sat up straight, then lifted the incense between the palms of his hands until his hands were resting on his forehead, his eyes open, declining his head slightly in prayer. I did the same. The gong sounded again, and the monks began to chant. My knee hurt again. I forced myself to ignore the pain and focus on the chanting. It had meant a lot to Gabriel to organize this, and it meant a lot to me, too.

Suddenly my thoughts were awash with the minds of the monks. I almost keeled over, but then Gabriel's thoughts came strongly into my mind.

"We've come a long way, my brother, and we had to do it alone. Now we can cast our demons aside and look to the future. We remember her, we remember him, just feel now. Open your mind and feel them."

Feelings, fleeting images, emotions felt and seen by Gabriel with Philip and Mariah began to enter my brain. I was overwhelmed. The chanting of the monks and the gong occasionally reverberating across the beach blended and focused my thoughts until I was in the well of Gabriel's mind. My eyes were open, but all I saw was the years that Gabriel had spent with Philip and the months with Mariah.

A clear piercing thought from Gabriel, "My gift to you, my brother." An image of my mother smiling down at me came to my mind. The image was sharp and came with the emotion of the love she felt.

I thought, "Thank you, my brother, this is a wonderful gift."

I realized that the gong hadn't sounded for a while, and the monks had stopped chanting. Thirty-five minutes had passed. A gong for each year since my parents had been taken from us. The head monk stood, and another monk picked up the wooden bowl with the water and the wax from the candle in it. We waied as he dipped a brush made from small twigs into the bowl and, saying a prayer, flicked the water over us three times. He moved away and walked over to the aborigines, blessing them in a similar fashion. Once he had covered the entire crowd of people, he returned to the carpet and sat down again.

Smoke wafted around me. Gabriel shuffled off the carpet and, waiing at the monks once more, stood up. I did the same. We stood together and faced the path of white stones.

***

Mariko, Marty and Sharon stood just inside the clearfilm doors, which were open to the deck. They looked out to the sea across the white sails partially covering the beach in front of them. Mariko walked forward across the deck, with Marty on her left and Sharon on her right. The baby in her arms was dressed in a long, flowing white gown.

As Mariko went down the steps to the beach, Sharon held her arm just above her elbow. She turned, smiled at Sharon, and said, "You're probably wondering why I asked you to get the gown for the naming ceremony," and she cocked an eyebrow.

Sharon flicked her eyebrows up in the affirmative, but didn't say anything.

Her eyes scanned the seated crowd, head calmly turning left and right. She hadn't been in any crowds since she'd been blinded, and it made her a little nervous.

"Well, the reason is that it's tradition that the child's godmother buys the gown." Mariko turned to face straight again, walking on the white, flat stones toward where Mark was standing. Sharon was shocked.

"Why me?" she asked as they walked.

"Because there's only one other woman who's maybe tougher, and perhaps smarter, in the entire world," she nodded her head sideways at Marty, "and she's pregnant with your other godchild. So you're my best choice."

Sharon looked at Marty around Mariko's shoulder. Marty smiled at her and nodded and held out her hand, which Sharon took in hers. Tears in her eyes, she understood that Mark and Mariko had given her what Sir Thomas had taken away. A family.

***

I walked around the fire until my back was to the ocean. Taking off my black jacket, I laid it on the sand next to me. Maloo and the elders began chanting in Waalpiri, their tribal language. Mariko walked up to Gabriel and held out our son. Gabriel took the boy and carefully unwrapped the gown until the baby was naked. He turned to Sharon and held out the child.

"As the boy's godmother, I ask you to carry him to his godfather," Gabriel said and nodded at Maloo chanting in the wafting smoke.

Sharon reached out and with a glance at Mark, who nodded and smiled, took the baby in her arms. She sat down in the sand next to Maloo, who was waving the smoke towards them.

The chanting by the elders increased in volume. There was not another sound on the beach. Maloo gestured to Marty, and she sat down next to him, gracefully folding her knees below her. Maloo gestured then to Mariko to sit by Sharon. Gabriel and I were next, Gabriel sitting alongside Marty and I next to Mariko. The chanting reached an even higher level, and suddenly I felt it again. This time the elders and Maloo came into my mind.

Maloo picked up the naked baby and held him high above the smoke. The smoke swirled around, and I felt Mariko's uneasy thought. It was smoothed with thoughts from Gabriel and Maloo. "It's okay. The baby will not be harmed. This is to cleanse the evil passed to him through us and protect him from sickness."

I saw Gabriel nod to Maloo, who handed the baby back to Sharon and showed her how to lay the baby's head with the top against Marty's stomach.

Marty got Sharon to take one of the baby's hands and Mariko the other. Then Maloo took Marty's hand and Sharon's in his, nodding to us, and I picked up Mariko's hand and Gabriel's. Now we were all physically connected.

The chanting of the Waalpiri elders was suddenly joined by that of the Tibetan monks, and I felt all of our minds connecting.

I breathed out slowly and let my mind float free. And there we were. All of us joined as a golden orb of feeling. Within the orb I could feel my son's mind and then, a surprise, the mind of another, almost indistinct, but there in Marty's stomach. Gabriel squeezed my hand.

Maloo's clear, loud thought came through as a feeling more than words, and the feeling was the path to the absolute present, reaching from the past to the future through the moment of now.

I felt my father and my mother. I felt them in our collective mind. They passed through us all and touched the mind of our son, Philip Gabriel Zumar.